#2

MY BOYFRIEND IS A MONSTER

Made for Each Other

OR

I MADE MY PROM DATE

OR

HUNKENSTEIN

OR

LOVE IN STITCHES

OR

OUR LOVE'S ALIIIIIIVE!!

PAUL D. STORRIE

Illustrated by ELDON COWGUR

GRAPHIC UNIVERSE™ · MINNEAPOLIS · NEW YORK

STORY BY
PAUL D. STORRIE

ART, LETTERING,
AND COVER BY
ELDON COWGUR

Copyright © 2011 by Lerner Publishing Group, Inc.

Graphic Universe™ is a trademark of Lerner Publishing Group, Inc.

Graphic Universe™
A division of Lerner Publishing Group, Inc.
241 First Avenue North
Minneapolis, MN 55401 U.S.A.

Website address: www.lernerbooks.com

Library of Congress Cataloging-in-Publication Data

Storrie, Paul D.
    Made for each other / by Paul D. Storrie ; illustrated by Eldon Cowgur.
        p.   cm. — (My boyfriend is a monster ; #2)
    Summary: High school students Maria and Tom are immediately attracted to each other, but an envious monster named Hedy will stop at nothing to destroy their romance.
    ISBN: 978–0–7613–5601–1 (lib. bdg. : alk. paper)
    1. Graphic novels. [1. Graphic novels. 2. Horror stories. 3. Monsters—Fiction. 4. High schools—Fiction. 5. Schools—Fiction.] I. Cowgur, Eldon, ill. II. Title.
PZ7.7.S756Mb 2011
741.5′973—dc22   2010028722

Manufactured in the United States of America
2 – BC – 1/31/12

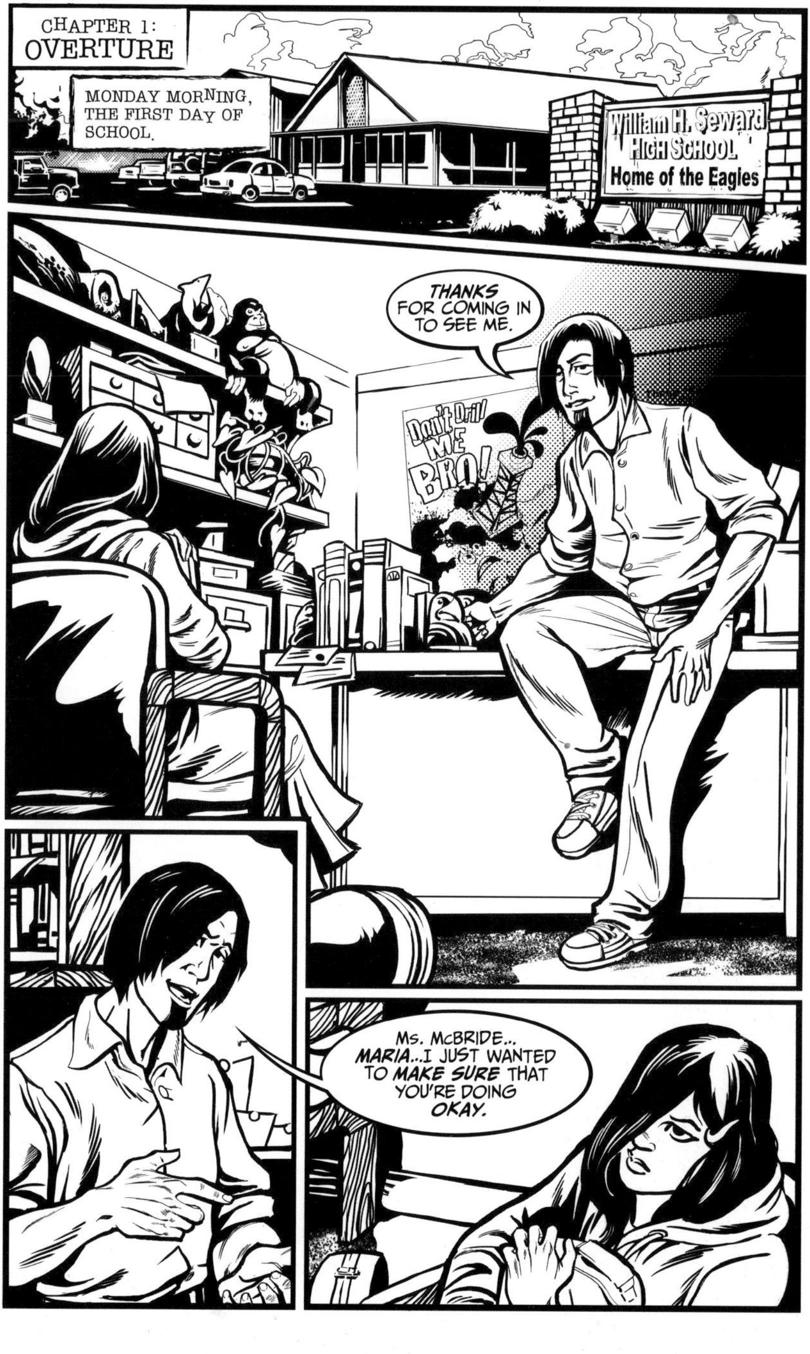
CHAPTER 1:
OVERTURE
MONDAY MORNING, THE FIRST DAY OF SCHOOL.
William H. Seward
HIGH SCHOOL
Home of the Eagles
THANKS FOR COMING IN TO SEE ME.
Don't Drill ME BRO!
Ms. McBRIDE... MARIA...I JUST WANTED TO MAKE SURE THAT YOU'RE DOING OKAY.

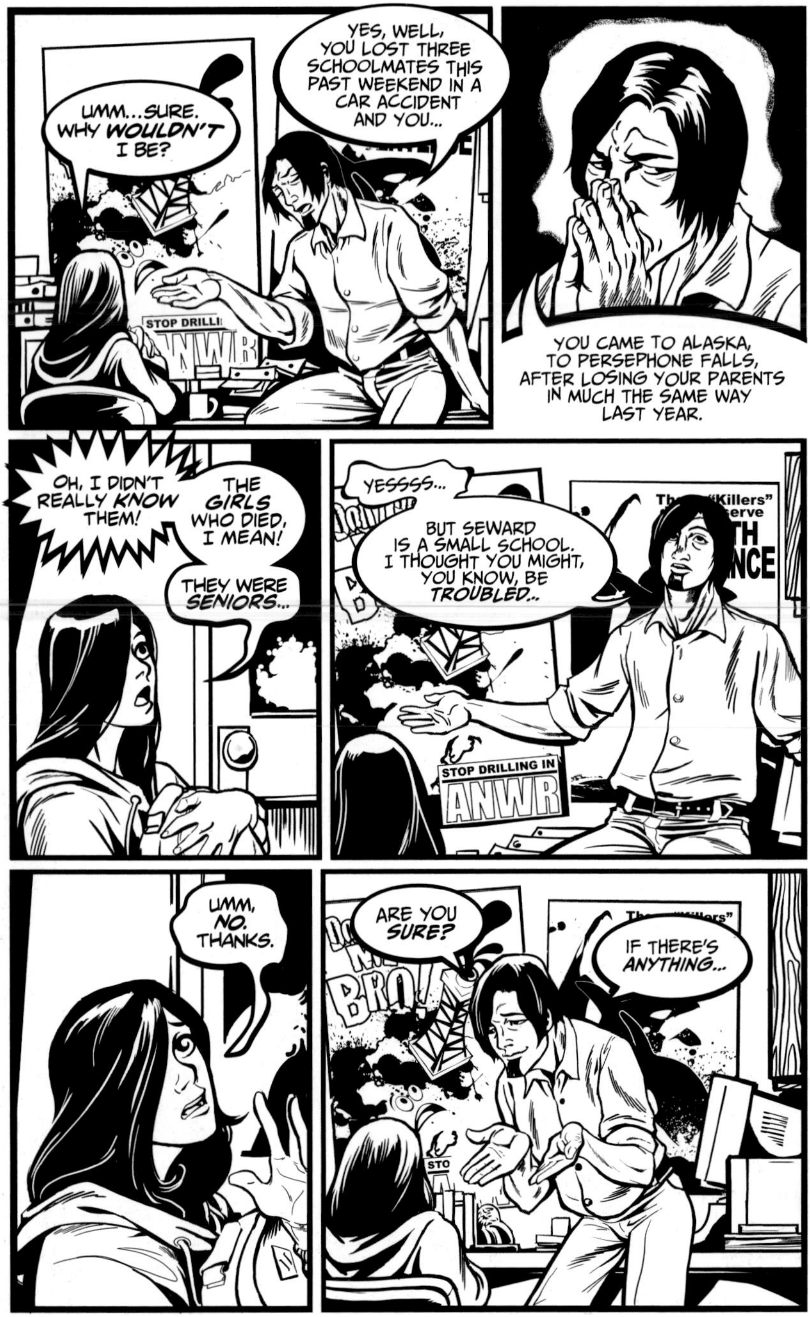
UMM...SURE. WHY WOULDN'T I BE?
YES, WELL, YOU LOST THREE SCHOOLMATES THIS PAST WEEKEND IN A CAR ACCIDENT AND YOU...
STOP DRILLI
ANWR
YOU CAME TO ALASKA, TO PERSEPHONE FALLS, AFTER LOSING YOUR PARENTS IN MUCH THE SAME WAY LAST YEAR.
OH, I DIDN'T REALLY KNOW THEM!
THE GIRLS WHO DIED, I MEAN!
THEY WERE SENIORS...
YESSSS...
BUT SEWARD IS A SMALL SCHOOL. I THOUGHT YOU MIGHT, YOU KNOW, BE TROUBLED...
STOP DRILLING IN
ANWR
UMM, NO. THANKS.
ARE YOU SURE?
IF THERE'S ANYTHING...

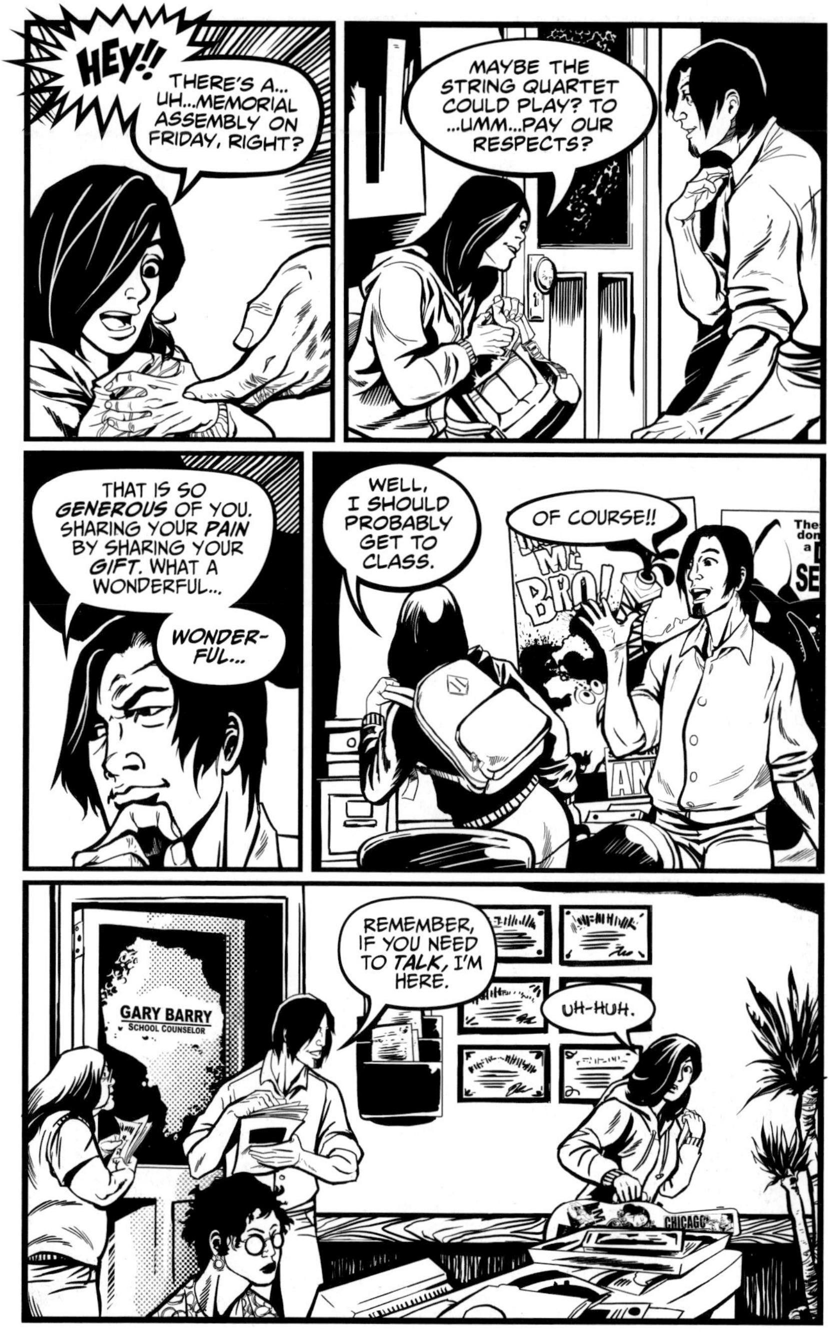
HEY!!
THERE'S A... UH...MEMORIAL ASSEMBLY ON FRIDAY, RIGHT?
MAYBE THE STRING QUARTET COULD PLAY? TO ...UMM...PAY OUR RESPECTS?
THAT IS SO *GENEROUS* OF YOU. SHARING YOUR *PAIN* BY SHARING YOUR *GIFT*. WHAT A WONDERFUL...
WONDER-FUL...
WELL, I SHOULD PROBABLY GET TO CLASS.
OF COURSE!!
REMEMBER, IF YOU NEED TO *TALK*, I'M HERE.
UH-HUH.
GARY BARRY
SCHOOL COUNSELOR
CHICAGO

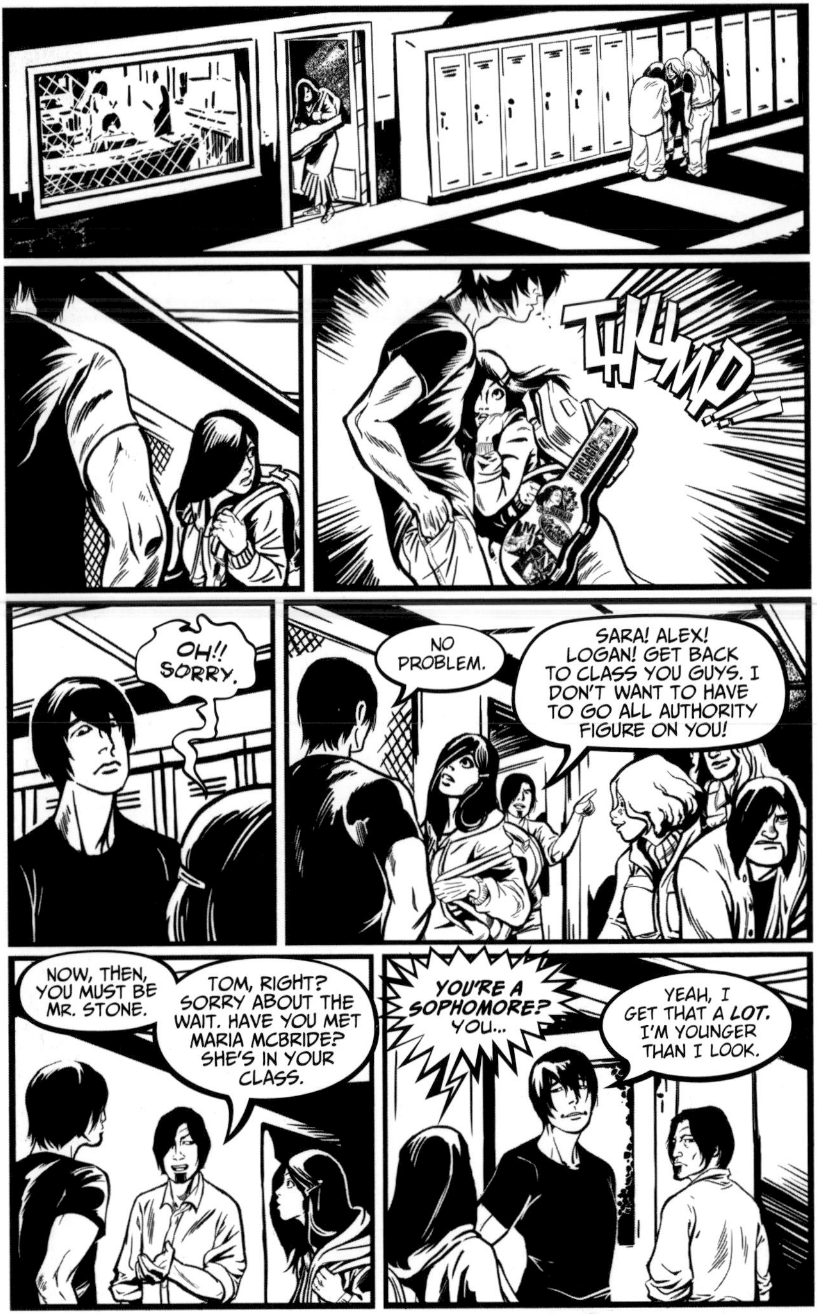
THUMP...!!
OH!! SORRY.
NO PROBLEM.
SARA! ALEX! LOGAN! GET BACK TO CLASS YOU GUYS. I DON'T WANT TO HAVE TO GO ALL AUTHORITY FIGURE ON YOU!
NOW, THEN, YOU MUST BE MR. STONE.
TOM, RIGHT? SORRY ABOUT THE WAIT. HAVE YOU MET MARIA MCBRIDE? SHE'S IN YOUR CLASS.
YOU'RE A SOPHOMORE? YOU...
YEAH, I GET THAT A **LOT.** I'M YOUNGER THAN I LOOK.

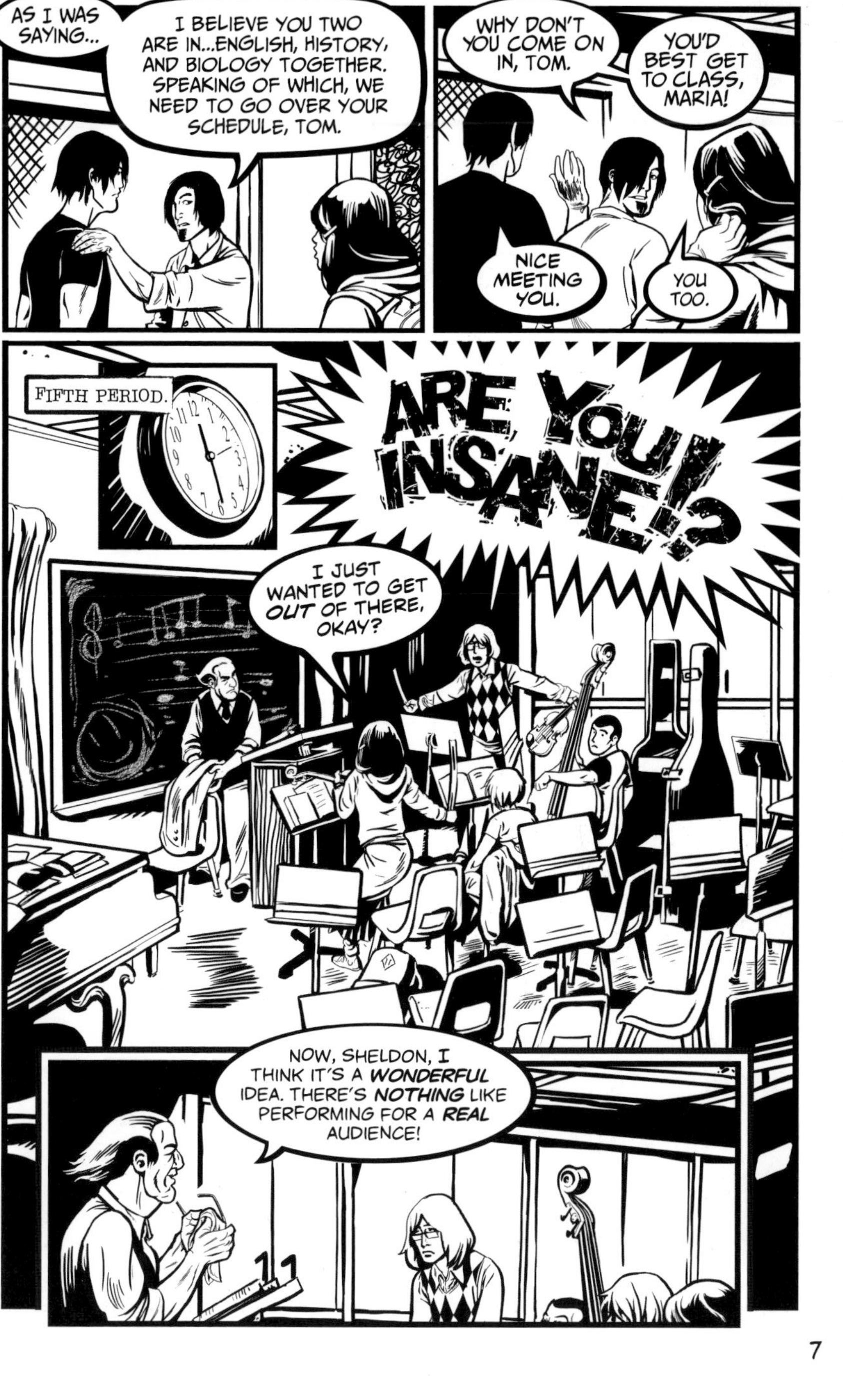
AS I WAS SAYING...
I BELIEVE YOU TWO ARE IN...ENGLISH, HISTORY, AND BIOLOGY TOGETHER. SPEAKING OF WHICH, WE NEED TO GO OVER YOUR SCHEDULE, TOM.
WHY DON'T YOU COME ON IN, TOM.
YOU'D BEST GET TO CLASS, MARIA!
NICE MEETING YOU.
YOU TOO.
FIFTH PERIOD.
ARE YOU INSANE!?
I JUST WANTED TO GET OUT OF THERE, OKAY?
NOW, SHELDON, I THINK IT'S A WONDERFUL IDEA. THERE'S NOTHING LIKE PERFORMING FOR A REAL AUDIENCE!

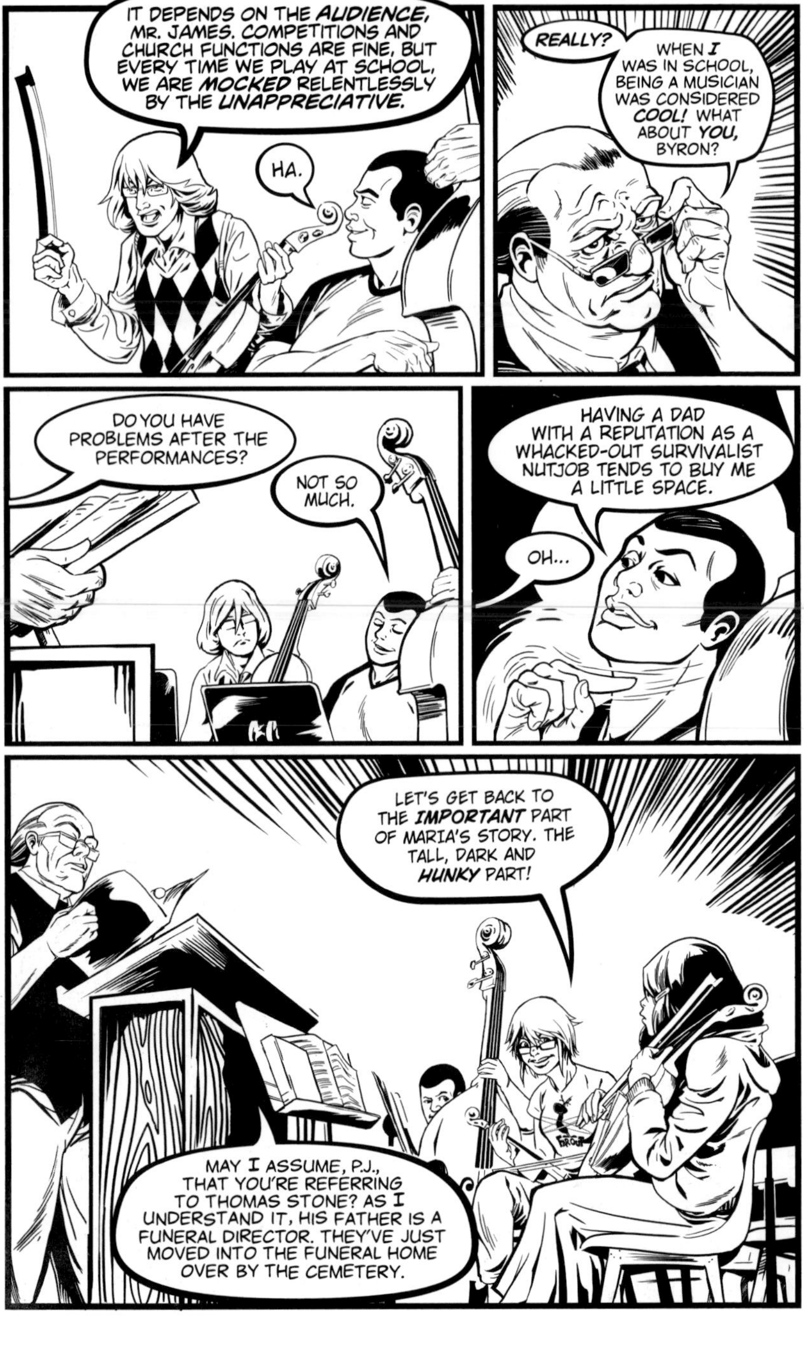
IT DEPENDS ON THE AUDIENCE, MR. JAMES. COMPETITIONS AND CHURCH FUNCTIONS ARE FINE, BUT EVERY TIME WE PLAY AT SCHOOL, WE ARE MOCKED RELENTLESSLY BY THE UNAPPRECIATIVE.
HA.
REALLY?
WHEN I WAS IN SCHOOL, BEING A MUSICIAN WAS CONSIDERED COOL! WHAT ABOUT YOU, BYRON?
DO YOU HAVE PROBLEMS AFTER THE PERFORMANCES?
NOT SO MUCH.
HAVING A DAD WITH A REPUTATION AS A WHACKED-OUT SURVIVALIST NUTJOB TENDS TO BUY ME A LITTLE SPACE.
OH...
LET'S GET BACK TO THE IMPORTANT PART OF MARIA'S STORY. THE TALL, DARK AND HUNKY PART!
MAY I ASSUME, P.J., THAT YOU'RE REFERRING TO THOMAS STONE? AS I UNDERSTAND IT, HIS FATHER IS A FUNERAL DIRECTOR. THEY'VE JUST MOVED INTO THE FUNERAL HOME OVER BY THE CEMETERY.

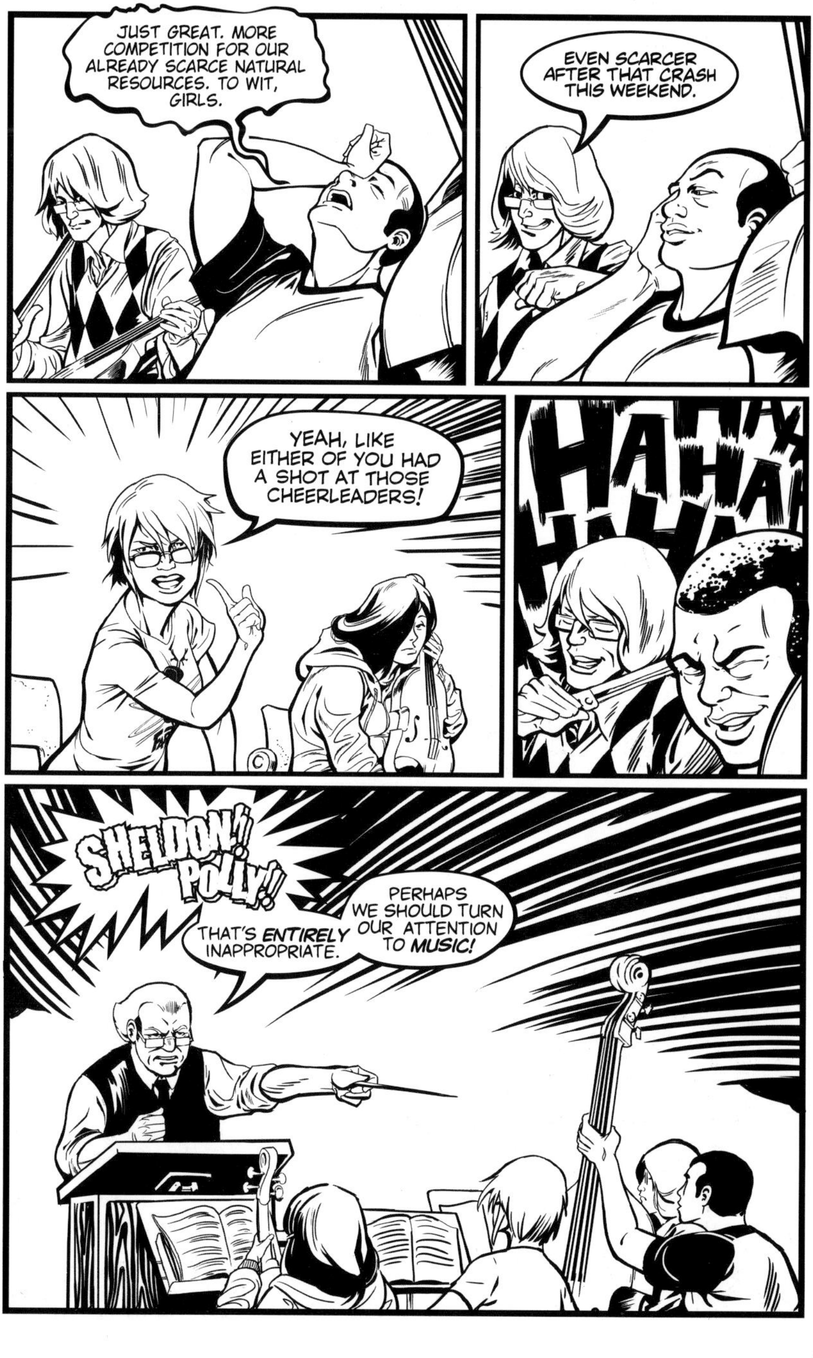

JUST GREAT. MORE COMPETITION FOR OUR ALREADY SCARCE NATURAL RESOURCES. TO WIT, GIRLS.
EVEN SCARCER AFTER THAT CRASH THIS WEEKEND.
YEAH, LIKE EITHER OF YOU HAD A SHOT AT THOSE CHEERLEADERS!
HAHAHA
SHELDON!! POLLY!!
THAT'S ENTIRELY INAPPROPRIATE.
PERHAPS WE SHOULD TURN OUR ATTENTION TO MUSIC!

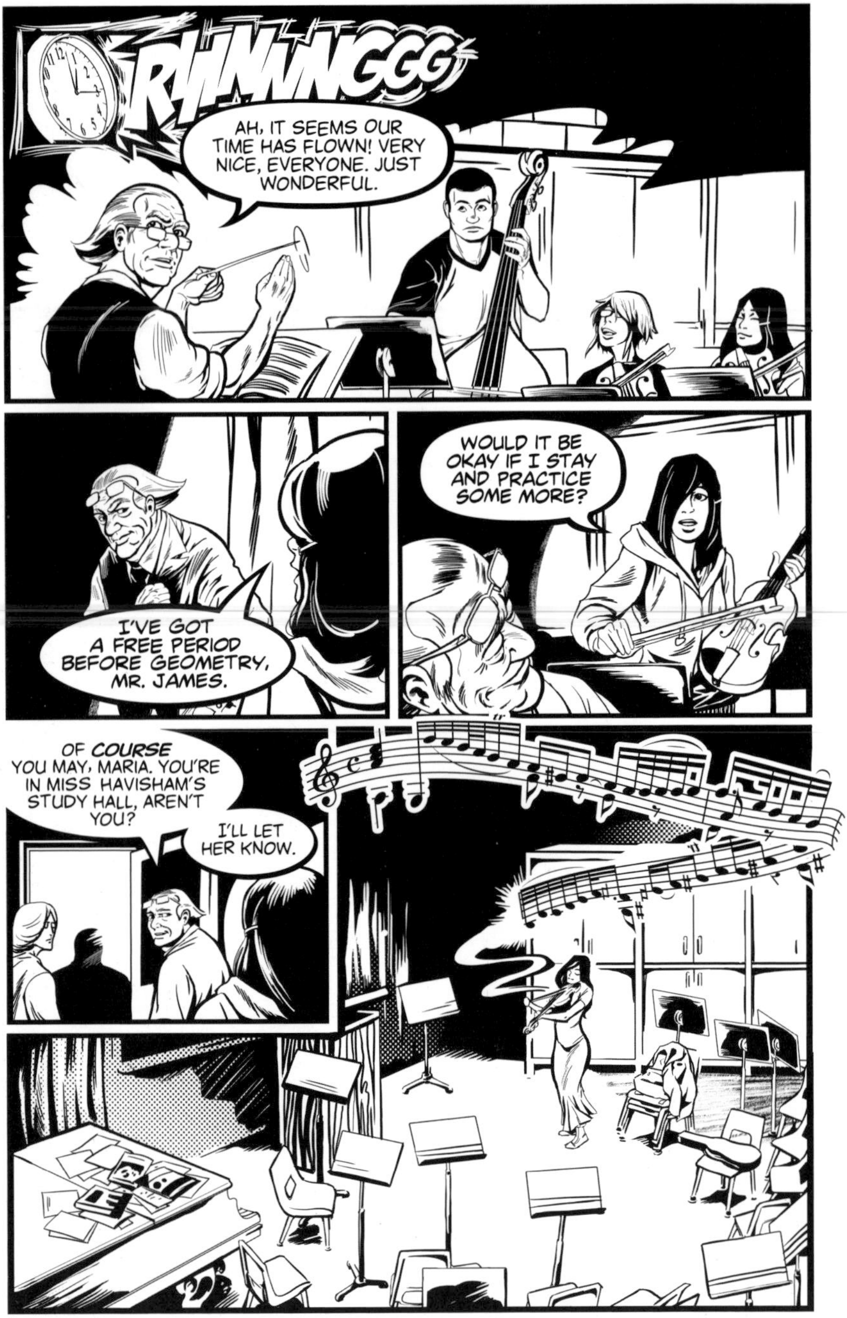
RHNNNNGGG
AH, IT SEEMS OUR TIME HAS FLOWN! VERY NICE, EVERYONE. JUST WONDERFUL.
I'VE GOT A FREE PERIOD BEFORE GEOMETRY, MR. JAMES.
WOULD IT BE OKAY IF I STAY AND PRACTICE SOME MORE?
OF **COURSE** YOU MAY, MARIA. YOU'RE IN MISS HAVISHAM'S STUDY HALL, AREN'T YOU?
I'LL LET HER KNOW.

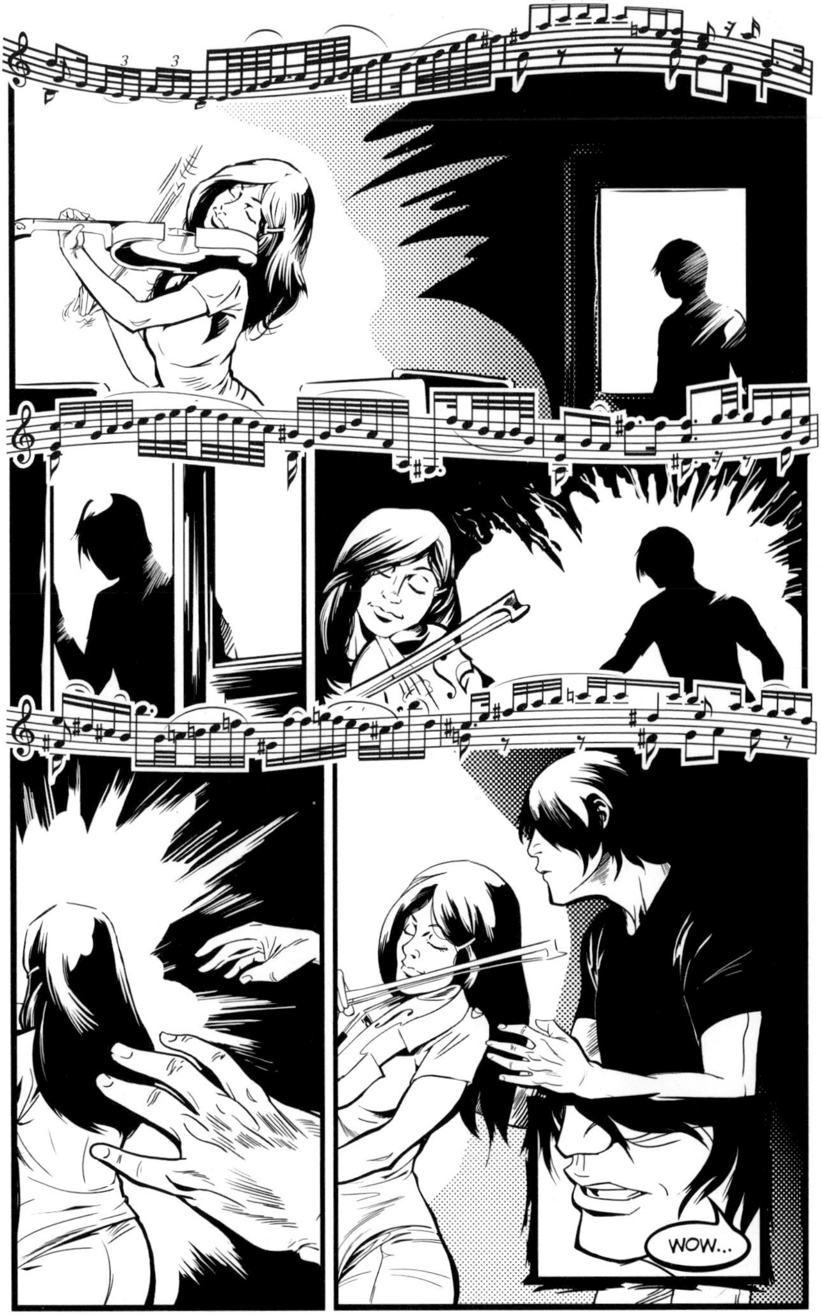
WOW...

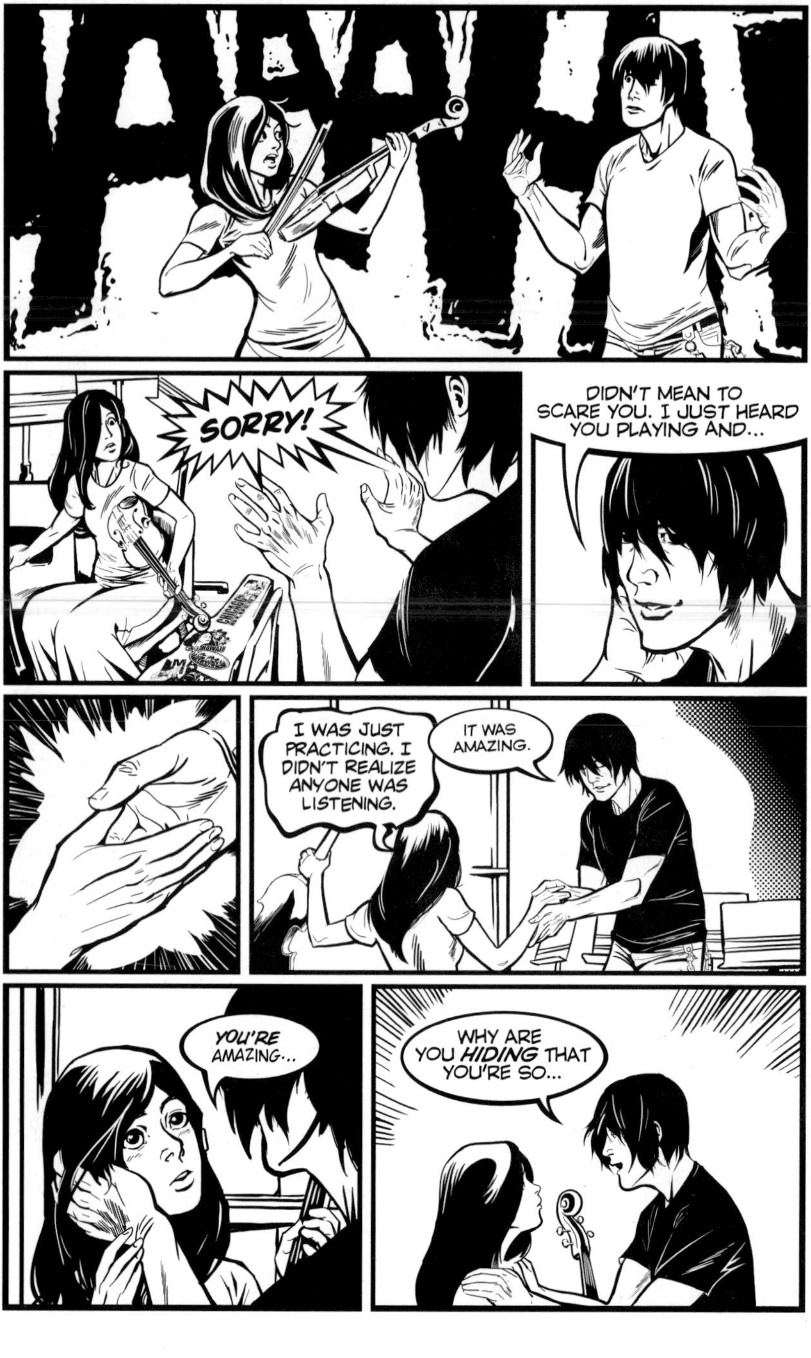
SORRY!
DIDN'T MEAN TO SCARE YOU. I JUST HEARD YOU PLAYING AND...
I WAS JUST PRACTICING. I DIDN'T REALIZE ANYONE WAS LISTENING.
IT WAS AMAZING.
YOU'RE AMAZING...
WHY ARE YOU HIDING THAT YOU'RE SO...

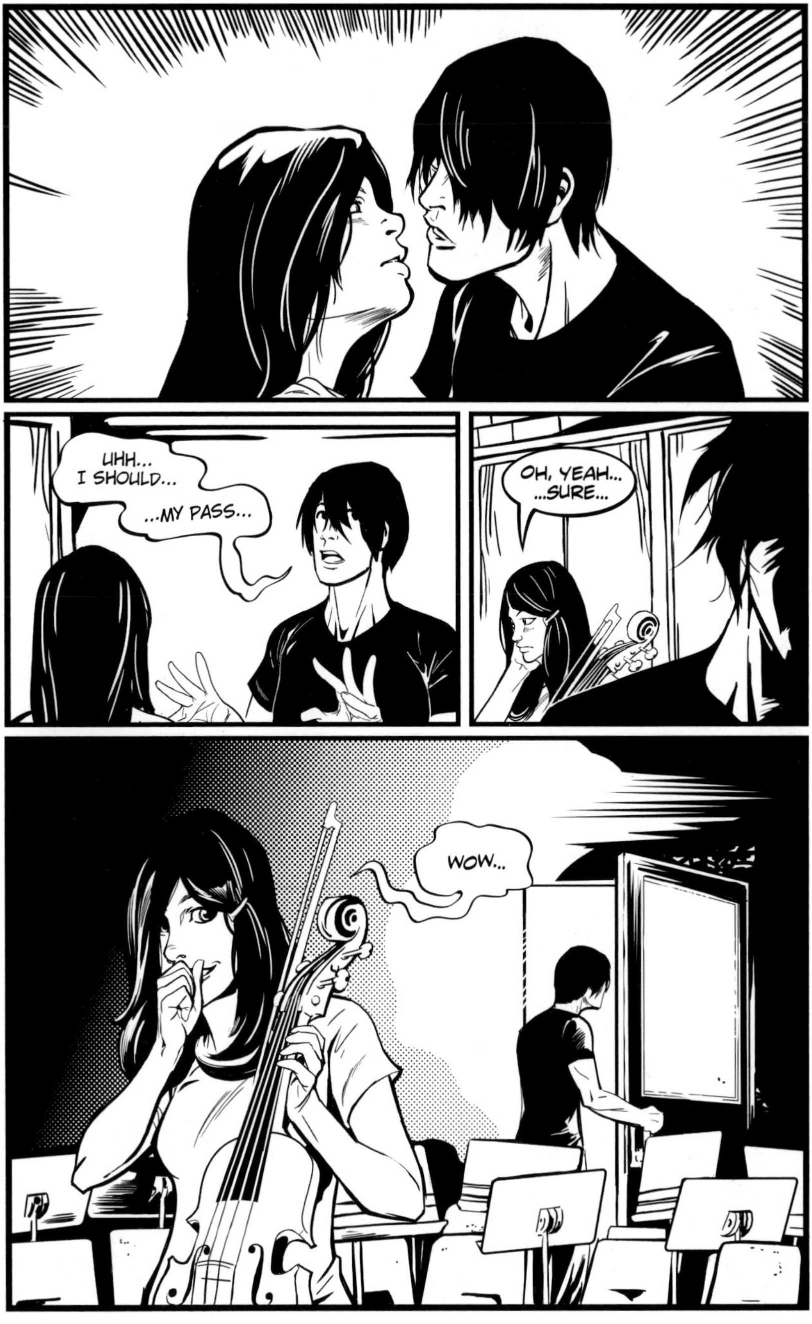
UHH...
I SHOULD...
...MY PASS...
OH, YEAH...
...SURE...
WOW...

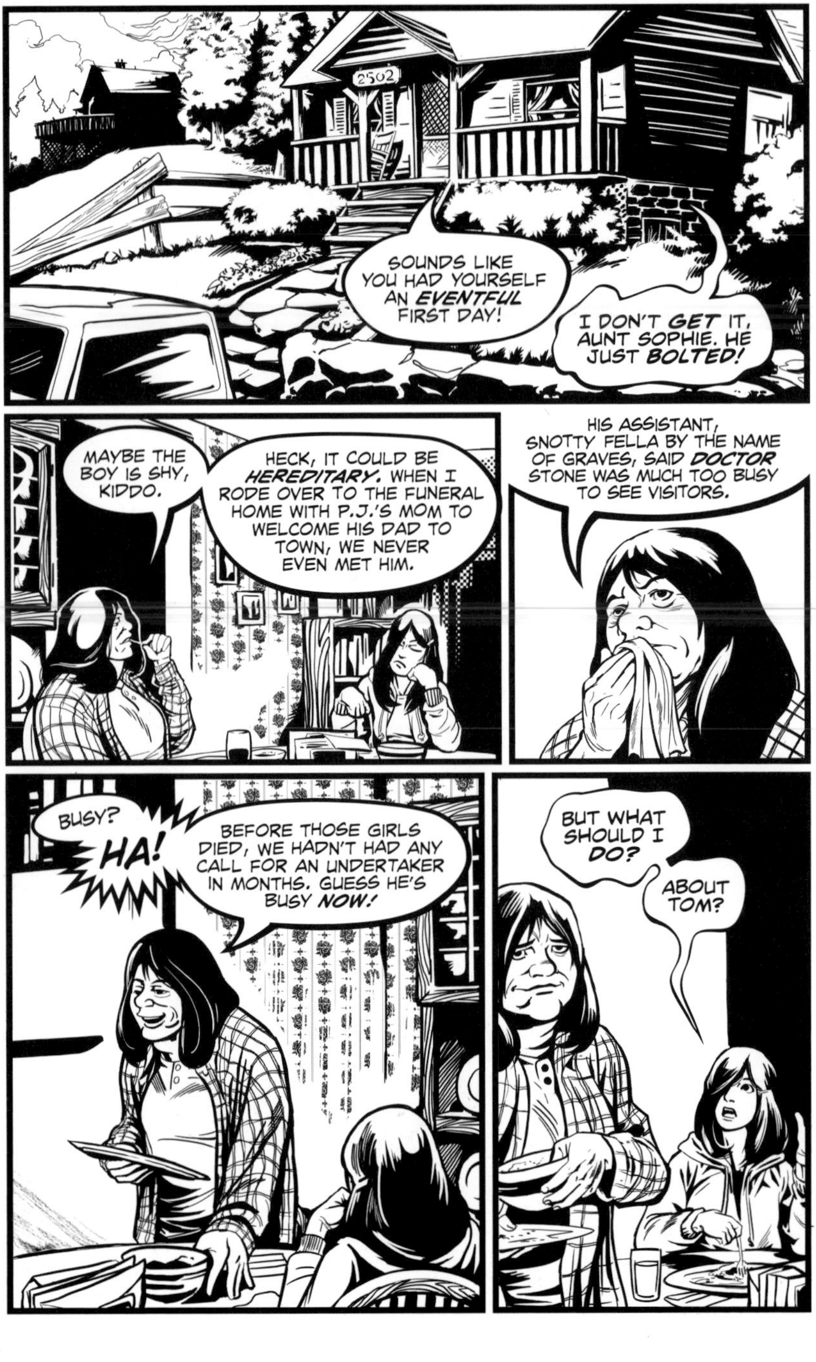
SOUNDS LIKE YOU HAD YOURSELF AN EVENTFUL FIRST DAY!
I DON'T GET IT, AUNT SOPHIE. HE JUST BOLTED!
MAYBE THE BOY IS SHY, KIDDO.
HECK, IT COULD BE HEREDITARY. WHEN I RODE OVER TO THE FUNERAL HOME WITH P.J.'S MOM TO WELCOME HIS DAD TO TOWN, WE NEVER EVEN MET HIM.
HIS ASSISTANT, SNOTTY FELLA BY THE NAME OF GRAVES, SAID DOCTOR STONE WAS MUCH TOO BUSY TO SEE VISITORS.
BUSY? HA!
BEFORE THOSE GIRLS DIED, WE HADN'T HAD ANY CALL FOR AN UNDERTAKER IN MONTHS. GUESS HE'S BUSY NOW!
BUT WHAT SHOULD I DO?
ABOUT TOM?

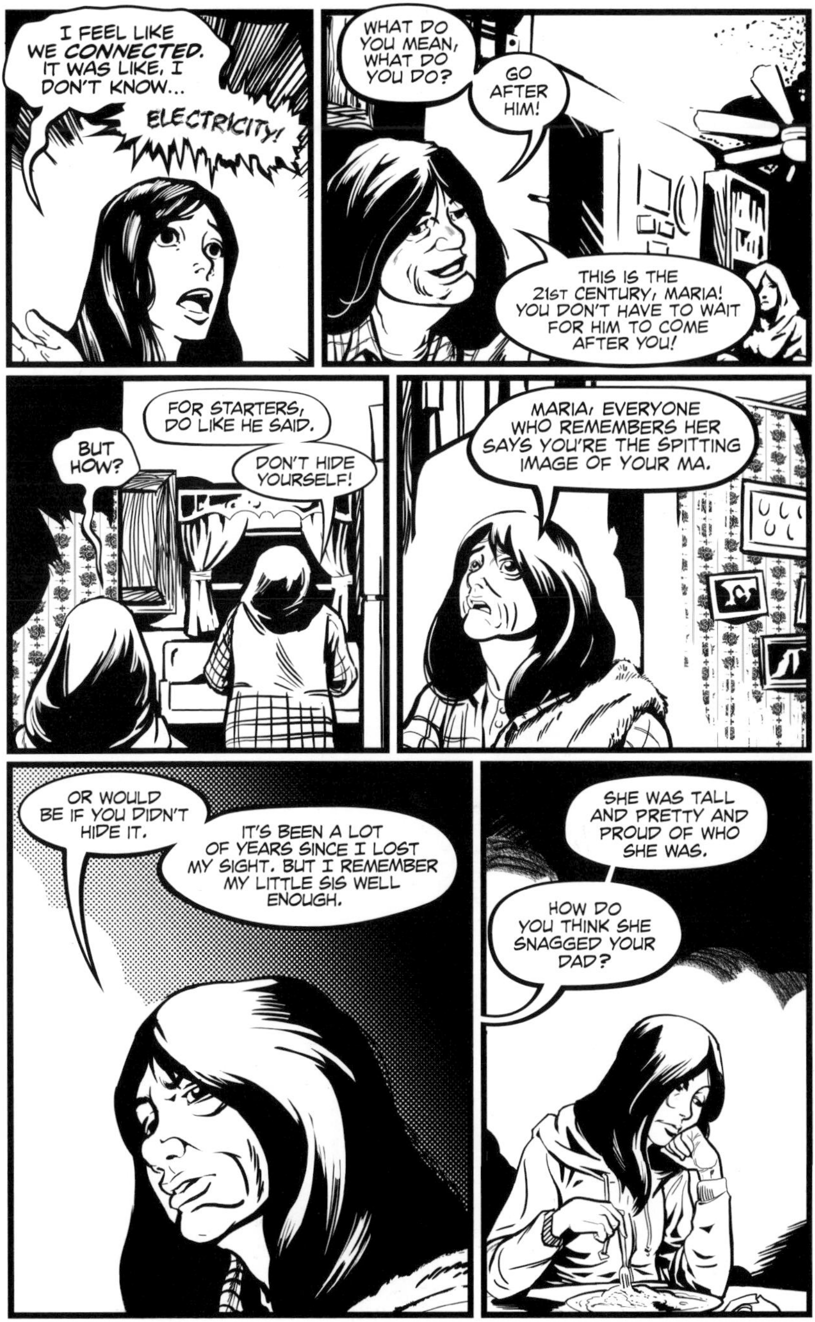
I FEEL LIKE WE CONNECTED. IT WAS LIKE, I DON'T KNOW...
ELECTRICITY!
WHAT DO YOU MEAN, WHAT DO YOU DO?
GO AFTER HIM!
THIS IS THE 21ST CENTURY, MARIA! YOU DON'T HAVE TO WAIT FOR HIM TO COME AFTER YOU!
BUT HOW?
FOR STARTERS, DO LIKE HE SAID.
DON'T HIDE YOURSELF!
MARIA, EVERYONE WHO REMEMBERS HER SAYS YOU'RE THE SPITTING IMAGE OF YOUR MA.
OR WOULD BE IF YOU DIDN'T HIDE IT.
IT'S BEEN A LOT OF YEARS SINCE I LOST MY SIGHT. BUT I REMEMBER MY LITTLE SIS WELL ENOUGH.
SHE WAS TALL AND PRETTY AND PROUD OF WHO SHE WAS.
HOW DO YOU THINK SHE SNAGGED YOUR DAD?

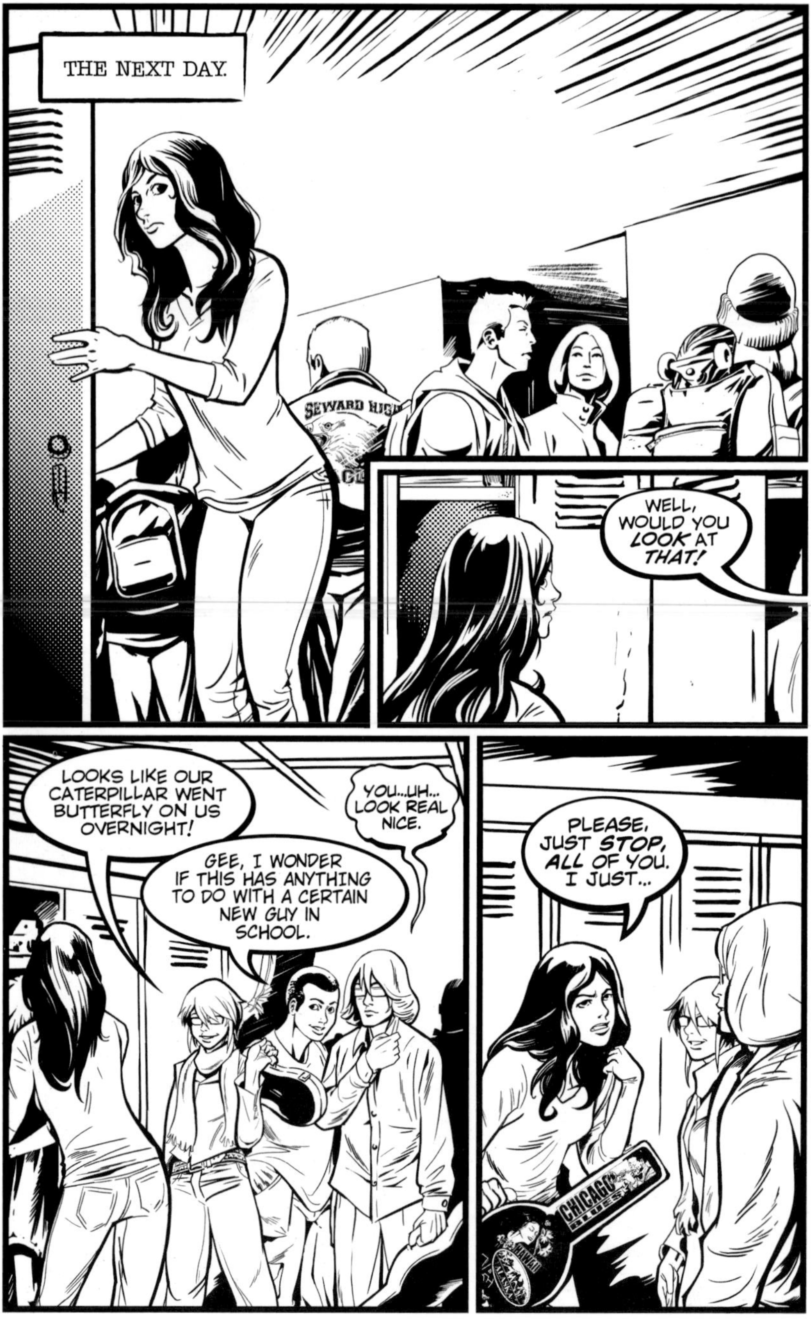

THE NEXT DAY.
SEWARD HIGH
WELL, WOULD YOU LOOK AT THAT!
LOOKS LIKE OUR CATERPILLAR WENT BUTTERFLY ON US OVERNIGHT!
YOU...UH... LOOK REAL NICE.
GEE, I WONDER IF THIS HAS ANYTHING TO DO WITH A CERTAIN NEW GUY IN SCHOOL.
PLEASE, JUST STOP, ALL OF YOU. I JUST...
CHICAGO BLUES

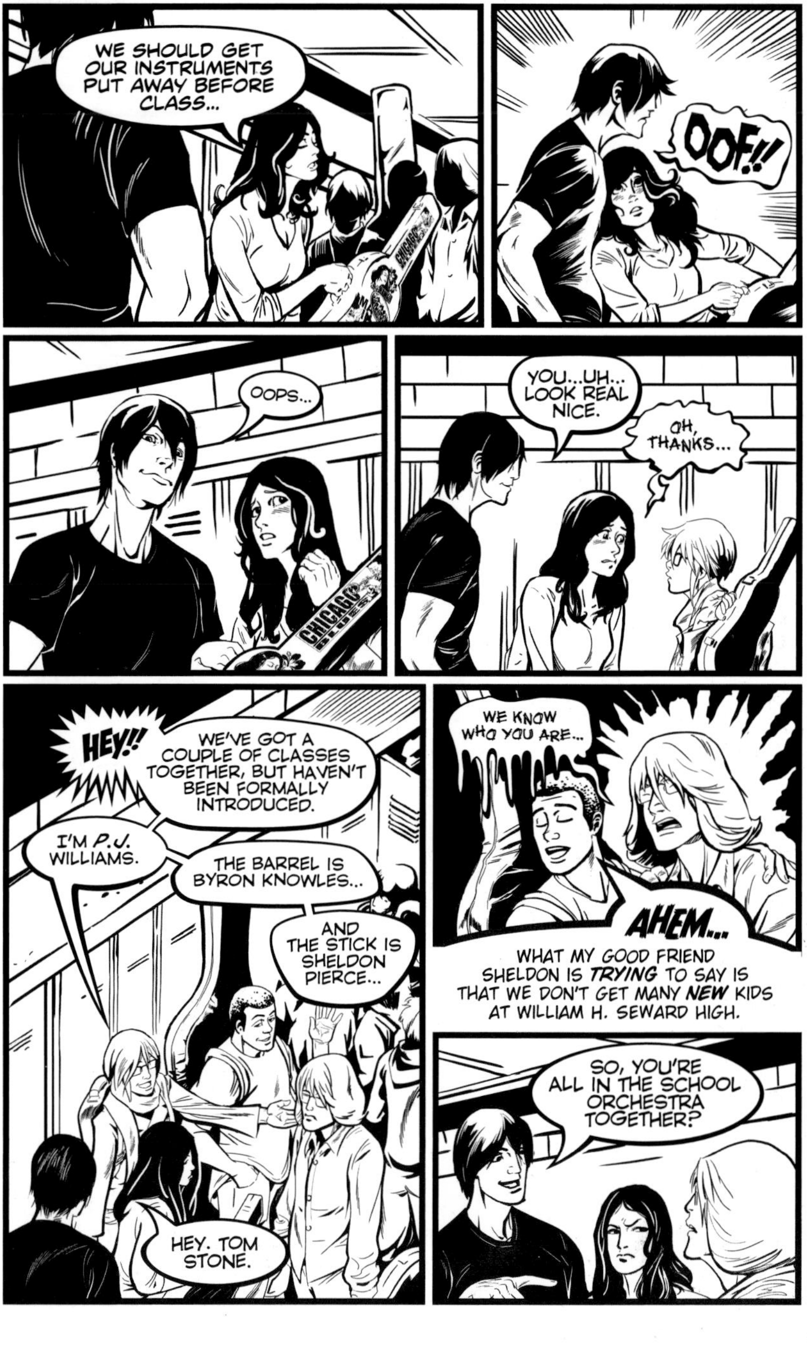

WE SHOULD GET OUR INSTRUMENTS PUT AWAY BEFORE CLASS...
OOF!!
OOPS...
YOU...UH... LOOK REAL NICE.
OH, THANKS...
HEY!!
WE'VE GOT A COUPLE OF CLASSES TOGETHER, BUT HAVEN'T BEEN FORMALLY INTRODUCED.
I'M P.J. WILLIAMS.
THE BARREL IS BYRON KNOWLES...
AND THE STICK IS SHELDON PIERCE...
HEY. TOM STONE.
WE KNOW WHO YOU ARE...
AHEM...
WHAT MY GOOD FRIEND SHELDON IS TRYING TO SAY IS THAT WE DON'T GET MANY NEW KIDS AT WILLIAM H. SEWARD HIGH.
SO, YOU'RE ALL IN THE SCHOOL ORCHESTRA TOGETHER?

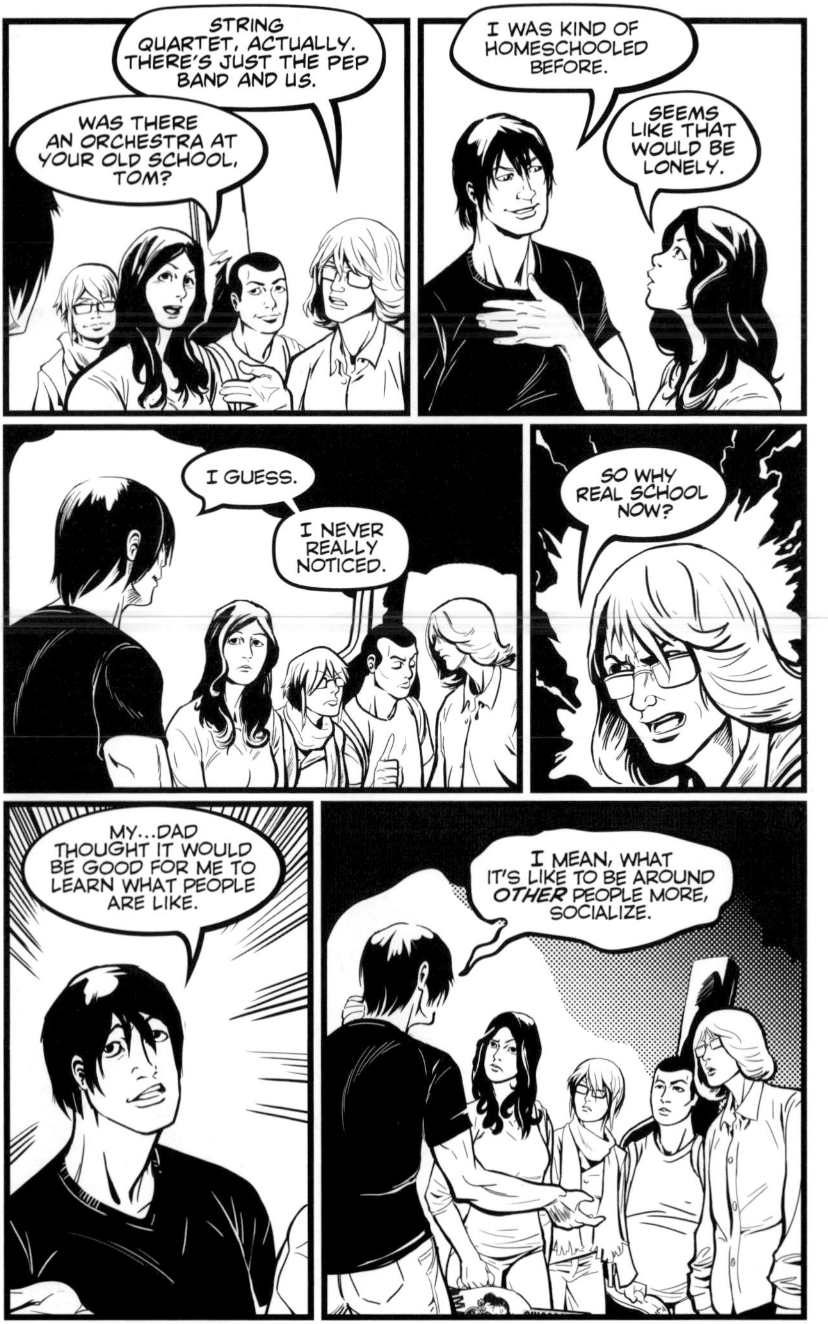
WAS THERE AN ORCHESTRA AT YOUR OLD SCHOOL, TOM?
STRING QUARTET, ACTUALLY. THERE'S JUST THE PEP BAND AND US.
I WAS KIND OF HOMESCHOOLED BEFORE.
SEEMS LIKE THAT WOULD BE LONELY.
I GUESS.
I NEVER REALLY NOTICED.
SO WHY REAL SCHOOL NOW?
MY...DAD THOUGHT IT WOULD BE GOOD FOR ME TO LEARN WHAT PEOPLE ARE LIKE.
I MEAN, WHAT IT'S LIKE TO BE AROUND *OTHER* PEOPLE MORE, SOCIALIZE.

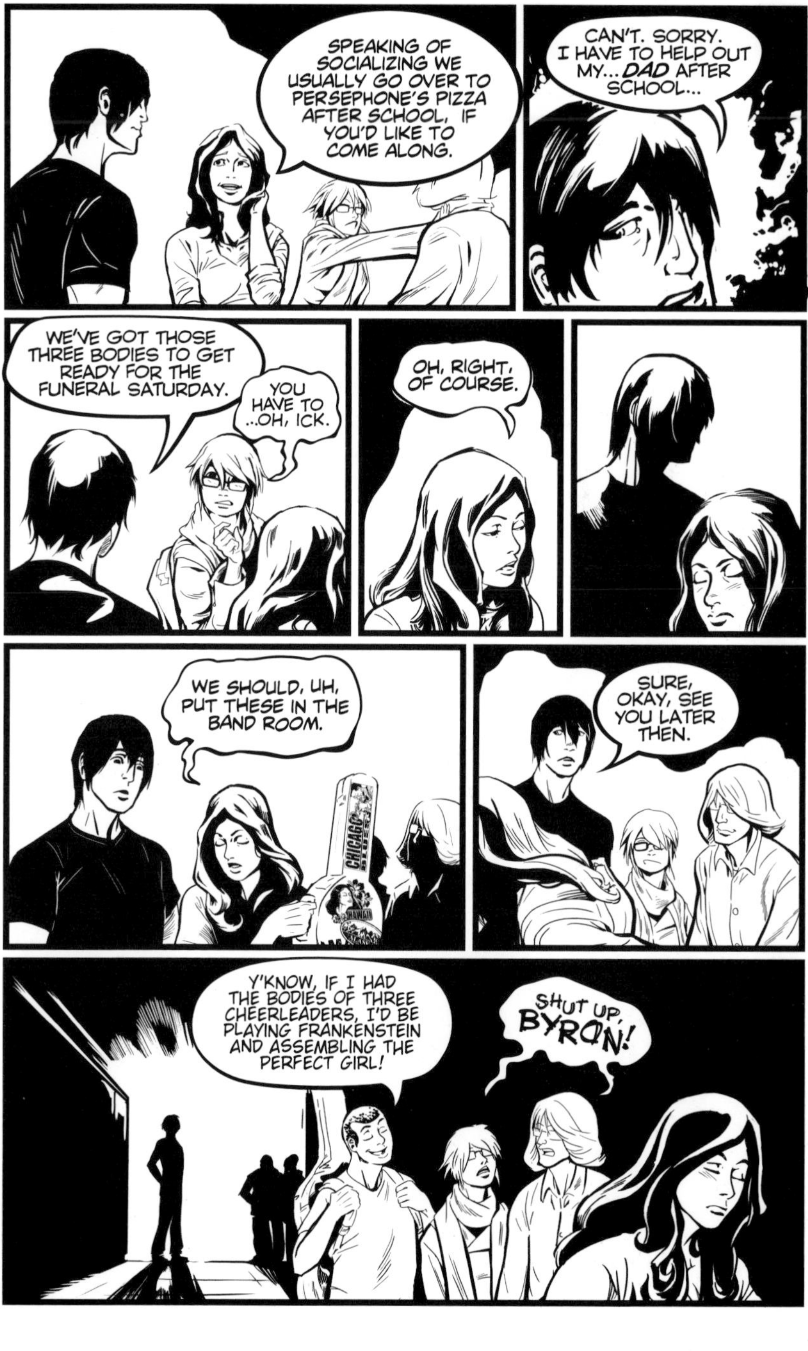
SPEAKING OF SOCIALIZING WE USUALLY GO OVER TO PERSEPHONE'S PIZZA AFTER SCHOOL, IF YOU'D LIKE TO COME ALONG.
CAN'T. SORRY. I HAVE TO HELP OUT MY...DAD AFTER SCHOOL...
WE'VE GOT THOSE THREE BODIES TO GET READY FOR THE FUNERAL SATURDAY.
YOU HAVE TO ..OH, ICK.
OH, RIGHT, OF COURSE.
WE SHOULD, UH, PUT THESE IN THE BAND ROOM.
CHICAGO BLUES
HAWAII
SURE, OKAY, SEE YOU LATER THEN.
Y'KNOW, IF I HAD THE BODIES OF THREE CHEERLEADERS, I'D BE PLAYING FRANKENSTEIN AND ASSEMBLING THE PERFECT GIRL!
SHUT UP, BYRON!

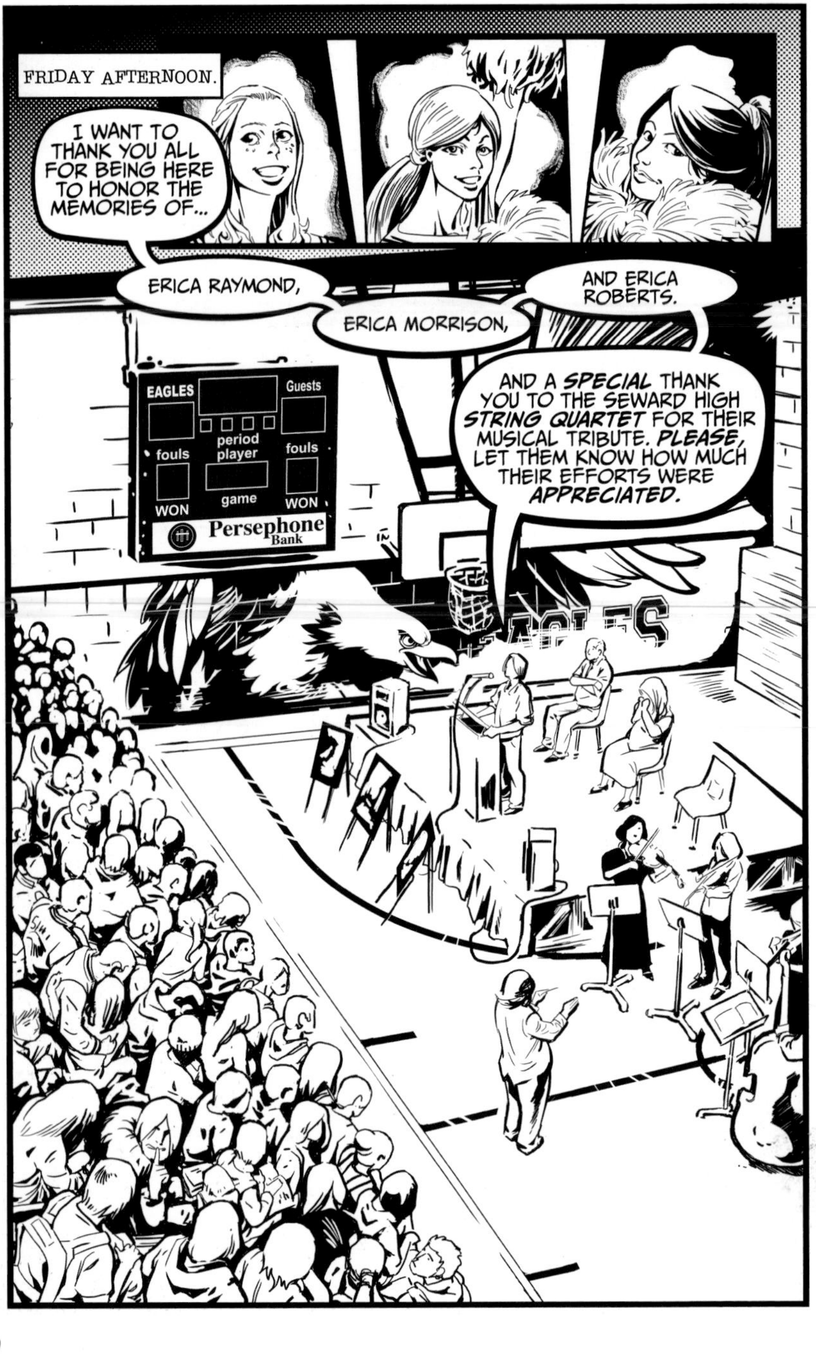
FRIDAY AFTERNOON.
I WANT TO THANK YOU ALL FOR BEING HERE TO HONOR THE MEMORIES OF...
ERICA RAYMOND,
ERICA MORRISON,
AND ERICA ROBERTS.
AND A SPECIAL THANK YOU TO THE SEWARD HIGH STRING QUARTET FOR THEIR MUSICAL TRIBUTE. PLEASE, LET THEM KNOW HOW MUCH THEIR EFFORTS WERE APPRECIATED.
EAGLES
Guests
period
player
fouls
fouls
game
WON
WON
Persephone Bank

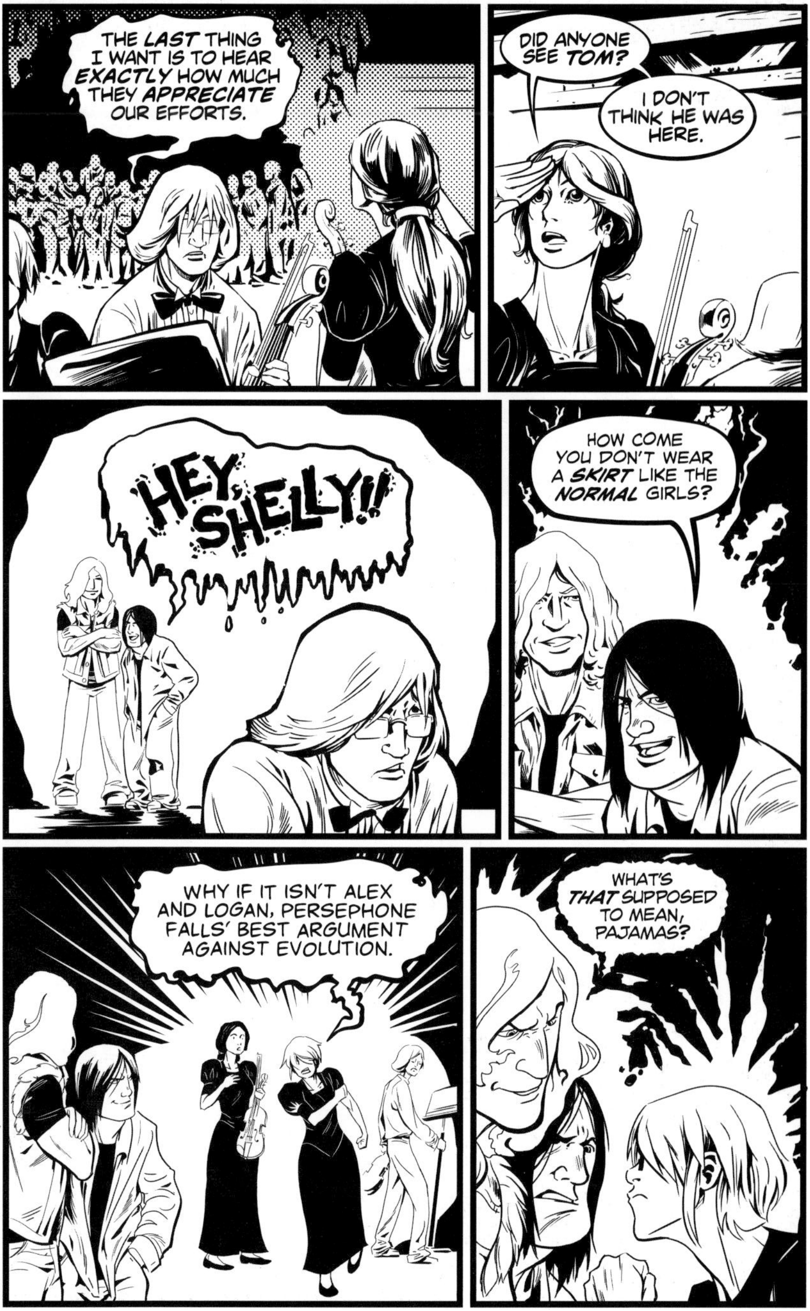
THE LAST THING I WANT IS TO HEAR EXACTLY HOW MUCH THEY APPRECIATE OUR EFFORTS.
DID ANYONE SEE TOM?
I DON'T THINK HE WAS HERE.
HEY, SHELLY!!
HOW COME YOU DON'T WEAR A SKIRT LIKE THE NORMAL GIRLS?
WHY IF IT ISN'T ALEX AND LOGAN, PERSEPHONE FALLS' BEST ARGUMENT AGAINST EVOLUTION.
WHAT'S THAT SUPPOSED TO MEAN, PAJAMAS?

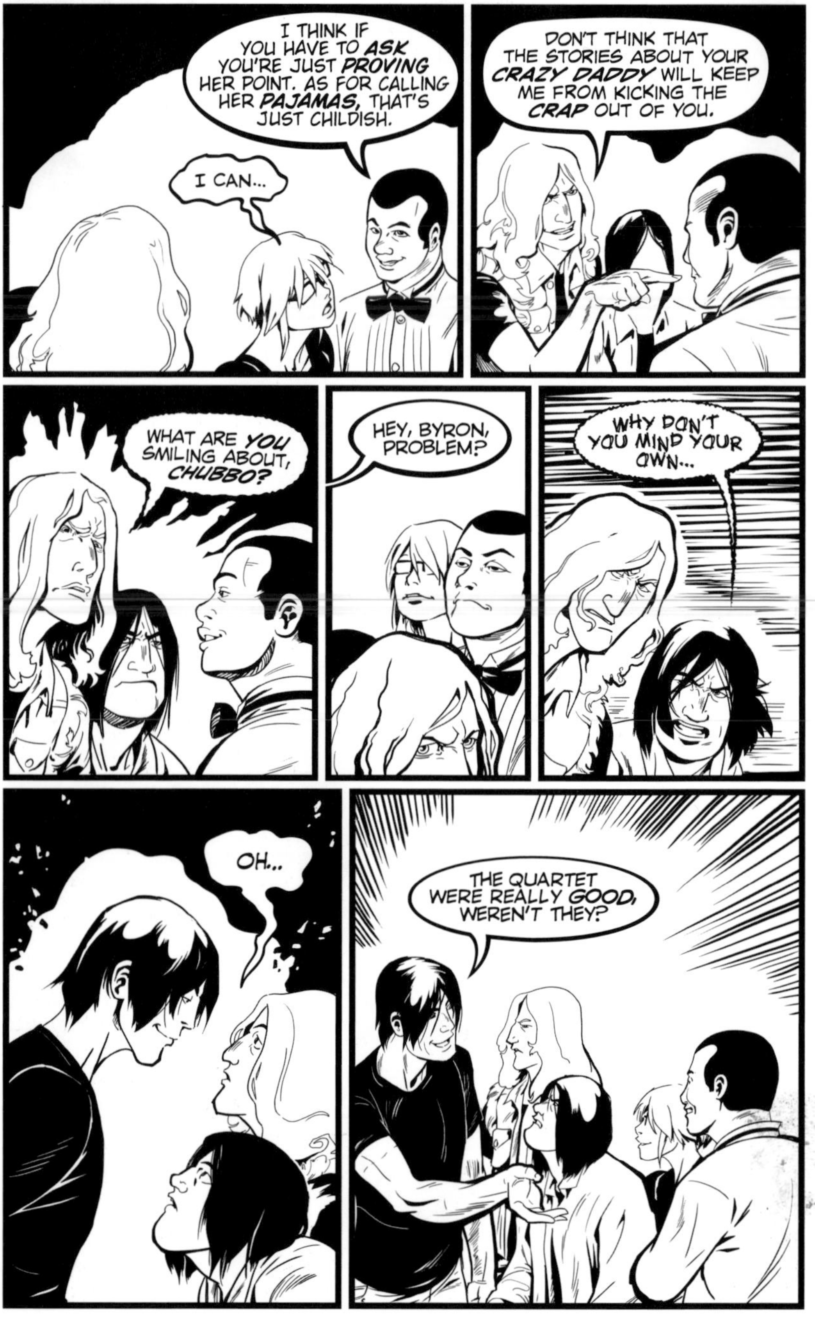
I THINK IF YOU HAVE TO ASK YOU'RE JUST PROVING HER POINT. AS FOR CALLING HER PAJAMAS, THAT'S JUST CHILDISH.
I CAN...
DON'T THINK THAT THE STORIES ABOUT YOUR CRAZY DADDY WILL KEEP ME FROM KICKING THE CRAP OUT OF YOU.
WHAT ARE YOU SMILING ABOUT, CHUBBO?
HEY, BYRON, PROBLEM?
WHY DON'T YOU MIND YOUR OWN...
OH...
THE QUARTET WERE REALLY GOOD, WEREN'T THEY?

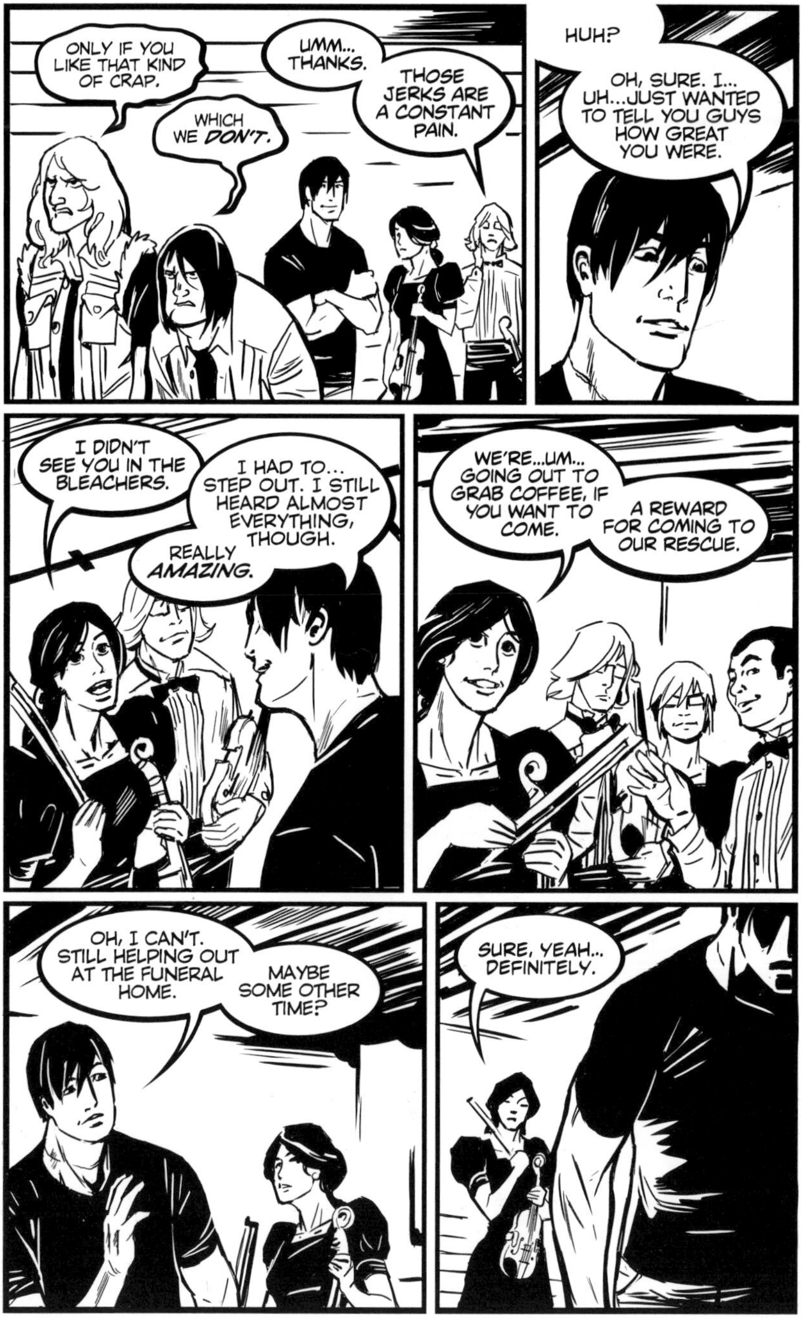

ONLY IF YOU LIKE THAT KIND OF CRAP.
WHICH WE DON'T.
UMM... THANKS.
THOSE JERKS ARE A CONSTANT PAIN.
HUH?
OH, SURE. I... UH...JUST WANTED TO TELL YOU GUYS HOW GREAT YOU WERE.
I DIDN'T SEE YOU IN THE BLEACHERS.
I HAD TO... STEP OUT. I STILL HEARD ALMOST EVERYTHING, THOUGH.
REALLY AMAZING.
WE'RE...UM... GOING OUT TO GRAB COFFEE, IF YOU WANT TO COME.
A REWARD FOR COMING TO OUR RESCUE.
OH, I CAN'T. STILL HELPING OUT AT THE FUNERAL HOME.
MAYBE SOME OTHER TIME?
SURE, YEAH... DEFINITELY.

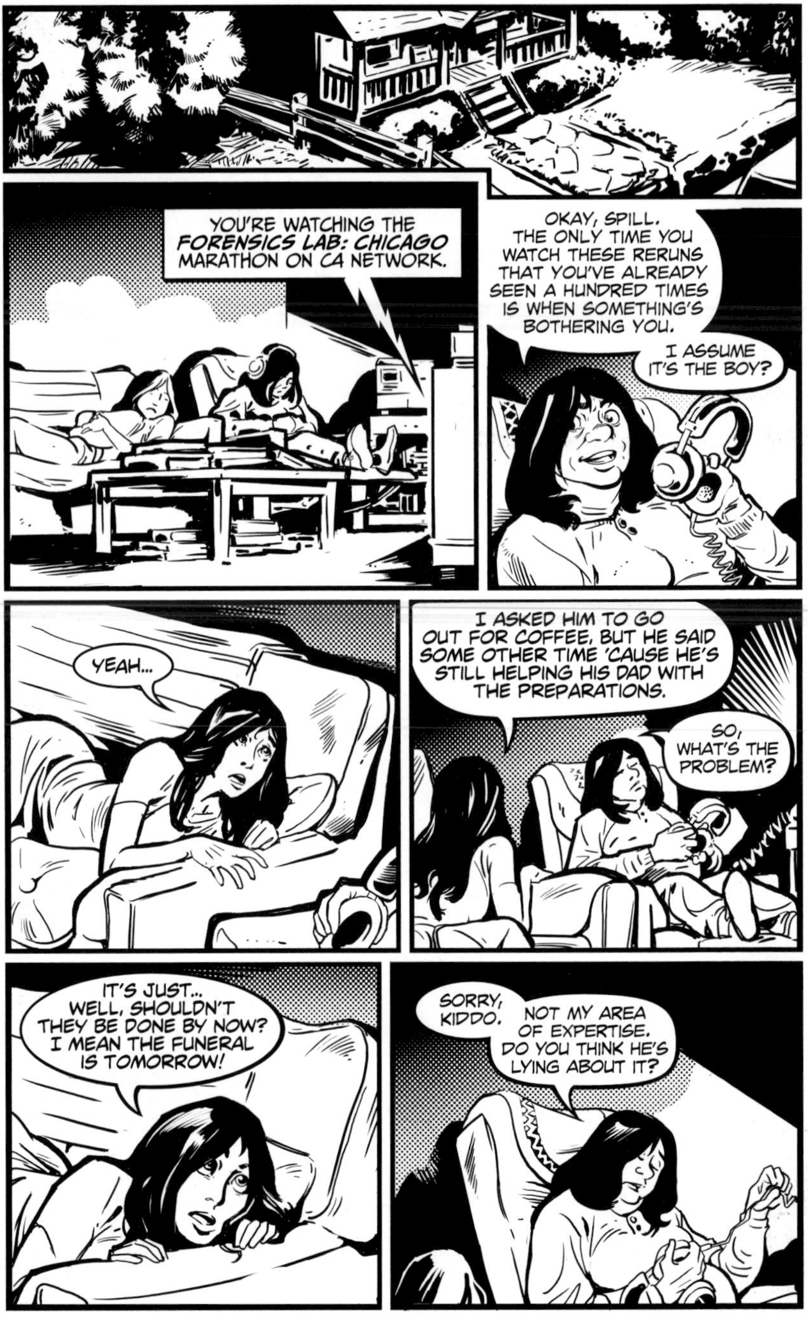
YOU'RE WATCHING THE FORENSICS LAB: CHICAGO MARATHON ON C4 NETWORK.
OKAY, SPILL. THE ONLY TIME YOU WATCH THESE RERUNS THAT YOU'VE ALREADY SEEN A HUNDRED TIMES IS WHEN SOMETHING'S BOTHERING YOU.
I ASSUME IT'S THE BOY?
YEAH...
I ASKED HIM TO GO OUT FOR COFFEE, BUT HE SAID SOME OTHER TIME 'CAUSE HE'S STILL HELPING HIS DAD WITH THE PREPARATIONS.
SO, WHAT'S THE PROBLEM?
IT'S JUST... WELL, SHOULDN'T THEY BE DONE BY NOW? I MEAN THE FUNERAL IS TOMORROW!
SORRY, KIDDO.
NOT MY AREA OF EXPERTISE. DO YOU THINK HE'S LYING ABOUT IT?

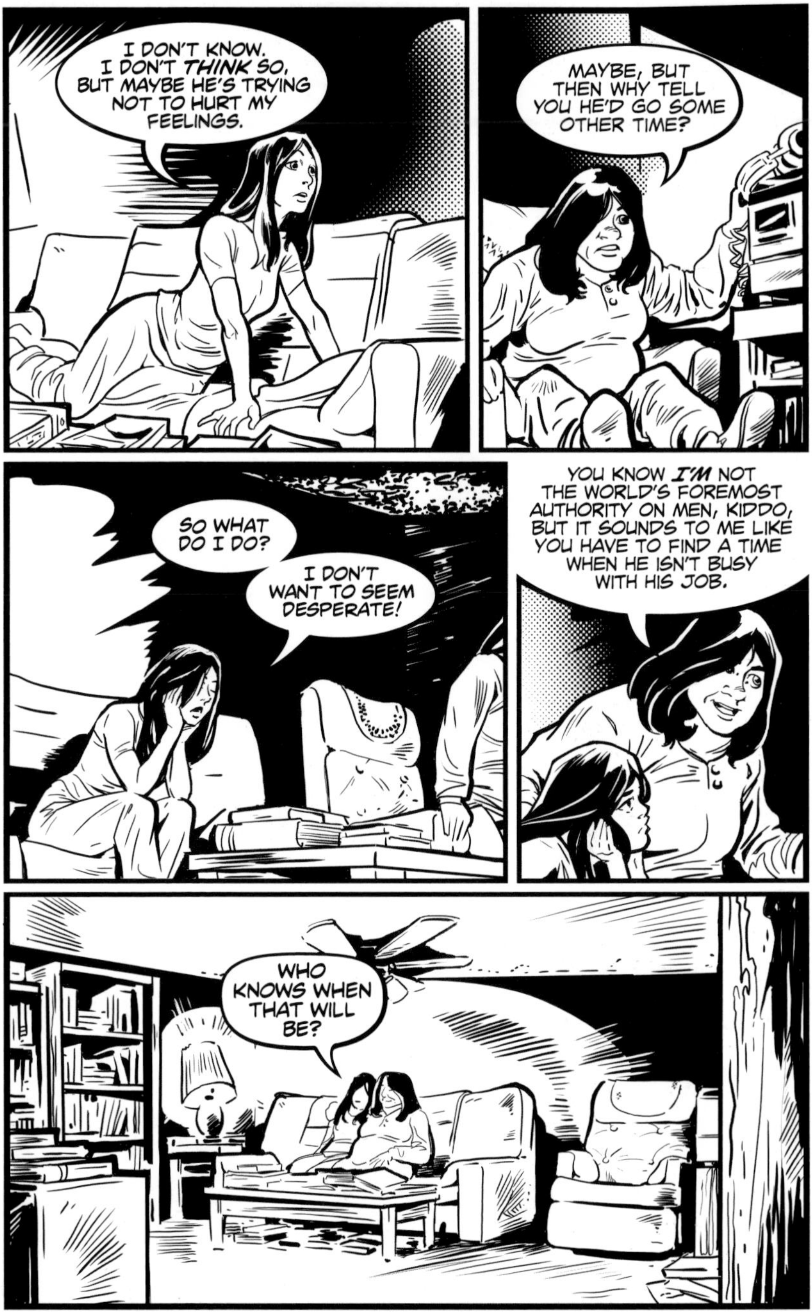
I DON'T KNOW. I DON'T THINK SO, BUT MAYBE HE'S TRYING NOT TO HURT MY FEELINGS.
MAYBE, BUT THEN WHY TELL YOU HE'D GO SOME OTHER TIME?
SO WHAT DO I DO?
I DON'T WANT TO SEEM DESPERATE!
YOU KNOW I'M NOT THE WORLD'S FOREMOST AUTHORITY ON MEN, KIDDO, BUT IT SOUNDS TO ME LIKE YOU HAVE TO FIND A TIME WHEN HE ISN'T BUSY WITH HIS JOB.
WHO KNOWS WHEN THAT WILL BE?

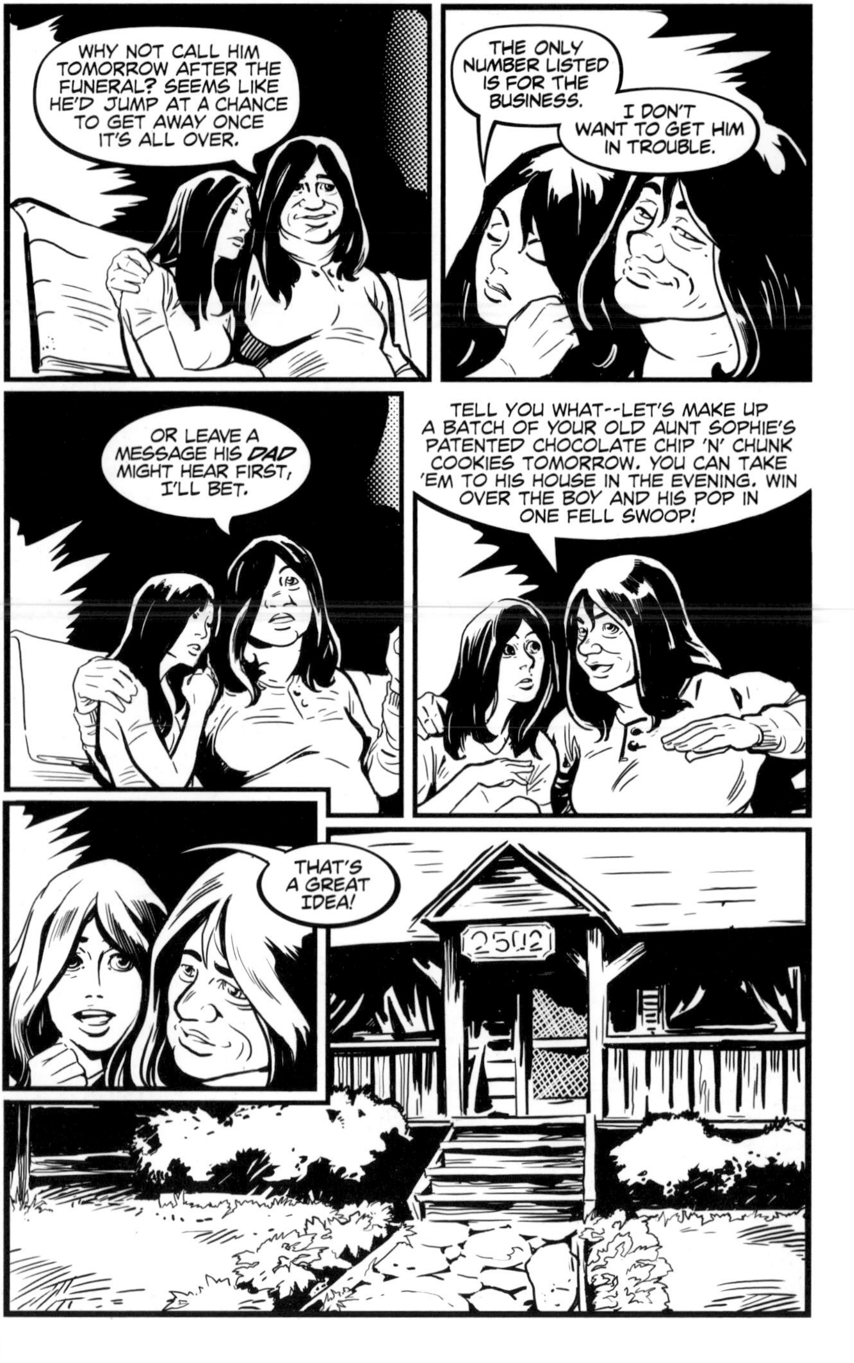
WHY NOT CALL HIM TOMORROW AFTER THE FUNERAL? SEEMS LIKE HE'D JUMP AT A CHANCE TO GET AWAY ONCE IT'S ALL OVER.
THE ONLY NUMBER LISTED IS FOR THE BUSINESS.
I DON'T WANT TO GET HIM IN TROUBLE.
OR LEAVE A MESSAGE HIS *DAD* MIGHT HEAR FIRST, I'LL BET.
TELL YOU WHAT--LET'S MAKE UP A BATCH OF YOUR OLD AUNT SOPHIE'S PATENTED CHOCOLATE CHIP 'N' CHUNK COOKIES TOMORROW. YOU CAN TAKE 'EM TO HIS HOUSE IN THE EVENING. WIN OVER THE BOY AND HIS POP IN ONE FELL SWOOP!
THAT'S A GREAT IDEA!
2502

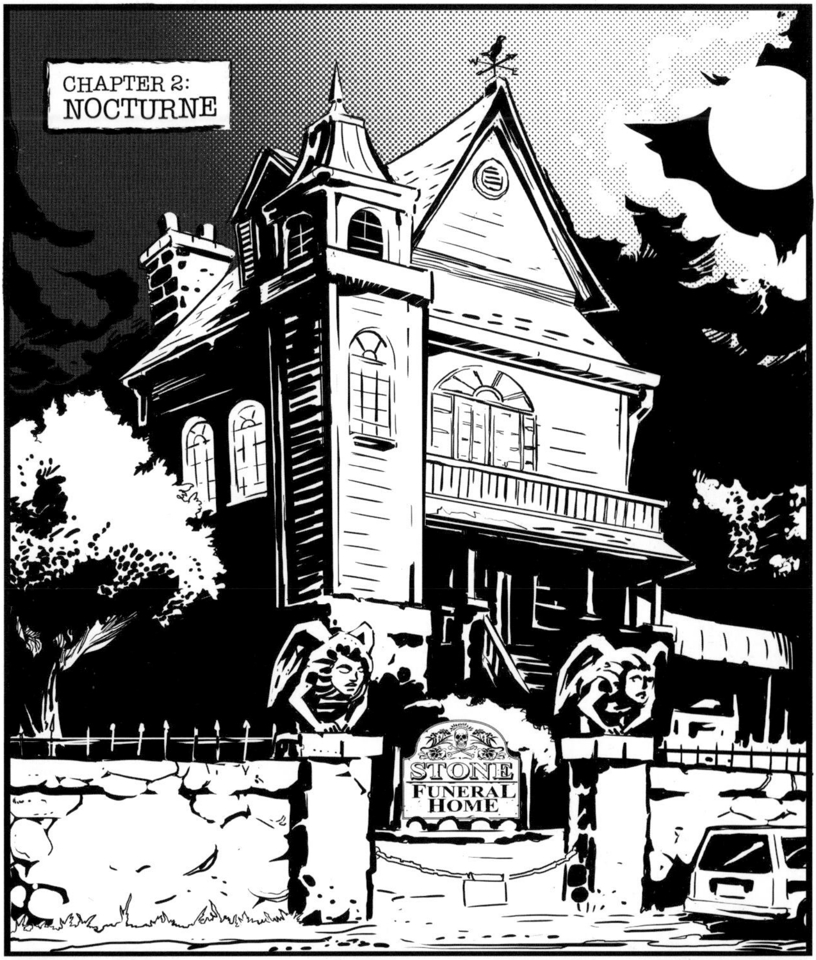
CHAPTER 2:
NOCTURNE
STONE
FUNERAL
HOME

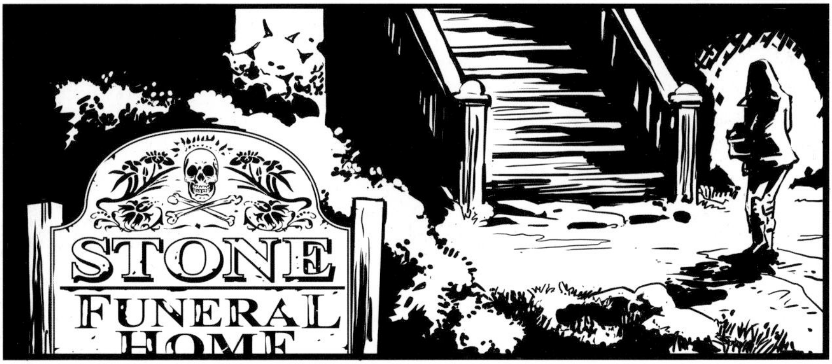
STONE
FUNERAL

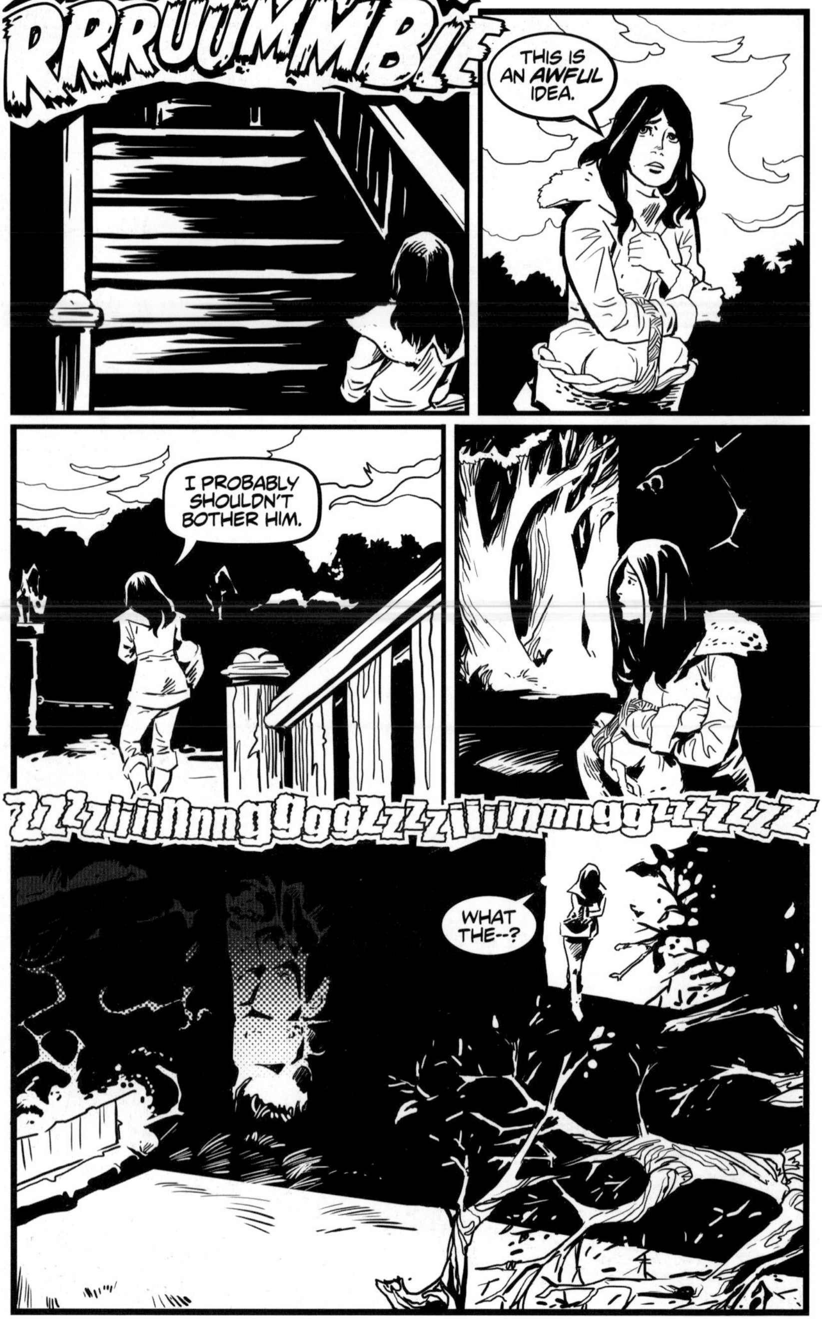
RRRUUMMBLE
THIS IS AN AWFUL IDEA.
I PROBABLY SHOULDN'T BOTHER HIM.
ZZZziiiiNnngGggZZZziiiinnnggZZZZZZ
WHAT THE--?

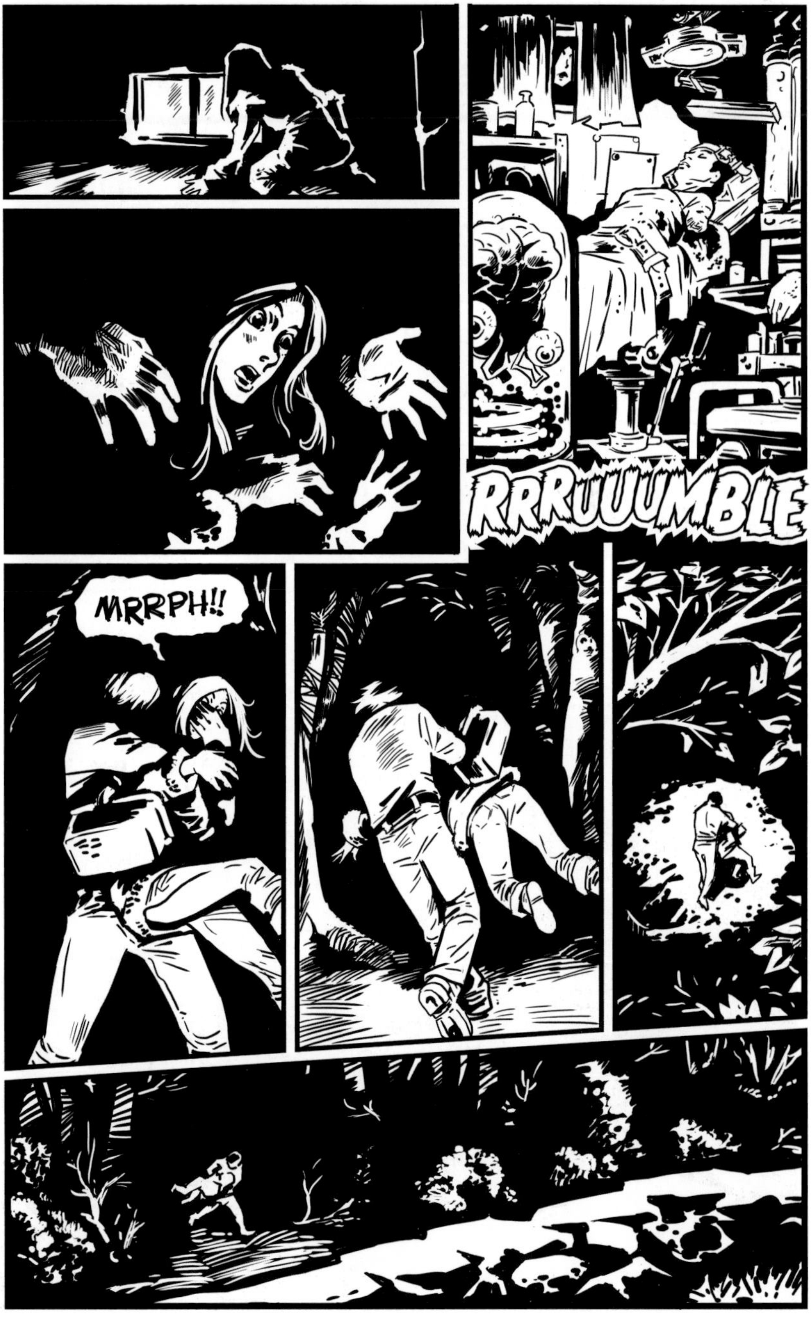
RRRUUUMBLE
MRRPH!!

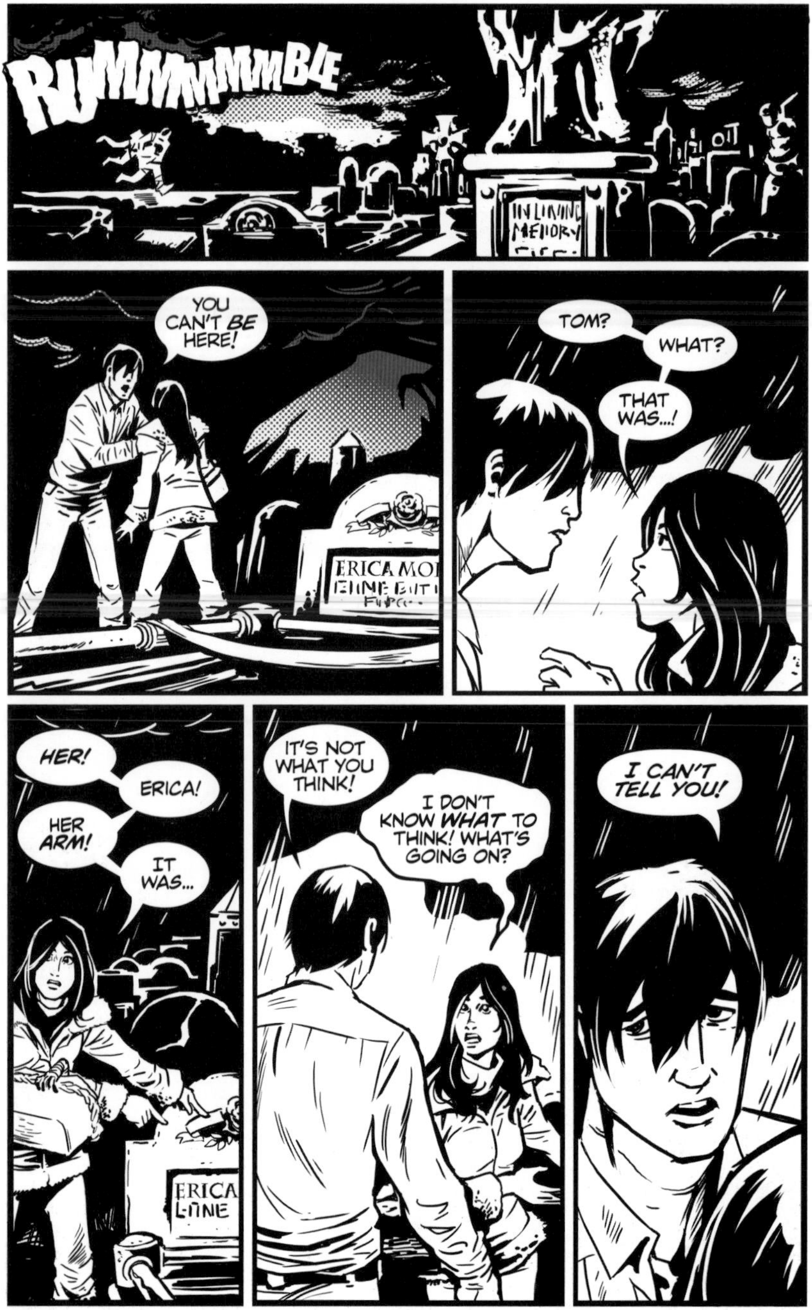
RUMMMMMMBLE
IN LOVING MEMORY
YOU CAN'T BE HERE!
ERICA MO
TOM?
WHAT?
THAT WAS...!
HER!
ERICA!
HER ARM!
IT WAS...
ERICA
IT'S NOT WHAT YOU THINK!
I DON'T KNOW WHAT TO THINK! WHAT'S GOING ON?
I CAN'T TELL YOU!

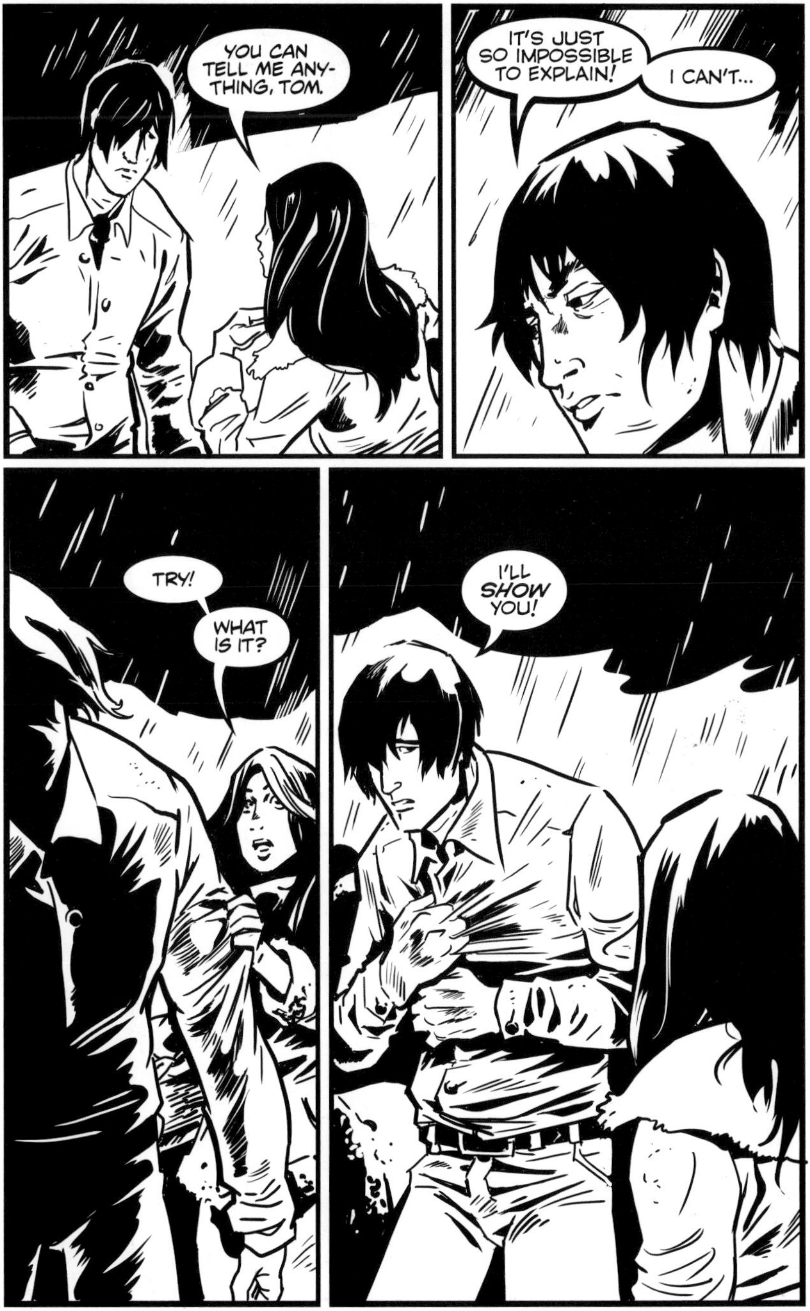
YOU CAN TELL ME ANY-THING, TOM.
IT'S JUST SO IMPOSSIBLE TO EXPLAIN!
I CAN'T...
TRY!
WHAT IS IT?
I'LL SHOW YOU!

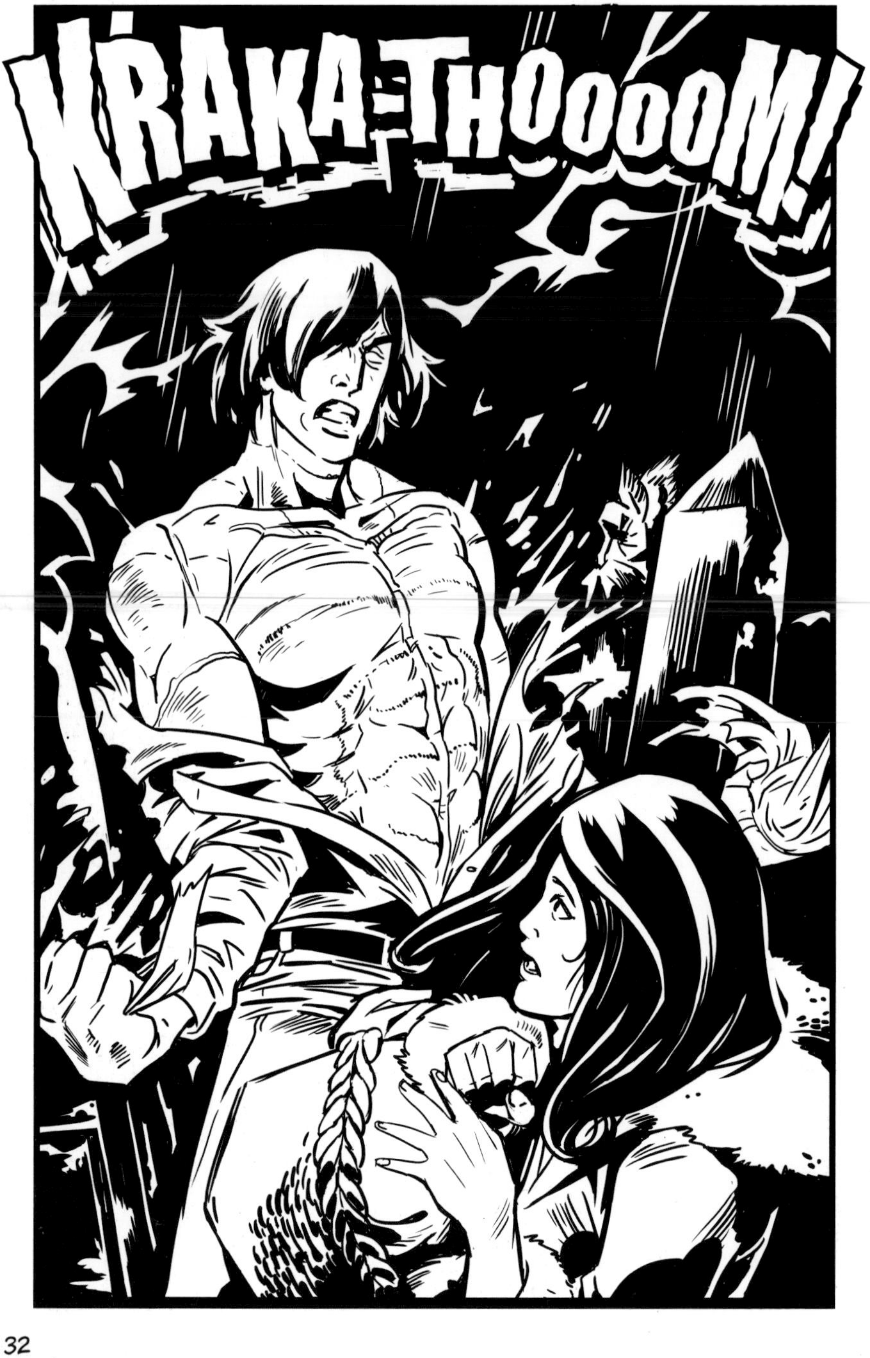
KRAKA-THOOOOOM!!

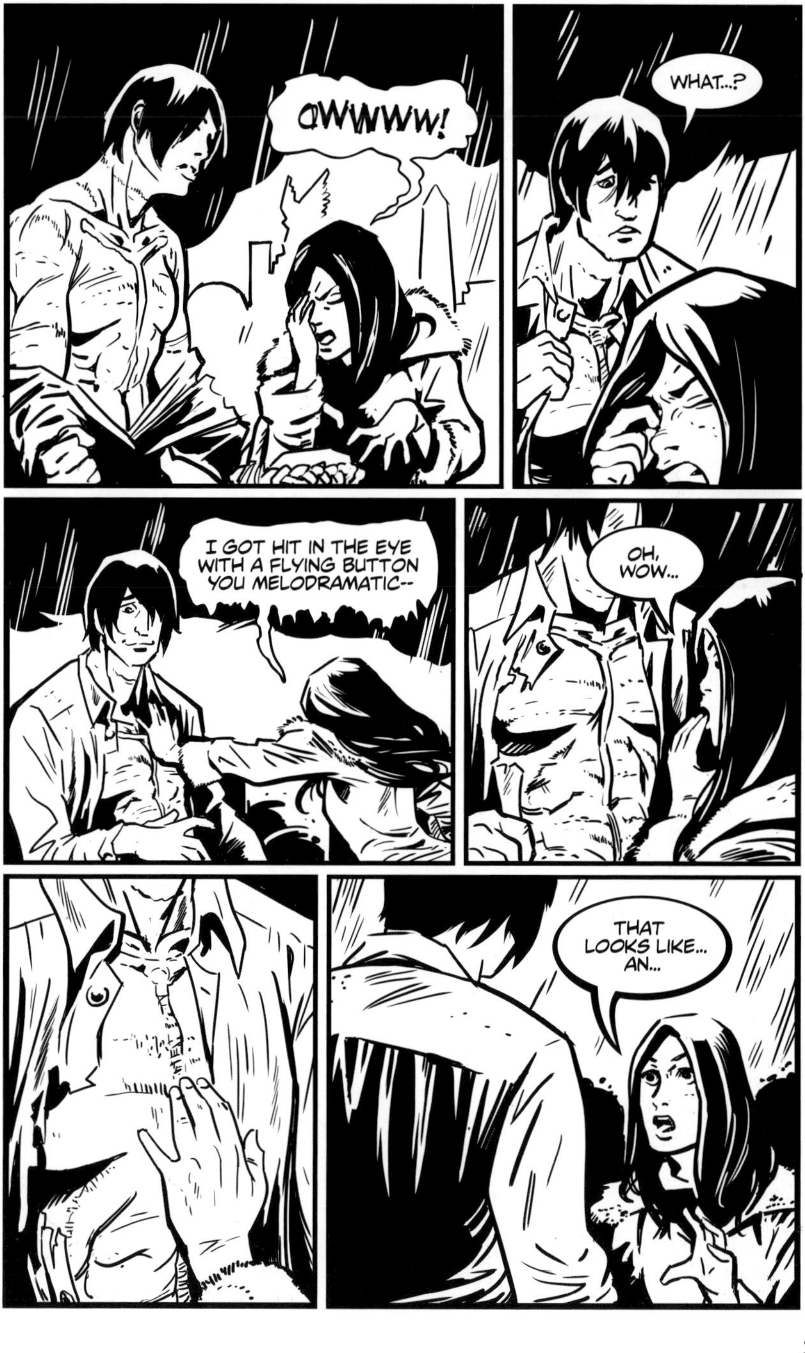
OWWWW!
WHAT...?
I GOT HIT IN THE EYE WITH A FLYING BUTTON YOU MELODRAMATIC--
OH, WOW...
THAT LOOKS LIKE... AN...

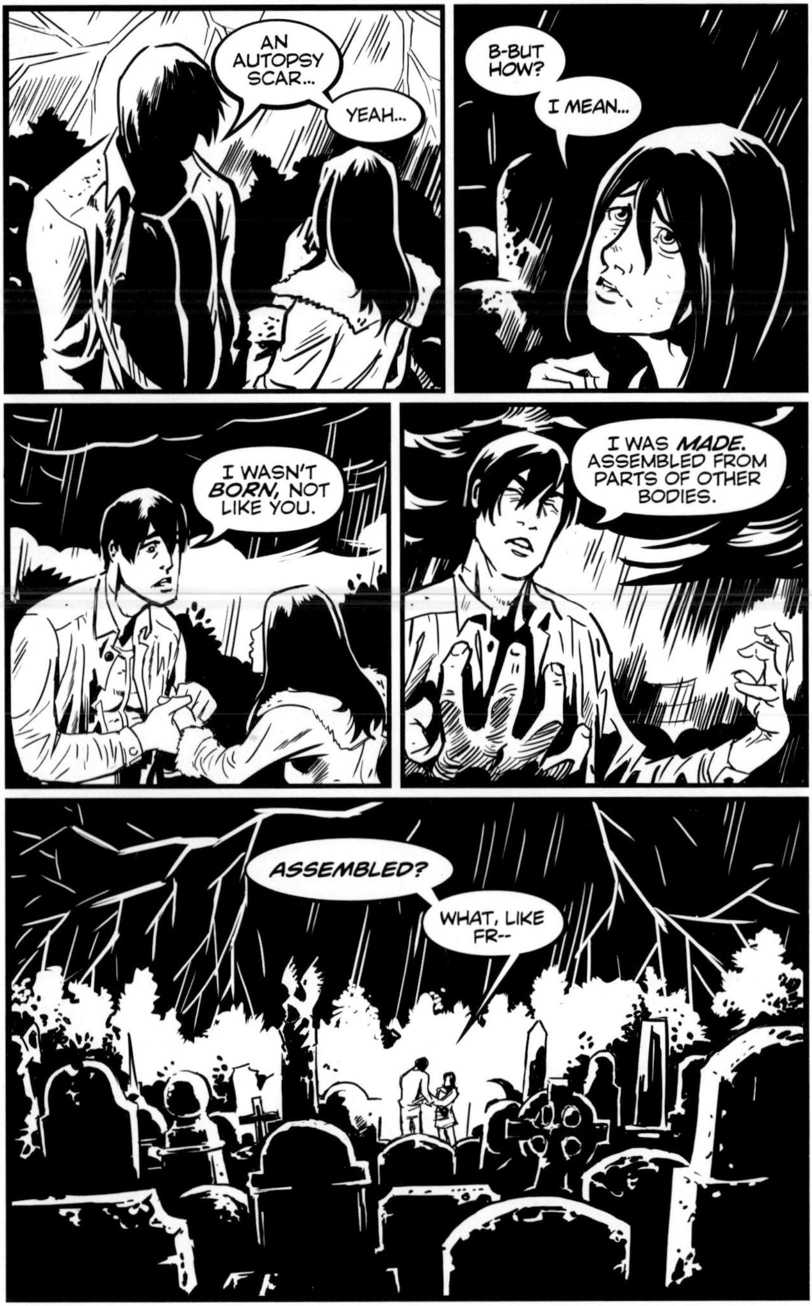
AN AUTOPSY SCAR...
YEAH...
B-BUT HOW?
I MEAN...
I WASN'T *BORN,* NOT LIKE YOU.
I WAS *MADE.* ASSEMBLED FROM PARTS OF OTHER BODIES.
ASSEMBLED?
WHAT, LIKE FR--

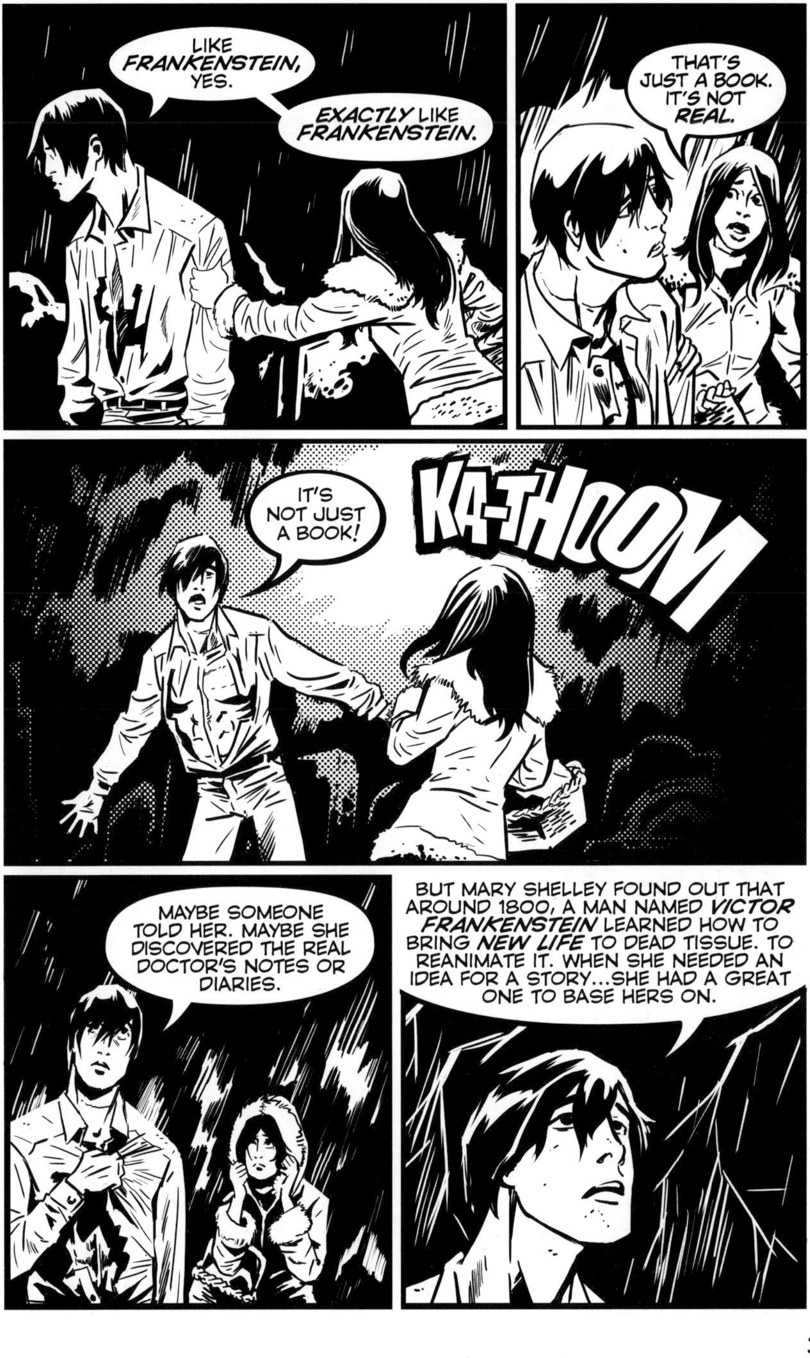

LIKE *FRANKENSTEIN,* YES.
EXACTLY LIKE *FRANKENSTEIN.*
THAT'S JUST A BOOK. IT'S NOT *REAL.*
IT'S NOT JUST A BOOK!
KA-THOOM
MAYBE SOMEONE TOLD HER. MAYBE SHE DISCOVERED THE REAL DOCTOR'S NOTES OR DIARIES.
BUT MARY SHELLEY FOUND OUT THAT AROUND 1800, A MAN NAMED *VICTOR FRANKENSTEIN* LEARNED HOW TO BRING *NEW LIFE* TO DEAD TISSUE. TO REANIMATE IT. WHEN SHE NEEDED AN IDEA FOR A STORY...SHE HAD A GREAT ONE TO BASE HERS ON.

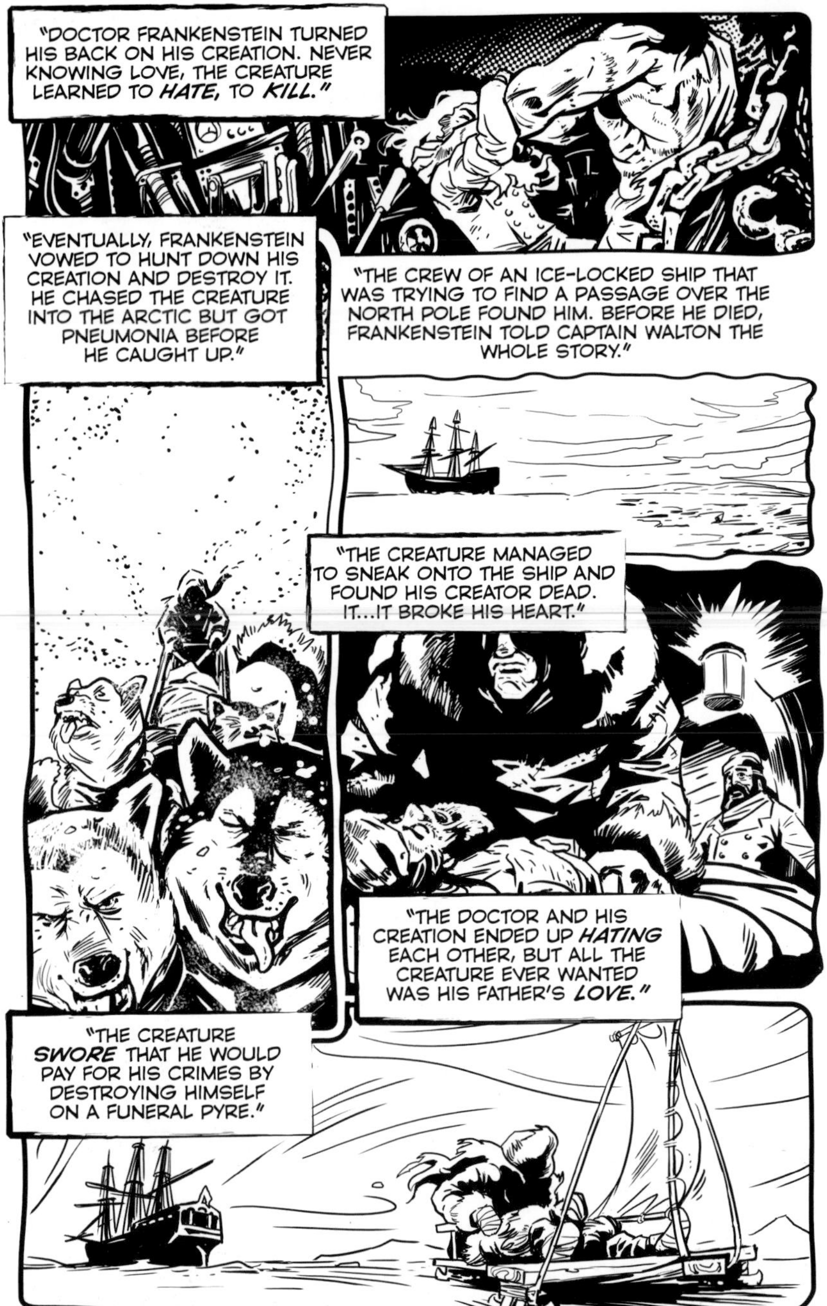
"DOCTOR FRANKENSTEIN TURNED HIS BACK ON HIS CREATION. NEVER KNOWING LOVE, THE CREATURE LEARNED TO *HATE*, TO *KILL*."
"EVENTUALLY, FRANKENSTEIN VOWED TO HUNT DOWN HIS CREATION AND DESTROY IT. HE CHASED THE CREATURE INTO THE ARCTIC BUT GOT PNEUMONIA BEFORE HE CAUGHT UP."
"THE CREW OF AN ICE-LOCKED SHIP THAT WAS TRYING TO FIND A PASSAGE OVER THE NORTH POLE FOUND HIM. BEFORE HE DIED, FRANKENSTEIN TOLD CAPTAIN WALTON THE WHOLE STORY."
"THE CREATURE MANAGED TO SNEAK ONTO THE SHIP AND FOUND HIS CREATOR DEAD. IT...IT BROKE HIS HEART."
"THE DOCTOR AND HIS CREATION ENDED UP *HATING* EACH OTHER, BUT ALL THE CREATURE EVER WANTED WAS HIS FATHER'S *LOVE*."
"THE CREATURE *SWORE* THAT HE WOULD PAY FOR HIS CRIMES BY DESTROYING HIMSELF ON A FUNERAL PYRE."

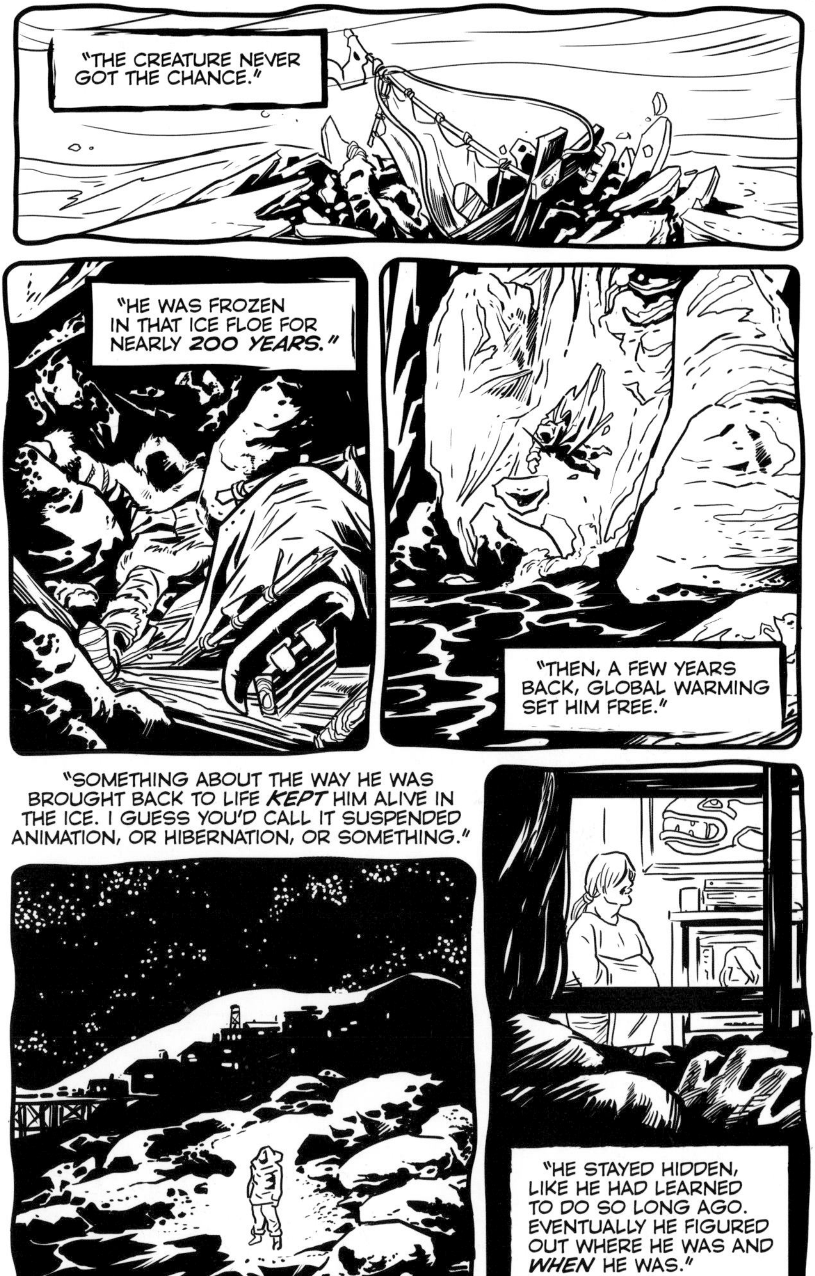
"THE CREATURE NEVER GOT THE CHANCE."
"HE WAS FROZEN IN THAT ICE FLOE FOR NEARLY **200 YEARS.**"
"THEN, A FEW YEARS BACK, GLOBAL WARMING SET HIM FREE."
"SOMETHING ABOUT THE WAY HE WAS BROUGHT BACK TO LIFE ***KEPT*** HIM ALIVE IN THE ICE. I GUESS YOU'D CALL IT SUSPENDED ANIMATION, OR HIBERNATION, OR SOMETHING."
"HE STAYED HIDDEN, LIKE HE HAD LEARNED TO DO SO LONG AGO. EVENTUALLY HE FIGURED OUT WHERE HE WAS AND ***WHEN*** HE WAS."

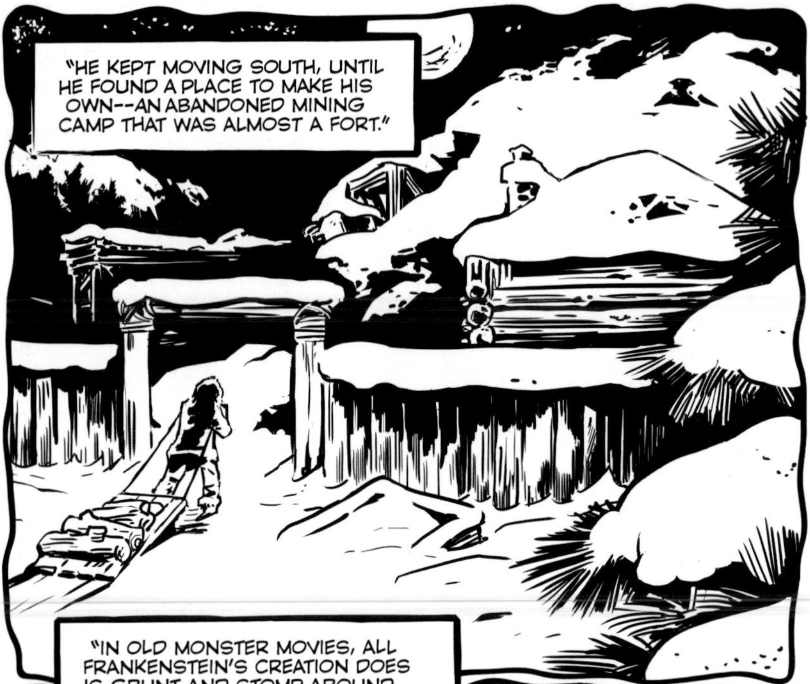
"HE KEPT MOVING SOUTH, UNTIL HE FOUND A PLACE TO MAKE HIS OWN--AN ABANDONED MINING CAMP THAT WAS ALMOST A FORT."

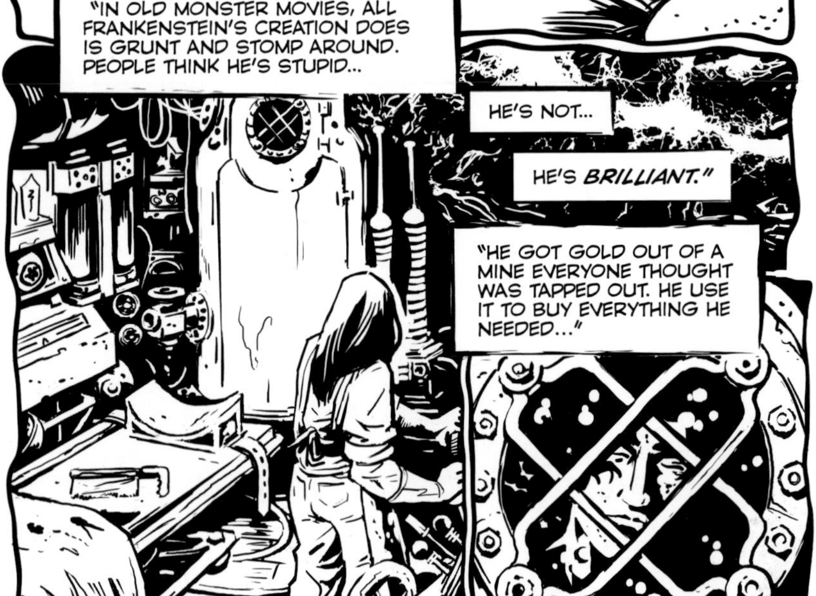
"IN OLD MONSTER MOVIES, ALL FRANKENSTEIN'S CREATION DOES IS GRUNT AND STOMP AROUND. PEOPLE THINK HE'S STUPID...
HE'S NOT...
HE'S BRILLIANT."
"HE GOT GOLD OUT OF A MINE EVERYONE THOUGHT WAS TAPPED OUT. HE USE IT TO BUY EVERYTHING HE NEEDED..."
"...TO MAKE ME!"

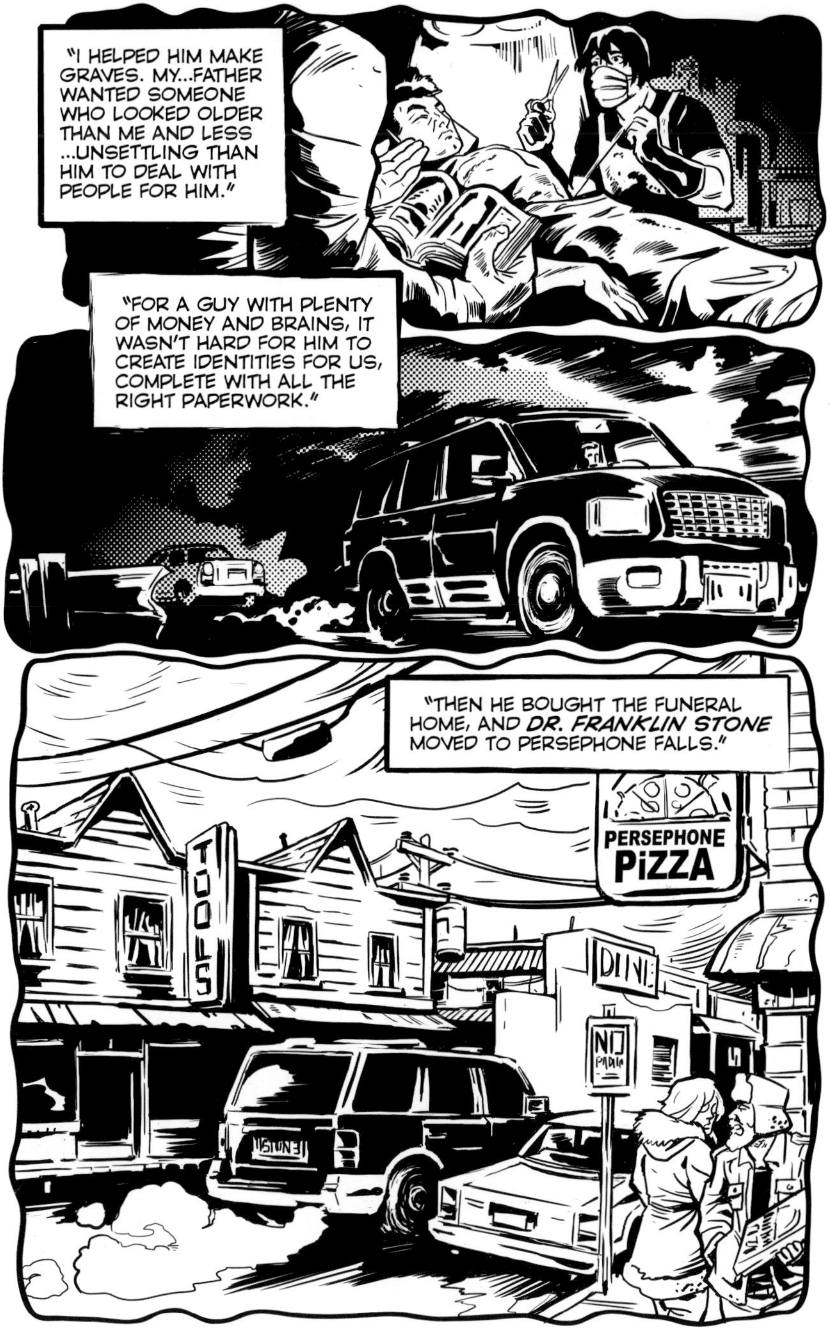
"I HELPED HIM MAKE GRAVES. MY...FATHER WANTED SOMEONE WHO LOOKED OLDER THAN ME AND LESS ...UNSETTLING THAN HIM TO DEAL WITH PEOPLE FOR HIM."
"FOR A GUY WITH PLENTY OF MONEY AND BRAINS, IT WASN'T HARD FOR HIM TO CREATE IDENTITIES FOR US, COMPLETE WITH ALL THE RIGHT PAPERWORK."
"THEN HE BOUGHT THE FUNERAL HOME, AND *DR. FRANKLIN STONE* MOVED TO PERSEPHONE FALLS."
PERSEPHONE PIZZA
TOOLS

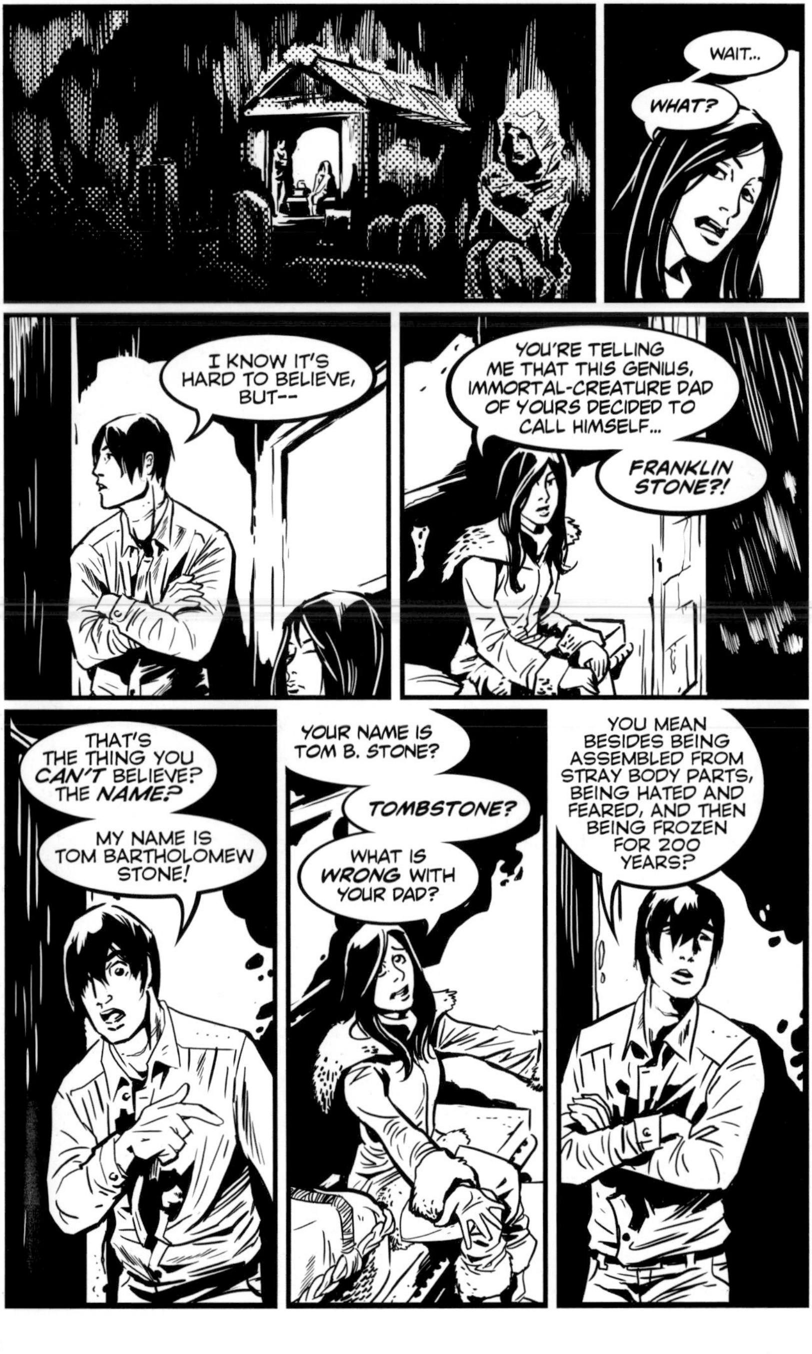
WAIT...
WHAT?
I KNOW IT'S HARD TO BELIEVE, BUT--
YOU'RE TELLING ME THAT THIS GENIUS, IMMORTAL-CREATURE DAD OF YOURS DECIDED TO CALL HIMSELF...
FRANKLIN STONE?!
THAT'S THE THING YOU CAN'T BELIEVE? THE NAME?
MY NAME IS TOM BARTHOLOMEW STONE!
YOUR NAME IS TOM B. STONE?
TOMBSTONE?
WHAT IS WRONG WITH YOUR DAD?
YOU MEAN BESIDES BEING ASSEMBLED FROM STRAY BODY PARTS, BEING HATED AND FEARED, AND THEN BEING FROZEN FOR 200 YEARS?

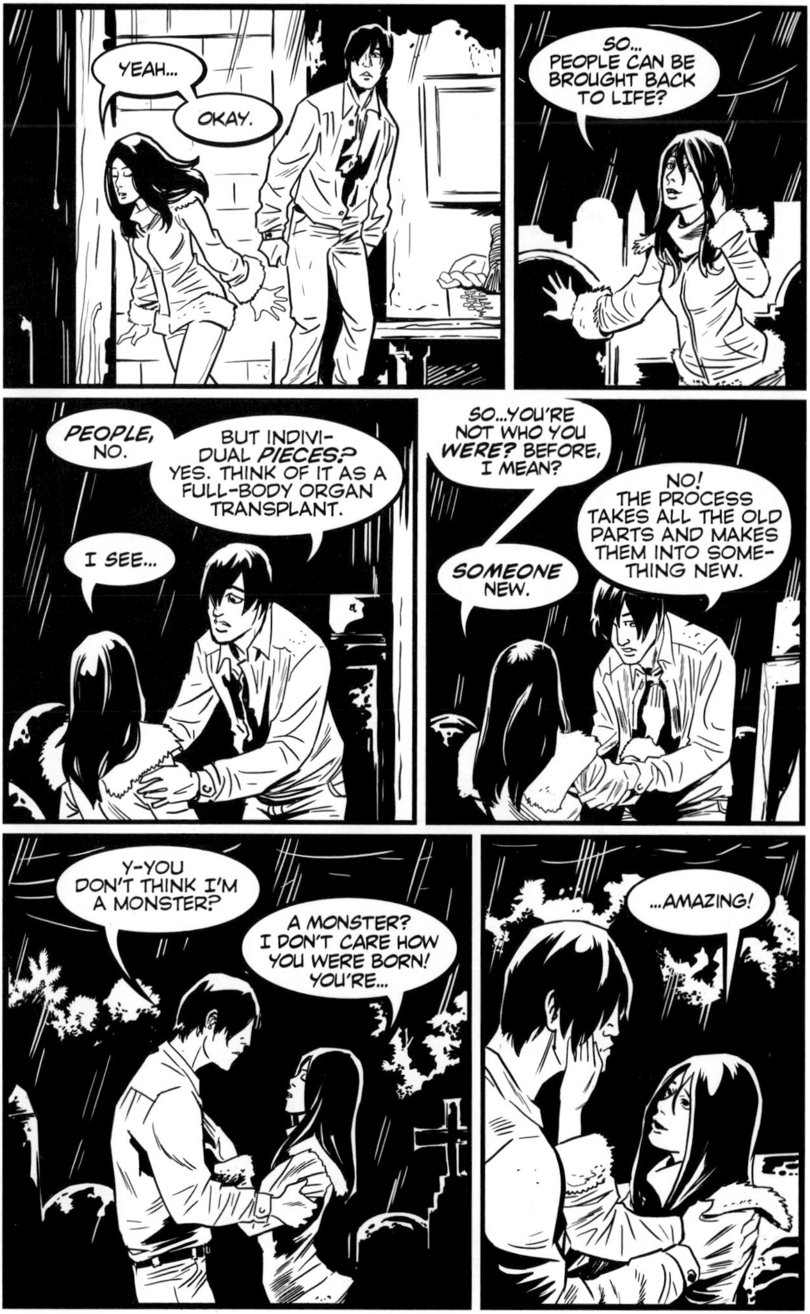
YEAH...
OKAY.
SO... PEOPLE CAN BE BROUGHT BACK TO LIFE?
PEOPLE, NO.
BUT INDIVI-DUAL PIECES? YES. THINK OF IT AS A FULL-BODY ORGAN TRANSPLANT.
I SEE...
SO...YOU'RE NOT WHO YOU WERE? BEFORE, I MEAN?
NO! THE PROCESS TAKES ALL THE OLD PARTS AND MAKES THEM INTO SOME-THING NEW.
SOMEONE NEW.
Y-YOU DON'T THINK I'M A MONSTER?
A MONSTER? I DON'T CARE HOW YOU WERE BORN! YOU'RE...
...AMAZING!

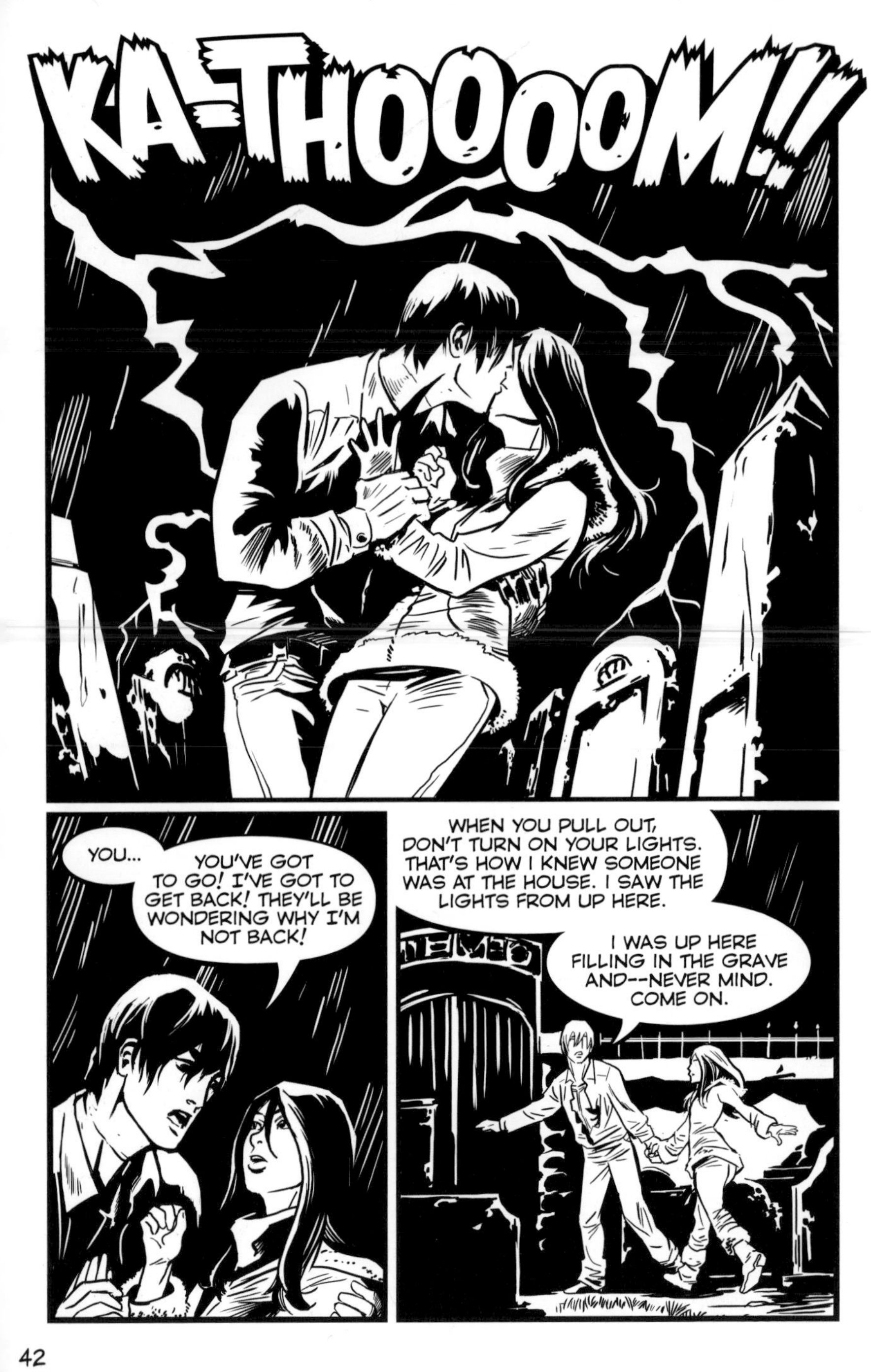
KA-THOOOOM!!
YOU...
YOU'VE GOT TO GO! I'VE GOT TO GET BACK! THEY'LL BE WONDERING WHY I'M NOT BACK!
WHEN YOU PULL OUT, DON'T TURN ON YOUR LIGHTS. THAT'S HOW I KNEW SOMEONE WAS AT THE HOUSE. I SAW THE LIGHTS FROM UP HERE.
I WAS UP HERE FILLING IN THE GRAVE AND--NEVER MIND. COME ON.

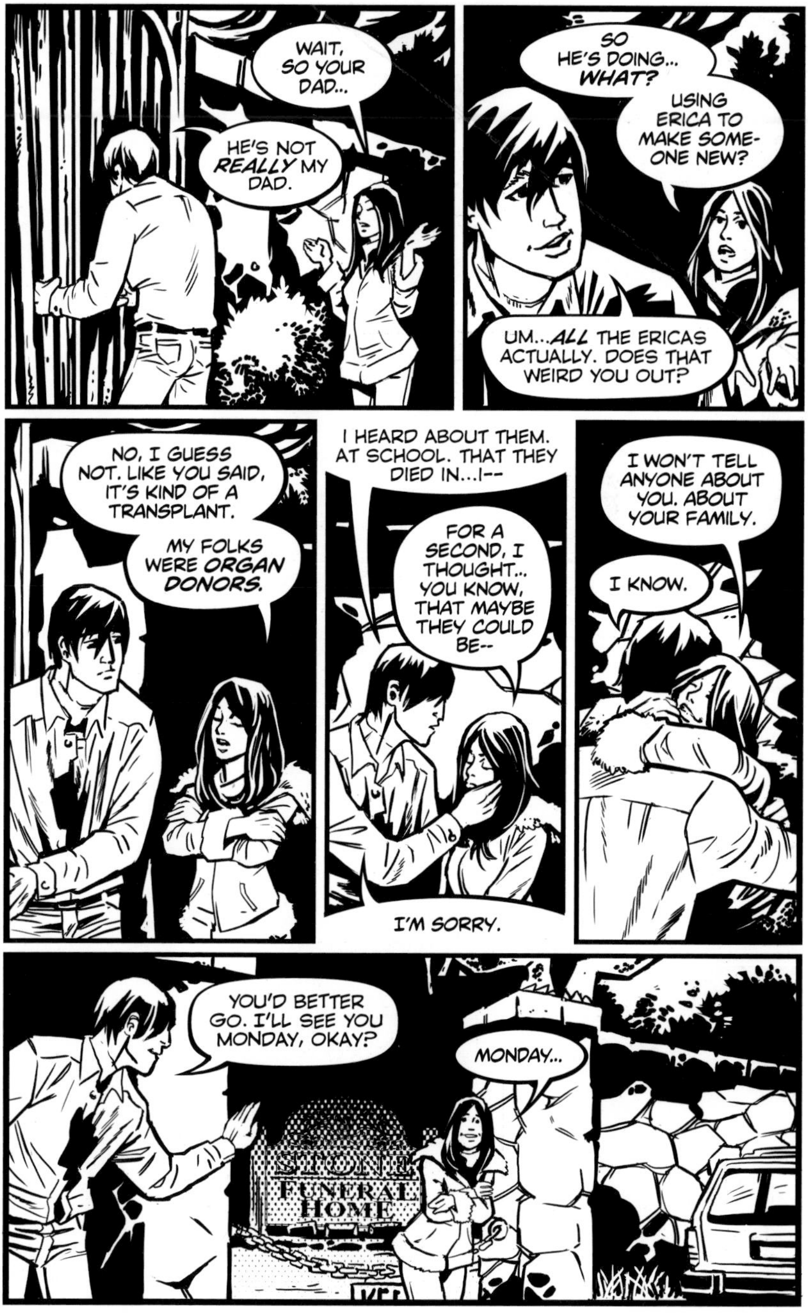
WAIT, SO YOUR DAD...
HE'S NOT *REALLY* MY DAD.
SO HE'S DOING... *WHAT?*
USING ERICA TO MAKE SOME-ONE NEW?
UM...*ALL* THE ERICAS ACTUALLY. DOES THAT WEIRD YOU OUT?
NO, I GUESS NOT. LIKE YOU SAID, IT'S KIND OF A TRANSPLANT.
MY FOLKS WERE *ORGAN DONORS.*
I HEARD ABOUT THEM. AT SCHOOL. THAT THEY DIED IN...I--
FOR A SECOND, I THOUGHT... YOU KNOW, THAT MAYBE THEY COULD BE--
I'M SORRY.
I WON'T TELL ANYONE ABOUT YOU. ABOUT YOUR FAMILY.
I KNOW.
YOU'D BETTER GO. I'LL SEE YOU MONDAY, OKAY?
MONDAY...
STONE FUNERAL HOME

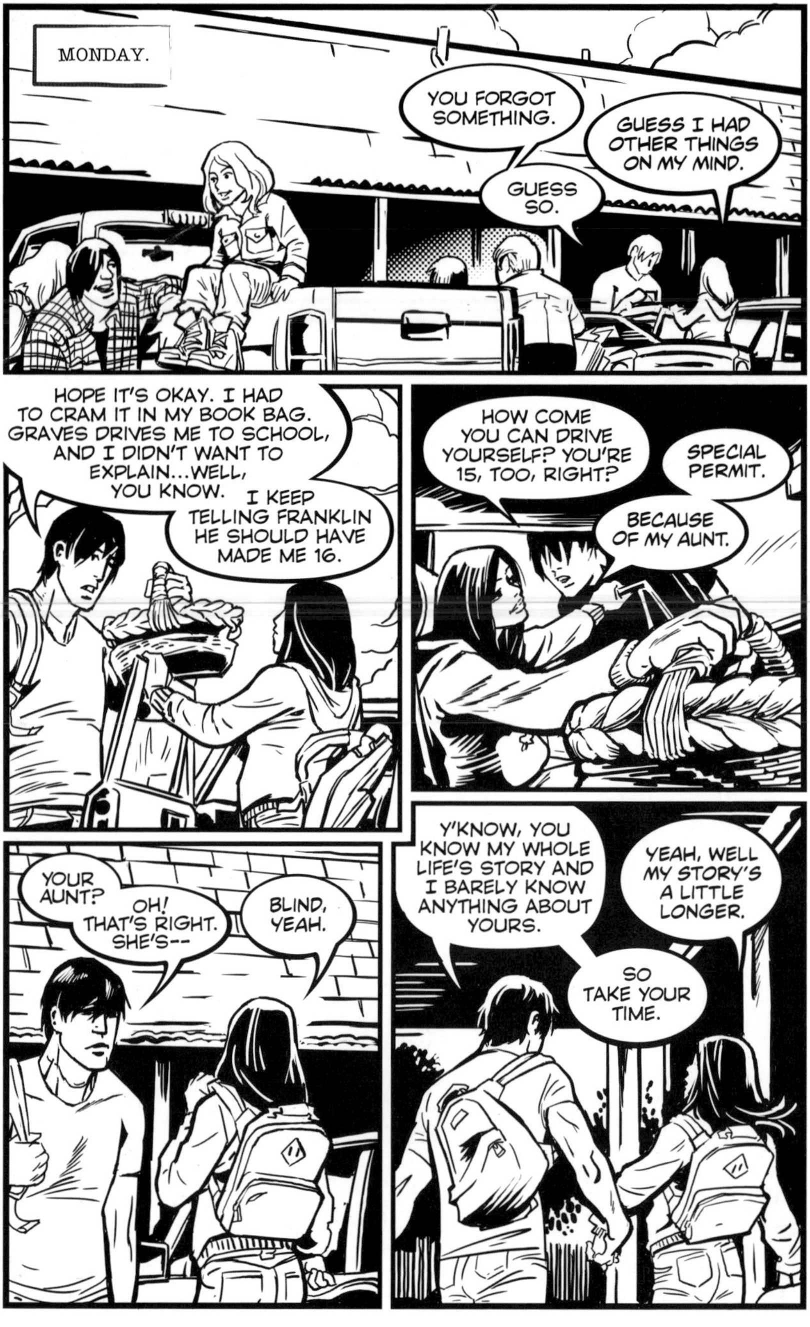

MONDAY.
YOU FORGOT SOMETHING.
GUESS SO.
GUESS I HAD OTHER THINGS ON MY MIND.
HOPE IT'S OKAY. I HAD TO CRAM IT IN MY BOOK BAG. GRAVES DRIVES ME TO SCHOOL, AND I DIDN'T WANT TO EXPLAIN...WELL, YOU KNOW.
I KEEP TELLING FRANKLIN HE SHOULD HAVE MADE ME 16.
HOW COME YOU CAN DRIVE YOURSELF? YOU'RE 15, TOO, RIGHT?
SPECIAL PERMIT.
BECAUSE OF MY AUNT.
YOUR AUNT?
OH! THAT'S RIGHT. SHE'S--
BLIND, YEAH.
Y'KNOW, YOU KNOW MY WHOLE LIFE'S STORY AND I BARELY KNOW ANYTHING ABOUT YOURS.
YEAH, WELL MY STORY'S A LITTLE LONGER.
SO TAKE YOUR TIME.

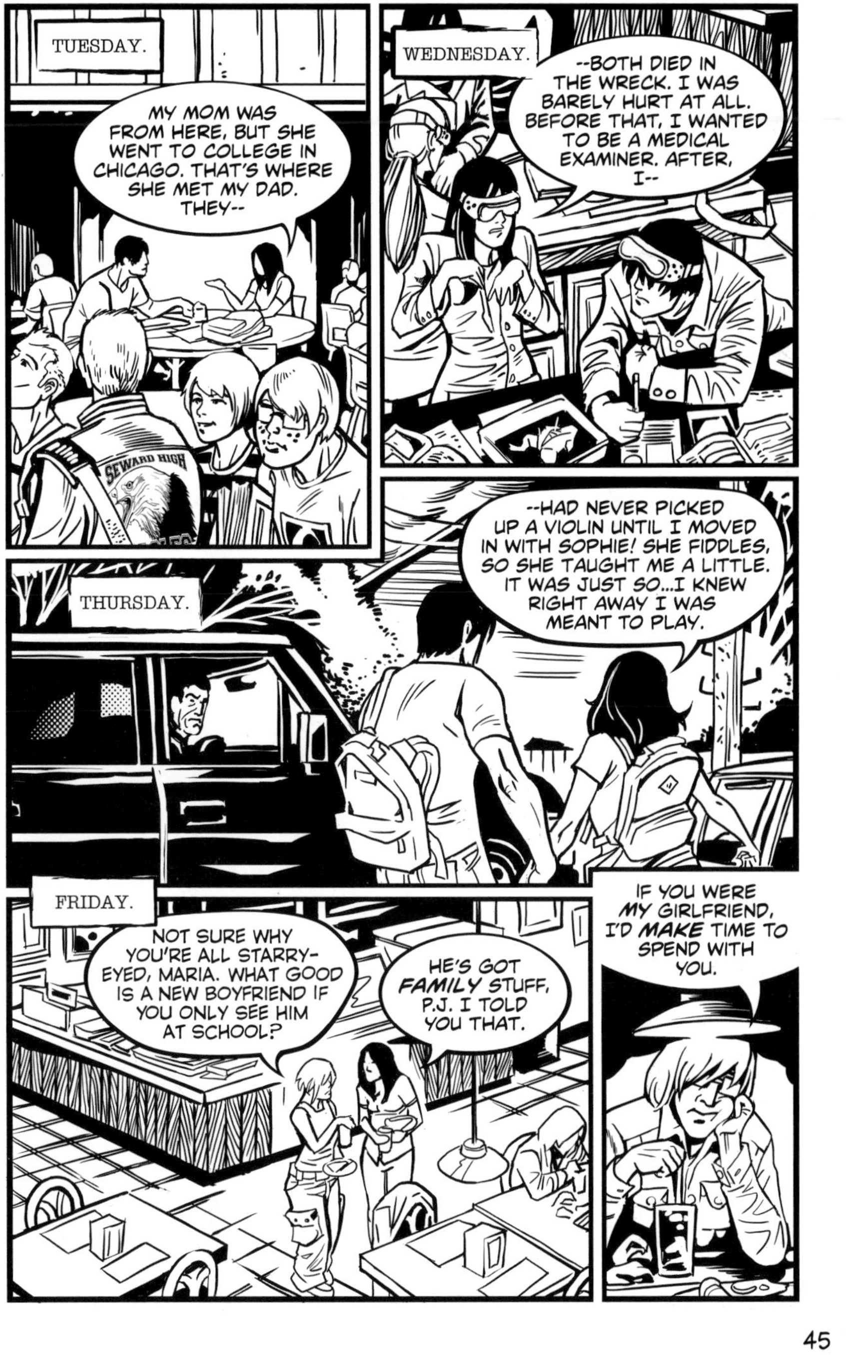
TUESDAY.
MY MOM WAS FROM HERE, BUT SHE WENT TO COLLEGE IN CHICAGO. THAT'S WHERE SHE MET MY DAD. THEY--
SEWARD HIGH
WEDNESDAY.
--BOTH DIED IN THE WRECK. I WAS BARELY HURT AT ALL. BEFORE THAT, I WANTED TO BE A MEDICAL EXAMINER. AFTER, I--
THURSDAY.
--HAD NEVER PICKED UP A VIOLIN UNTIL I MOVED IN WITH SOPHIE! SHE FIDDLES, SO SHE TAUGHT ME A LITTLE. IT WAS JUST SO...I KNEW RIGHT AWAY I WAS MEANT TO PLAY.
FRIDAY.
NOT SURE WHY YOU'RE ALL STARRY-EYED, MARIA. WHAT GOOD IS A NEW BOYFRIEND IF YOU ONLY SEE HIM AT SCHOOL?
HE'S GOT *FAMILY* STUFF, P.J. I TOLD YOU THAT.
IF YOU WERE *MY* GIRLFRIEND, I'D *MAKE* TIME TO SPEND WITH YOU.

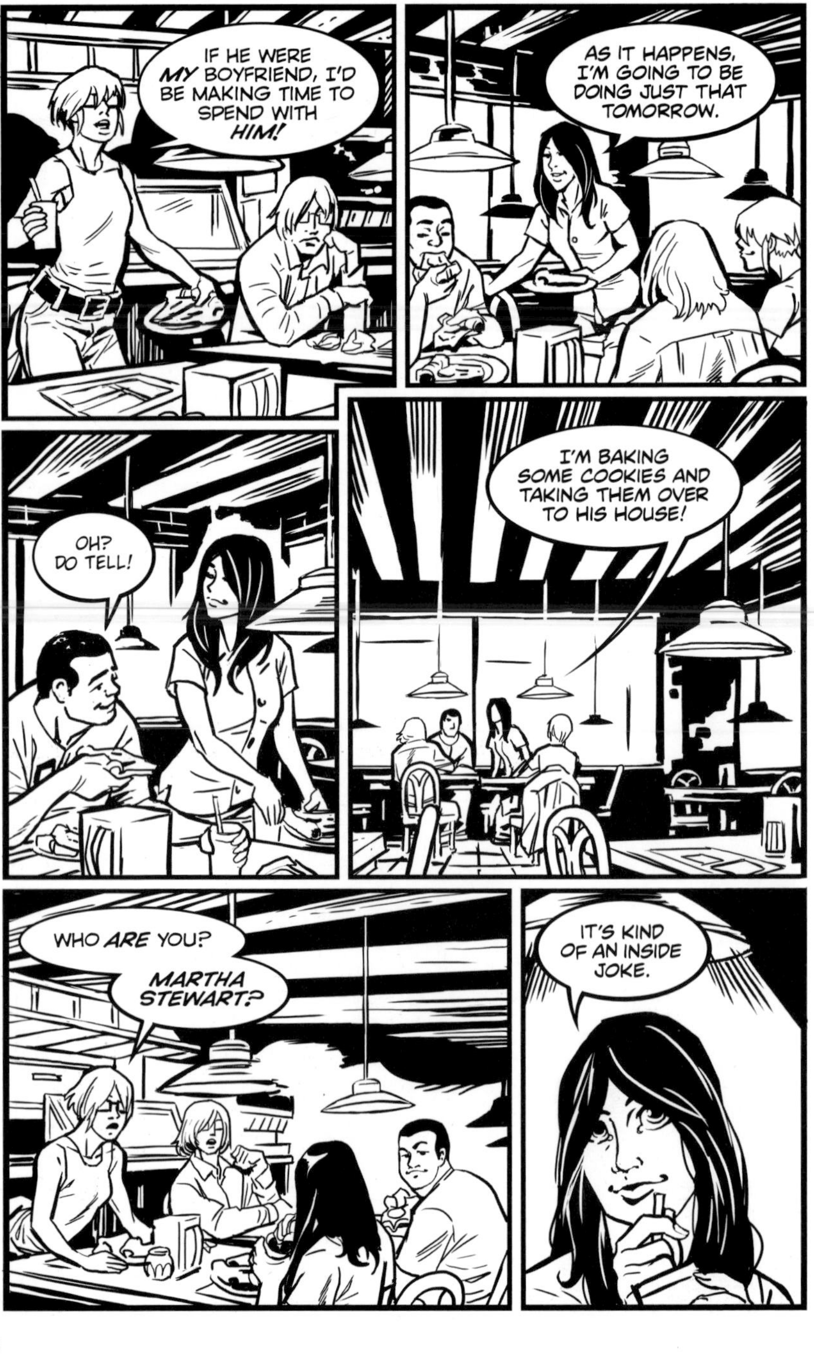
IF HE WERE *MY* BOYFRIEND, I'D BE MAKING TIME TO SPEND WITH *HIM!*
AS IT HAPPENS, I'M GOING TO BE DOING JUST THAT TOMORROW.
OH? DO TELL!
I'M BAKING SOME COOKIES AND TAKING THEM OVER TO HIS HOUSE!
WHO *ARE* YOU?
MARTHA STEWART?
IT'S KIND OF AN INSIDE JOKE.

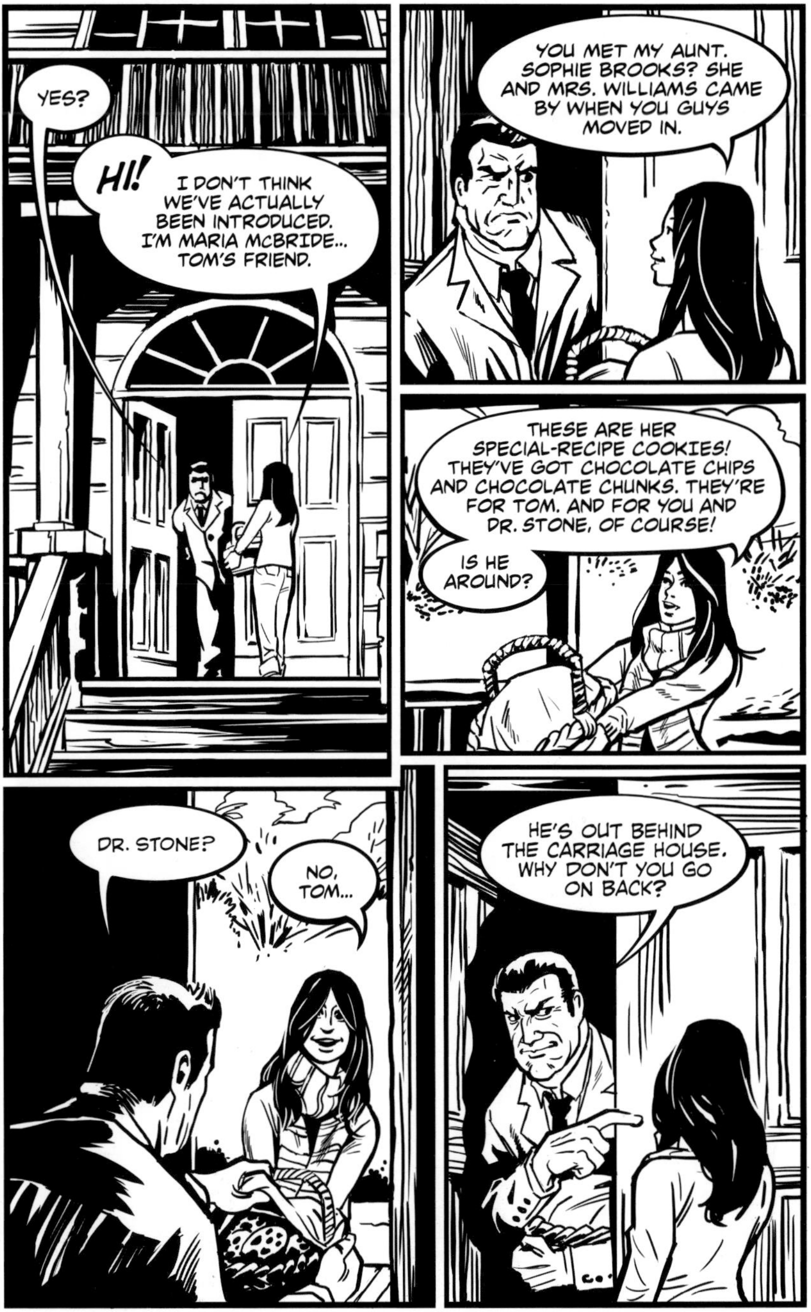
YES?
HI!
I DON'T THINK WE'VE ACTUALLY BEEN INTRODUCED. I'M MARIA McBRIDE... TOM'S FRIEND.
YOU MET MY AUNT. SOPHIE BROOKS? SHE AND MRS. WILLIAMS CAME BY WHEN YOU GUYS MOVED IN.
THESE ARE HER SPECIAL-RECIPE COOKIES! THEY'VE GOT CHOCOLATE CHIPS AND CHOCOLATE CHUNKS. THEY'RE FOR TOM. AND FOR YOU AND DR. STONE, OF COURSE!
IS HE AROUND?
DR. STONE?
NO, TOM...
HE'S OUT BEHIND THE CARRIAGE HOUSE. WHY DON'T YOU GO ON BACK?

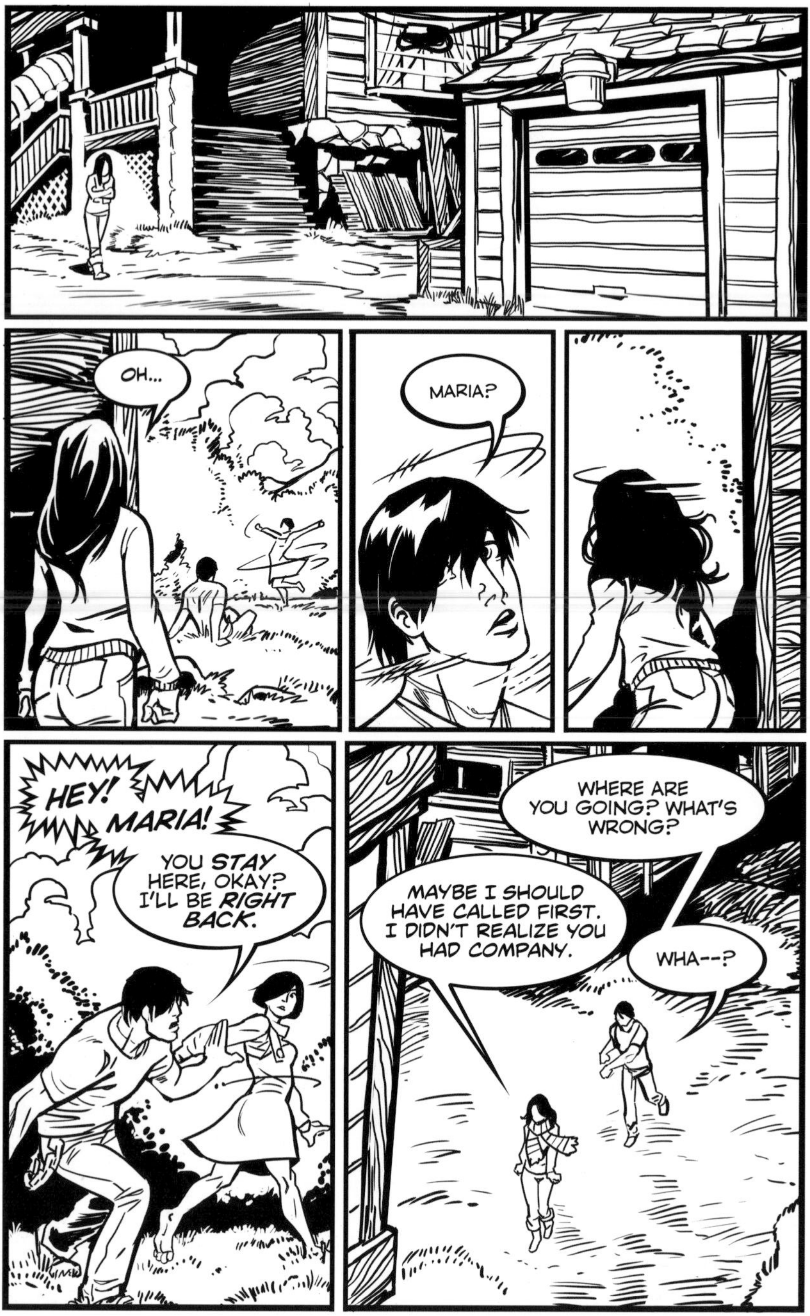
OH...
MARIA?
HEY! MARIA!
YOU STAY HERE, OKAY? I'LL BE RIGHT BACK.
WHERE ARE YOU GOING? WHAT'S WRONG?
MAYBE I SHOULD HAVE CALLED FIRST. I DIDN'T REALIZE YOU HAD COMPANY.
WHA--?

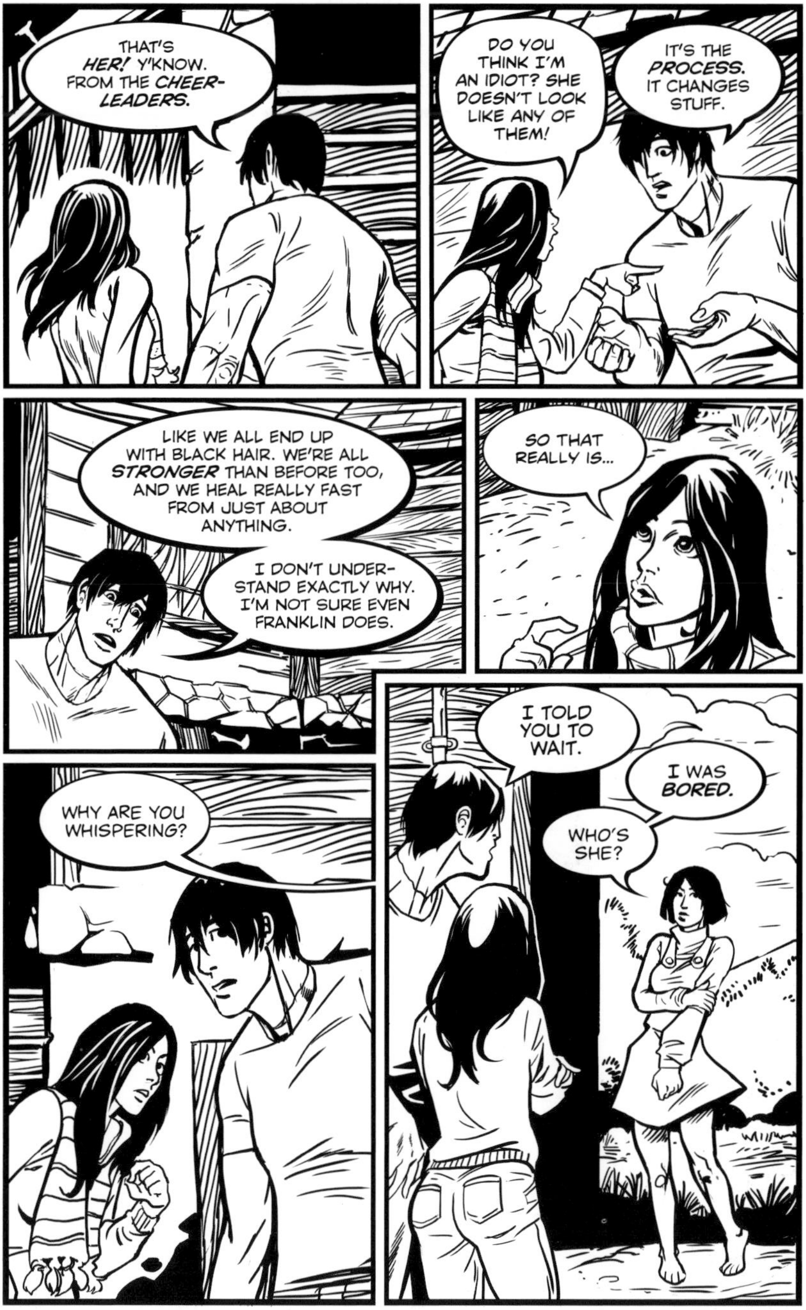
THAT'S HER! Y'KNOW. FROM THE CHEER-LEADERS.
DO YOU THINK I'M AN IDIOT? SHE DOESN'T LOOK LIKE ANY OF THEM!
IT'S THE PROCESS. IT CHANGES STUFF.
LIKE WE ALL END UP WITH BLACK HAIR. WE'RE ALL STRONGER THAN BEFORE TOO, AND WE HEAL REALLY FAST FROM JUST ABOUT ANYTHING.
I DON'T UNDER-STAND EXACTLY WHY. I'M NOT SURE EVEN FRANKLIN DOES.
SO THAT REALLY IS...
WHY ARE YOU WHISPERING?
I TOLD YOU TO WAIT.
I WAS BORED.
WHO'S SHE?

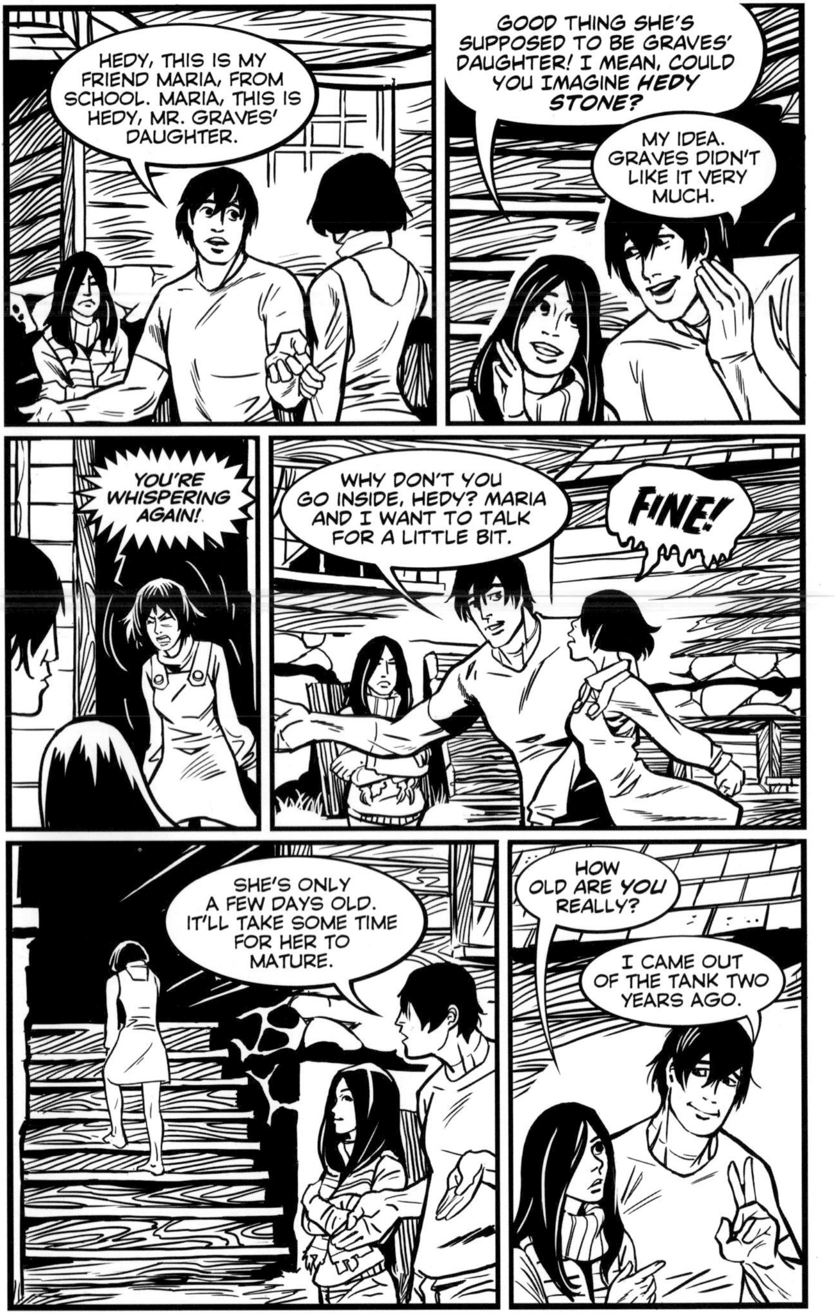
HEDY, THIS IS MY FRIEND MARIA, FROM SCHOOL. MARIA, THIS IS HEDY, MR. GRAVES' DAUGHTER.
GOOD THING SHE'S SUPPOSED TO BE GRAVES' DAUGHTER! I MEAN, COULD YOU IMAGINE *HEDY STONE?*
MY IDEA. GRAVES DIDN'T LIKE IT VERY MUCH.
YOU'RE WHISPERING AGAIN!
WHY DON'T YOU GO INSIDE, HEDY? MARIA AND I WANT TO TALK FOR A LITTLE BIT.
FINE!
SHE'S ONLY A FEW DAYS OLD. IT'LL TAKE SOME TIME FOR HER TO MATURE.
HOW OLD ARE *YOU* REALLY?
I CAME OUT OF THE TANK TWO YEARS AGO.

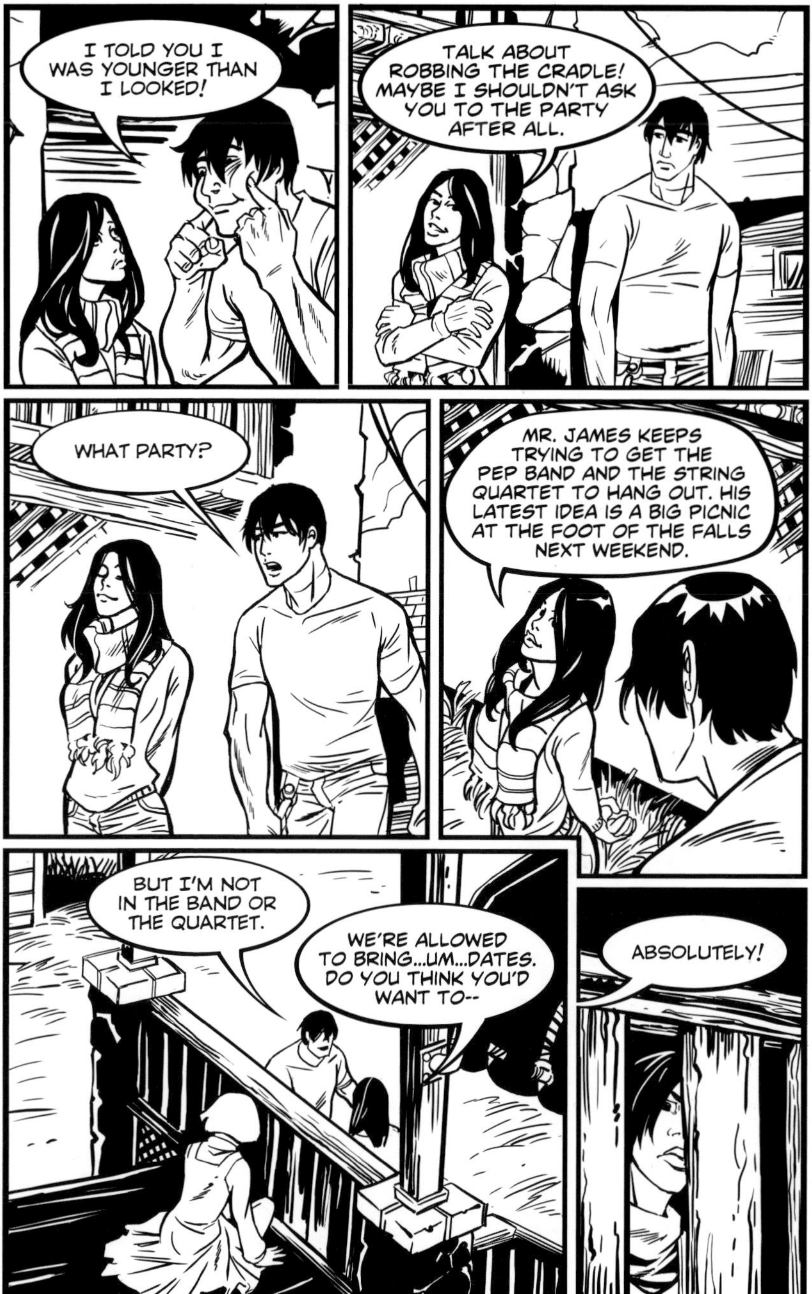
I TOLD YOU I WAS YOUNGER THAN I LOOKED!
TALK ABOUT ROBBING THE CRADLE! MAYBE I SHOULDN'T ASK YOU TO THE PARTY AFTER ALL.
WHAT PARTY?
MR. JAMES KEEPS TRYING TO GET THE PEP BAND AND THE STRING QUARTET TO HANG OUT. HIS LATEST IDEA IS A BIG PICNIC AT THE FOOT OF THE FALLS NEXT WEEKEND.
BUT I'M NOT IN THE BAND OR THE QUARTET.
WE'RE ALLOWED TO BRING...UM...DATES. DO YOU THINK YOU'D WANT TO--
ABSOLUTELY!

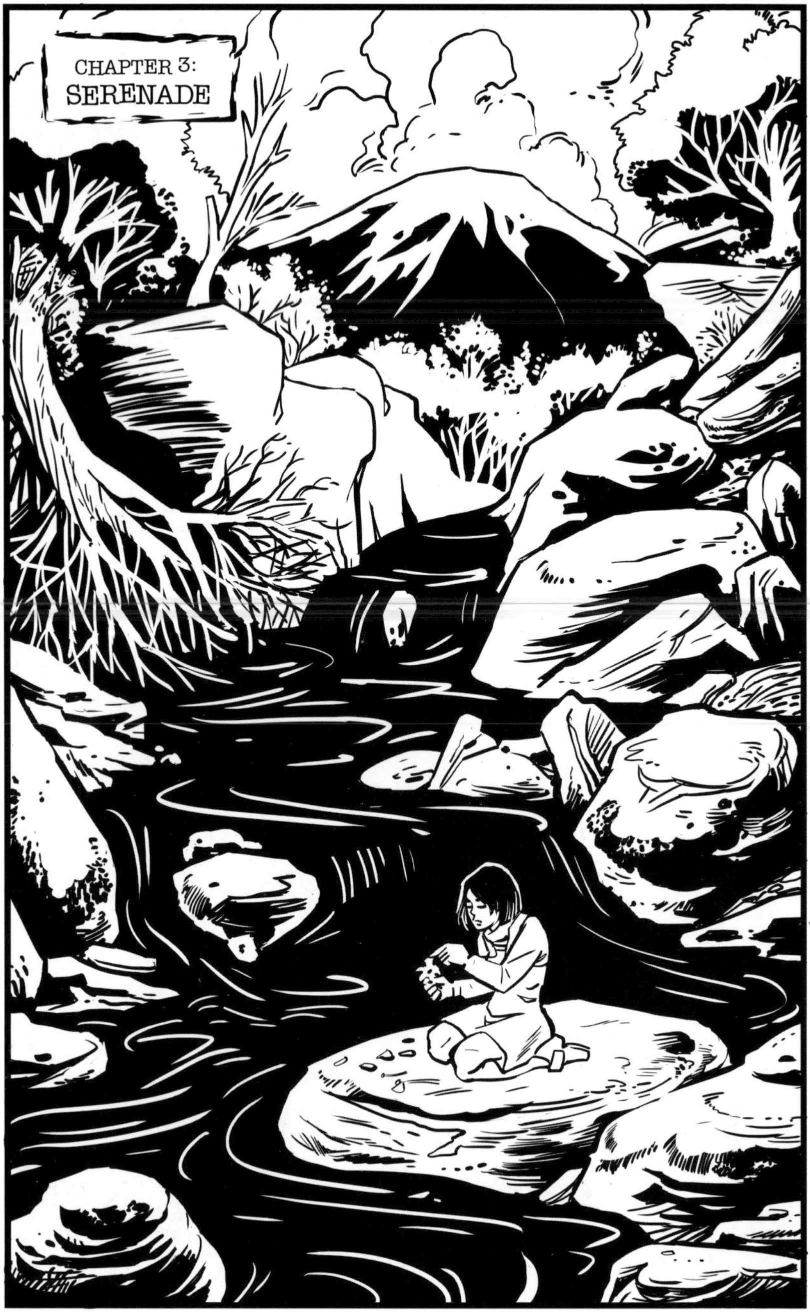
CHAPTER 3:
SERENADE

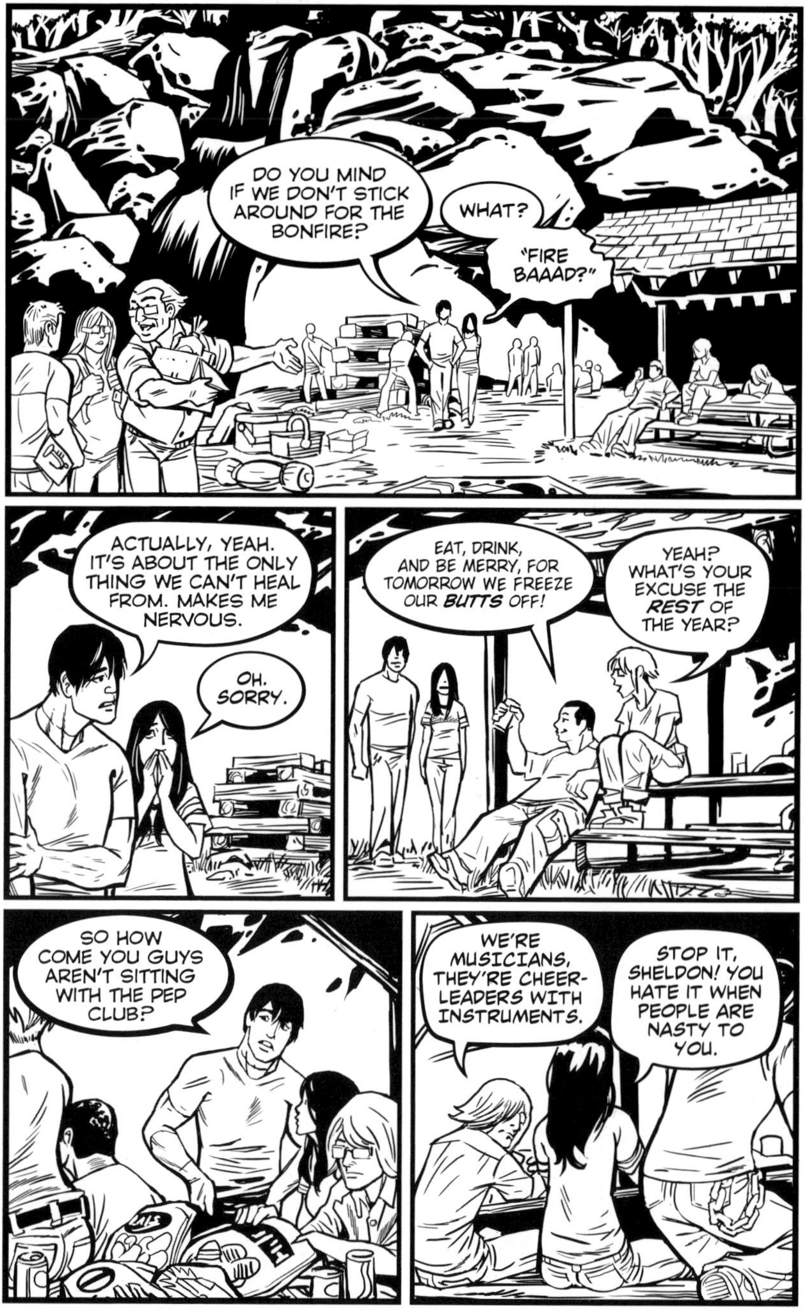
DO YOU MIND IF WE DON'T STICK AROUND FOR THE BONFIRE?
WHAT?
"FIRE BAAAD?"
ACTUALLY, YEAH. IT'S ABOUT THE ONLY THING WE CAN'T HEAL FROM. MAKES ME NERVOUS.
OH. SORRY.
EAT, DRINK, AND BE MERRY, FOR TOMORROW WE FREEZE OUR BUTTS OFF!
YEAH? WHAT'S YOUR EXCUSE THE REST OF THE YEAR?
SO HOW COME YOU GUYS AREN'T SITTING WITH THE PEP CLUB?
WE'RE MUSICIANS, THEY'RE CHEER-LEADERS WITH INSTRUMENTS.
STOP IT, SHELDON! YOU HATE IT WHEN PEOPLE ARE NASTY TO YOU.

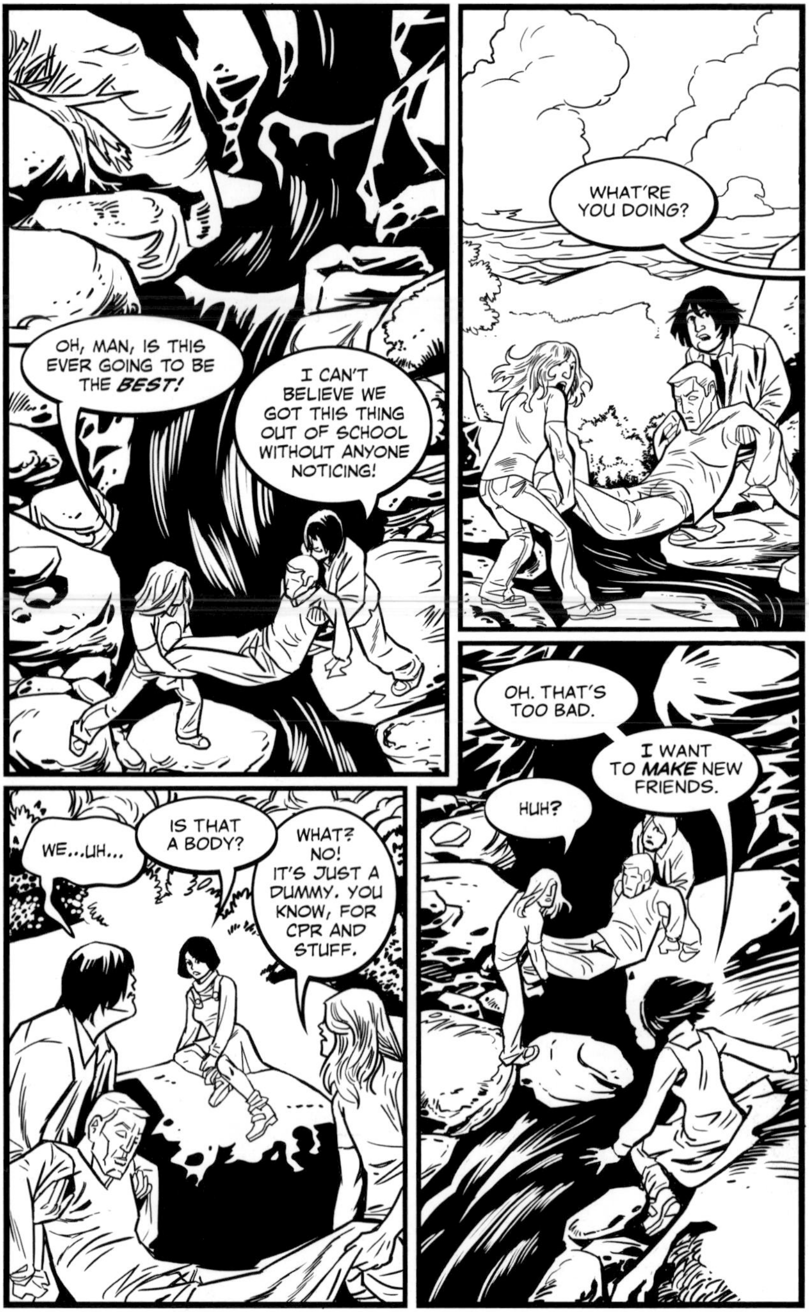
OH, MAN, IS THIS EVER GOING TO BE THE **BEST!**
I CAN'T BELIEVE WE GOT THIS THING OUT OF SCHOOL WITHOUT ANYONE NOTICING!
WHAT'RE YOU DOING?
WE...UH...
IS THAT A BODY?
WHAT? NO! IT'S JUST A DUMMY. YOU KNOW, FOR CPR AND STUFF.
OH. THAT'S TOO BAD.
I WANT TO **MAKE** NEW FRIENDS.
HUH?

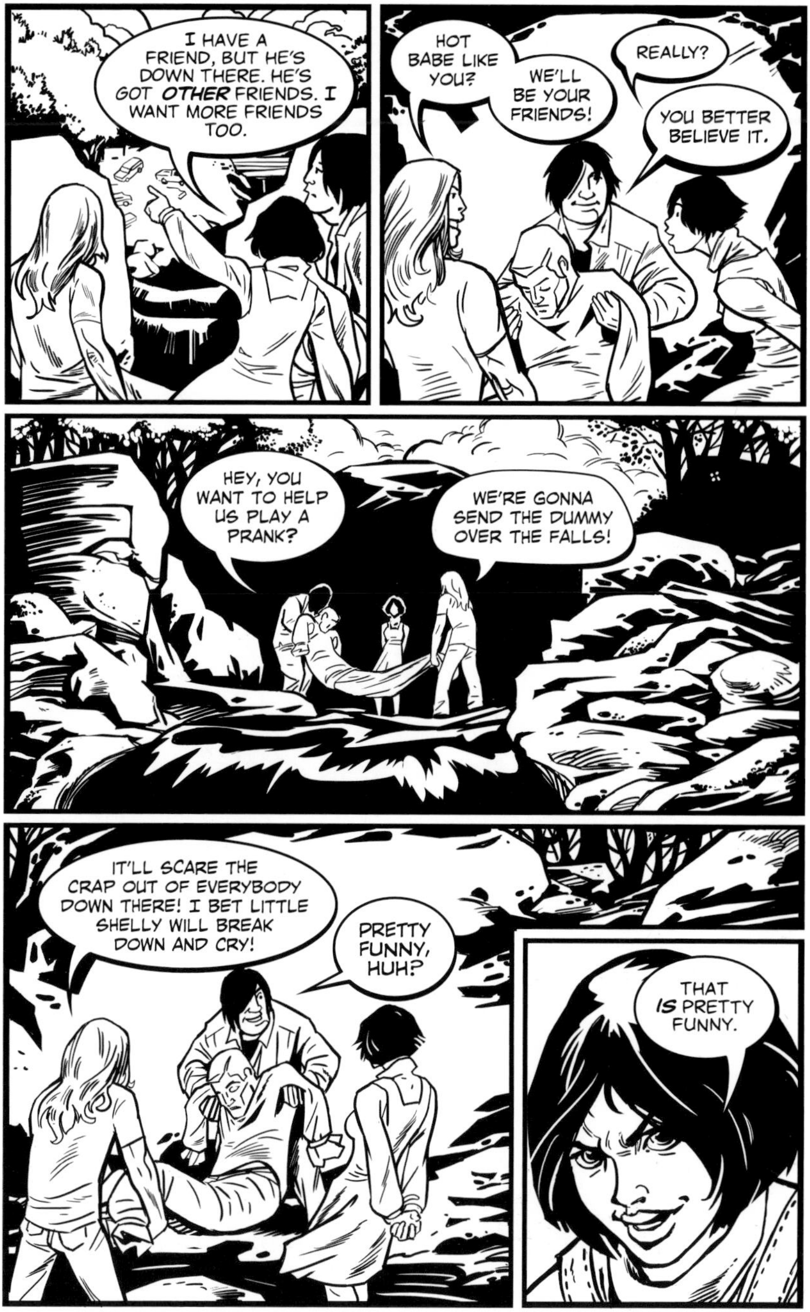
I HAVE A FRIEND, BUT HE'S DOWN THERE. HE'S GOT OTHER FRIENDS. I WANT MORE FRIENDS TOO.
HOT BABE LIKE YOU?
WE'LL BE YOUR FRIENDS!
REALLY?
YOU BETTER BELIEVE IT.
HEY, YOU WANT TO HELP US PLAY A PRANK?
WE'RE GONNA SEND THE DUMMY OVER THE FALLS!
IT'LL SCARE THE CRAP OUT OF EVERYBODY DOWN THERE! I BET LITTLE SHELLY WILL BREAK DOWN AND CRY!
PRETTY FUNNY, HUH?
THAT IS PRETTY FUNNY.

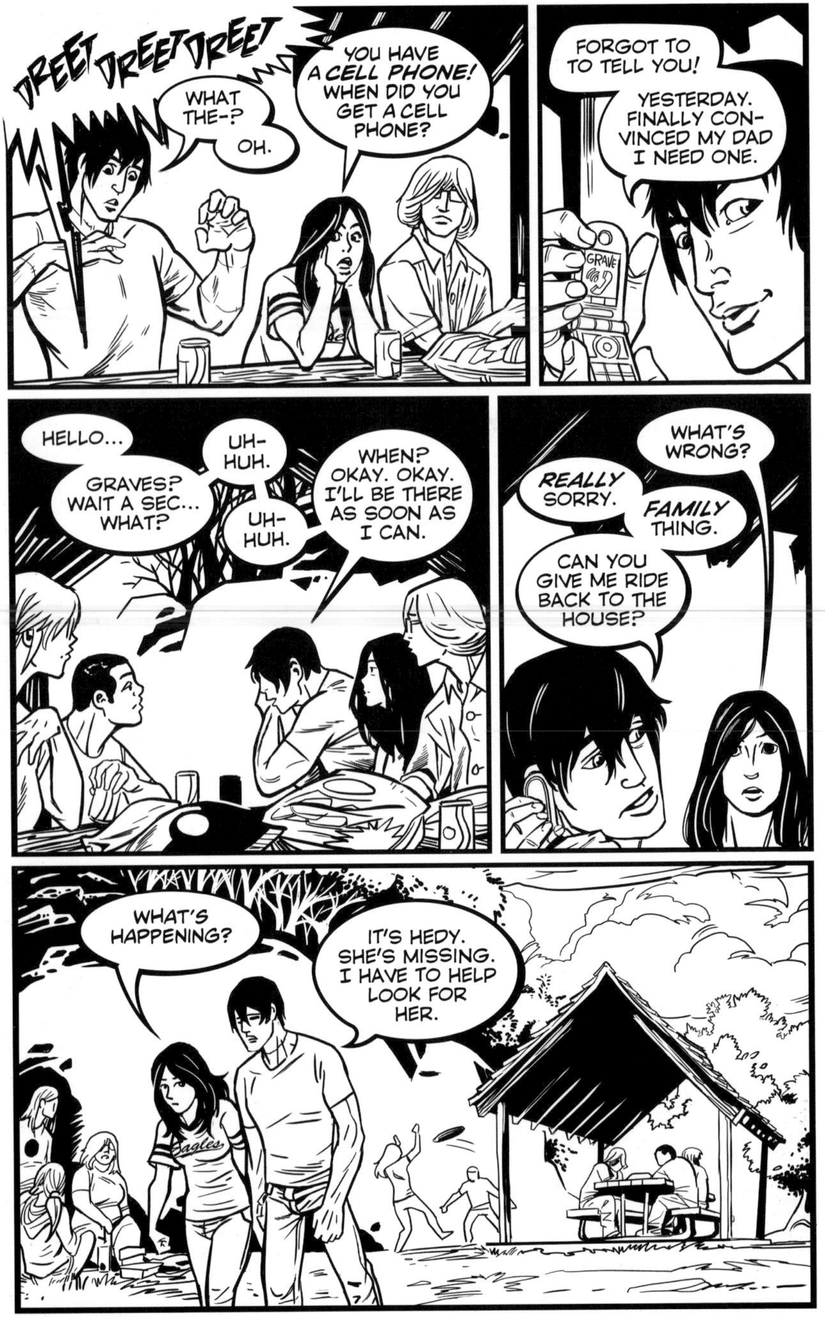

DREET DREET DREET
WHAT THE-? OH.
YOU HAVE A CELL PHONE! WHEN DID YOU GET A CELL PHONE?
FORGOT TO TO TELL YOU!
YESTERDAY. FINALLY CON-VINCED MY DAD I NEED ONE.
GRAVE
HELLO...
GRAVES? WAIT A SEC... WHAT?
UH-HUH.
UH-HUH.
WHEN? OKAY. OKAY. I'LL BE THERE AS SOON AS I CAN.
WHAT'S WRONG?
REALLY SORRY.
FAMILY THING.
CAN YOU GIVE ME RIDE BACK TO THE HOUSE?
WHAT'S HAPPENING?
IT'S HEDY. SHE'S MISSING. I HAVE TO HELP LOOK FOR HER.
Eagles

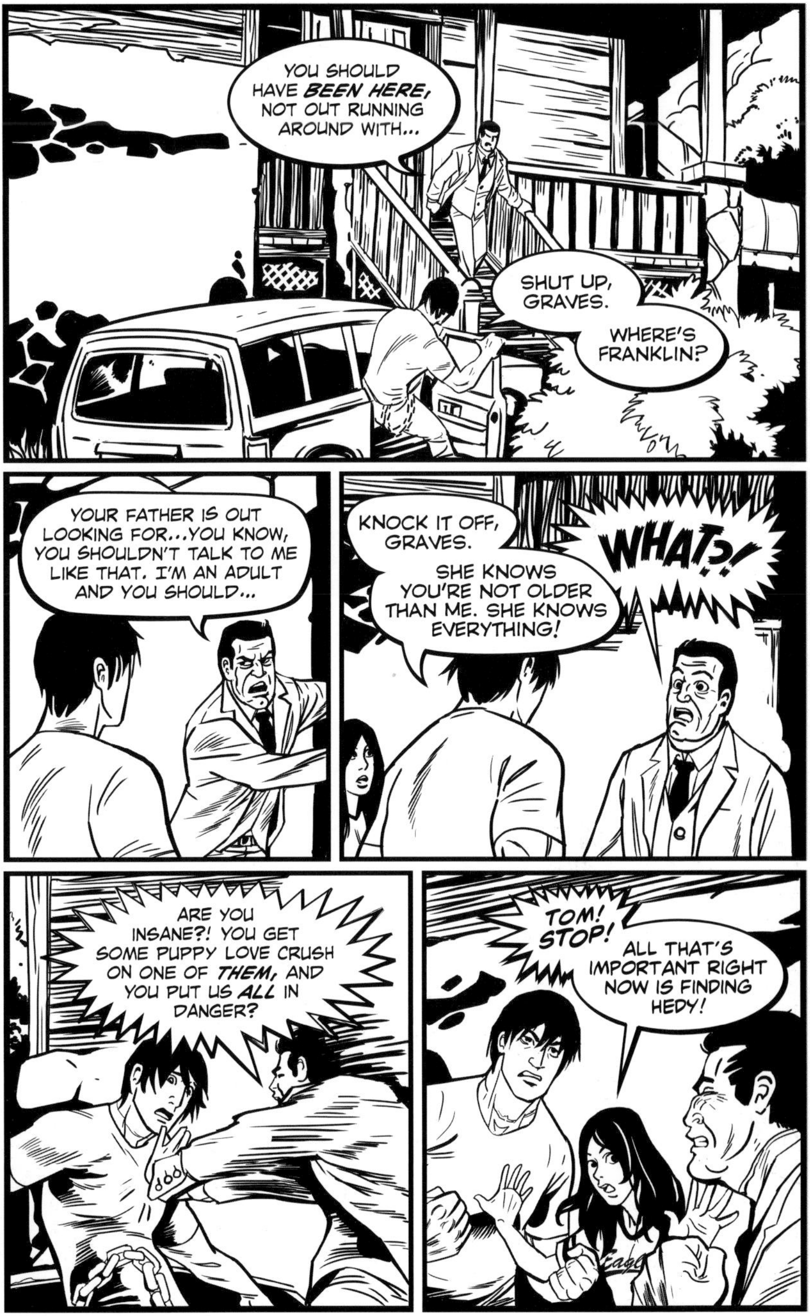
YOU SHOULD HAVE BEEN HERE, NOT OUT RUNNING AROUND WITH...
SHUT UP, GRAVES.
WHERE'S FRANKLIN?
YOUR FATHER IS OUT LOOKING FOR...YOU KNOW, YOU SHOULDN'T TALK TO ME LIKE THAT. I'M AN ADULT AND YOU SHOULD...
KNOCK IT OFF, GRAVES.
SHE KNOWS YOU'RE NOT OLDER THAN ME. SHE KNOWS EVERYTHING!
WHAT?!
ARE YOU INSANE?! YOU GET SOME PUPPY LOVE CRUSH ON ONE OF THEM, AND YOU PUT US ALL IN DANGER?
TOM! STOP!
ALL THAT'S IMPORTANT RIGHT NOW IS FINDING HEDY!

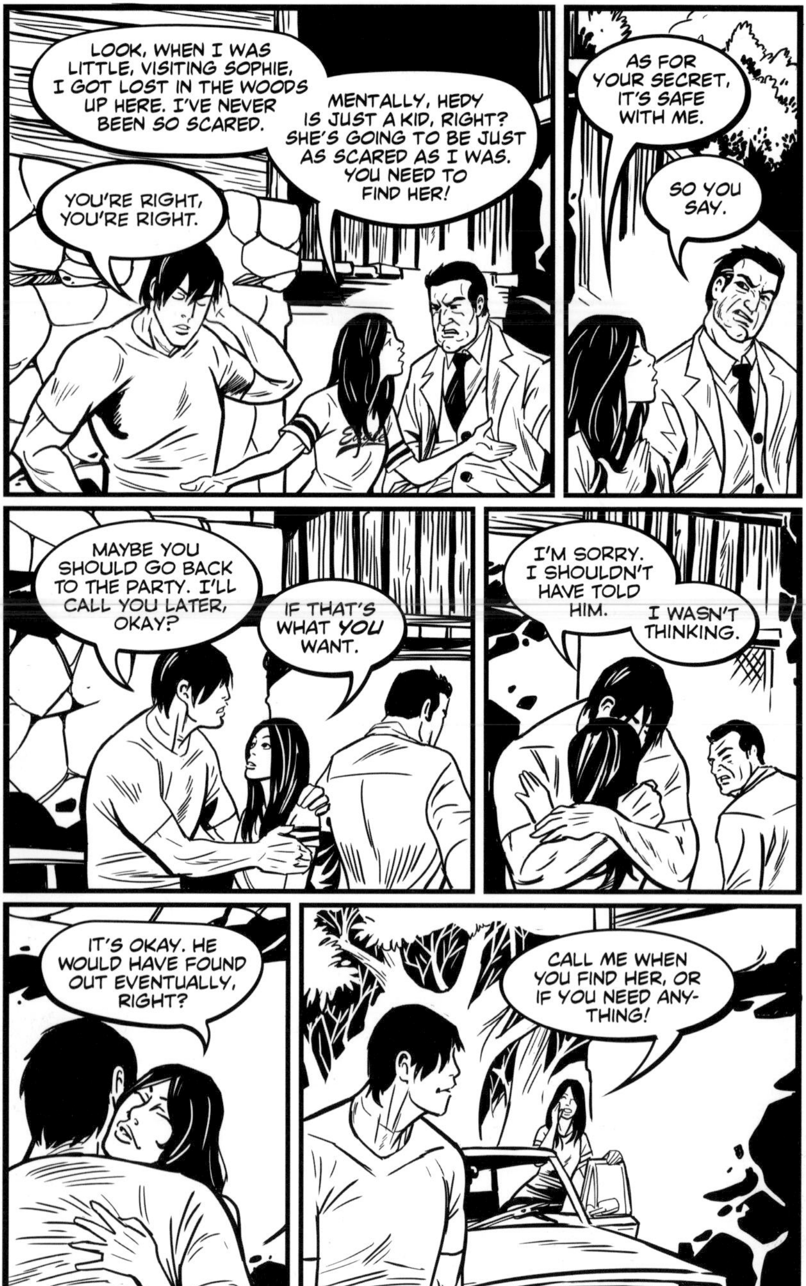
LOOK, WHEN I WAS LITTLE, VISITING SOPHIE, I GOT LOST IN THE WOODS UP HERE. I'VE NEVER BEEN SO SCARED.
MENTALLY, HEDY IS JUST A KID, RIGHT? SHE'S GOING TO BE JUST AS SCARED AS I WAS. YOU NEED TO FIND HER!
YOU'RE RIGHT, YOU'RE RIGHT.
AS FOR YOUR SECRET, IT'S SAFE WITH ME.
SO YOU SAY.
MAYBE YOU SHOULD GO BACK TO THE PARTY. I'LL CALL YOU LATER, OKAY?
IF THAT'S WHAT YOU WANT.
I'M SORRY. I SHOULDN'T HAVE TOLD HIM.
I WASN'T THINKING.
IT'S OKAY. HE WOULD HAVE FOUND OUT EVENTUALLY, RIGHT?
CALL ME WHEN YOU FIND HER, OR IF YOU NEED ANY-THING!

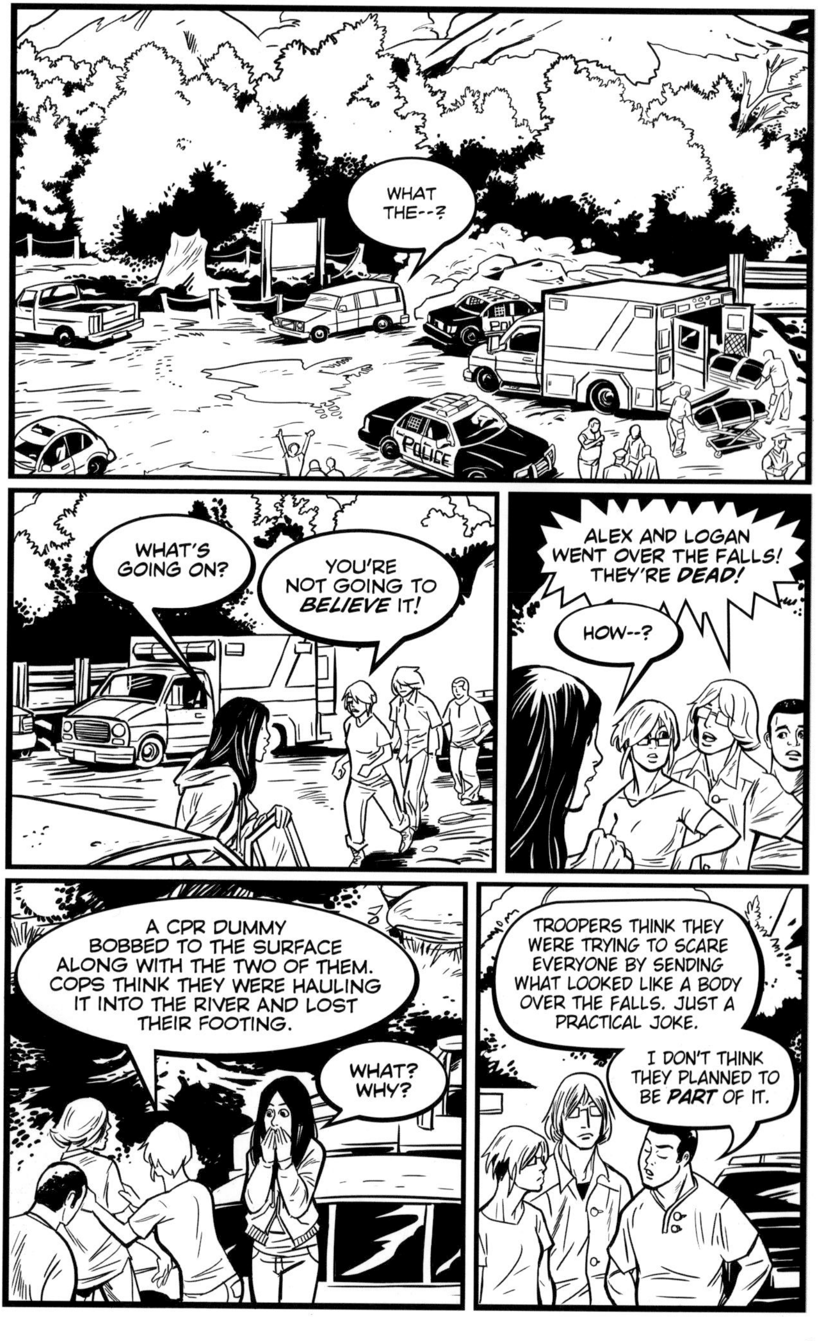
WHAT THE--?
POLICE
WHAT'S GOING ON?
YOU'RE NOT GOING TO *BELIEVE* IT!
ALEX AND LOGAN WENT OVER THE FALLS! THEY'RE *DEAD!*
HOW--?
A CPR DUMMY BOBBED TO THE SURFACE ALONG WITH THE TWO OF THEM. COPS THINK THEY WERE HAULING IT INTO THE RIVER AND LOST THEIR FOOTING.
WHAT? WHY?
TROOPERS THINK THEY WERE TRYING TO SCARE EVERYONE BY SENDING WHAT LOOKED LIKE A BODY OVER THE FALLS. JUST A PRACTICAL JOKE.
I DON'T THINK THEY PLANNED TO BE *PART* OF IT.

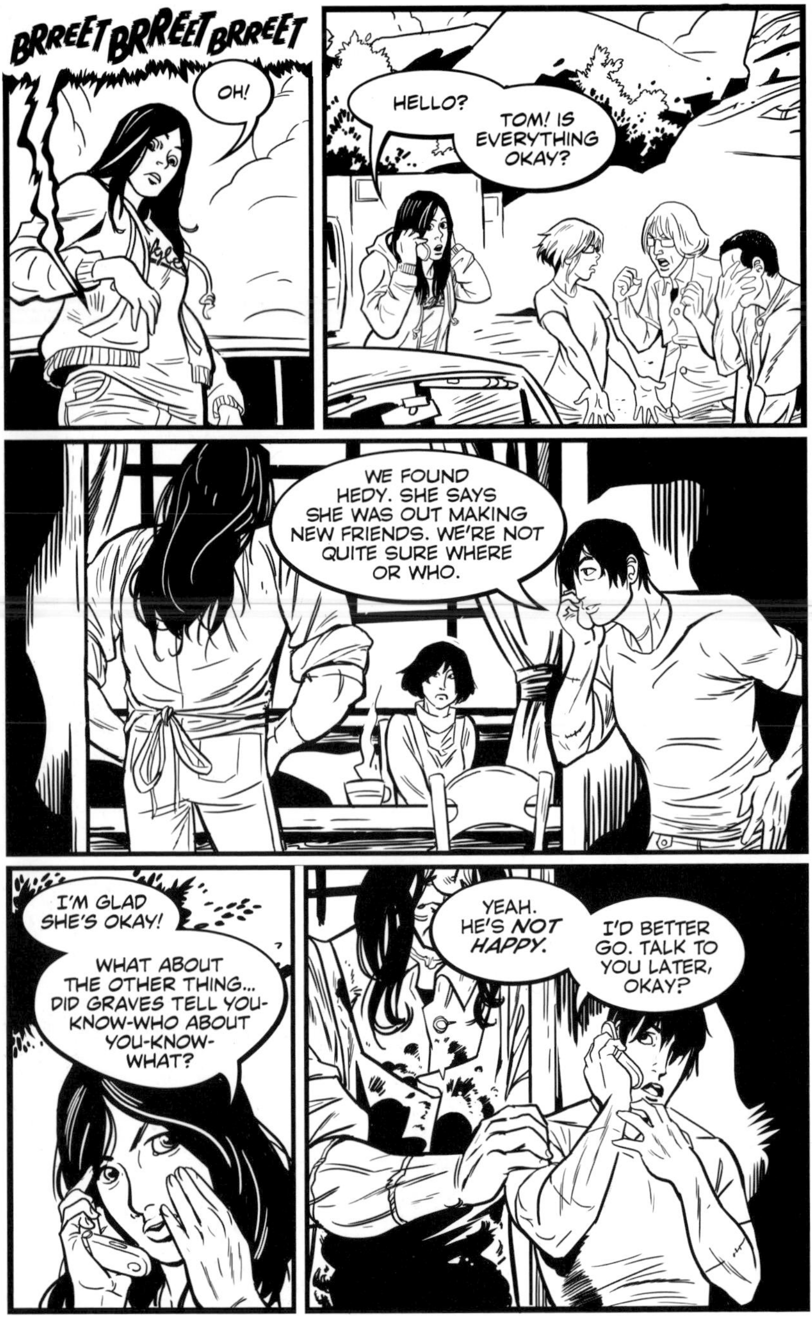
BRREET BRREET BRREET
OH!
HELLO?
TOM! IS EVERYTHING OKAY?
WE FOUND HEDY. SHE SAYS SHE WAS OUT MAKING NEW FRIENDS. WE'RE NOT QUITE SURE WHERE OR WHO.
I'M GLAD SHE'S OKAY!
WHAT ABOUT THE OTHER THING... DID GRAVES TELL YOU-KNOW-WHO ABOUT YOU-KNOW-WHAT?
YEAH. HE'S *NOT HAPPY.*
I'D BETTER GO. TALK TO YOU LATER, OKAY?

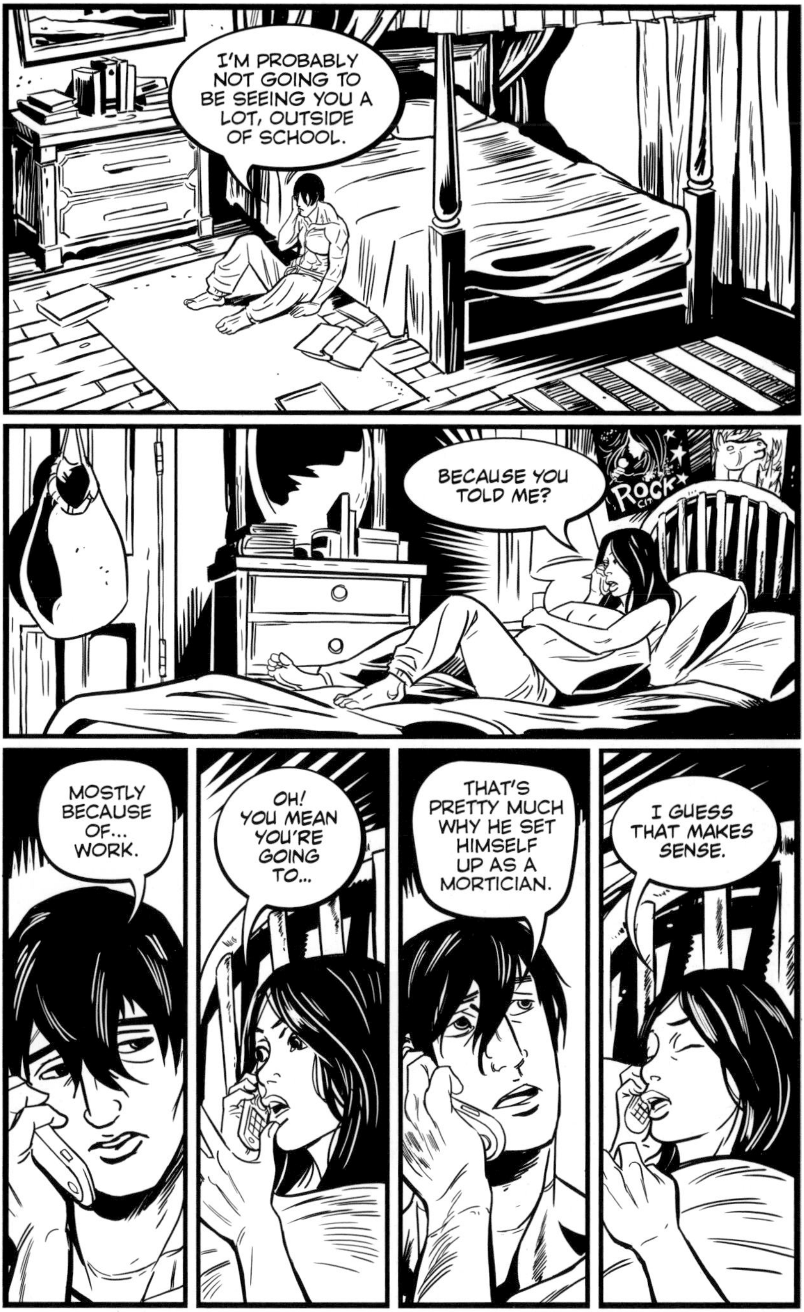
I'M PROBABLY NOT GOING TO BE SEEING YOU A LOT, OUTSIDE OF SCHOOL.
BECAUSE YOU TOLD ME?
ROCK
MOSTLY BECAUSE OF... WORK.
OH! YOU MEAN YOU'RE GOING TO...
THAT'S PRETTY MUCH WHY HE SET HIMSELF UP AS A MORTICIAN.
I GUESS THAT MAKES SENSE.

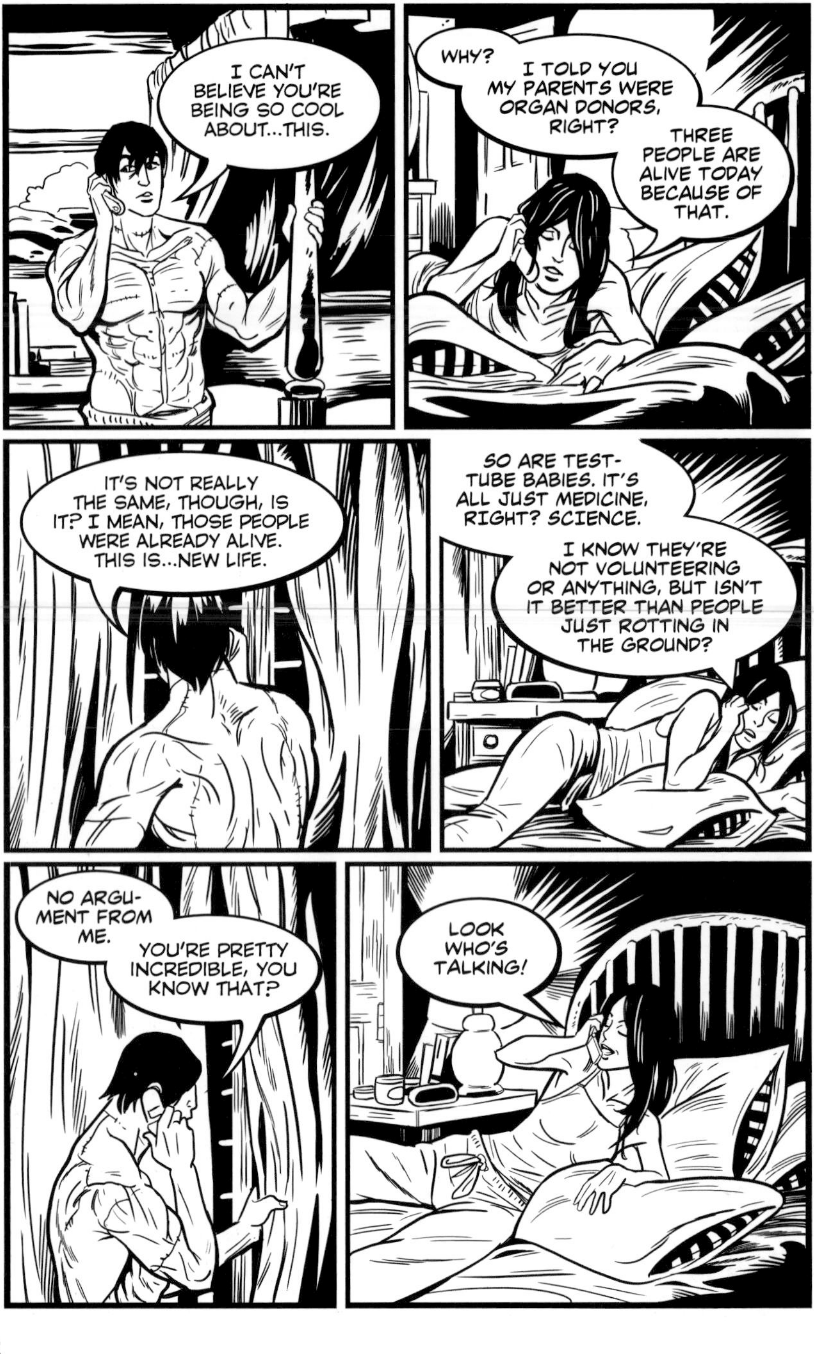
I CAN'T BELIEVE YOU'RE BEING SO COOL ABOUT...THIS.
WHY?
I TOLD YOU MY PARENTS WERE ORGAN DONORS, RIGHT?
THREE PEOPLE ARE ALIVE TODAY BECAUSE OF THAT.
IT'S NOT REALLY THE SAME, THOUGH, IS IT? I MEAN, THOSE PEOPLE WERE ALREADY ALIVE. THIS IS...NEW LIFE.
SO ARE TEST-TUBE BABIES. IT'S ALL JUST MEDICINE, RIGHT? SCIENCE.
I KNOW THEY'RE NOT VOLUNTEERING OR ANYTHING, BUT ISN'T IT BETTER THAN PEOPLE JUST ROTTING IN THE GROUND?
NO ARGUMENT FROM ME.
YOU'RE PRETTY INCREDIBLE, YOU KNOW THAT?
LOOK WHO'S TALKING!

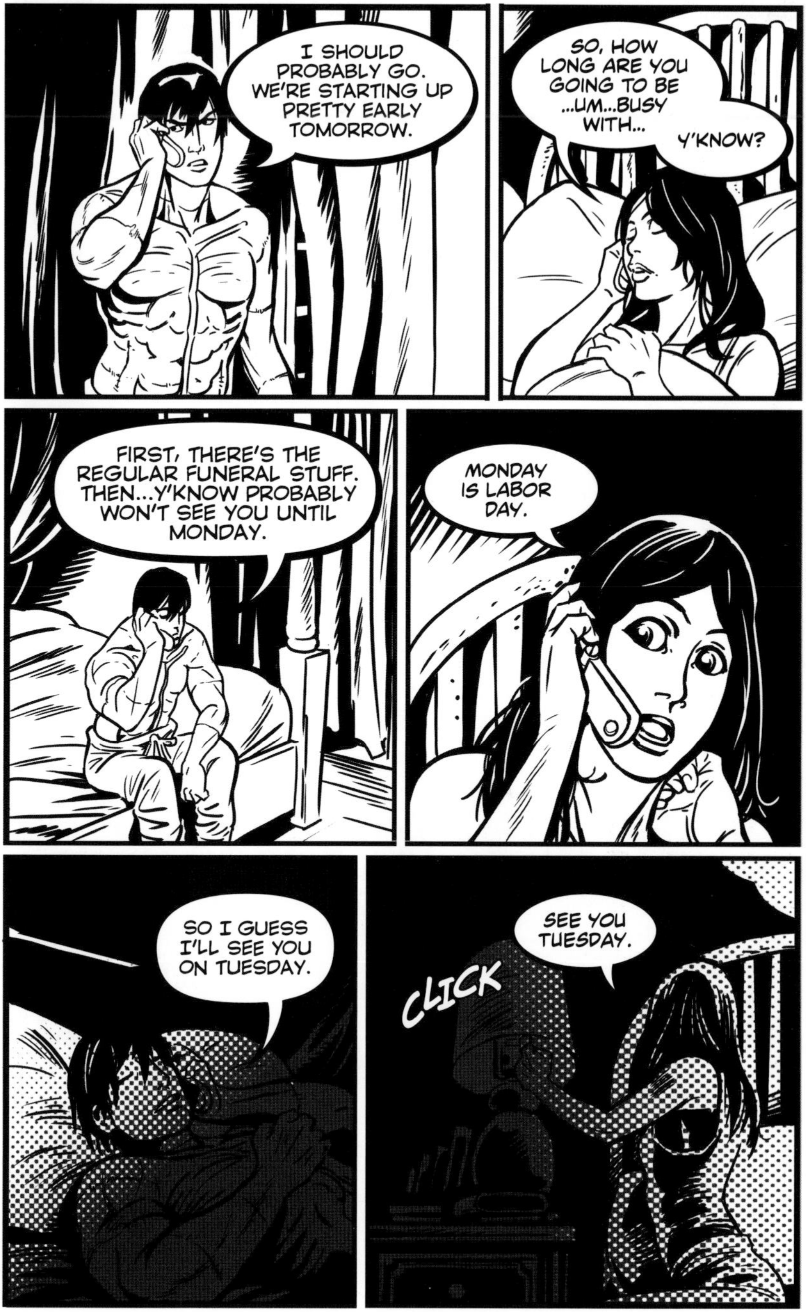
I SHOULD PROBABLY GO. WE'RE STARTING UP PRETTY EARLY TOMORROW.
SO, HOW LONG ARE YOU GOING TO BE ...UM...BUSY WITH...
Y'KNOW?
FIRST, THERE'S THE REGULAR FUNERAL STUFF. THEN...Y'KNOW PROBABLY WON'T SEE YOU UNTIL MONDAY.
MONDAY IS LABOR DAY.
SO I GUESS I'LL SEE YOU ON TUESDAY.
SEE YOU TUESDAY.
CLICK

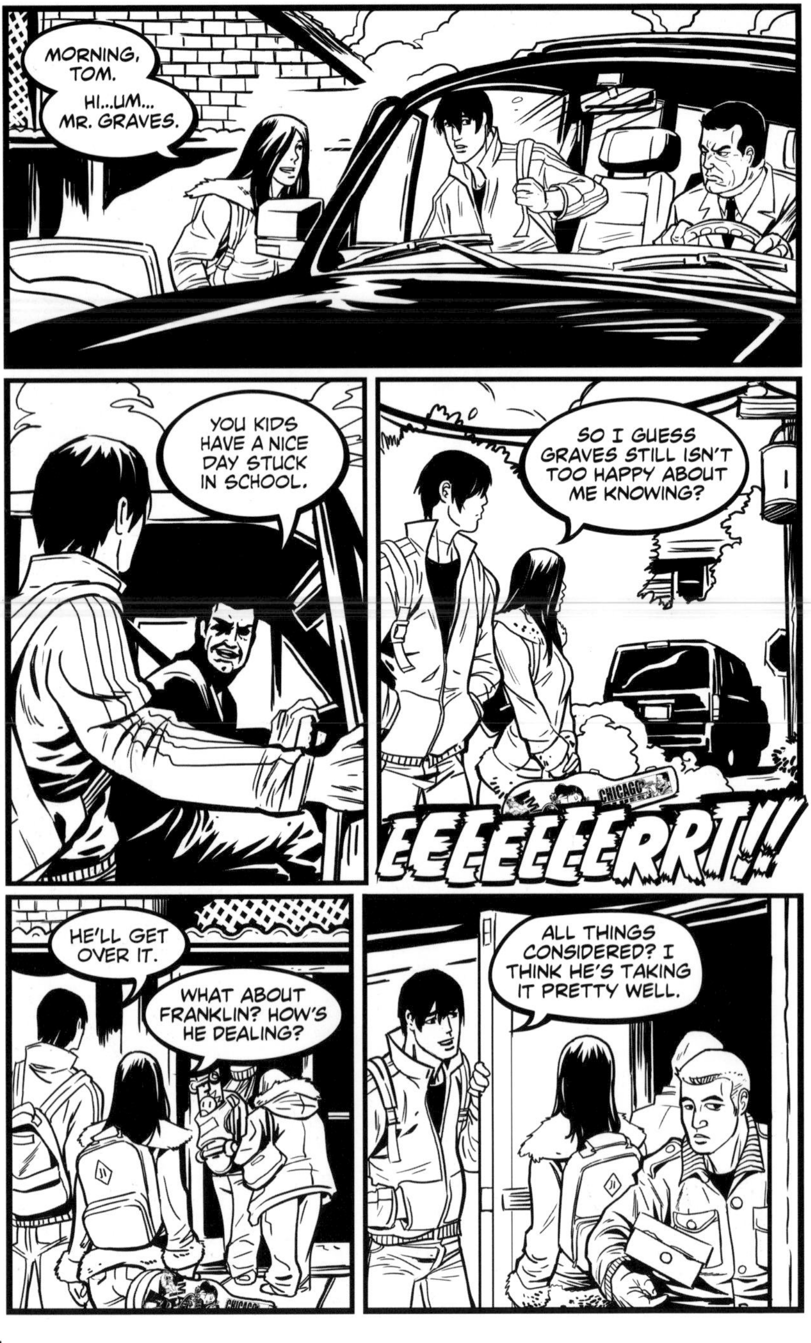
MORNING, TOM.
HI...UM... MR. GRAVES.
YOU KIDS HAVE A NICE DAY STUCK IN SCHOOL.
SO I GUESS GRAVES STILL ISN'T TOO HAPPY ABOUT ME KNOWING?
EEEEEEERRT!!
HE'LL GET OVER IT.
WHAT ABOUT FRANKLIN? HOW'S HE DEALING?
ALL THINGS CONSIDERED? I THINK HE'S TAKING IT PRETTY WELL.

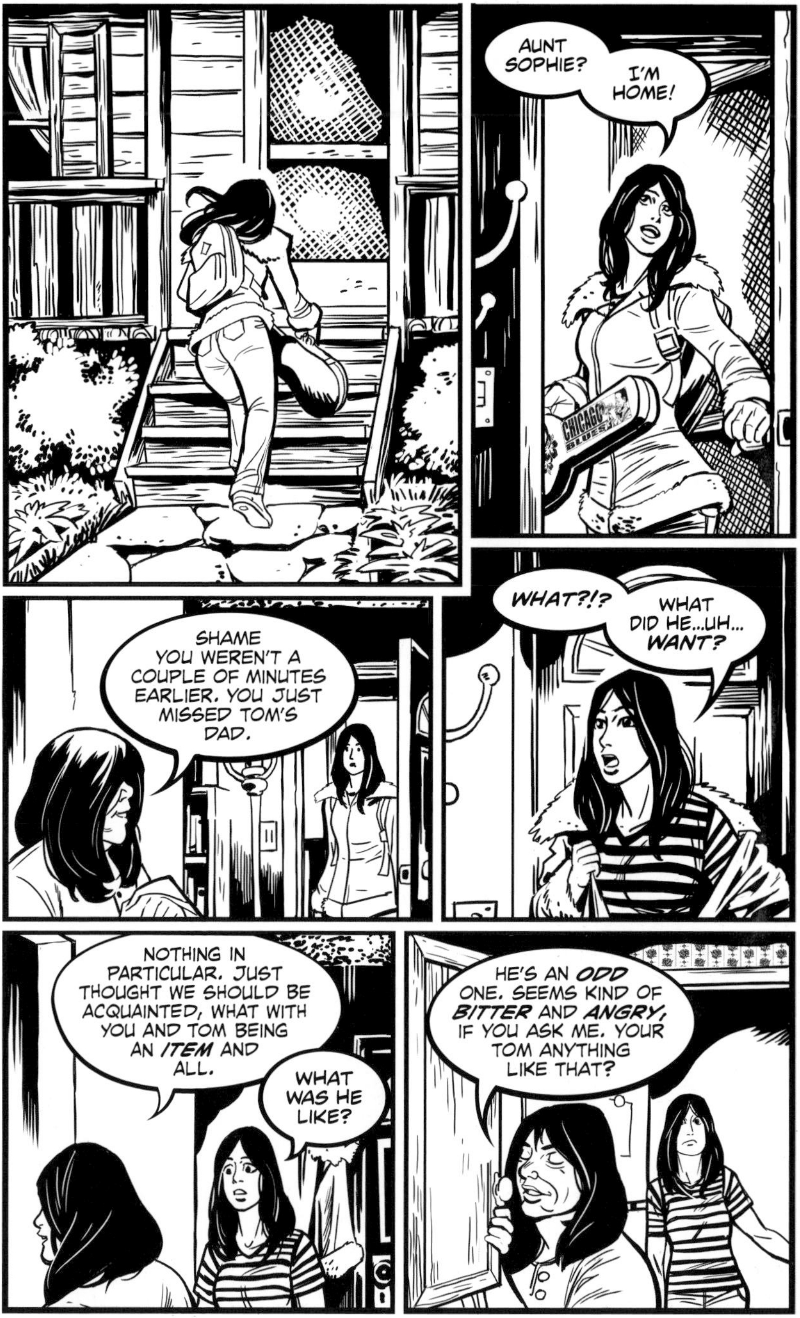
AUNT SOPHIE?
I'M HOME!
CHICAGO BLUES
SHAME YOU WEREN'T A COUPLE OF MINUTES EARLIER. YOU JUST MISSED TOM'S DAD.
WHAT?!?
WHAT DID HE...UH... WANT?
NOTHING IN PARTICULAR. JUST THOUGHT WE SHOULD BE ACQUAINTED, WHAT WITH YOU AND TOM BEING AN ITEM AND ALL.
WHAT WAS HE LIKE?
HE'S AN ODD ONE. SEEMS KIND OF BITTER AND ANGRY, IF YOU ASK ME. YOUR TOM ANYTHING LIKE THAT?

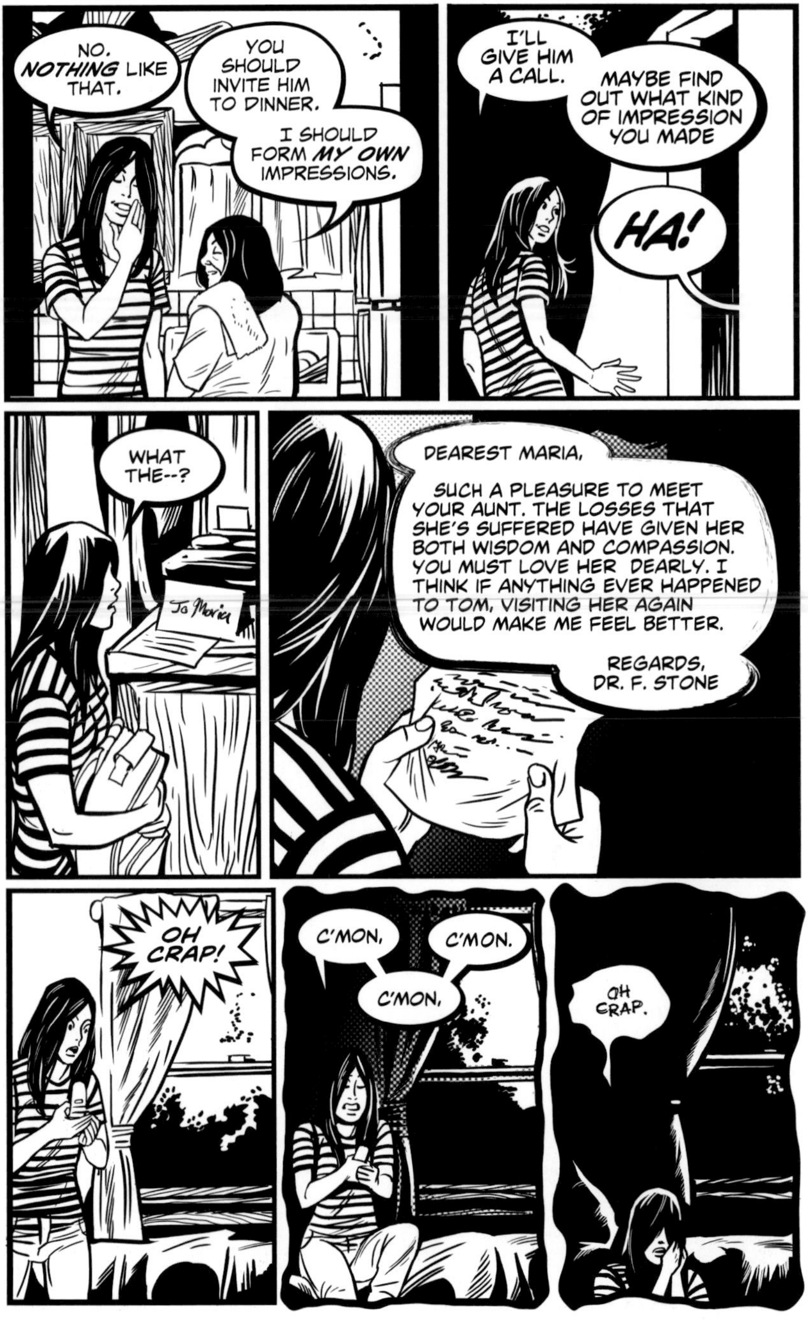
NO. NOTHING LIKE THAT.
YOU SHOULD INVITE HIM TO DINNER.
I SHOULD FORM MY OWN IMPRESSIONS.
I'LL GIVE HIM A CALL.
MAYBE FIND OUT WHAT KIND OF IMPRESSION YOU MADE
HA!
WHAT THE--?
To Maria
DEAREST MARIA,
SUCH A PLEASURE TO MEET YOUR AUNT. THE LOSSES THAT SHE'S SUFFERED HAVE GIVEN HER BOTH WISDOM AND COMPASSION. YOU MUST LOVE HER DEARLY. I THINK IF ANYTHING EVER HAPPENED TO TOM, VISITING HER AGAIN WOULD MAKE ME FEEL BETTER.
REGARDS, DR. F. STONE
OH CRAP!
C'MON,
C'MON,
C'MON.
OH CRAP.

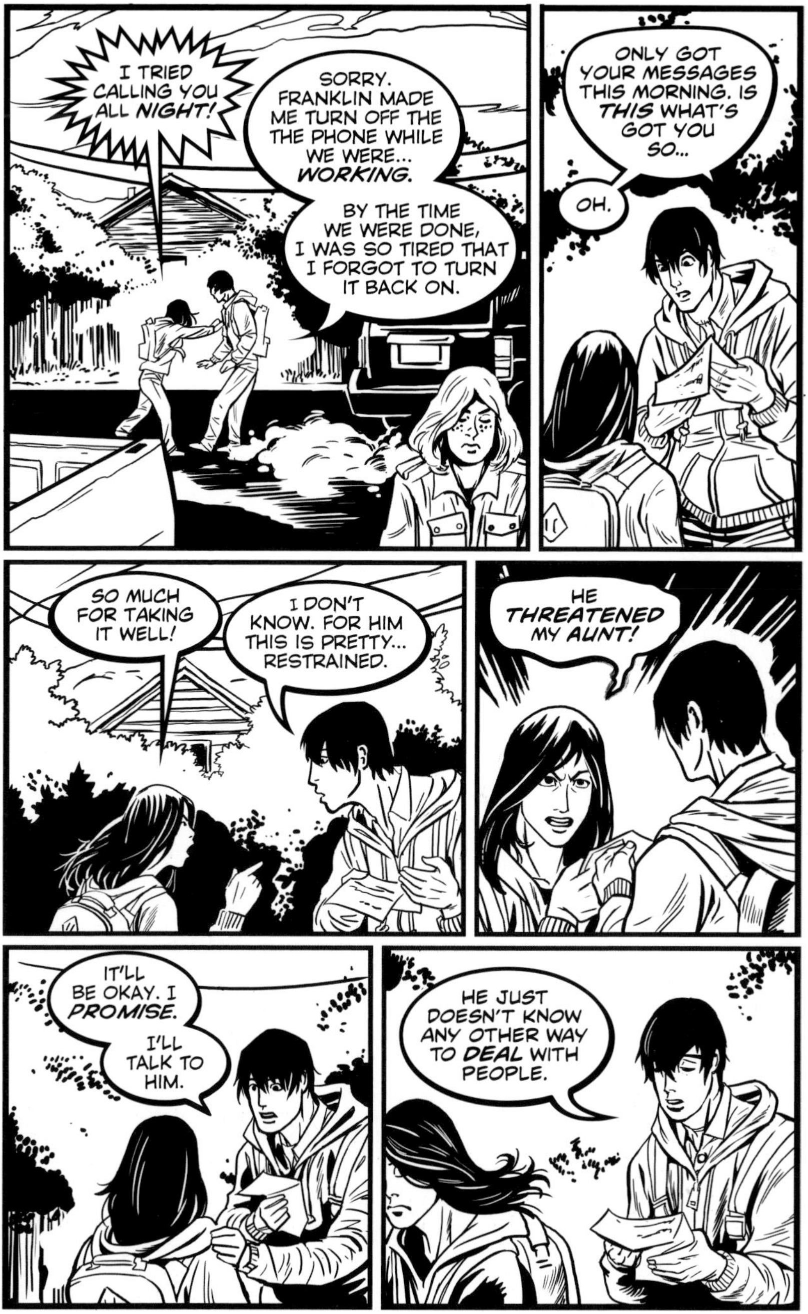
I TRIED CALLING YOU ALL NIGHT!
SORRY. FRANKLIN MADE ME TURN OFF THE THE PHONE WHILE WE WERE... WORKING.
BY THE TIME WE WERE DONE, I WAS SO TIRED THAT I FORGOT TO TURN IT BACK ON.
ONLY GOT YOUR MESSAGES THIS MORNING. IS THIS WHAT'S GOT YOU SO...
OH.
SO MUCH FOR TAKING IT WELL!
I DON'T KNOW. FOR HIM THIS IS PRETTY... RESTRAINED.
HE THREATENED MY AUNT!
IT'LL BE OKAY. I PROMISE.
I'LL TALK TO HIM.
HE JUST DOESN'T KNOW ANY OTHER WAY TO DEAL WITH PEOPLE.

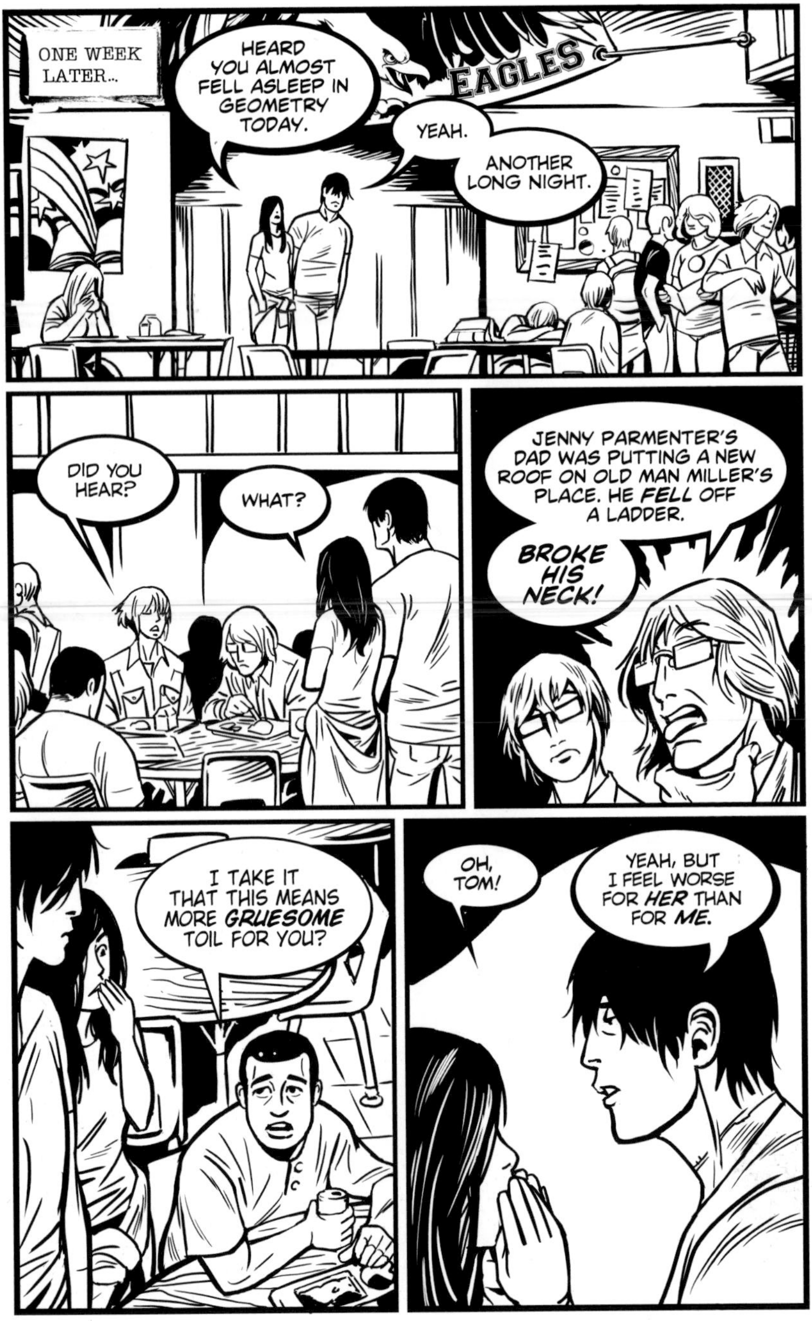

ONE WEEK LATER...
HEARD YOU ALMOST FELL ASLEEP IN GEOMETRY TODAY.
EAGLES
YEAH.
ANOTHER LONG NIGHT.
DID YOU HEAR?
WHAT?
JENNY PARMENTER'S DAD WAS PUTTING A NEW ROOF ON OLD MAN MILLER'S PLACE. HE FELL OFF A LADDER.
BROKE HIS NECK!
I TAKE IT THAT THIS MEANS MORE GRUESOME TOIL FOR YOU?
OH, TOM!
YEAH, BUT I FEEL WORSE FOR HER THAN FOR ME.

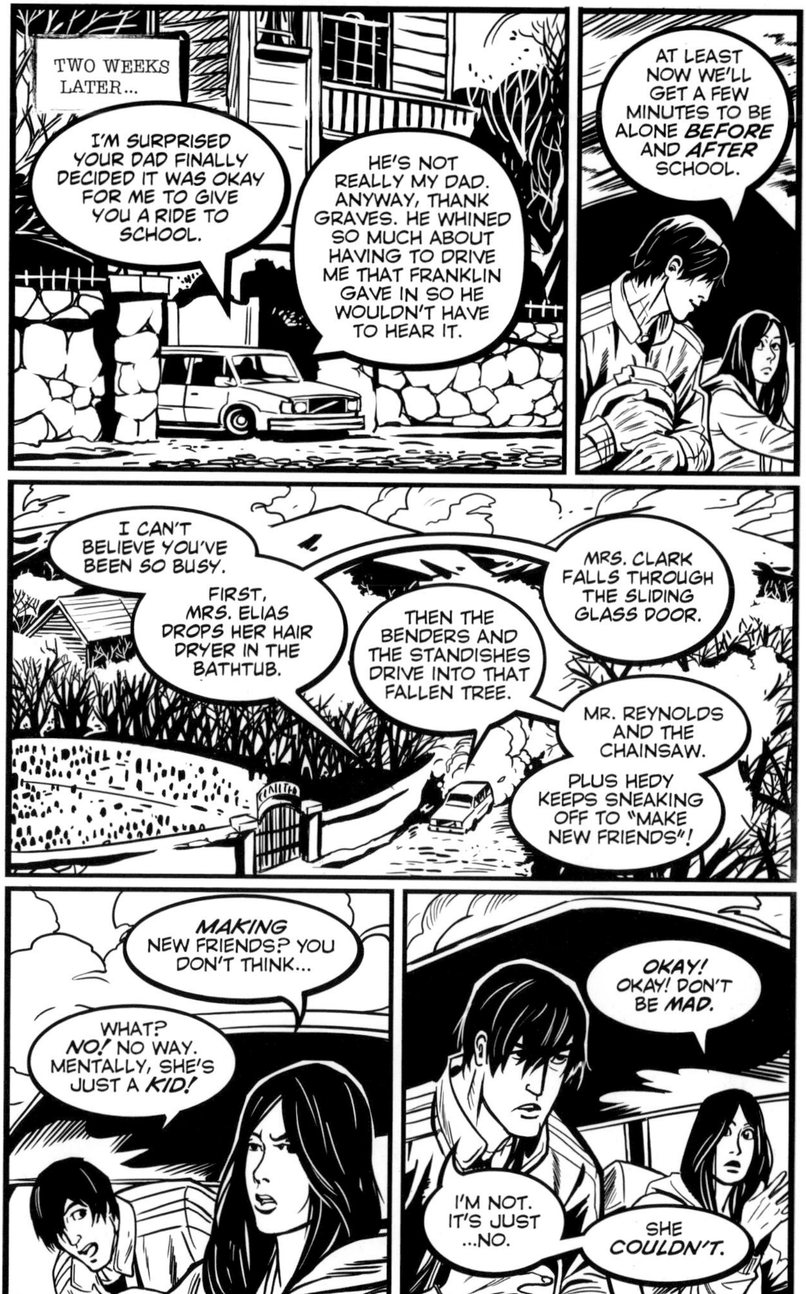
TWO WEEKS LATER...
I'M SURPRISED YOUR DAD FINALLY DECIDED IT WAS OKAY FOR ME TO GIVE YOU A RIDE TO SCHOOL.
HE'S NOT REALLY MY DAD. ANYWAY, THANK GRAVES. HE WHINED SO MUCH ABOUT HAVING TO DRIVE ME THAT FRANKLIN GAVE IN SO HE WOULDN'T HAVE TO HEAR IT.
AT LEAST NOW WE'LL GET A FEW MINUTES TO BE ALONE *BEFORE* AND *AFTER* SCHOOL.
I CAN'T BELIEVE YOU'VE BEEN SO BUSY.
FIRST, MRS. ELIAS DROPS HER HAIR DRYER IN THE BATHTUB.
THEN THE BENDERS AND THE STANDISHES DRIVE INTO THAT FALLEN TREE.
MRS. CLARK FALLS THROUGH THE SLIDING GLASS DOOR.
MR. REYNOLDS AND THE CHAINSAW.
PLUS HEDY KEEPS SNEAKING OFF TO "MAKE NEW FRIENDS"!
MAKING NEW FRIENDS? YOU DON'T THINK...
WHAT? *NO!* NO WAY. MENTALLY, SHE'S JUST A *KID!*
OKAY! OKAY! DON'T BE *MAD.*
I'M NOT. IT'S JUST ...NO.
SHE *COULDN'T.*

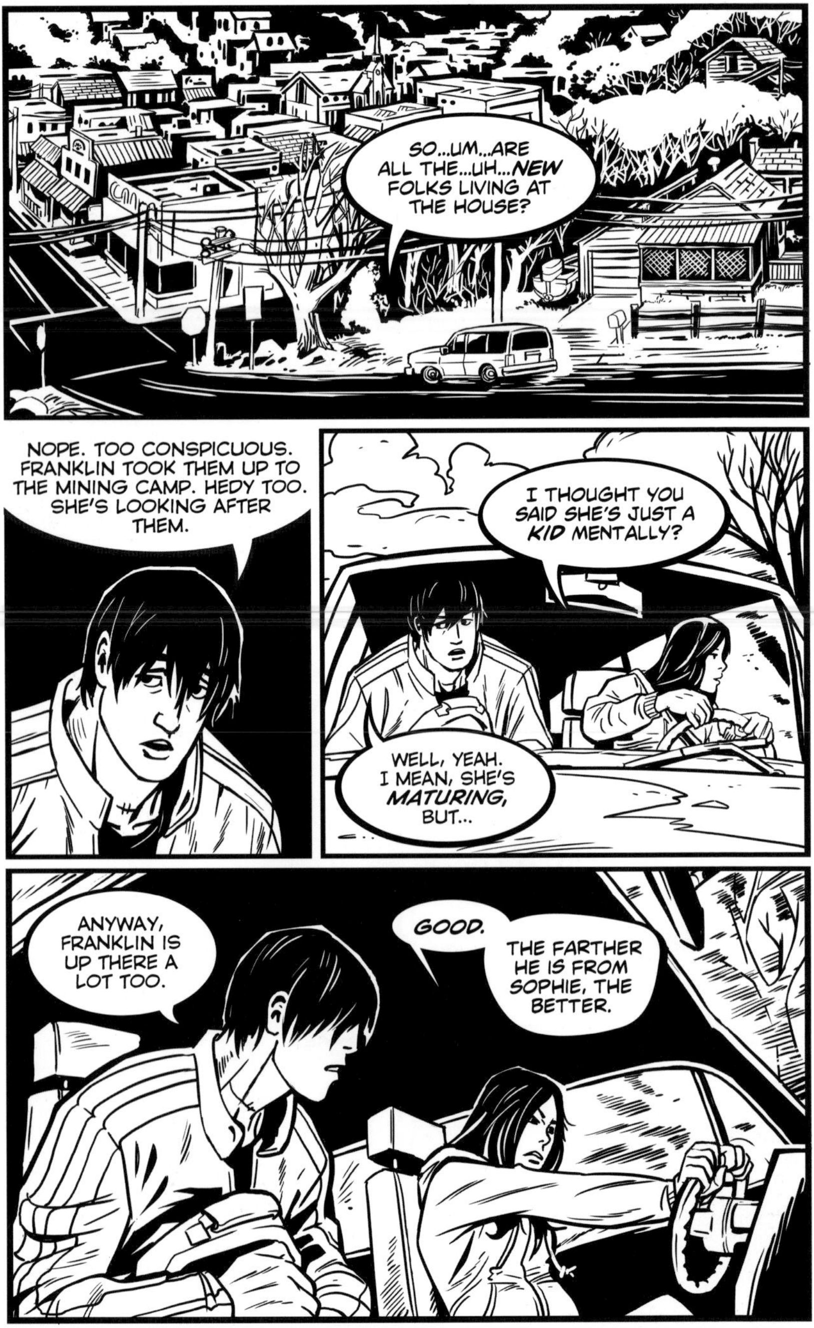
SO...UM...ARE ALL THE...UH...NEW FOLKS LIVING AT THE HOUSE?
NOPE. TOO CONSPICUOUS. FRANKLIN TOOK THEM UP TO THE MINING CAMP. HEDY TOO. SHE'S LOOKING AFTER THEM.
I THOUGHT YOU SAID SHE'S JUST A KID MENTALLY?
WELL, YEAH. I MEAN, SHE'S MATURING, BUT...
ANYWAY, FRANKLIN IS UP THERE A LOT TOO.
GOOD.
THE FARTHER HE IS FROM SOPHIE, THE BETTER.

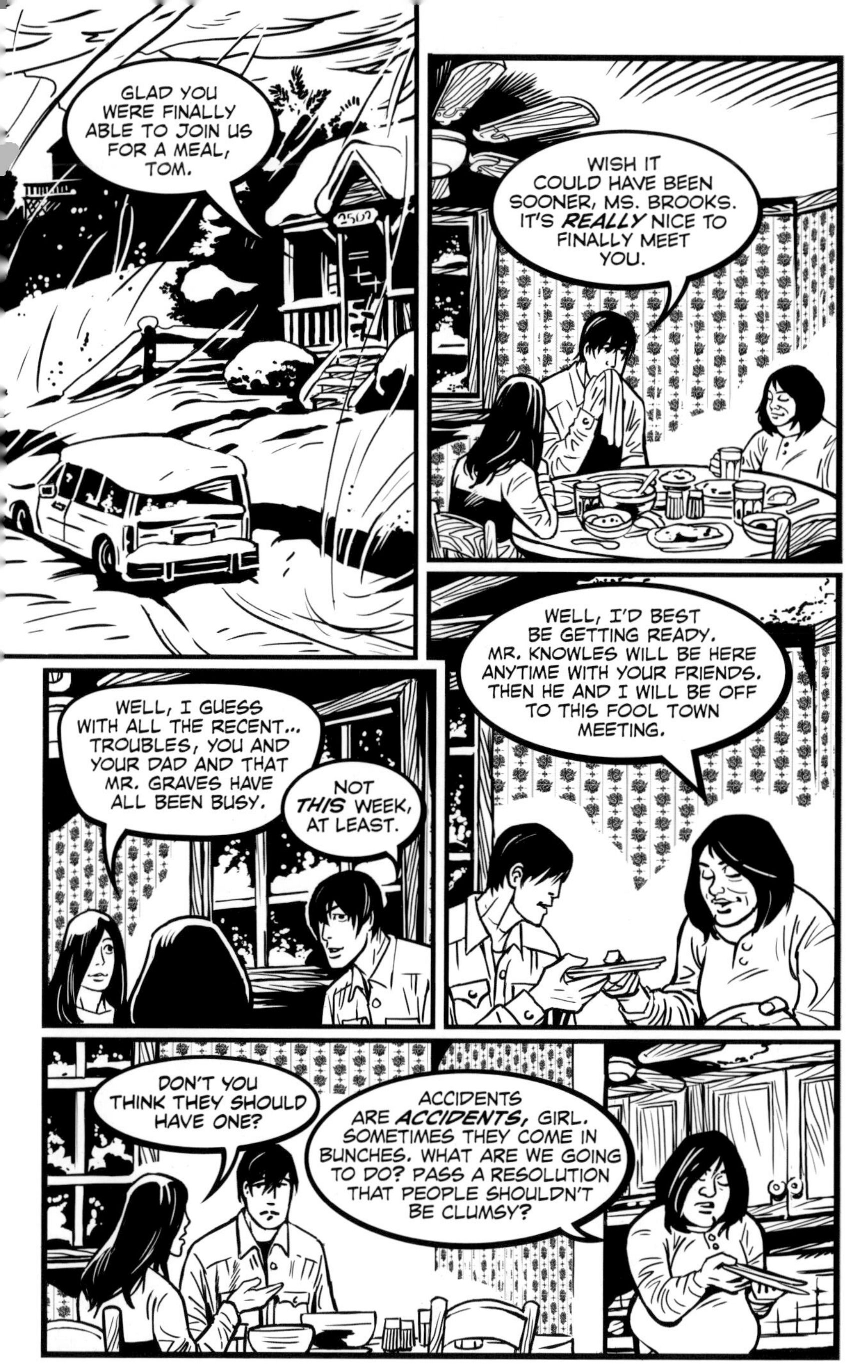
GLAD YOU WERE FINALLY ABLE TO JOIN US FOR A MEAL, TOM.
2502
WISH IT COULD HAVE BEEN SOONER, MS. BROOKS. IT'S *REALLY* NICE TO FINALLY MEET YOU.
WELL, I GUESS WITH ALL THE RECENT... TROUBLES, YOU AND YOUR DAD AND THAT MR. GRAVES HAVE ALL BEEN BUSY.
NOT *THIS* WEEK, AT LEAST.
WELL, I'D BEST BE GETTING READY. MR. KNOWLES WILL BE HERE ANYTIME WITH YOUR FRIENDS. THEN HE AND I WILL BE OFF TO THIS FOOL TOWN MEETING.
DON'T YOU THINK THEY SHOULD HAVE ONE?
ACCIDENTS ARE *ACCIDENTS,* GIRL. SOMETIMES THEY COME IN BUNCHES. WHAT ARE WE GOING TO DO? PASS A RESOLUTION THAT PEOPLE SHOULDN'T BE CLUMSY?

AFTER DINNER.

YOU KIDS BEHAVE YOUR-SELVES UNTIL WE GET BACK! SHOULD ONLY BE AN HOUR OR *TWO.*

HA! WE SHOULD *BE SO LUCKY.*

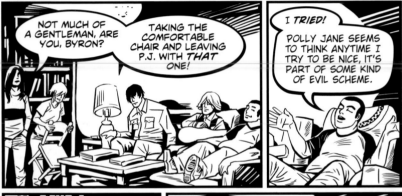

NOT MUCH OF A GENTLEMAN, ARE YOU, BYRON?

TAKING THE COMFORTABLE CHAIR AND LEAVING P.J. WITH *THAT* ONE!

I *TRIED!*

POLLY JANE SEEMS TO THINK ANYTIME I TRY TO BE NICE, IT'S PART OF SOME KIND OF EVIL SCHEME.

CAN YOU BLAME ME? HE'S *DEVIOUS.*

OR MAYBE HE JUST LIKES YOU?

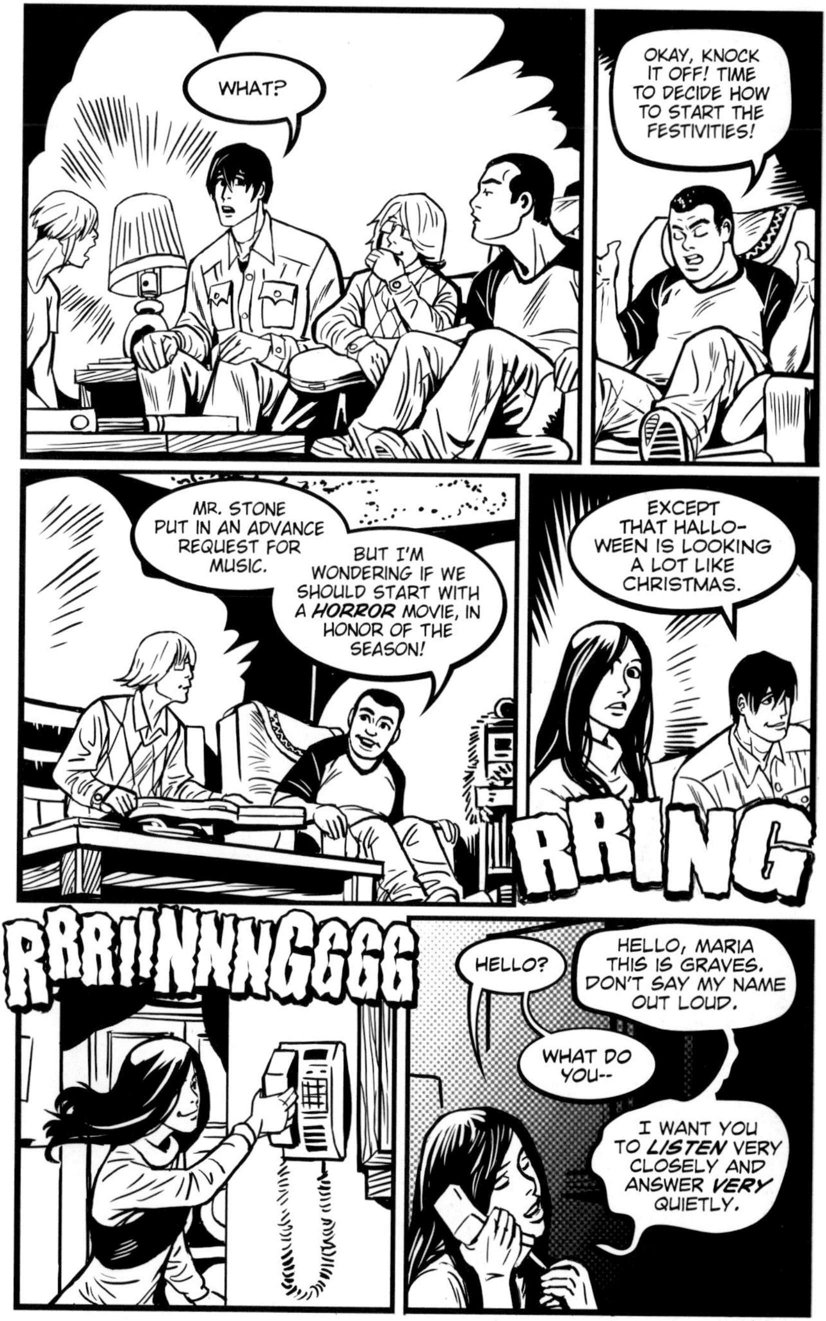
WHAT?
OKAY, KNOCK IT OFF! TIME TO DECIDE HOW TO START THE FESTIVITIES!
MR. STONE PUT IN AN ADVANCE REQUEST FOR MUSIC.
BUT I'M WONDERING IF WE SHOULD START WITH A HORROR MOVIE, IN HONOR OF THE SEASON!
EXCEPT THAT HALLO-WEEN IS LOOKING A LOT LIKE CHRISTMAS.
RRING
RRRIINNNGGGG
HELLO?
HELLO, MARIA THIS IS GRAVES. DON'T SAY MY NAME OUT LOUD.
WHAT DO YOU--
I WANT YOU TO LISTEN VERY CLOSELY AND ANSWER VERY QUIETLY.

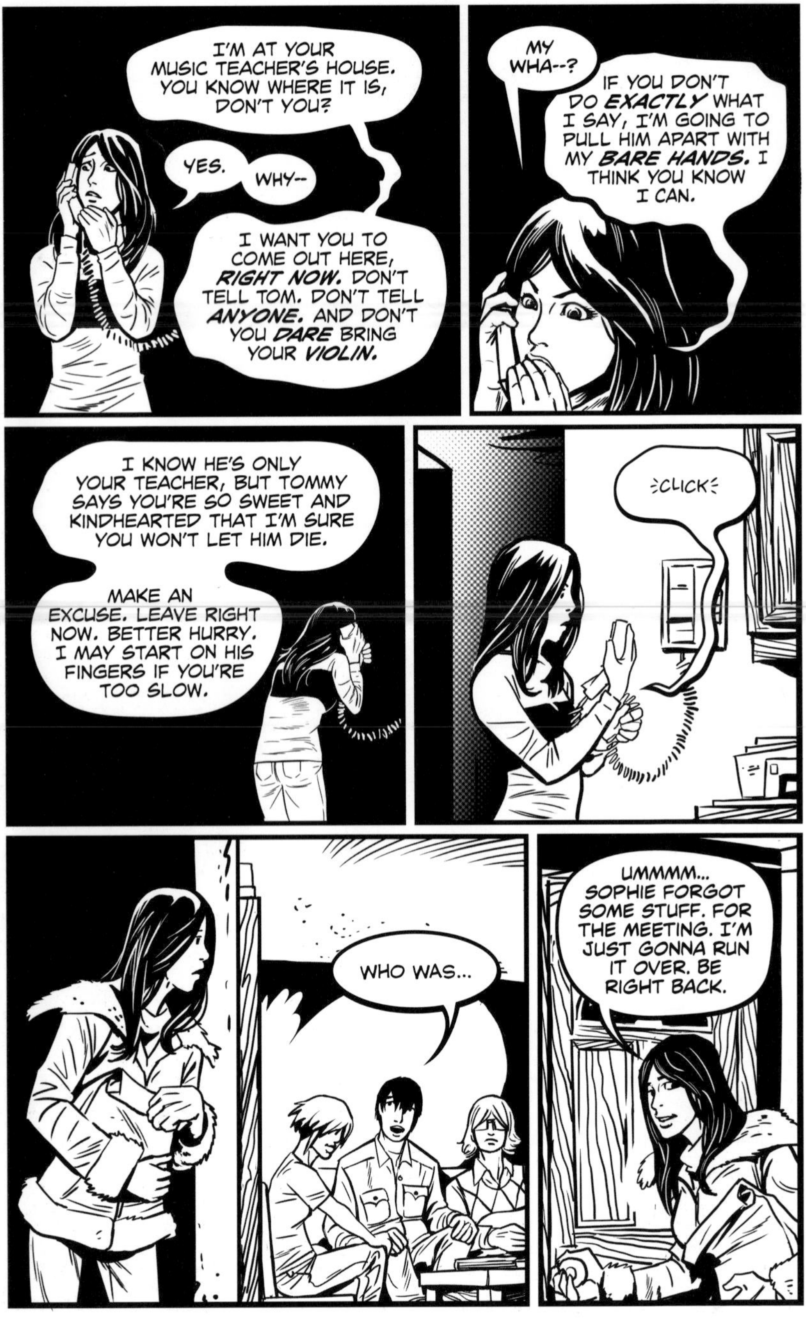
I'M AT YOUR MUSIC TEACHER'S HOUSE. YOU KNOW WHERE IT IS, DON'T YOU?
YES.
WHY--
I WANT YOU TO COME OUT HERE, RIGHT NOW. DON'T TELL TOM. DON'T TELL ANYONE. AND DON'T YOU DARE BRING YOUR VIOLIN.
MY WHA--?
IF YOU DON'T DO EXACTLY WHAT I SAY, I'M GOING TO PULL HIM APART WITH MY BARE HANDS. I THINK YOU KNOW I CAN.
I KNOW HE'S ONLY YOUR TEACHER, BUT TOMMY SAYS YOU'RE SO SWEET AND KINDHEARTED THAT I'M SURE YOU WON'T LET HIM DIE.
MAKE AN EXCUSE. LEAVE RIGHT NOW. BETTER HURRY. I MAY START ON HIS FINGERS IF YOU'RE TOO SLOW.
CLICK
WHO WAS...
UMMMM... SOPHIE FORGOT SOME STUFF. FOR THE MEETING. I'M JUST GONNA RUN IT OVER. BE RIGHT BACK.

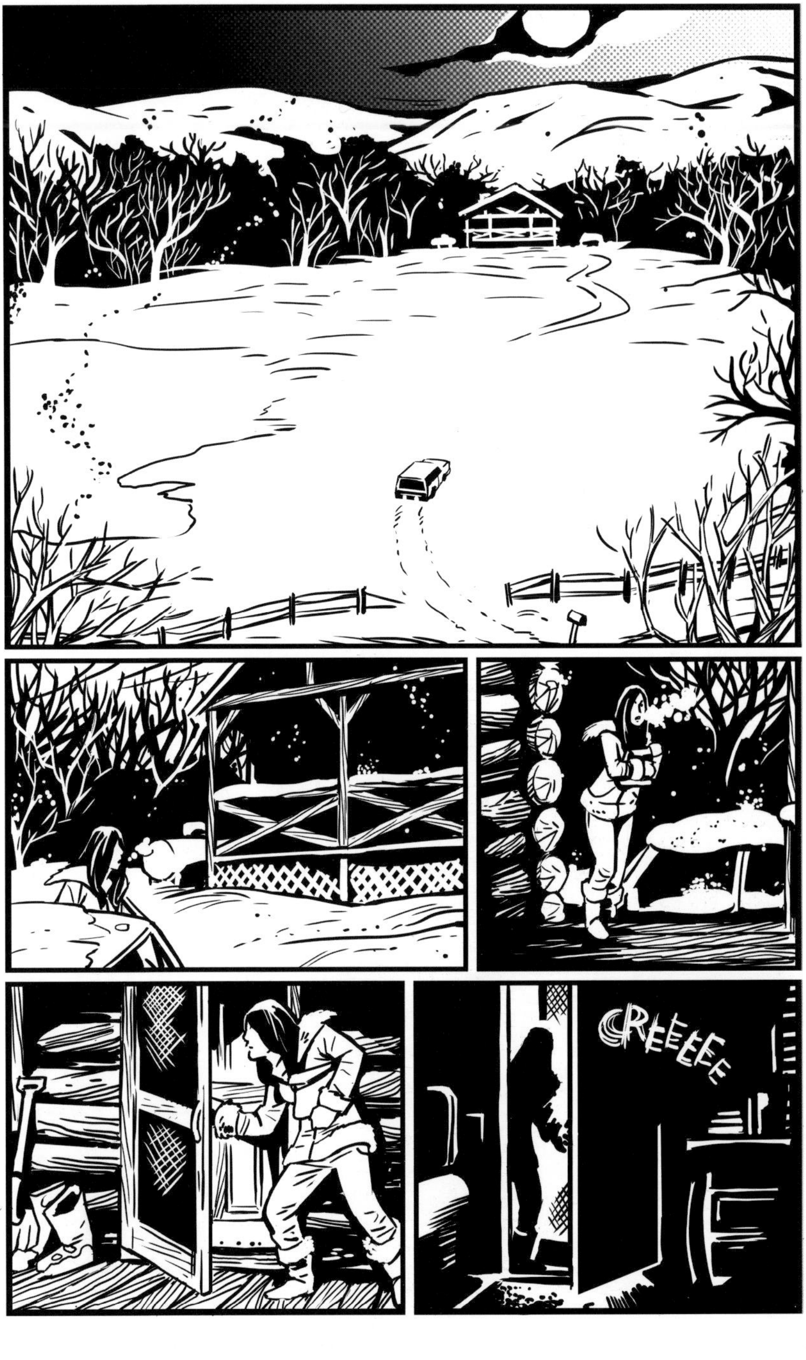
CREEEEE

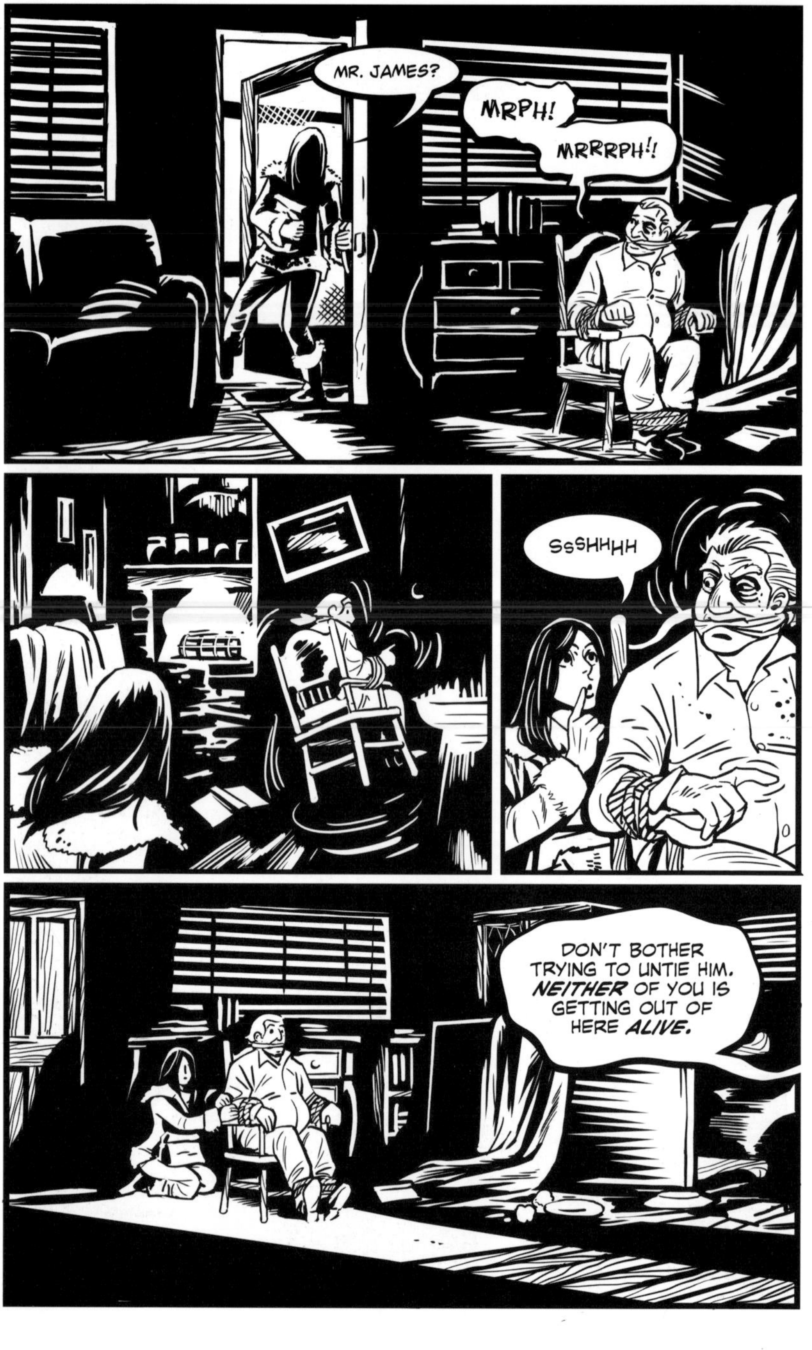
MR. JAMES?
MRPH!
MRRRPH!!
SsSHHHH
DON'T BOTHER TRYING TO UNTIE HIM. ***NEITHER*** OF YOU IS GETTING OUT OF HERE ***ALIVE.***

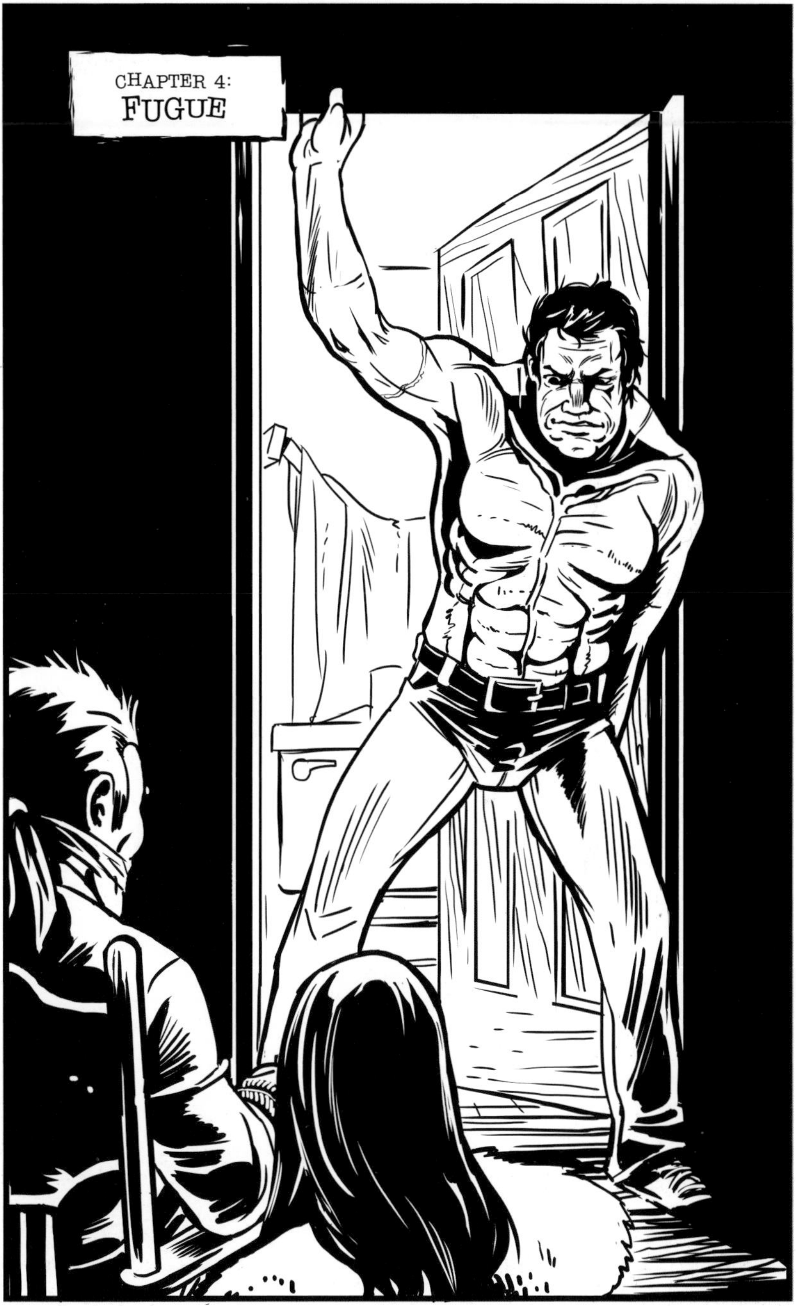
CHAPTER 4:
FUGUE

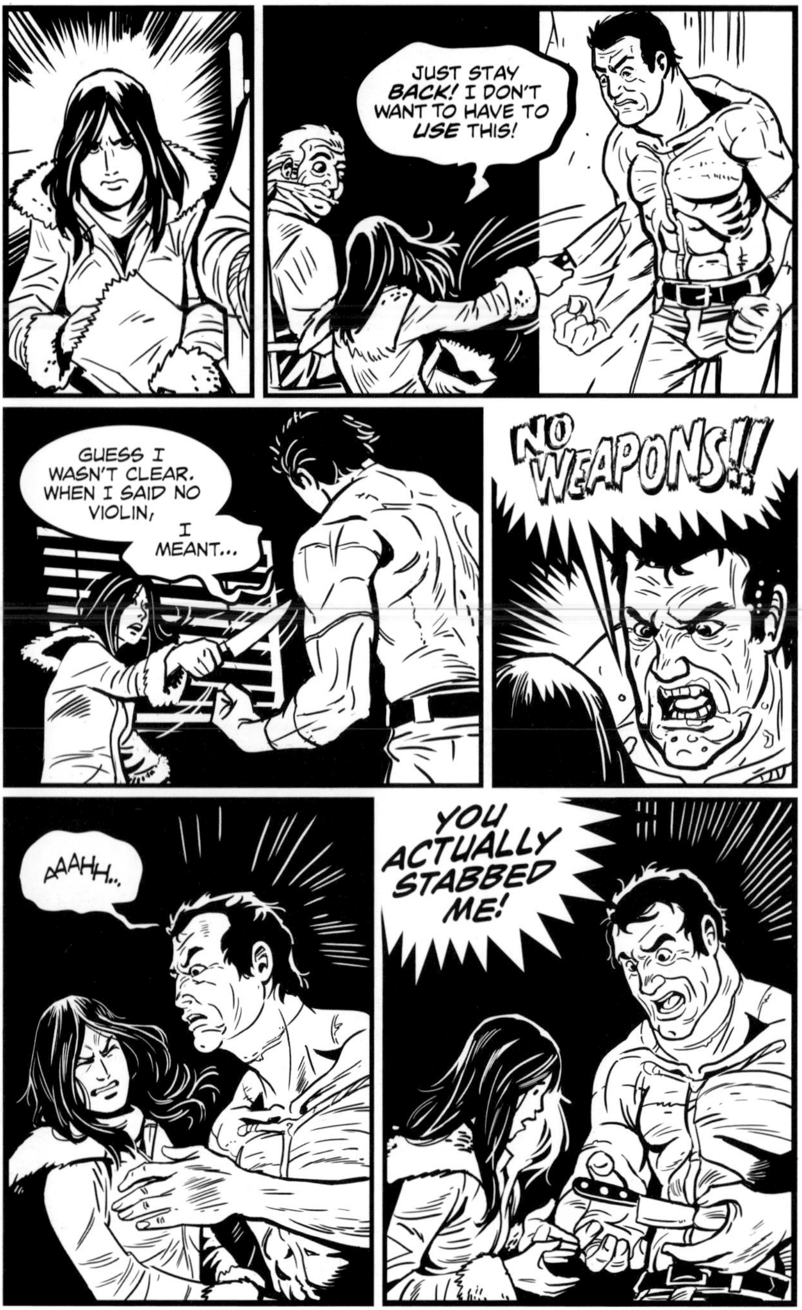
JUST STAY BACK! I DON'T WANT TO HAVE TO USE THIS!
GUESS I WASN'T CLEAR. WHEN I SAID NO VIOLIN,
I MEANT...
NO WEAPONS!!
AAAHH...
YOU ACTUALLY STABBED ME!

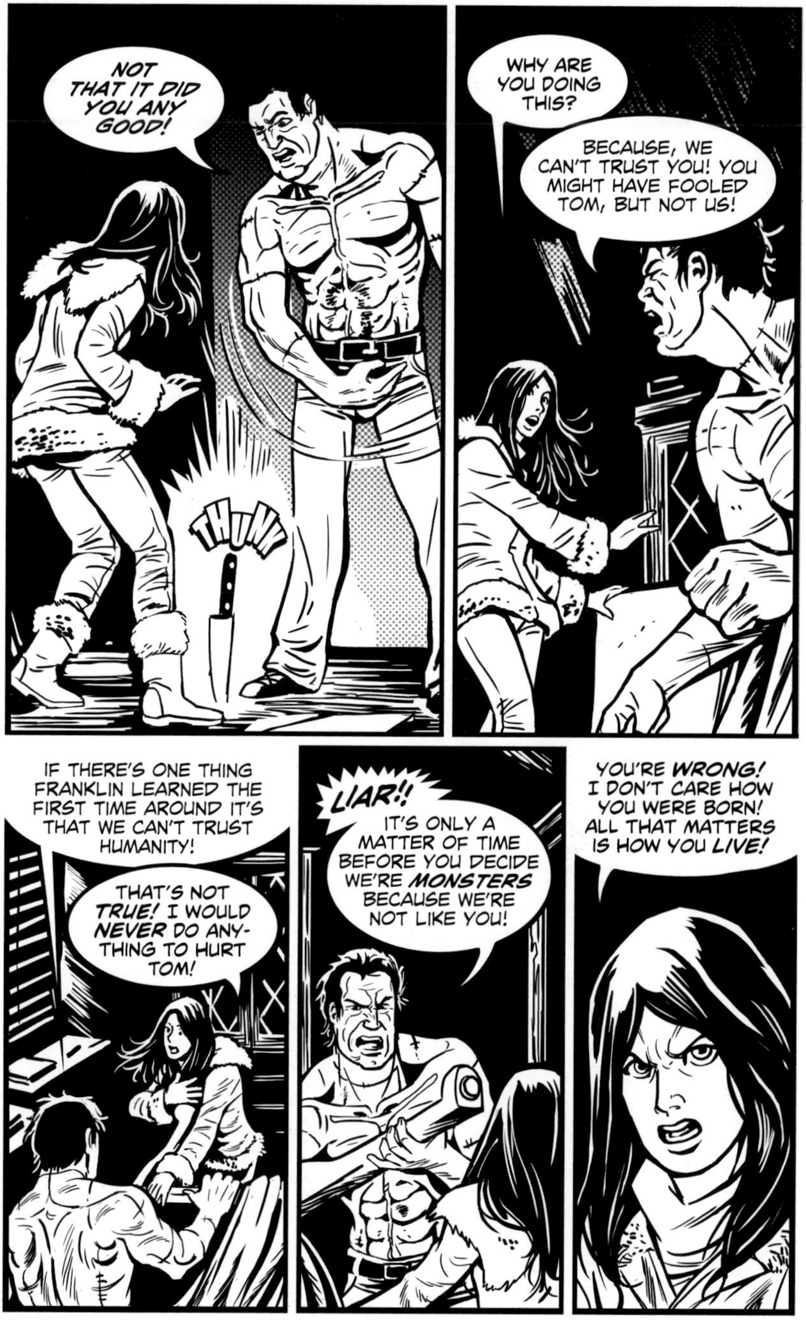
NOT THAT IT DID YOU ANY GOOD!
THUNK
WHY ARE YOU DOING THIS?
BECAUSE, WE CAN'T TRUST YOU! YOU MIGHT HAVE FOOLED TOM, BUT NOT US!
IF THERE'S ONE THING FRANKLIN LEARNED THE FIRST TIME AROUND IT'S THAT WE CAN'T TRUST HUMANITY!
THAT'S NOT TRUE! I WOULD NEVER DO ANY-THING TO HURT TOM!
LIAR!!
IT'S ONLY A MATTER OF TIME BEFORE YOU DECIDE WE'RE MONSTERS BECAUSE WE'RE NOT LIKE YOU!
YOU'RE WRONG! I DON'T CARE HOW YOU WERE BORN! ALL THAT MATTERS IS HOW YOU LIVE!

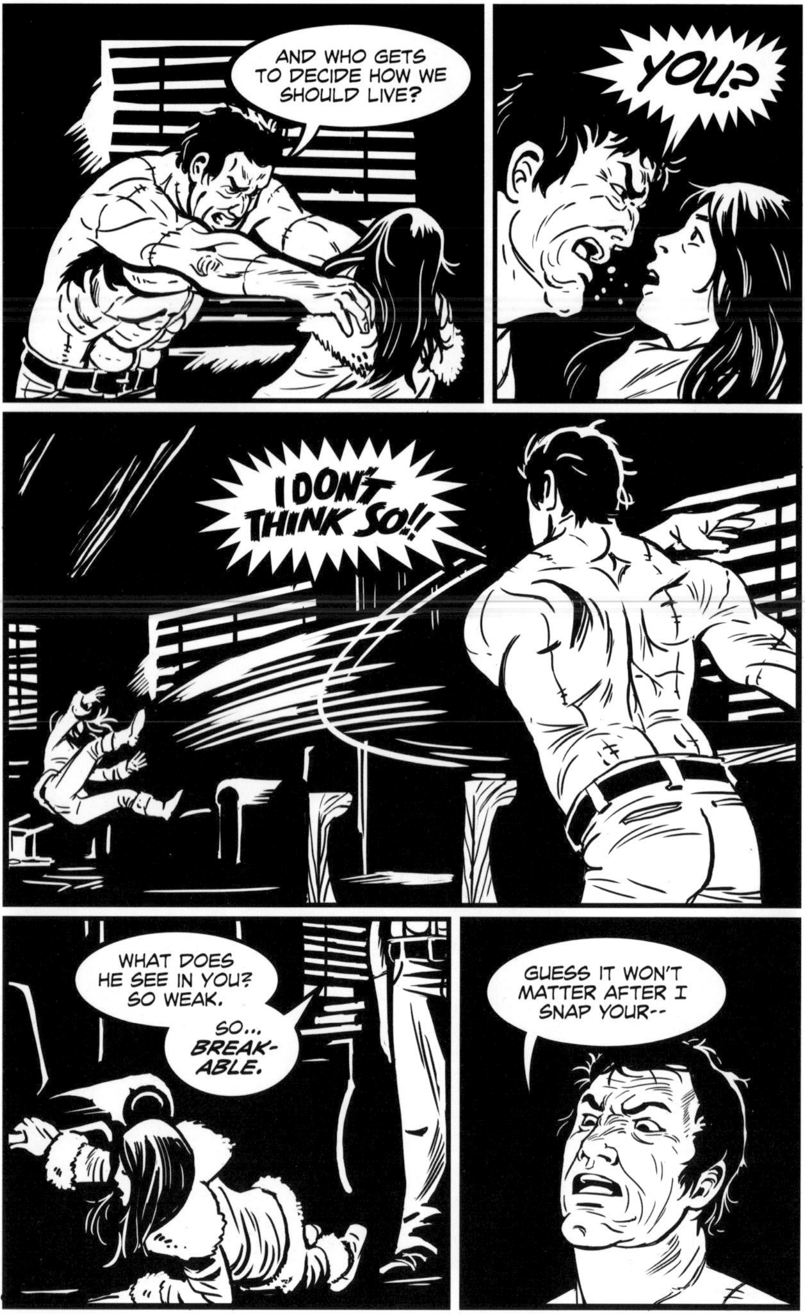
AND WHO GETS TO DECIDE HOW WE SHOULD LIVE?
YOU?
I DON'T THINK SO!!
WHAT DOES HE SEE IN YOU? SO WEAK.
SO... BREAK-ABLE.
GUESS IT WON'T MATTER AFTER I SNAP YOUR--

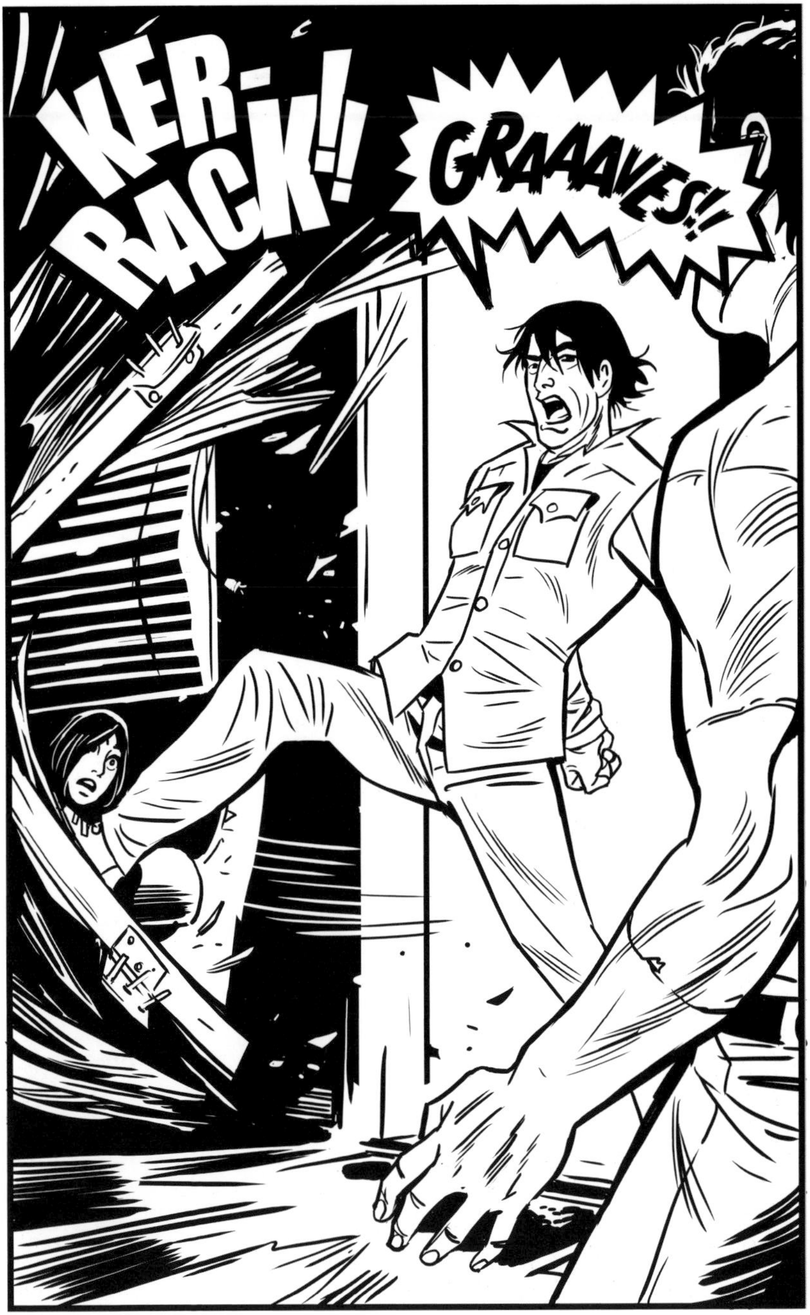
KER-RACK!!
GRAAAVES!!

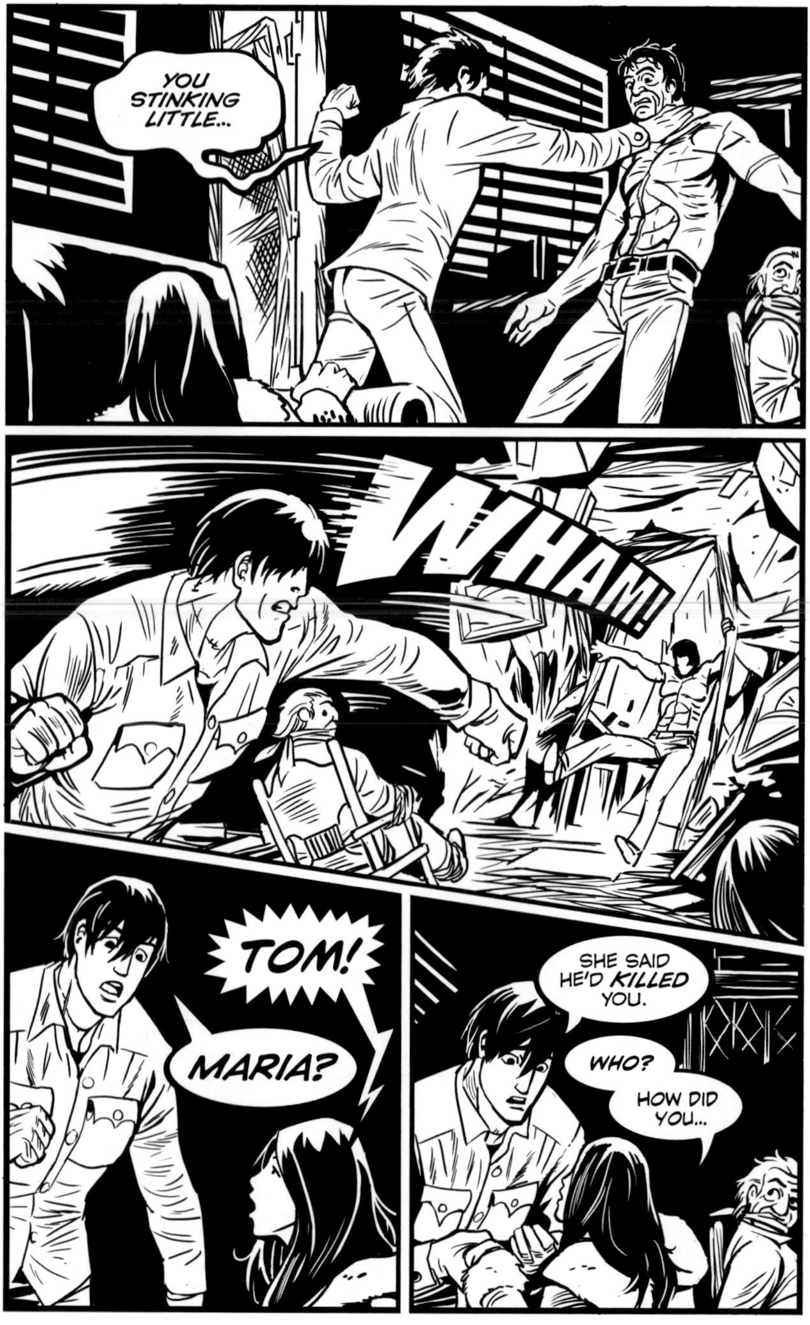
YOU STINKING LITTLE...
WHAM!
TOM!
MARIA?
SHE SAID HE'D *KILLED* YOU.
WHO?
HOW DID YOU...

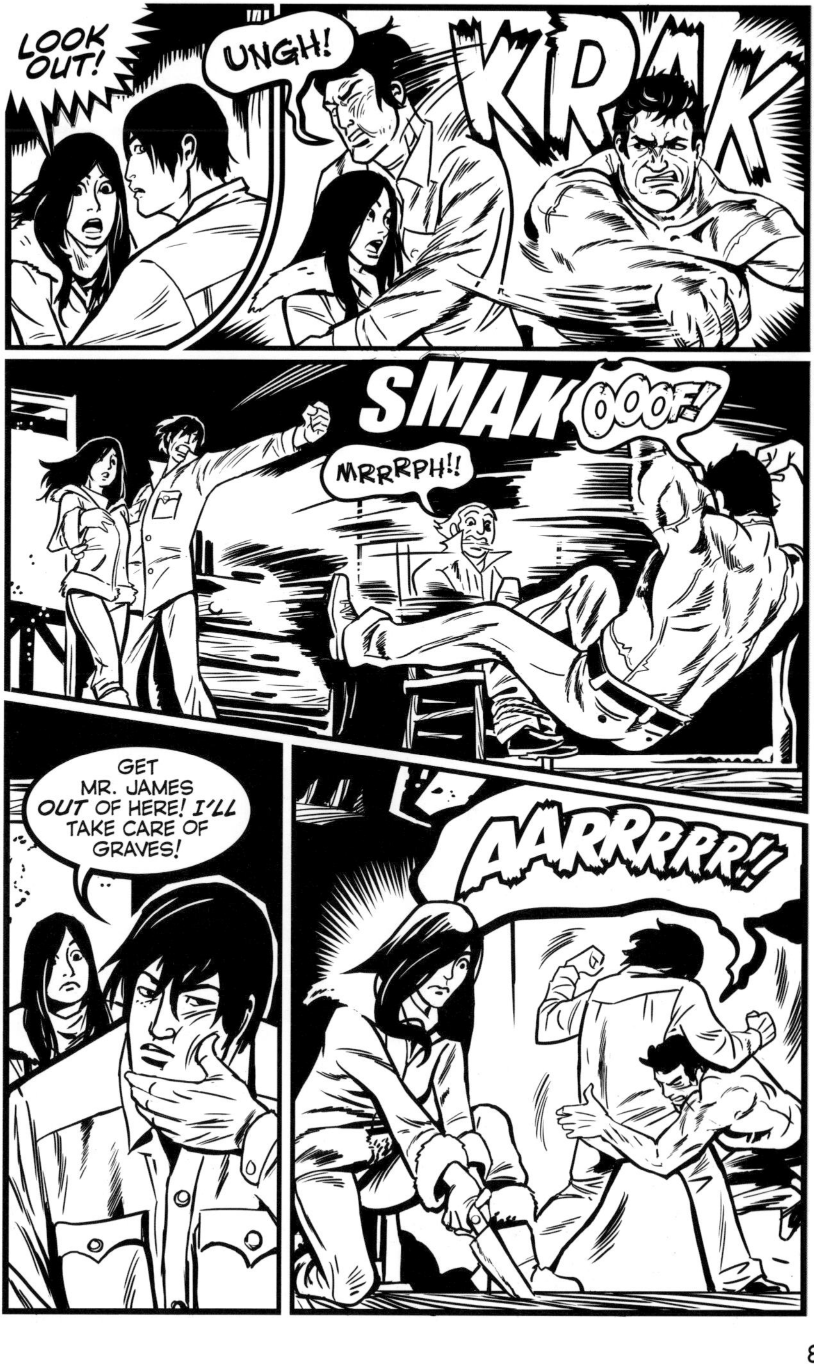
LOOK OUT!
UNGH!
KRAK
SMAK
OOOF!
MRRRPH!!
GET MR. JAMES OUT OF HERE! I'LL TAKE CARE OF GRAVES!
AARRRRR!

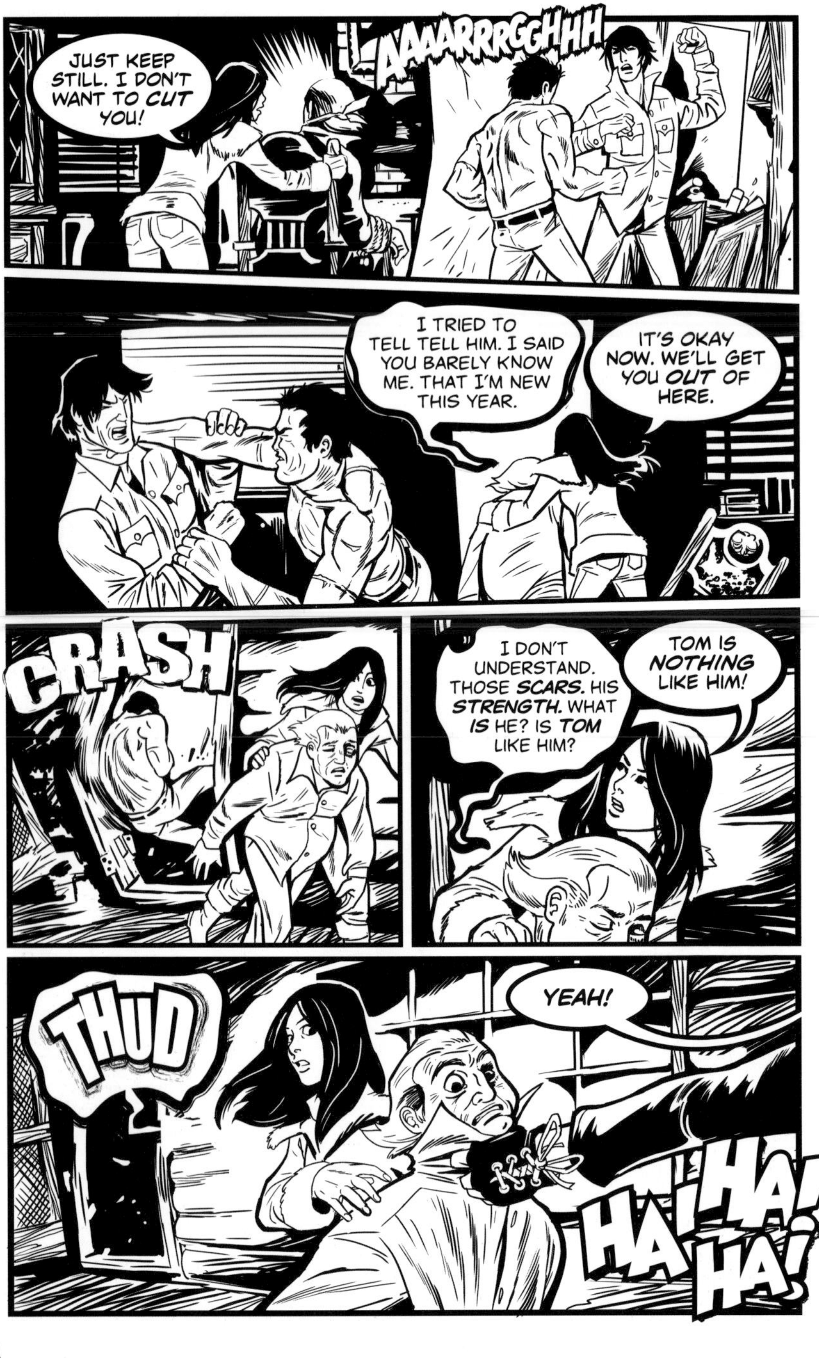
JUST KEEP STILL. I DON'T WANT TO CUT YOU!
AAAARRRGGHHH
I TRIED TO TELL TELL HIM. I SAID YOU BARELY KNOW ME. THAT I'M NEW THIS YEAR.
IT'S OKAY NOW. WE'LL GET YOU OUT OF HERE.
CRASH
I DON'T UNDERSTAND. THOSE SCARS. HIS STRENGTH. WHAT IS HE? IS TOM LIKE HIM?
TOM IS NOTHING LIKE HIM!
THUD
YEAH!
HA! HA! HA! HA!

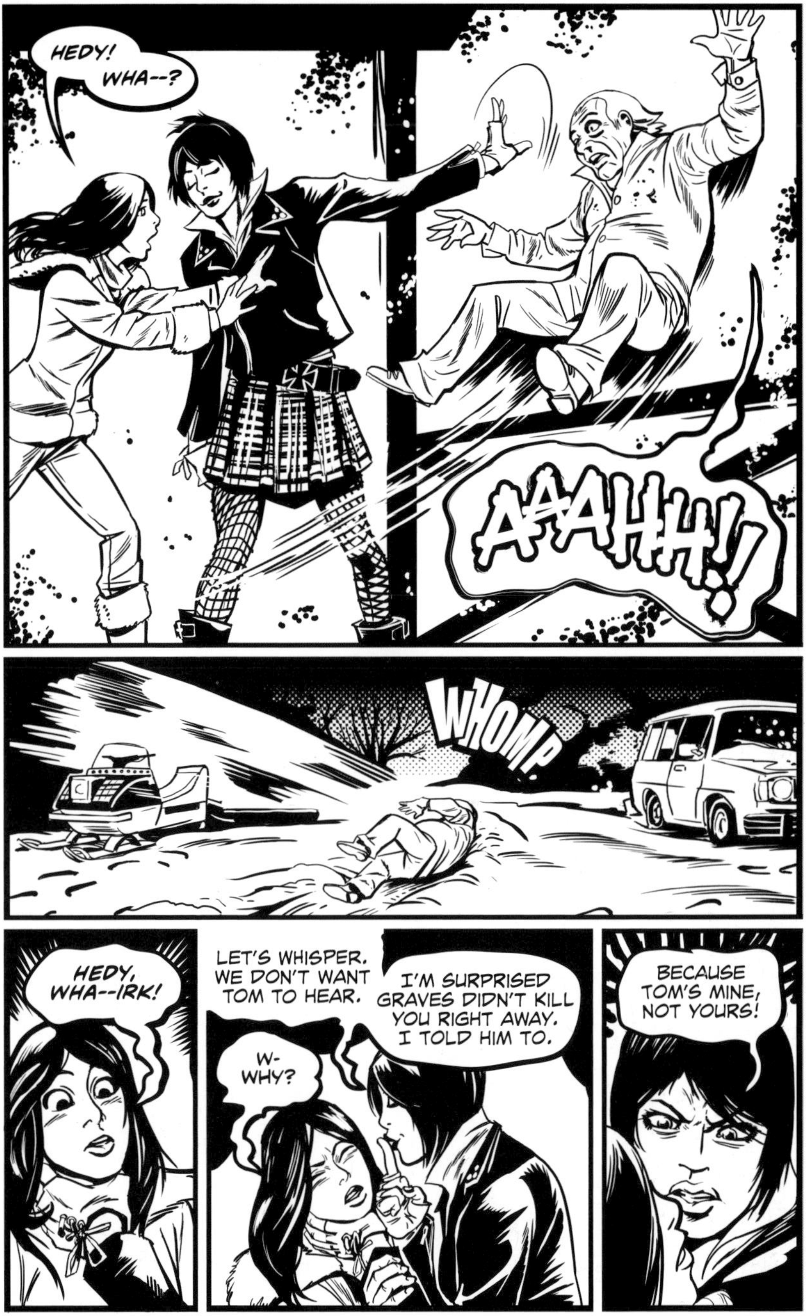
HEDY! WHA--?
AAAHH!!
WHOMP
HEDY, WHA--IRK!
LET'S WHISPER. WE DON'T WANT TOM TO HEAR.
W- WHY?
I'M SURPRISED GRAVES DIDN'T KILL YOU RIGHT AWAY. I TOLD HIM TO.
BECAUSE TOM'S MINE, NOT YOURS!

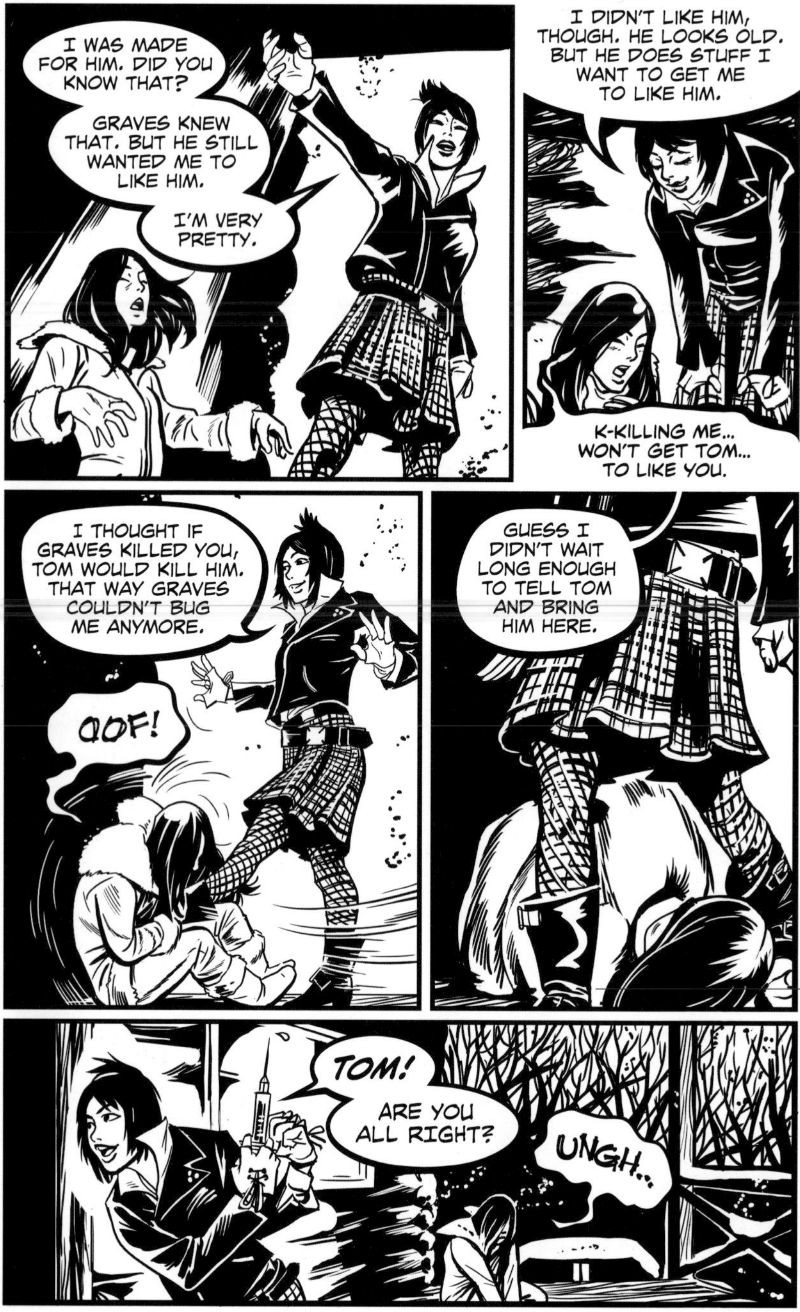
I WAS MADE FOR HIM. DID YOU KNOW THAT?
GRAVES KNEW THAT. BUT HE STILL WANTED ME TO LIKE HIM.
I'M VERY PRETTY.
I DIDN'T LIKE HIM, THOUGH. HE LOOKS OLD. BUT HE DOES STUFF I WANT TO GET ME TO LIKE HIM.
K-KILLING ME... WON'T GET TOM... TO LIKE YOU.
I THOUGHT IF GRAVES KILLED YOU, TOM WOULD KILL HIM. THAT WAY GRAVES COULDN'T BUG ME ANYMORE.
OOF!
GUESS I DIDN'T WAIT LONG ENOUGH TO TELL TOM AND BRING HIM HERE.
TOM!
ARE YOU ALL RIGHT?
UNGH...

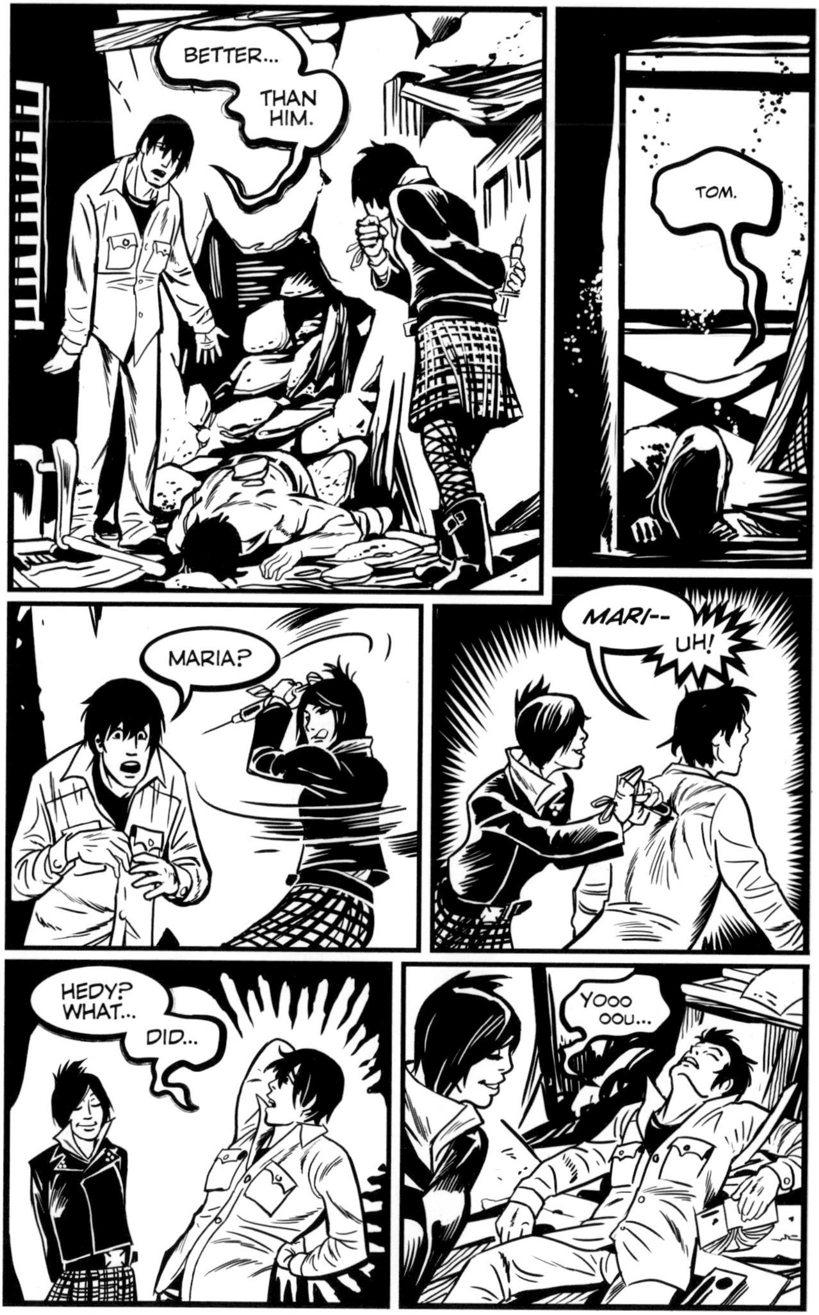
BETTER...
THAN HIM.
TOM.
MARIA?
MARI--
UH!
HEDY? WHAT...
DID...
YOOO OOU...

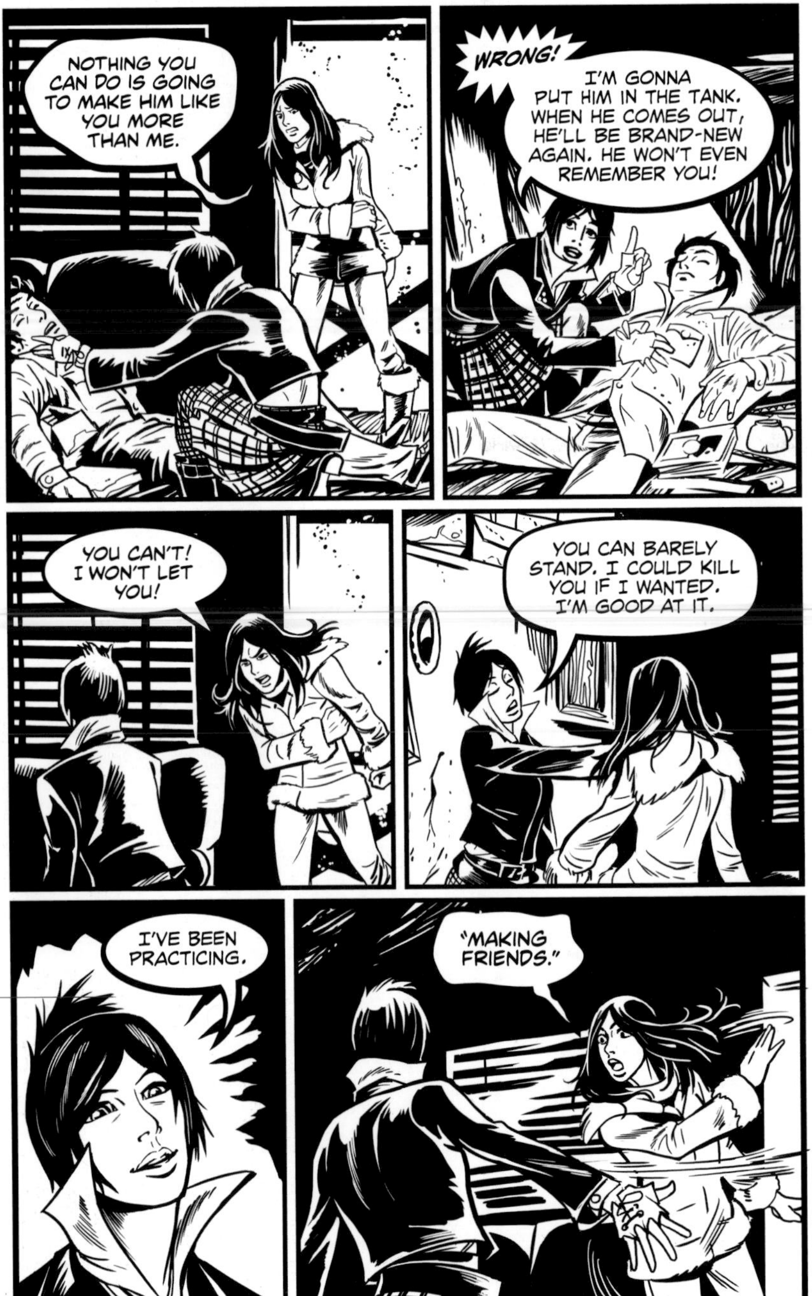
NOTHING YOU CAN DO IS GOING TO MAKE HIM LIKE YOU MORE THAN ME.
WRONG!
I'M GONNA PUT HIM IN THE TANK. WHEN HE COMES OUT, HE'LL BE BRAND-NEW AGAIN. HE WON'T EVEN REMEMBER YOU!
YOU CAN'T! I WON'T LET YOU!
YOU CAN BARELY STAND. I COULD KILL YOU IF I WANTED. I'M GOOD AT IT.
I'VE BEEN PRACTICING.
"MAKING FRIENDS."

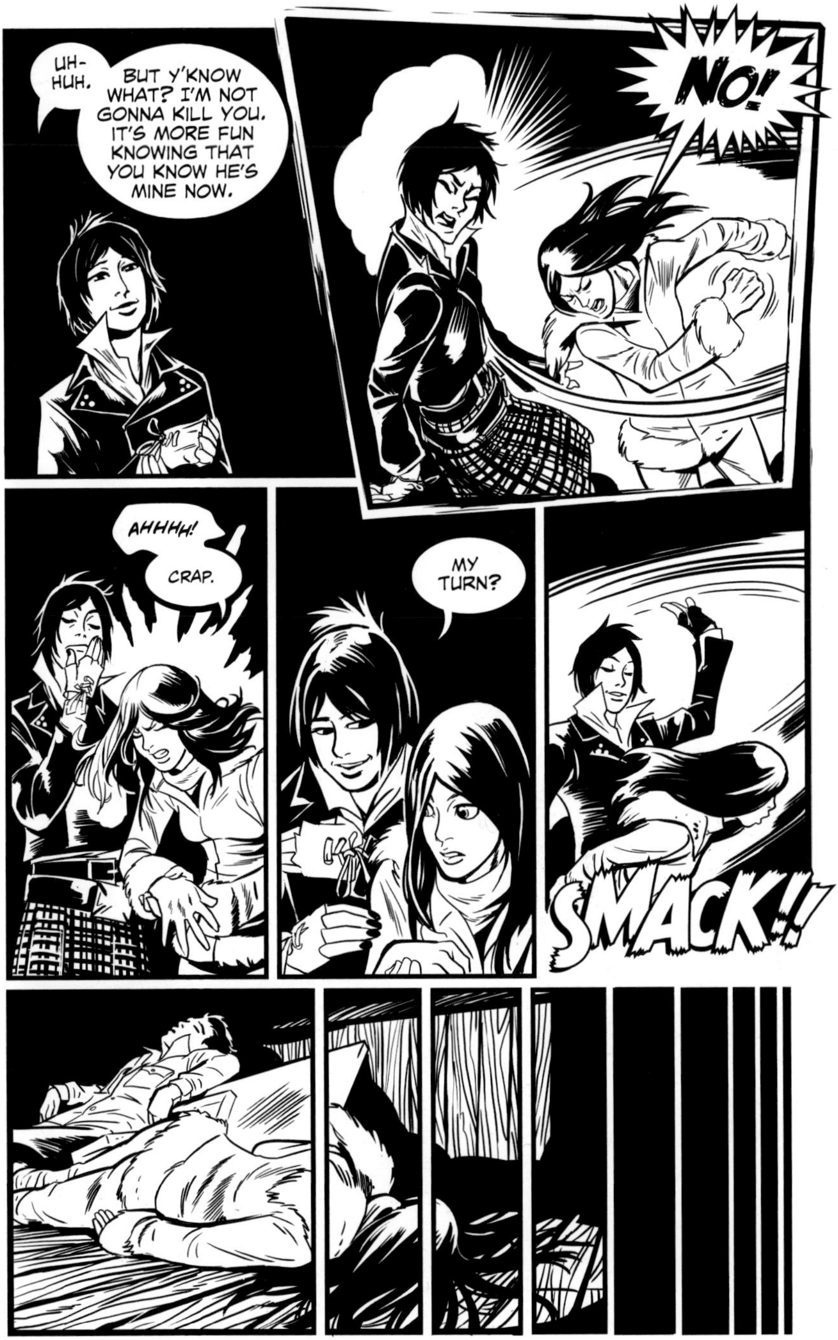
UH-HUH.
BUT Y'KNOW WHAT? I'M NOT GONNA KILL YOU. IT'S MORE FUN KNOWING THAT YOU KNOW HE'S MINE NOW.
NO!
AAAAAA
AHHHH!
CRAP.
MY TURN?
SMACK!!

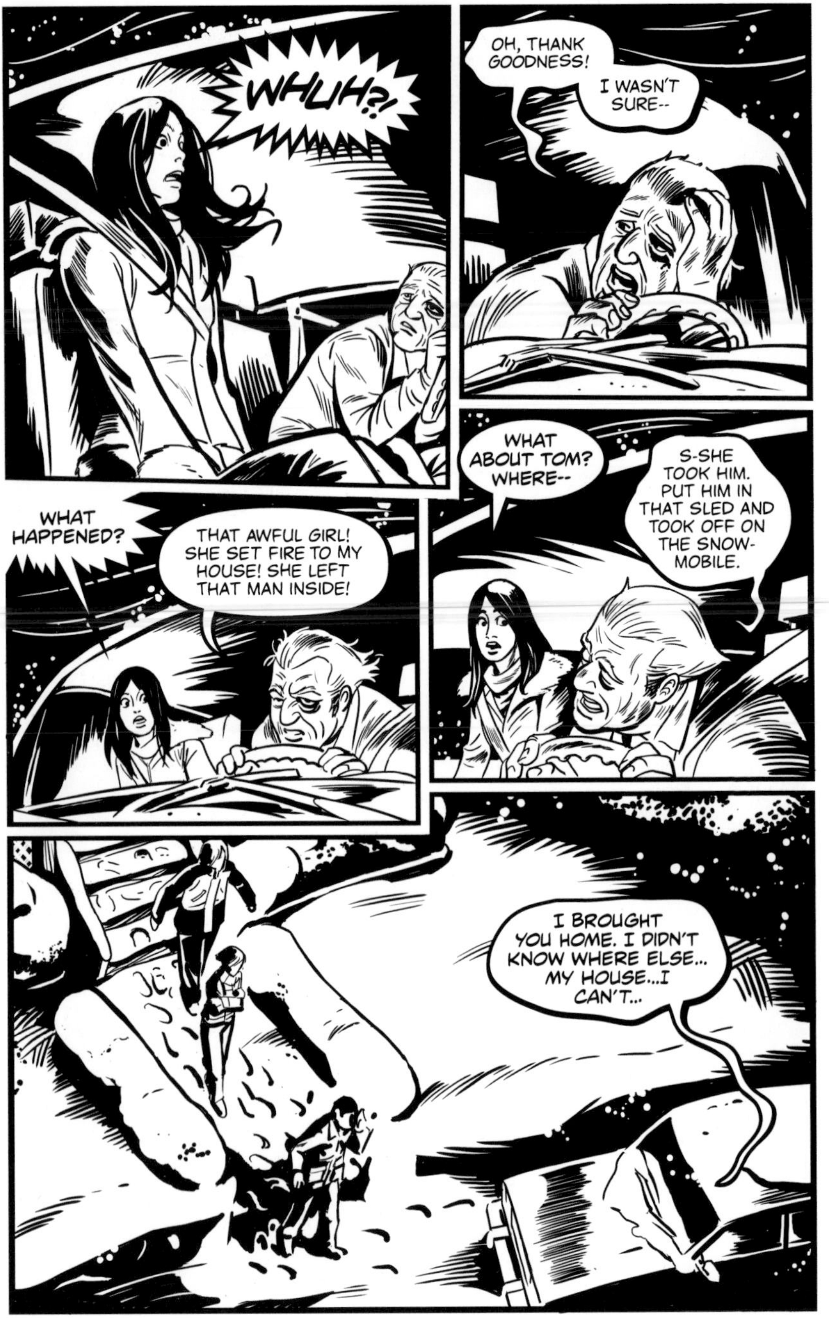
WHUH?!
OH, THANK GOODNESS!
I WASN'T SURE--
WHAT HAPPENED?
THAT AWFUL GIRL! SHE SET FIRE TO MY HOUSE! SHE LEFT THAT MAN INSIDE!
WHAT ABOUT TOM? WHERE--
S-SHE TOOK HIM. PUT HIM IN THAT SLED AND TOOK OFF ON THE SNOW-MOBILE.
I BROUGHT YOU HOME. I DIDN'T KNOW WHERE ELSE... MY HOUSE...I CAN'T...

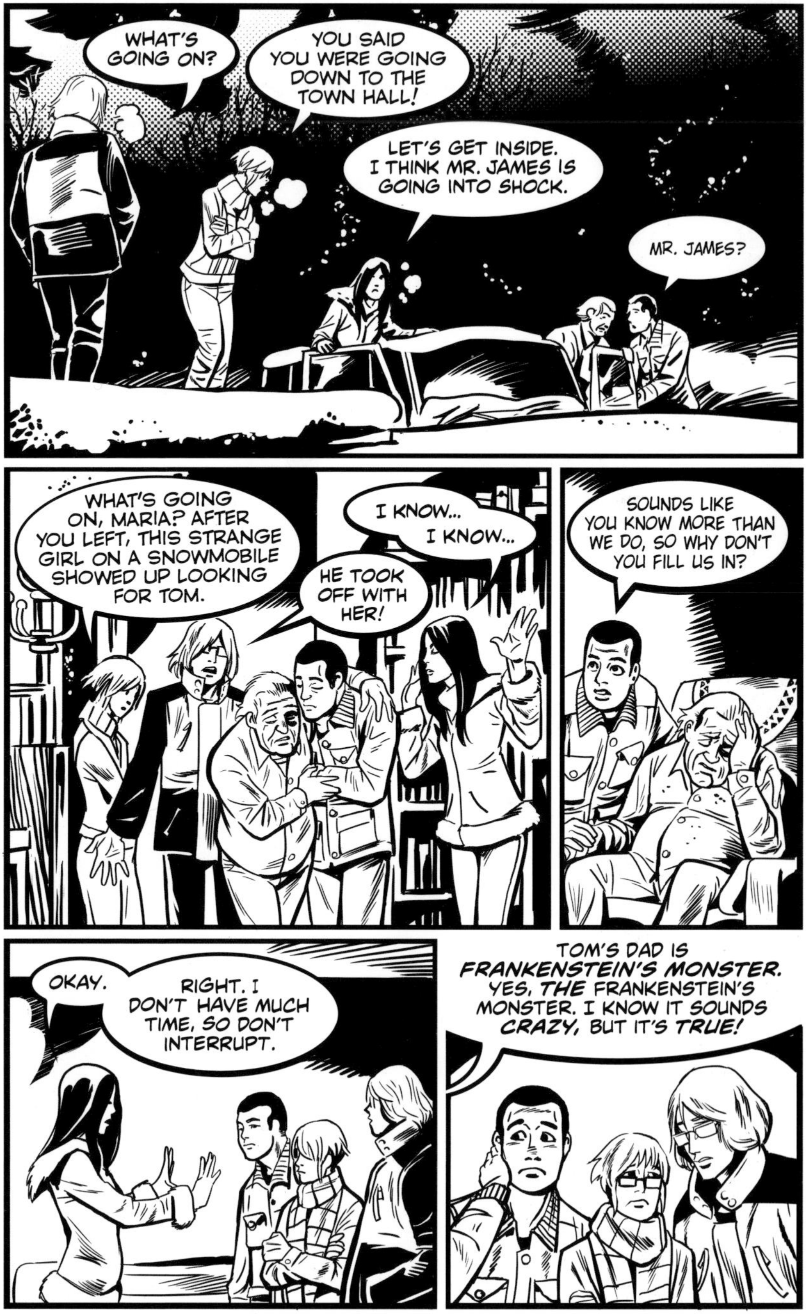
WHAT'S GOING ON?
YOU SAID YOU WERE GOING DOWN TO THE TOWN HALL!
LET'S GET INSIDE. I THINK MR. JAMES IS GOING INTO SHOCK.
MR. JAMES?
WHAT'S GOING ON, MARIA? AFTER YOU LEFT, THIS STRANGE GIRL ON A SNOWMOBILE SHOWED UP LOOKING FOR TOM.
HE TOOK OFF WITH HER!
I KNOW...
I KNOW...
SOUNDS LIKE YOU KNOW MORE THAN WE DO, SO WHY DON'T YOU FILL US IN?
OKAY.
RIGHT. I DON'T HAVE MUCH TIME, SO DON'T INTERRUPT.
TOM'S DAD IS FRANKENSTEIN'S MONSTER. YES, THE FRANKENSTEIN'S MONSTER. I KNOW IT SOUNDS CRAZY, BUT IT'S TRUE!

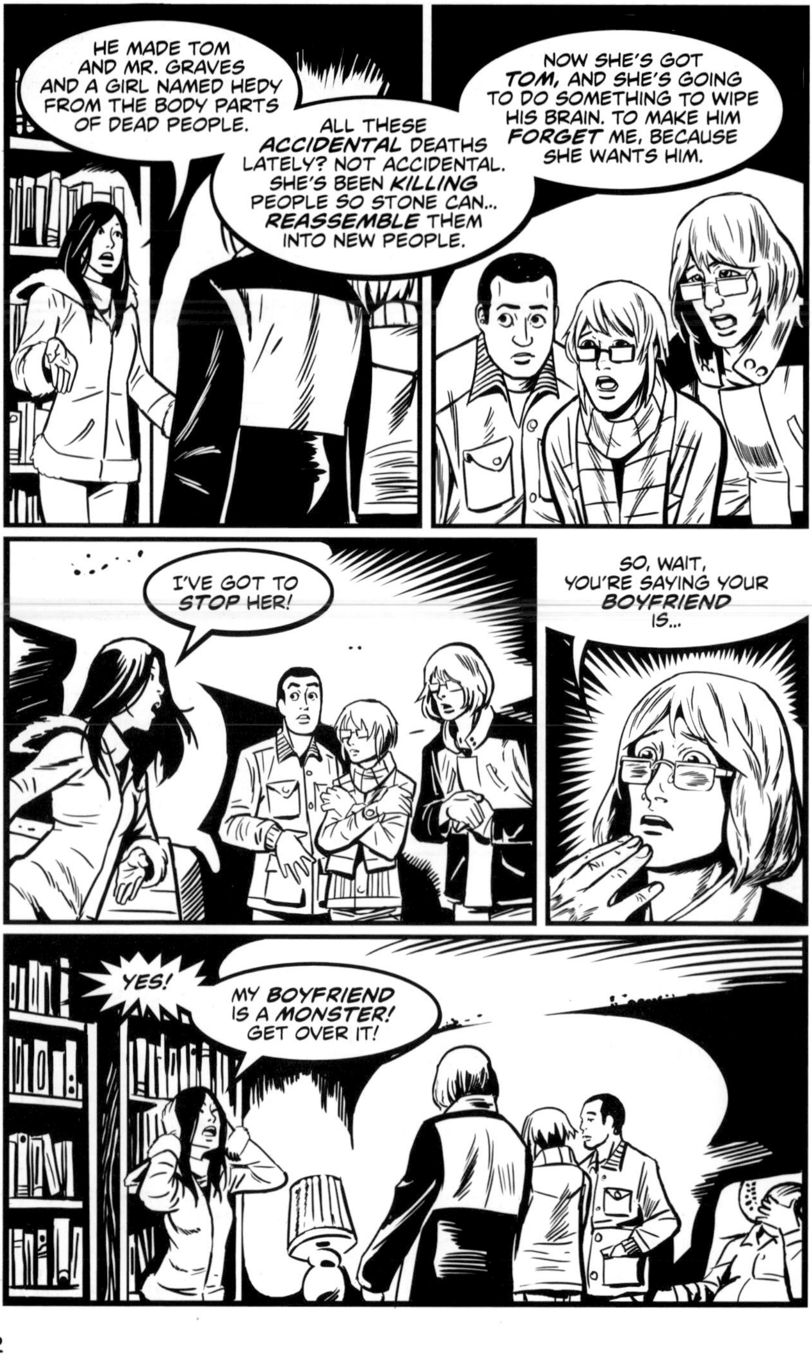
HE MADE TOM AND MR. GRAVES AND A GIRL NAMED HEDY FROM THE BODY PARTS OF DEAD PEOPLE.
ALL THESE ACCIDENTAL DEATHS LATELY? NOT ACCIDENTAL. SHE'S BEEN KILLING PEOPLE SO STONE CAN... REASSEMBLE THEM INTO NEW PEOPLE.
NOW SHE'S GOT TOM, AND SHE'S GOING TO DO SOMETHING TO WIPE HIS BRAIN. TO MAKE HIM FORGET ME, BECAUSE SHE WANTS HIM.
I'VE GOT TO STOP HER!
SO, WAIT, YOU'RE SAYING YOUR BOYFRIEND IS...
YES!
MY BOYFRIEND IS A MONSTER! GET OVER IT!

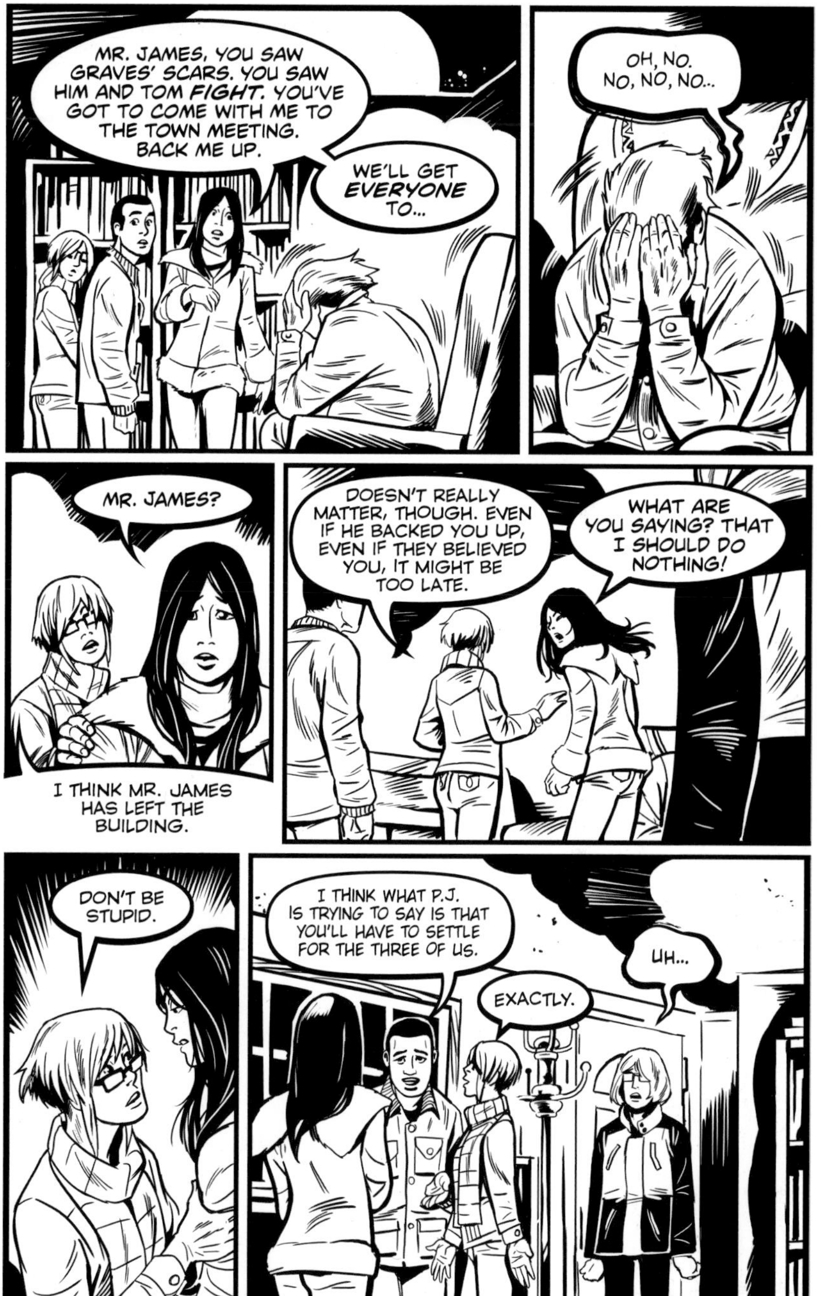
MR. JAMES, YOU SAW GRAVES' SCARS. YOU SAW HIM AND TOM FIGHT. YOU'VE GOT TO COME WITH ME TO THE TOWN MEETING. BACK ME UP.
WE'LL GET EVERYONE TO...
OH, NO. NO, NO, NO...
MR. JAMES?
I THINK MR. JAMES HAS LEFT THE BUILDING.
DOESN'T REALLY MATTER, THOUGH. EVEN IF HE BACKED YOU UP, EVEN IF THEY BELIEVED YOU, IT MIGHT BE TOO LATE.
WHAT ARE YOU SAYING? THAT I SHOULD DO NOTHING!
DON'T BE STUPID.
I THINK WHAT P.J. IS TRYING TO SAY IS THAT YOU'LL HAVE TO SETTLE FOR THE THREE OF US.
EXACTLY.
UH...

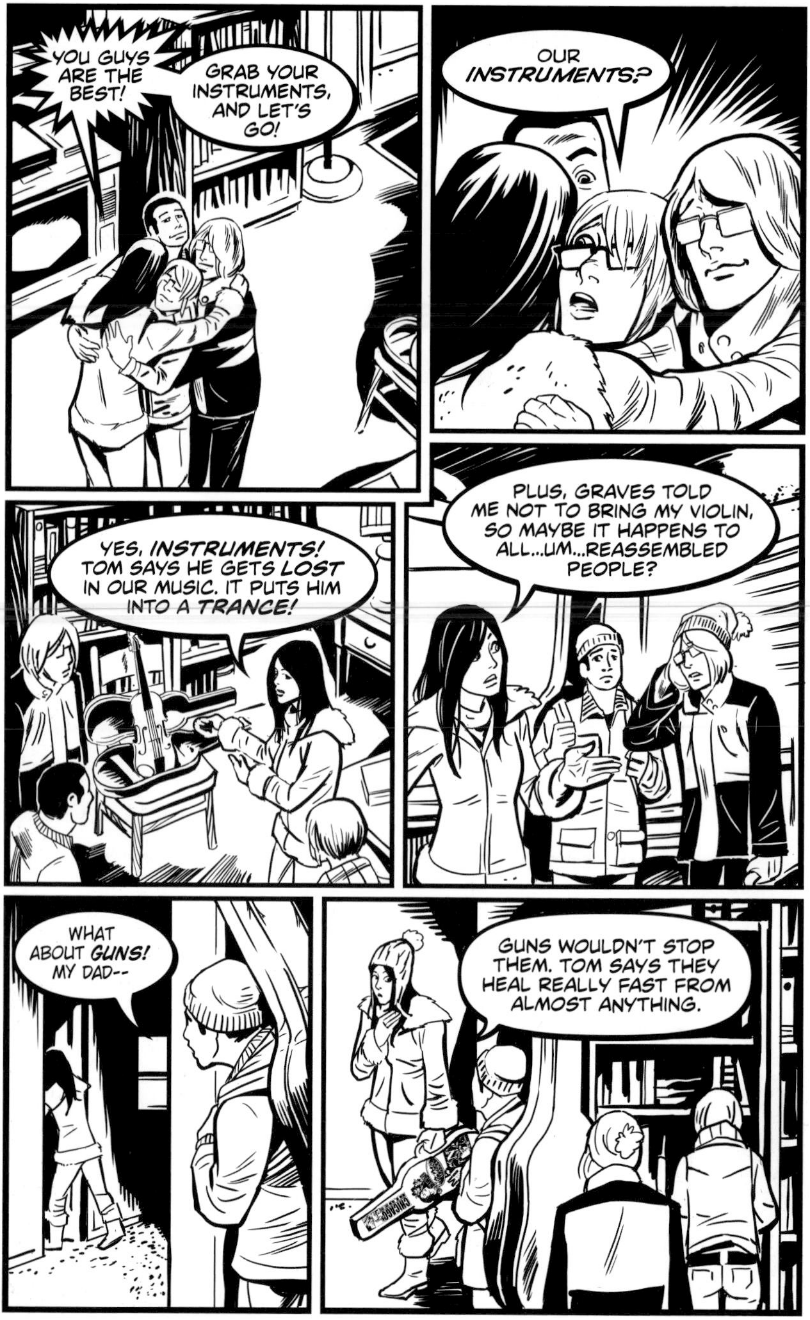
YOU GUYS ARE THE BEST!
GRAB YOUR INSTRUMENTS, AND LET'S GO!
OUR INSTRUMENTS?
YES, INSTRUMENTS! TOM SAYS HE GETS LOST IN OUR MUSIC. IT PUTS HIM INTO A TRANCE!
PLUS, GRAVES TOLD ME NOT TO BRING MY VIOLIN, SO MAYBE IT HAPPENS TO ALL...UM...REASSEMBLED PEOPLE?
WHAT ABOUT GUNS! MY DAD--
GUNS WOULDN'T STOP THEM. TOM SAYS THEY HEAL REALLY FAST FROM ALMOST ANYTHING.

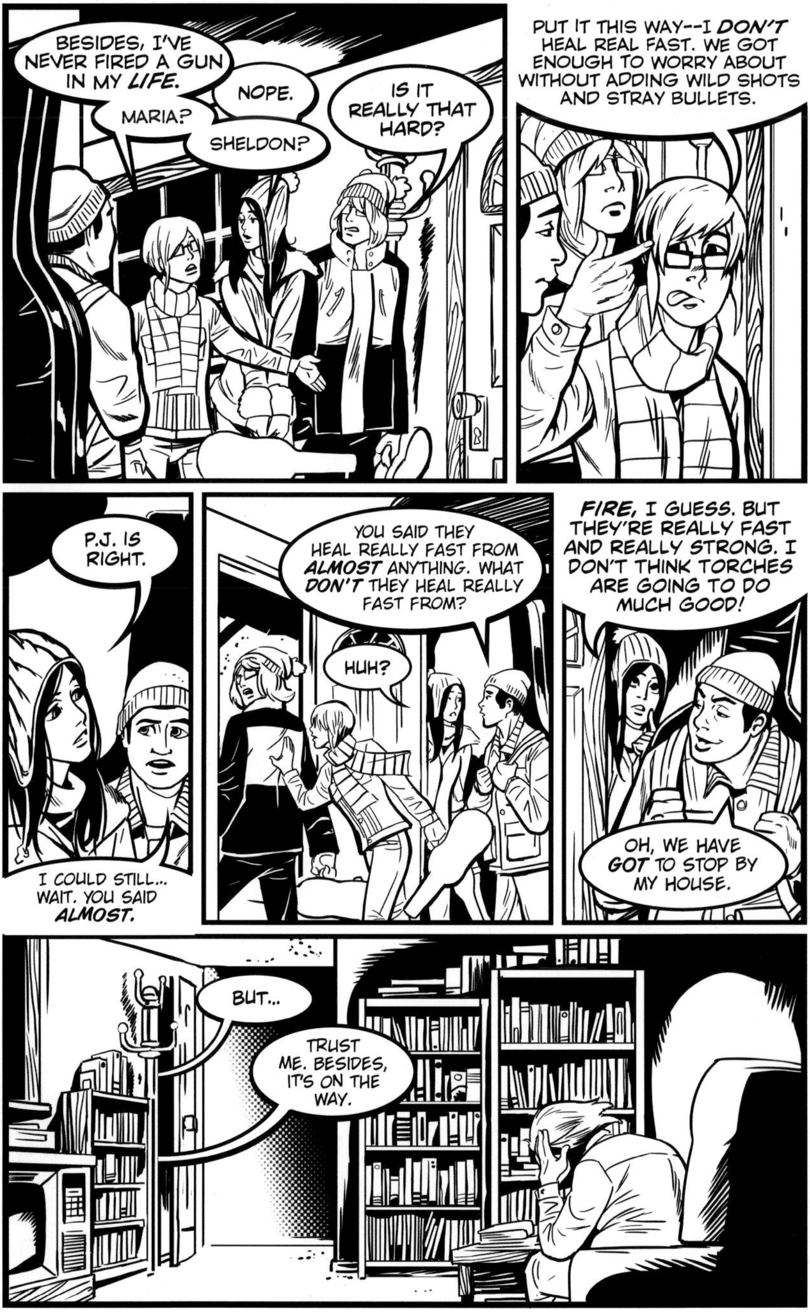
BESIDES, I'VE NEVER FIRED A GUN IN MY *LIFE.*
MARIA?
NOPE.
SHELDON?
IS IT REALLY THAT HARD?
PUT IT THIS WAY--I *DON'T* HEAL REAL FAST. WE GOT ENOUGH TO WORRY ABOUT WITHOUT ADDING WILD SHOTS AND STRAY BULLETS.
P.J. IS RIGHT.
I COULD STILL... WAIT. YOU SAID *ALMOST.*
YOU SAID THEY HEAL REALLY FAST FROM *ALMOST* ANYTHING. WHAT *DON'T* THEY HEAL REALLY FAST FROM?
HUH?
FIRE, I GUESS. BUT THEY'RE REALLY FAST AND REALLY STRONG. I DON'T THINK TORCHES ARE GOING TO DO MUCH GOOD!
OH, WE HAVE *GOT* TO STOP BY MY HOUSE.
BUT...
TRUST ME. BESIDES, IT'S ON THE WAY.

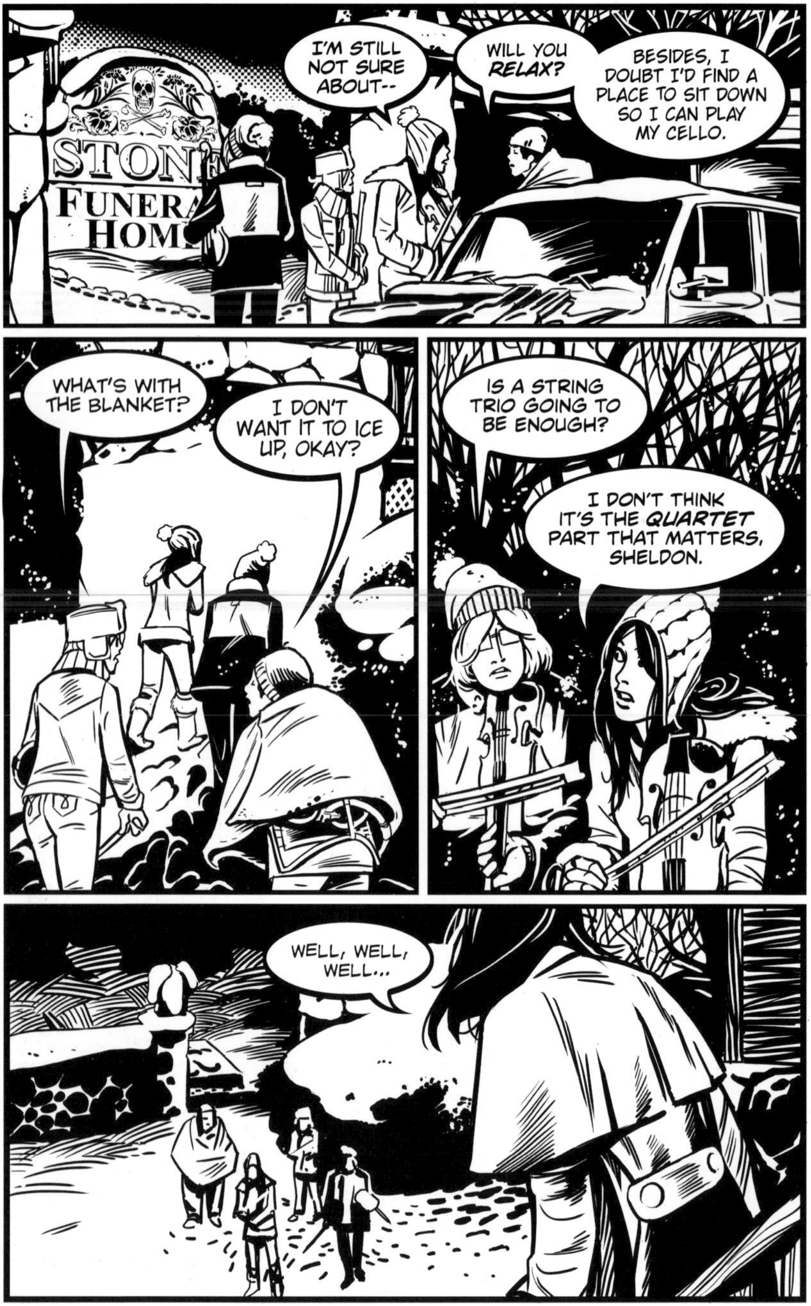
STONE FUNERAL HOME
I'M STILL NOT SURE ABOUT--
WILL YOU *RELAX?*
BESIDES, I DOUBT I'D FIND A PLACE TO SIT DOWN SO I CAN PLAY MY CELLO.
WHAT'S WITH THE BLANKET?
I DON'T WANT IT TO ICE UP, OKAY?
IS A STRING TRIO GOING TO BE ENOUGH?
I DON'T THINK IT'S THE *QUARTET* PART THAT MATTERS, SHELDON.
WELL, WELL, WELL...

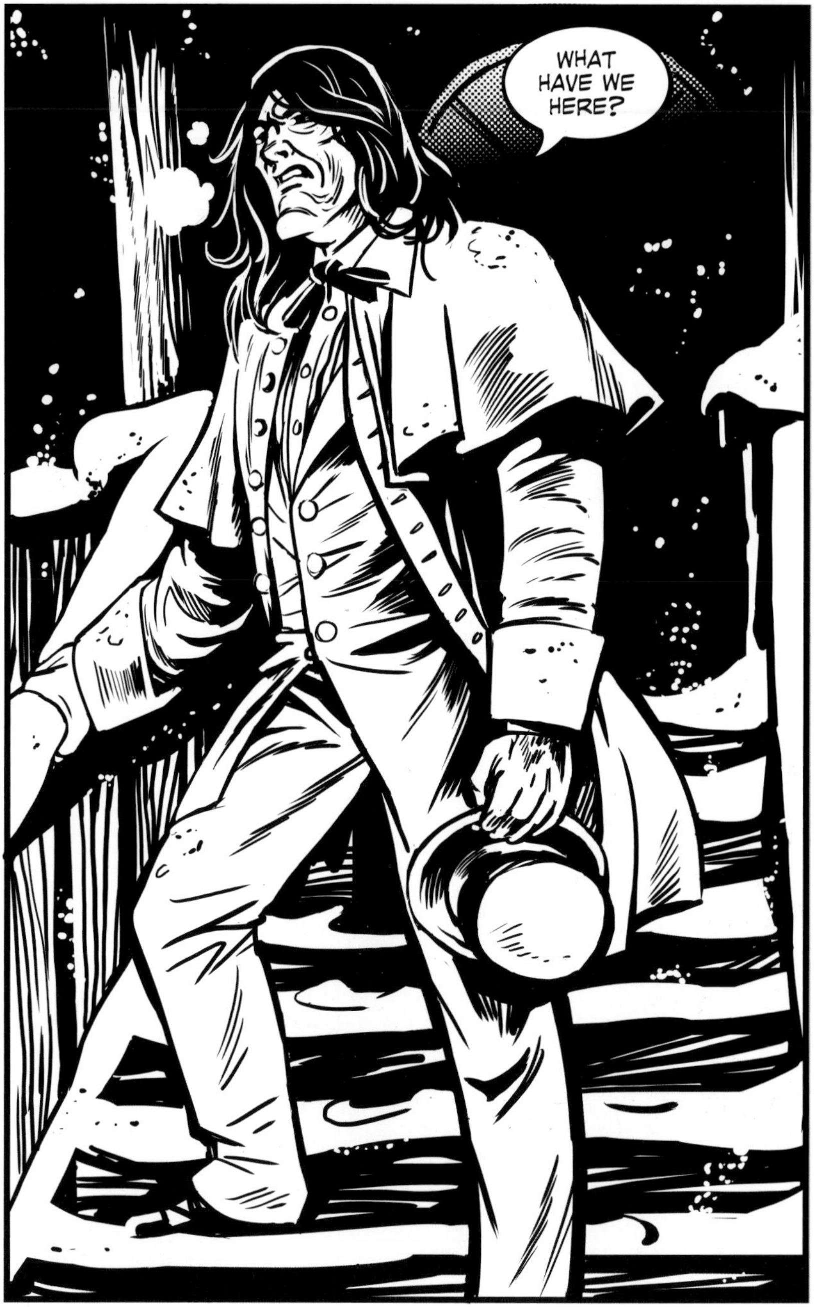
WHAT HAVE WE HERE?

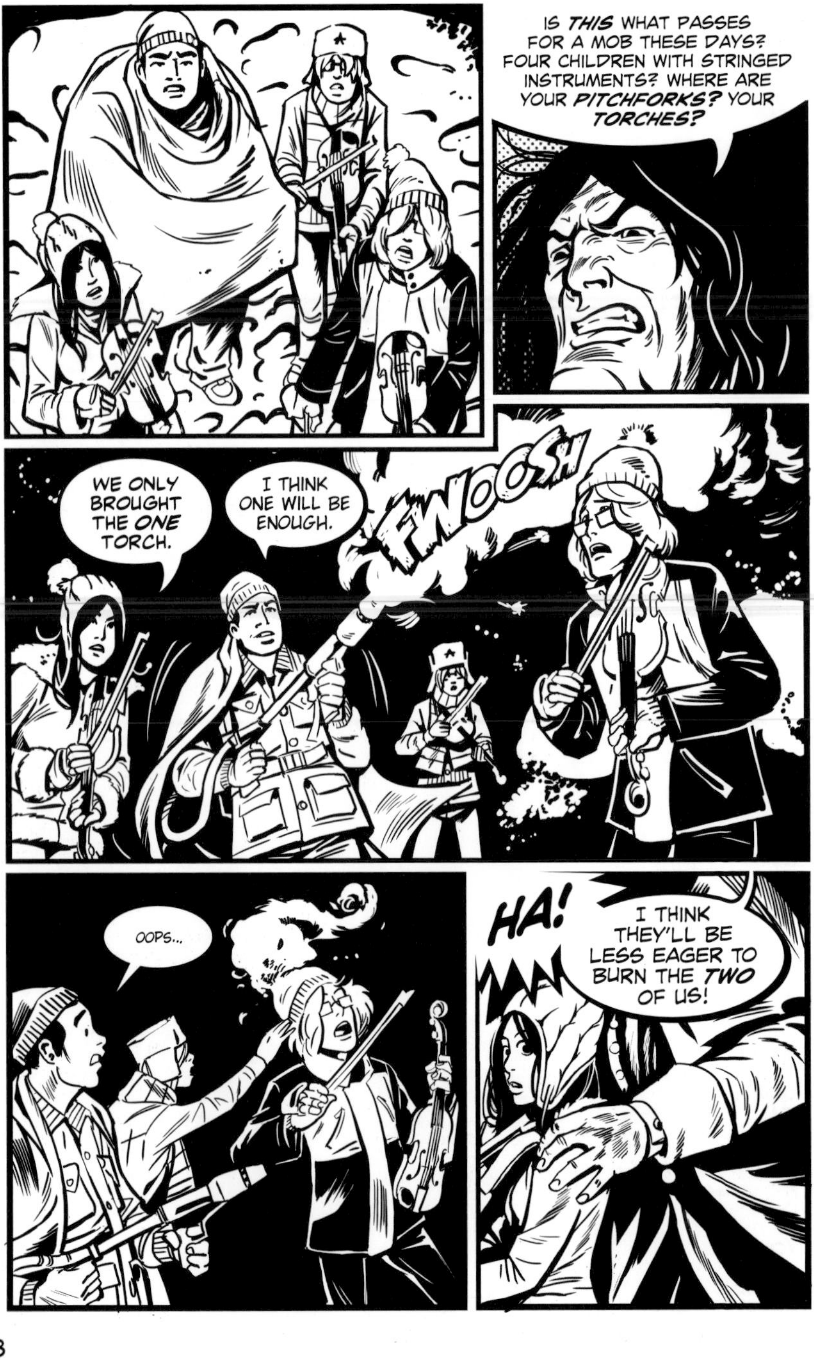

IS *THIS* WHAT PASSES FOR A MOB THESE DAYS? FOUR CHILDREN WITH STRINGED INSTRUMENTS? WHERE ARE YOUR *PITCHFORKS?* YOUR *TORCHES?*
WE ONLY BROUGHT THE *ONE* TORCH.
I THINK ONE WILL BE ENOUGH.
FWOOSH
OOPS...
HA!
I THINK THEY'LL BE LESS EAGER TO BURN THE *TWO* OF US!

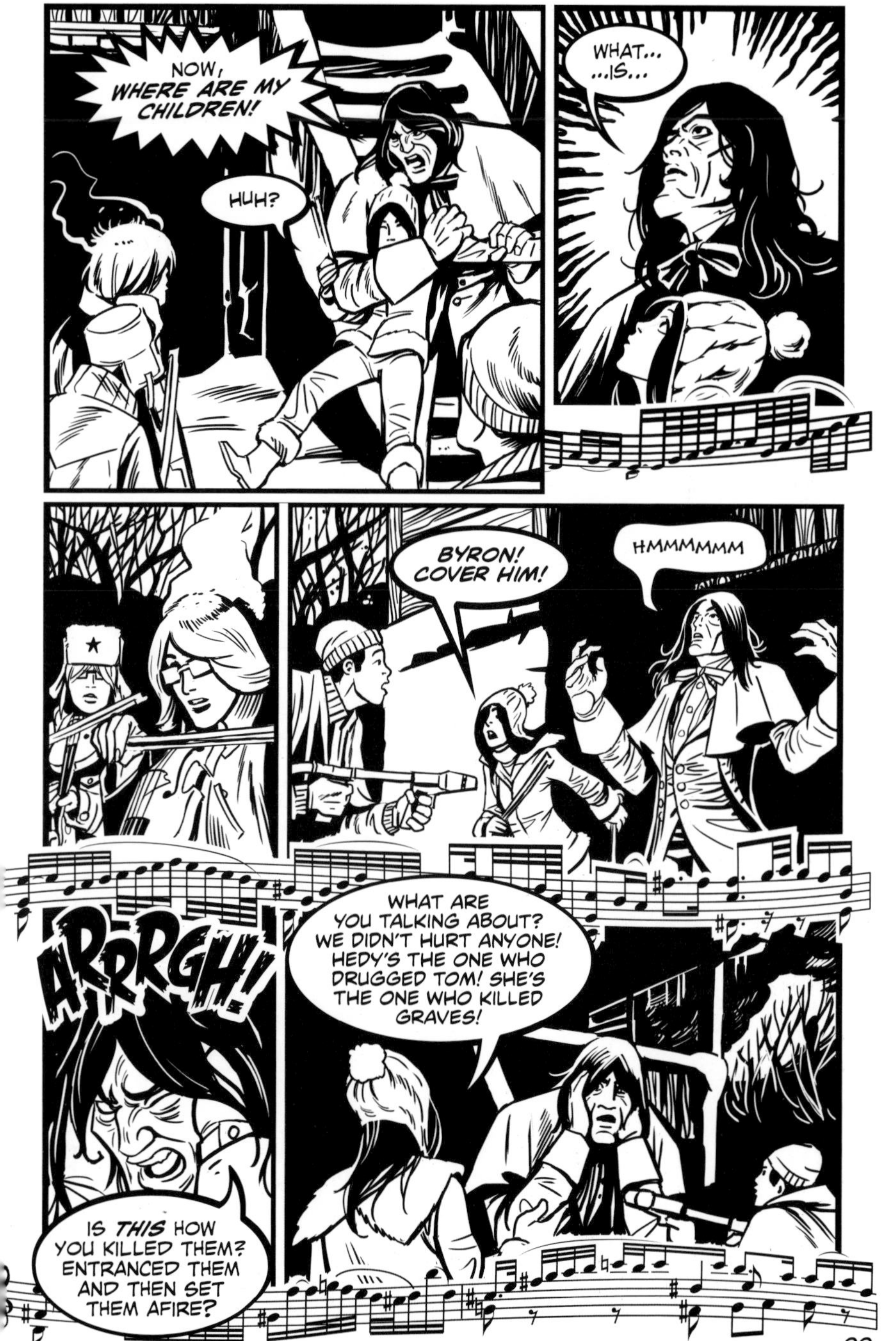
NOW, *WHERE ARE MY CHILDREN!*
HUH?
WHAT... ...IS...
BYRON! COVER HIM!
HMMMMMM
ARRRGH!
IS *THIS* HOW YOU KILLED THEM? ENTRANCED THEM AND THEN SET THEM AFIRE?
WHAT ARE YOU TALKING ABOUT? WE DIDN'T HURT ANYONE! HEDY'S THE ONE WHO DRUGGED TOM! SHE'S THE ONE WHO KILLED GRAVES!

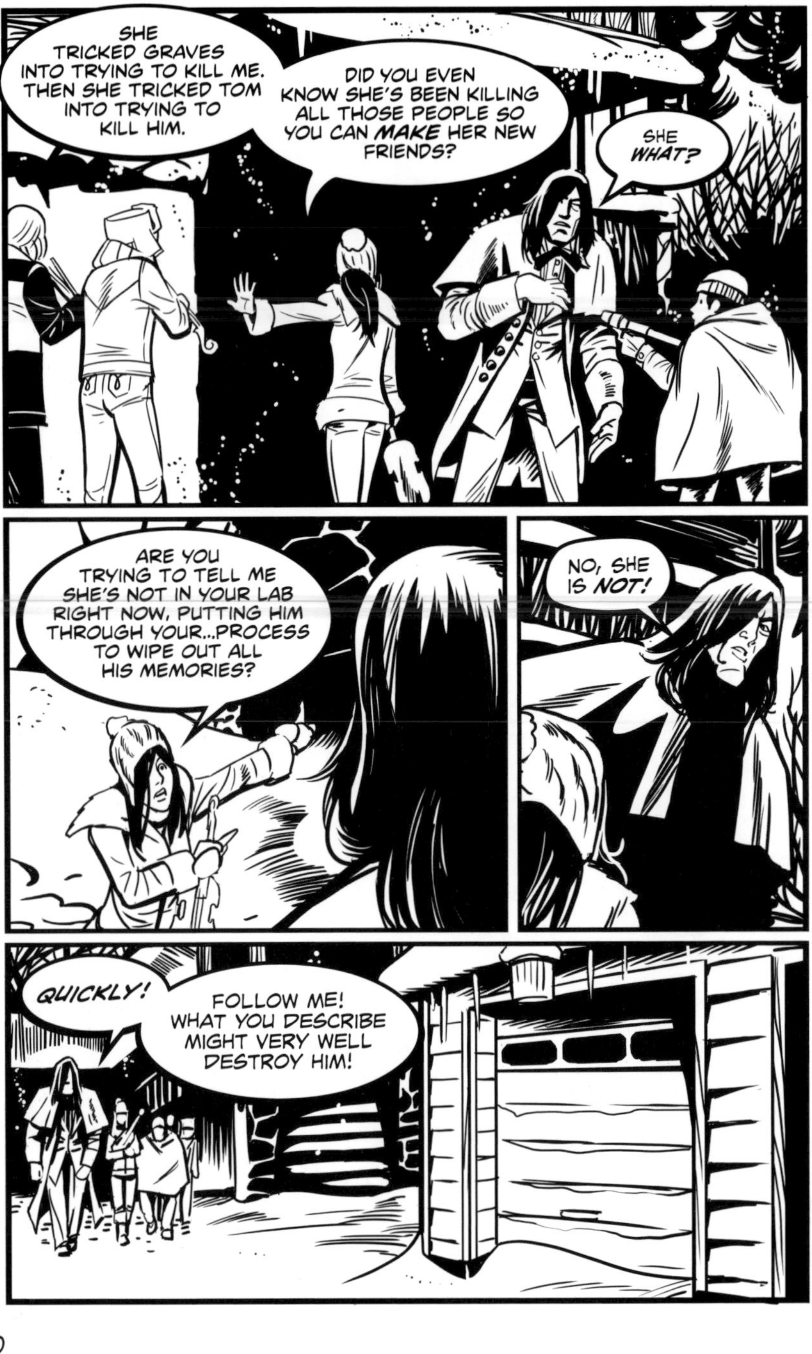
SHE TRICKED GRAVES INTO TRYING TO KILL ME. THEN SHE TRICKED TOM INTO TRYING TO KILL HIM.
DID YOU EVEN KNOW SHE'S BEEN KILLING ALL THOSE PEOPLE SO YOU CAN *MAKE* HER NEW FRIENDS?
SHE *WHAT?*
ARE YOU TRYING TO TELL ME SHE'S NOT IN YOUR LAB RIGHT NOW, PUTTING HIM THROUGH YOUR...PROCESS TO WIPE OUT ALL HIS MEMORIES?
NO, SHE IS *NOT!*
QUICKLY!
FOLLOW ME! WHAT YOU DESCRIBE MIGHT VERY WELL DESTROY HIM!

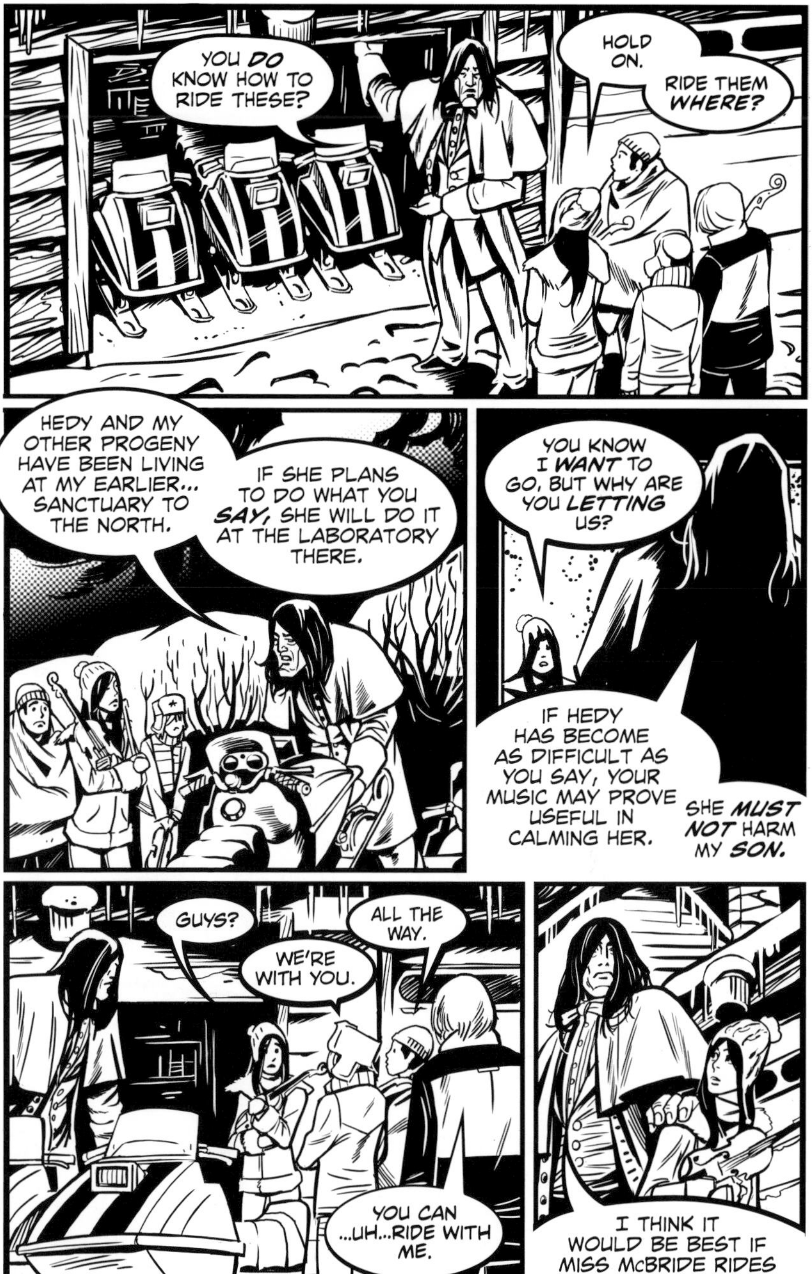
YOU DO KNOW HOW TO RIDE THESE?
HOLD ON.
RIDE THEM WHERE?
HEDY AND MY OTHER PROGENY HAVE BEEN LIVING AT MY EARLIER... SANCTUARY TO THE NORTH.
IF SHE PLANS TO DO WHAT YOU SAY, SHE WILL DO IT AT THE LABORATORY THERE.
YOU KNOW I WANT TO GO, BUT WHY ARE YOU LETTING US?
IF HEDY HAS BECOME AS DIFFICULT AS YOU SAY, YOUR MUSIC MAY PROVE USEFUL IN CALMING HER.
SHE MUST NOT HARM MY SON.
GUYS?
WE'RE WITH YOU.
ALL THE WAY.
YOU CAN ...UH...RIDE WITH ME.
I THINK IT WOULD BE BEST IF MISS McBRIDE RIDES WITH ME.

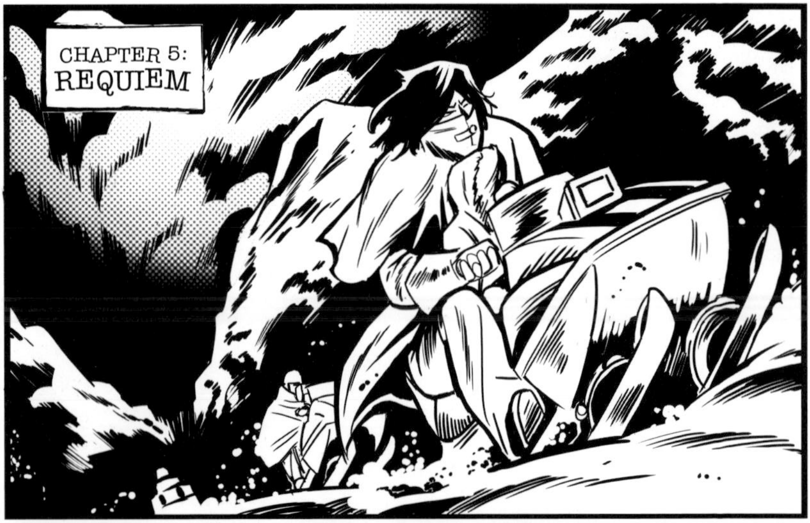
CHAPTER 5:
REQUIEM

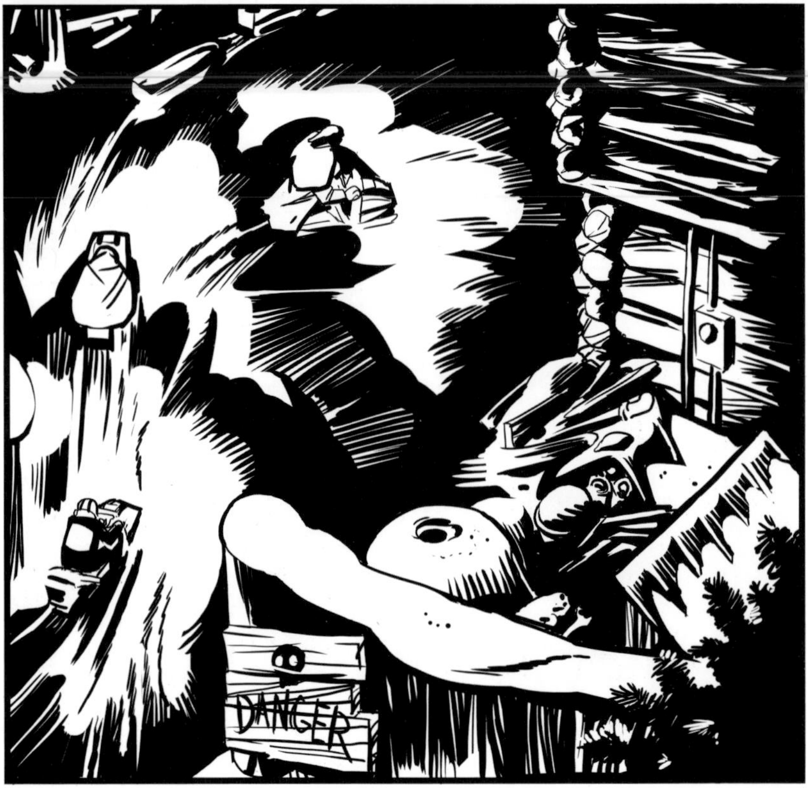
DANGER

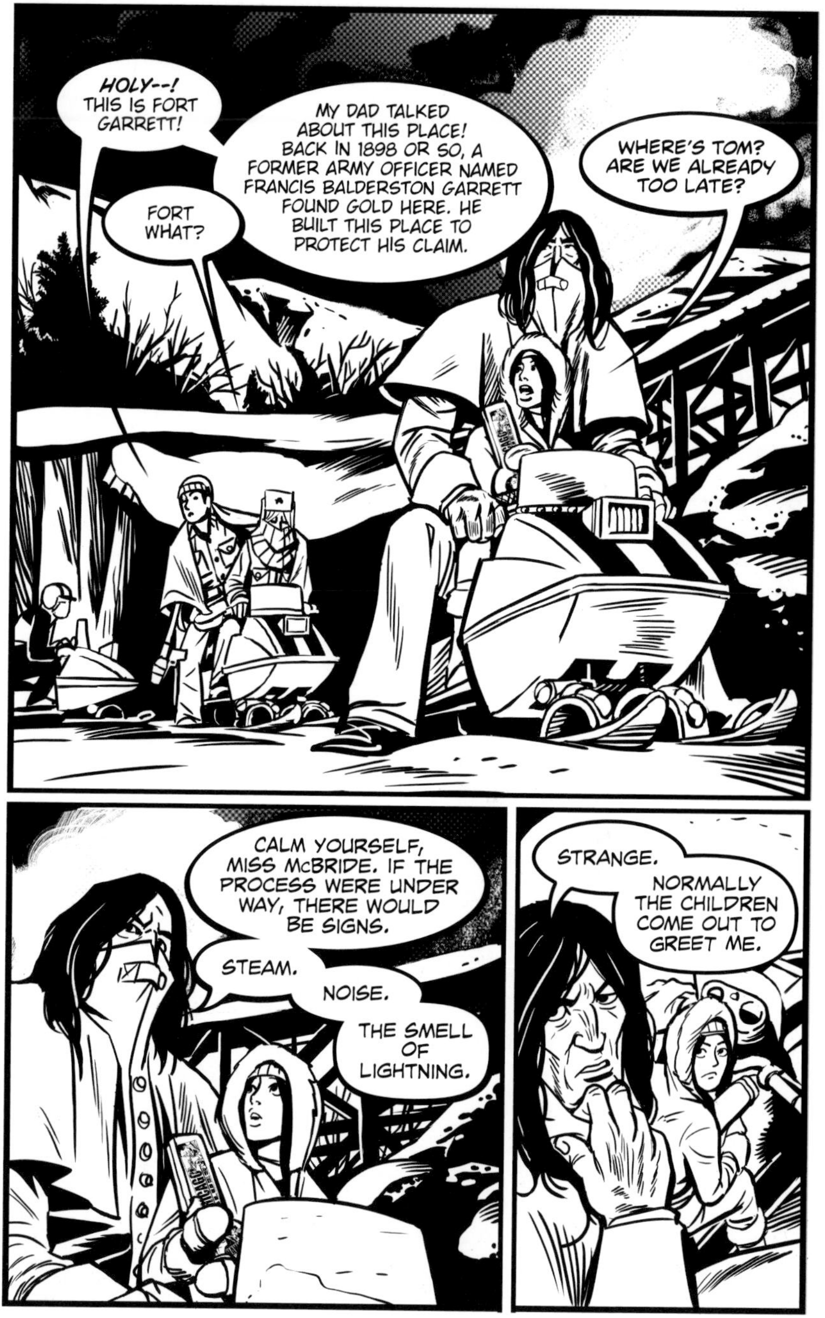
HOLY--! THIS IS FORT GARRETT!
FORT WHAT?
MY DAD TALKED ABOUT THIS PLACE! BACK IN 1898 OR SO, A FORMER ARMY OFFICER NAMED FRANCIS BALDERSTON GARRETT FOUND GOLD HERE. HE BUILT THIS PLACE TO PROTECT HIS CLAIM.
WHERE'S TOM? ARE WE ALREADY TOO LATE?
CALM YOURSELF, MISS McBRIDE. IF THE PROCESS WERE UNDER WAY, THERE WOULD BE SIGNS.
STEAM.
NOISE.
THE SMELL OF LIGHTNING.
STRANGE.
NORMALLY THE CHILDREN COME OUT TO GREET ME.

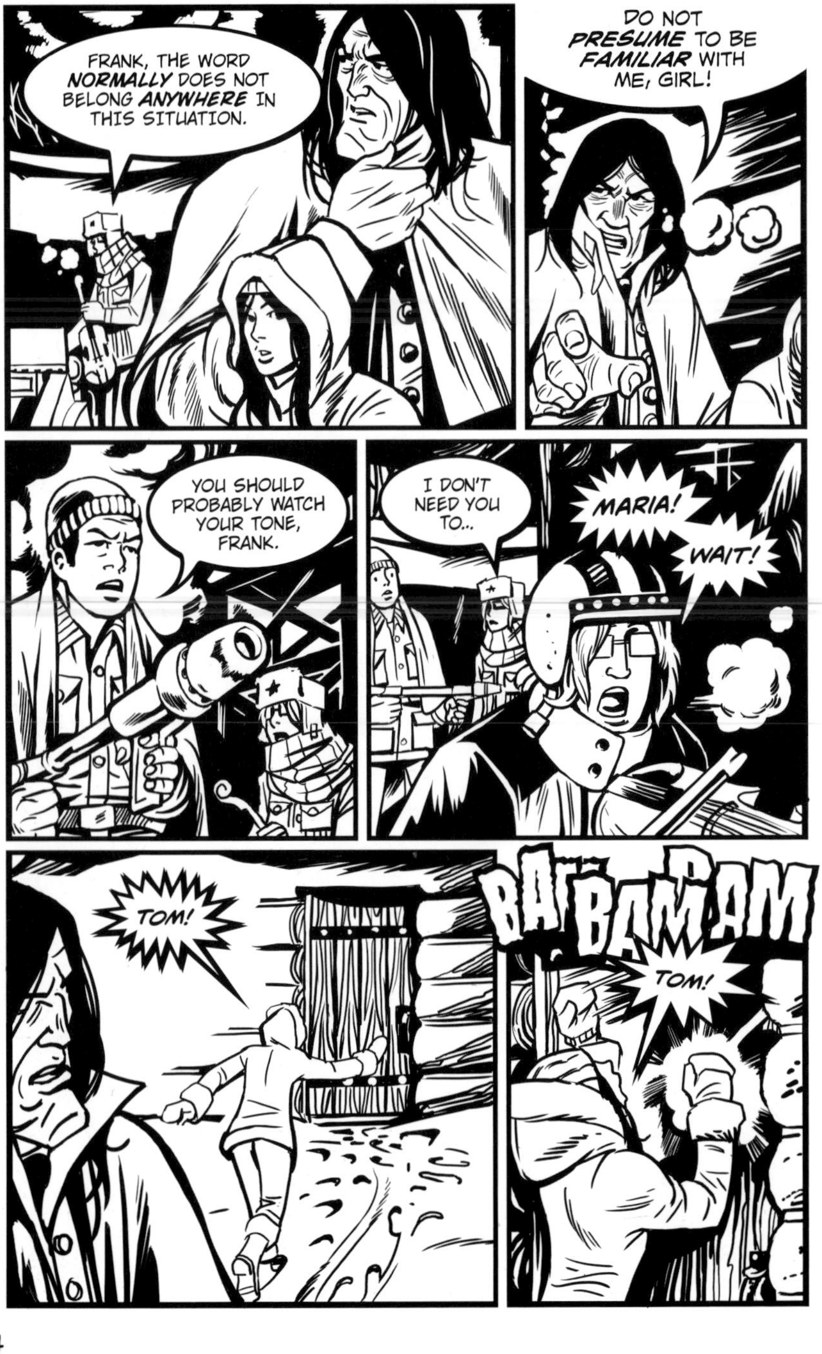
FRANK, THE WORD NORMALLY DOES NOT BELONG ANYWHERE IN THIS SITUATION.
DO NOT PRESUME TO BE FAMILIAR WITH ME, GIRL!
YOU SHOULD PROBABLY WATCH YOUR TONE, FRANK.
I DON'T NEED YOU TO...
MARIA!
WAIT!
TOM!
BAM BAM BAM
TOM!

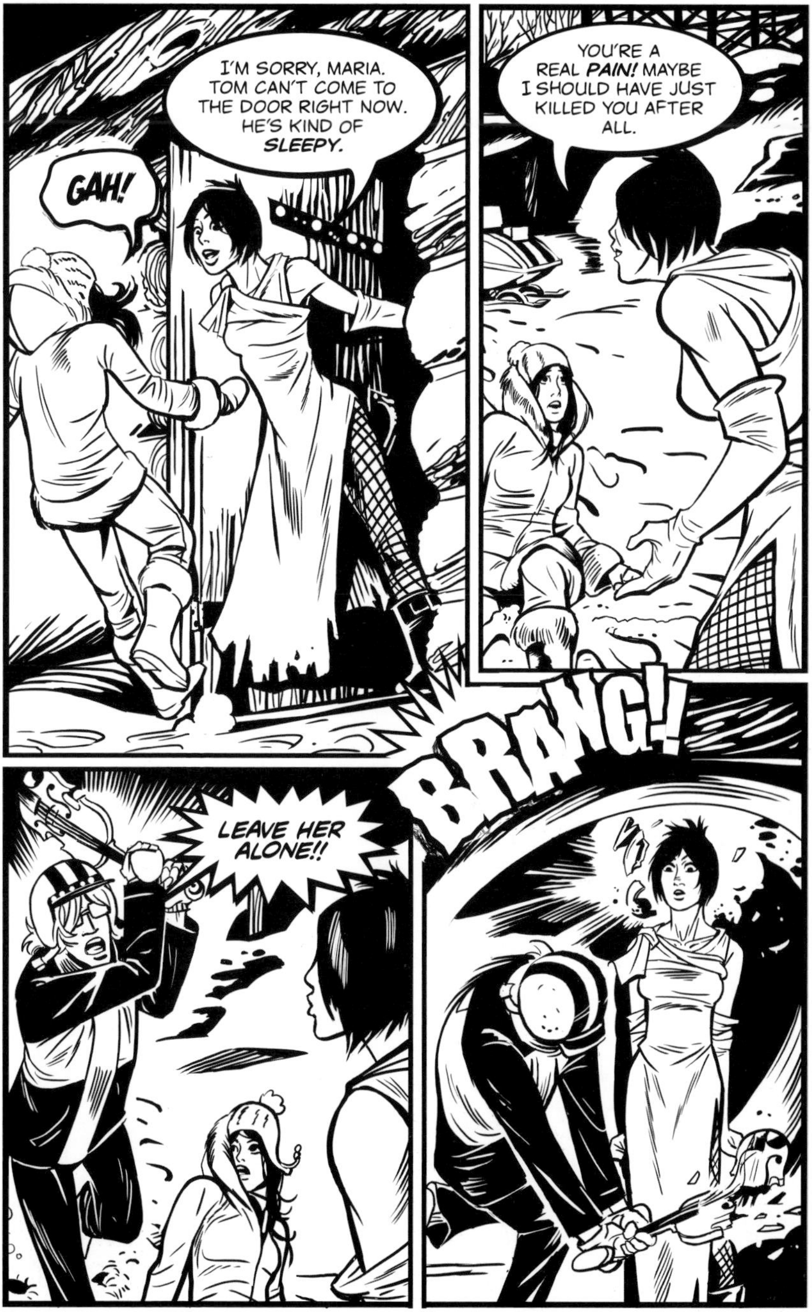
GAH!
I'M SORRY, MARIA. TOM CAN'T COME TO THE DOOR RIGHT NOW. HE'S KIND OF SLEEPY.
YOU'RE A REAL PAIN! MAYBE I SHOULD HAVE JUST KILLED YOU AFTER ALL.
LEAVE HER ALONE!!
BRANG!!

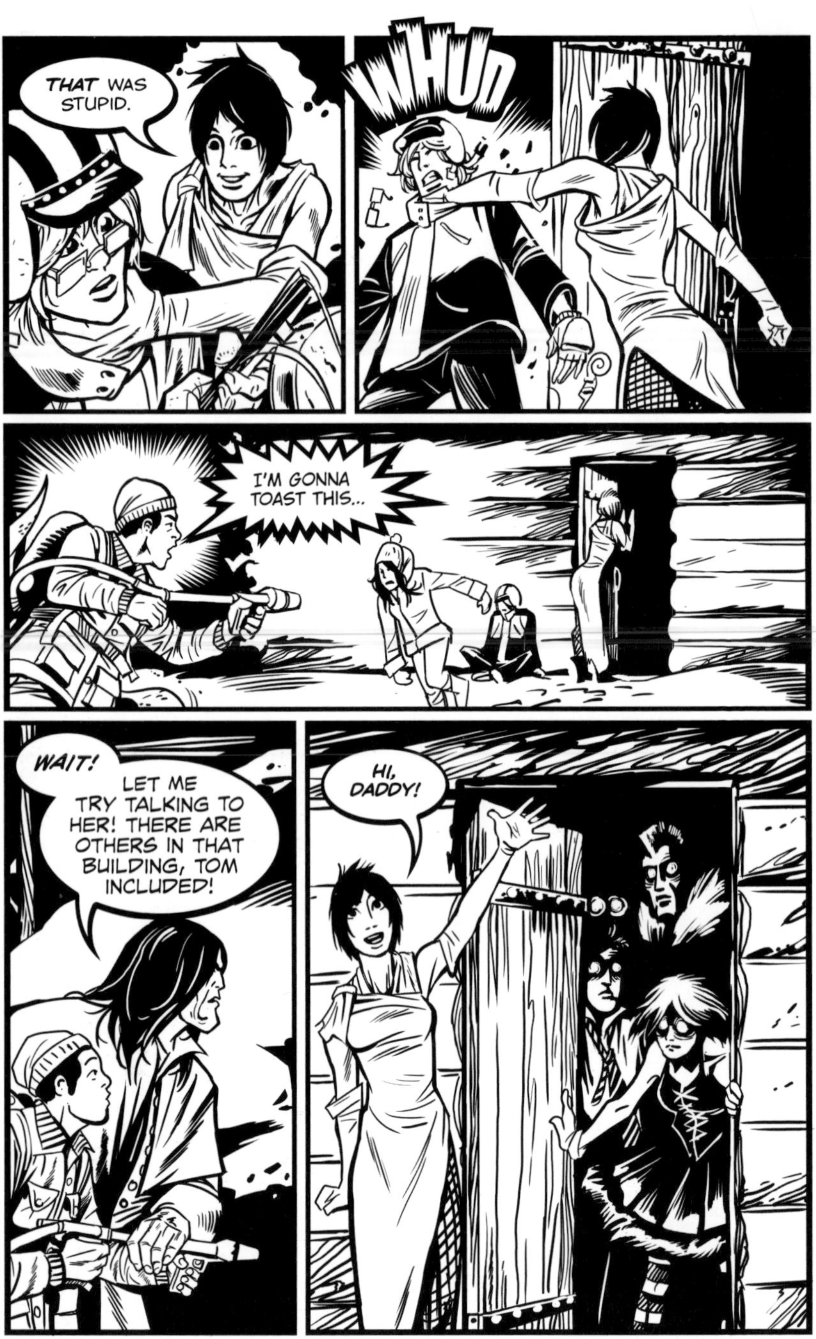
THAT WAS STUPID.
WHUD
I'M GONNA TOAST THIS...
WAIT!
LET ME TRY TALKING TO HER! THERE ARE OTHERS IN THAT BUILDING, TOM INCLUDED!
HI, DADDY!

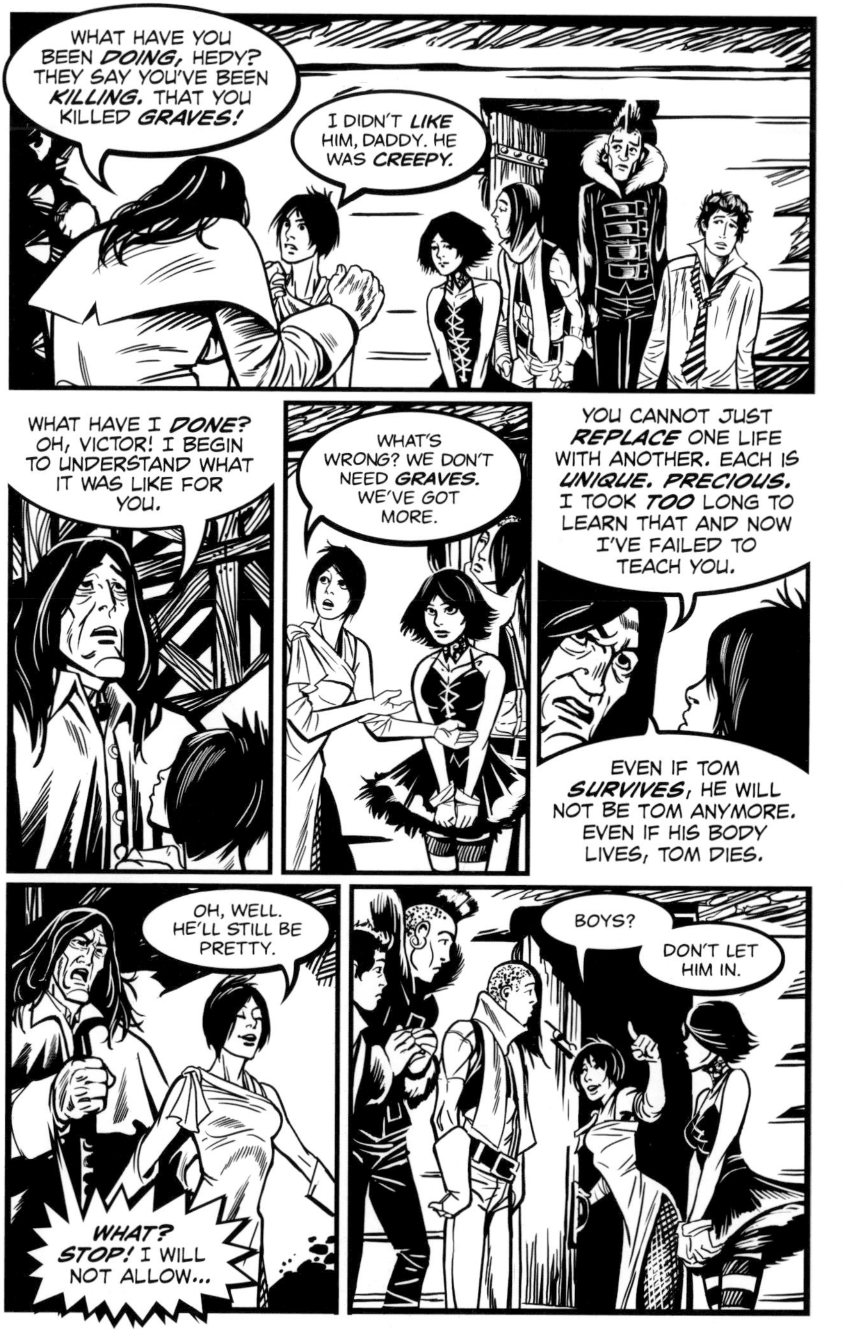
WHAT HAVE YOU BEEN DOING, HEDY? THEY SAY YOU'VE BEEN KILLING. THAT YOU KILLED GRAVES!
I DIDN'T LIKE HIM, DADDY. HE WAS CREEPY.
WHAT HAVE I DONE? OH, VICTOR! I BEGIN TO UNDERSTAND WHAT IT WAS LIKE FOR YOU.
WHAT'S WRONG? WE DON'T NEED GRAVES. WE'VE GOT MORE.
YOU CANNOT JUST REPLACE ONE LIFE WITH ANOTHER. EACH IS UNIQUE. PRECIOUS. I TOOK TOO LONG TO LEARN THAT AND NOW I'VE FAILED TO TEACH YOU.
EVEN IF TOM SURVIVES, HE WILL NOT BE TOM ANYMORE. EVEN IF HIS BODY LIVES, TOM DIES.
OH, WELL. HE'LL STILL BE PRETTY.
WHAT? STOP! I WILL NOT ALLOW...
BOYS?
DON'T LET HIM IN.

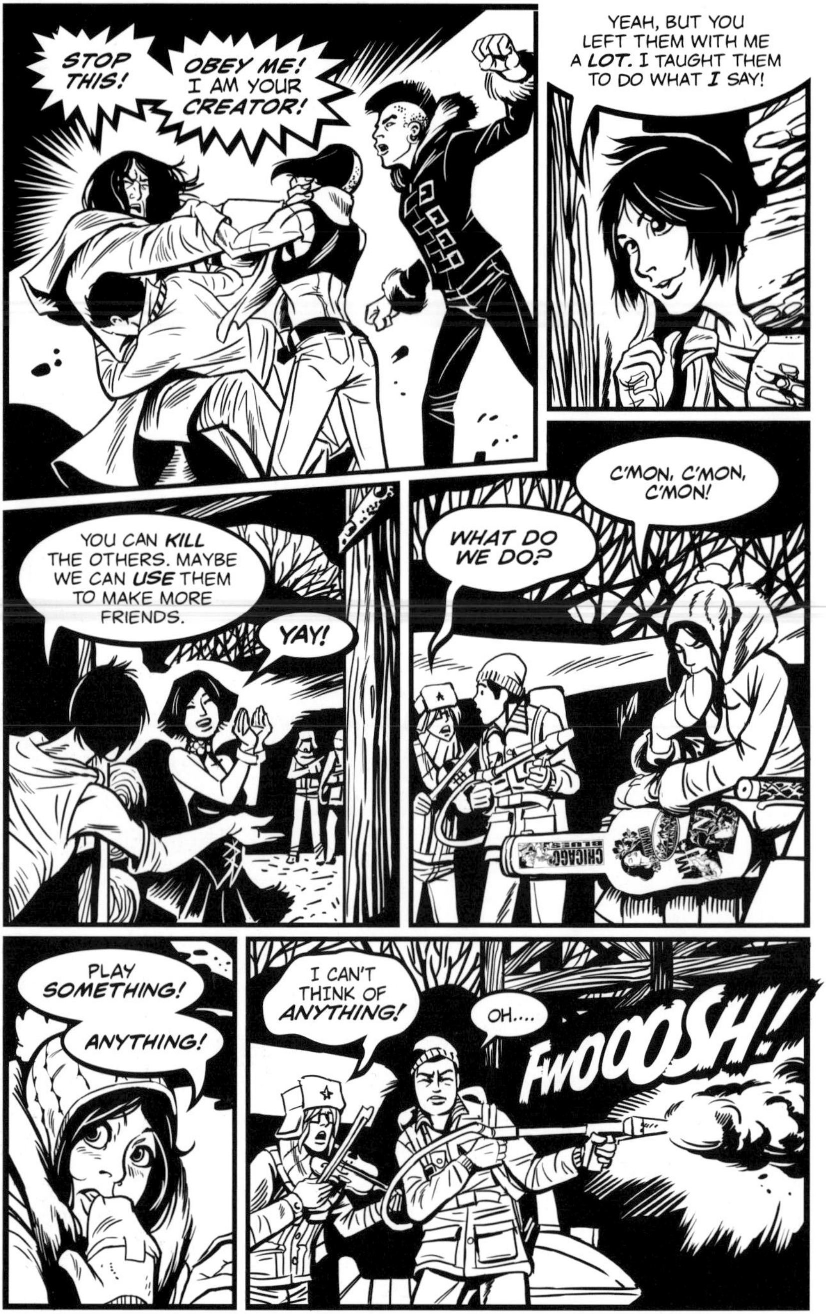
STOP THIS!
OBEY ME! I AM YOUR CREATOR!
YEAH, BUT YOU LEFT THEM WITH ME A LOT. I TAUGHT THEM TO DO WHAT I SAY!
YOU CAN KILL THE OTHERS. MAYBE WE CAN USE THEM TO MAKE MORE FRIENDS.
YAY!
C'MON, C'MON, C'MON!
WHAT DO WE DO?
CHICAGO BLUES
PLAY SOMETHING!
ANYTHING!
I CAN'T THINK OF ANYTHING!
OH....
FWOOOSH!

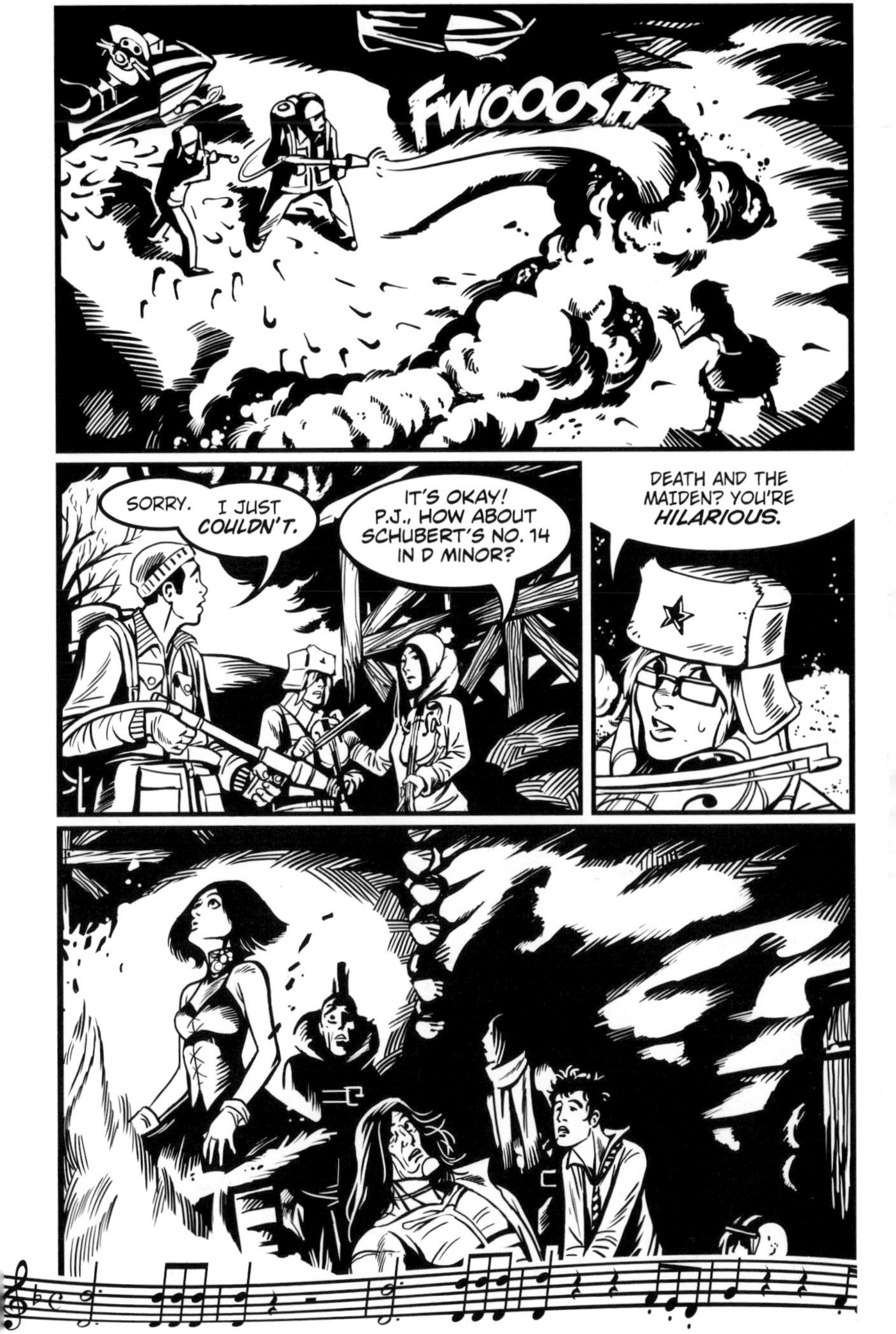
FWOOOSH
SORRY.
I JUST COULDN'T.
IT'S OKAY! P.J., HOW ABOUT SCHUBERT'S NO. 14 IN D MINOR?
DEATH AND THE MAIDEN? YOU'RE HILARIOUS.

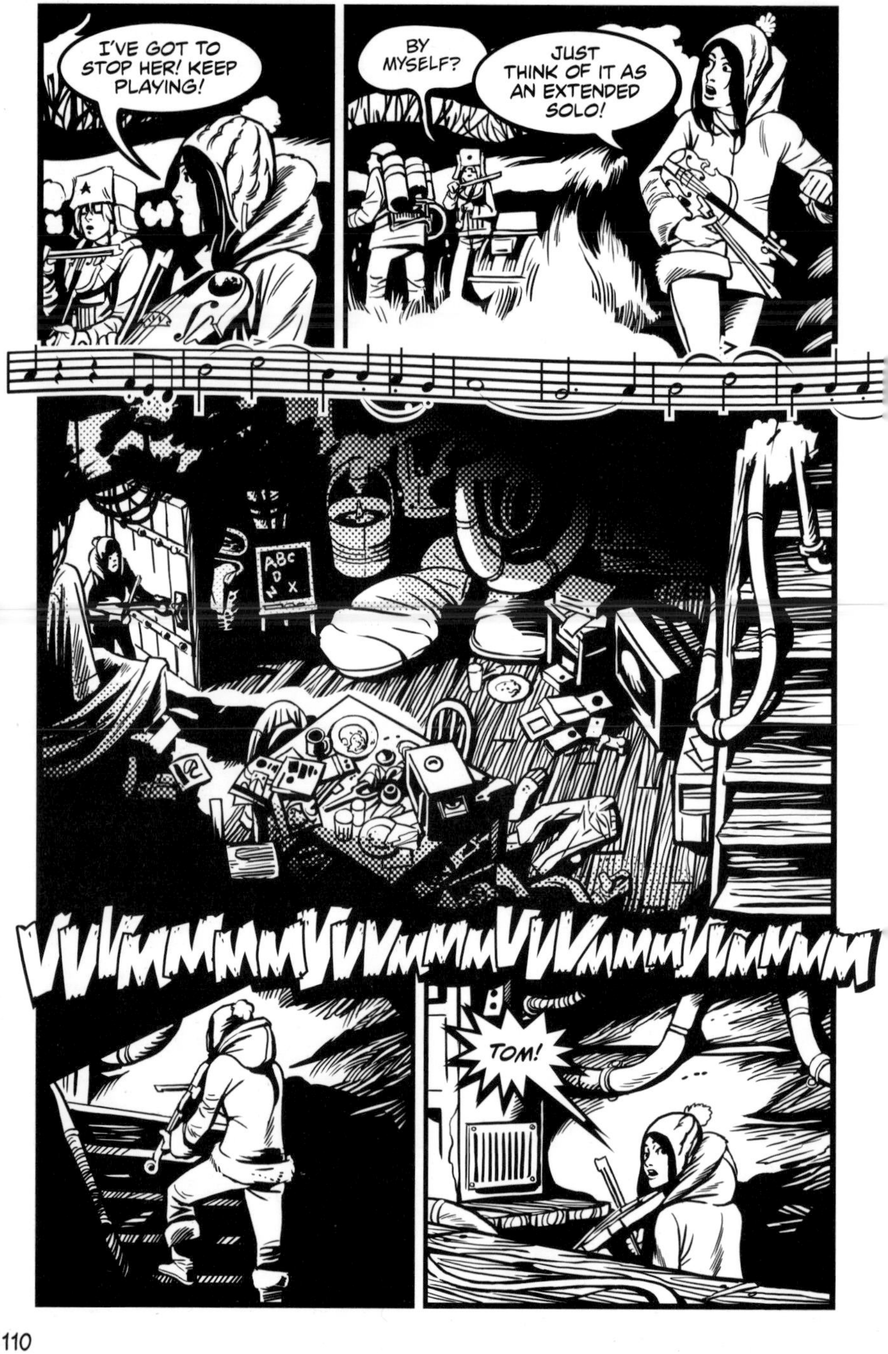
I'VE GOT TO STOP HER! KEEP PLAYING!
BY MYSELF?
JUST THINK OF IT AS AN EXTENDED SOLO!
ABC
D
N X
VVVMMMMMMVVVMMMMVVVMMMMVVMMNMM
TOM!

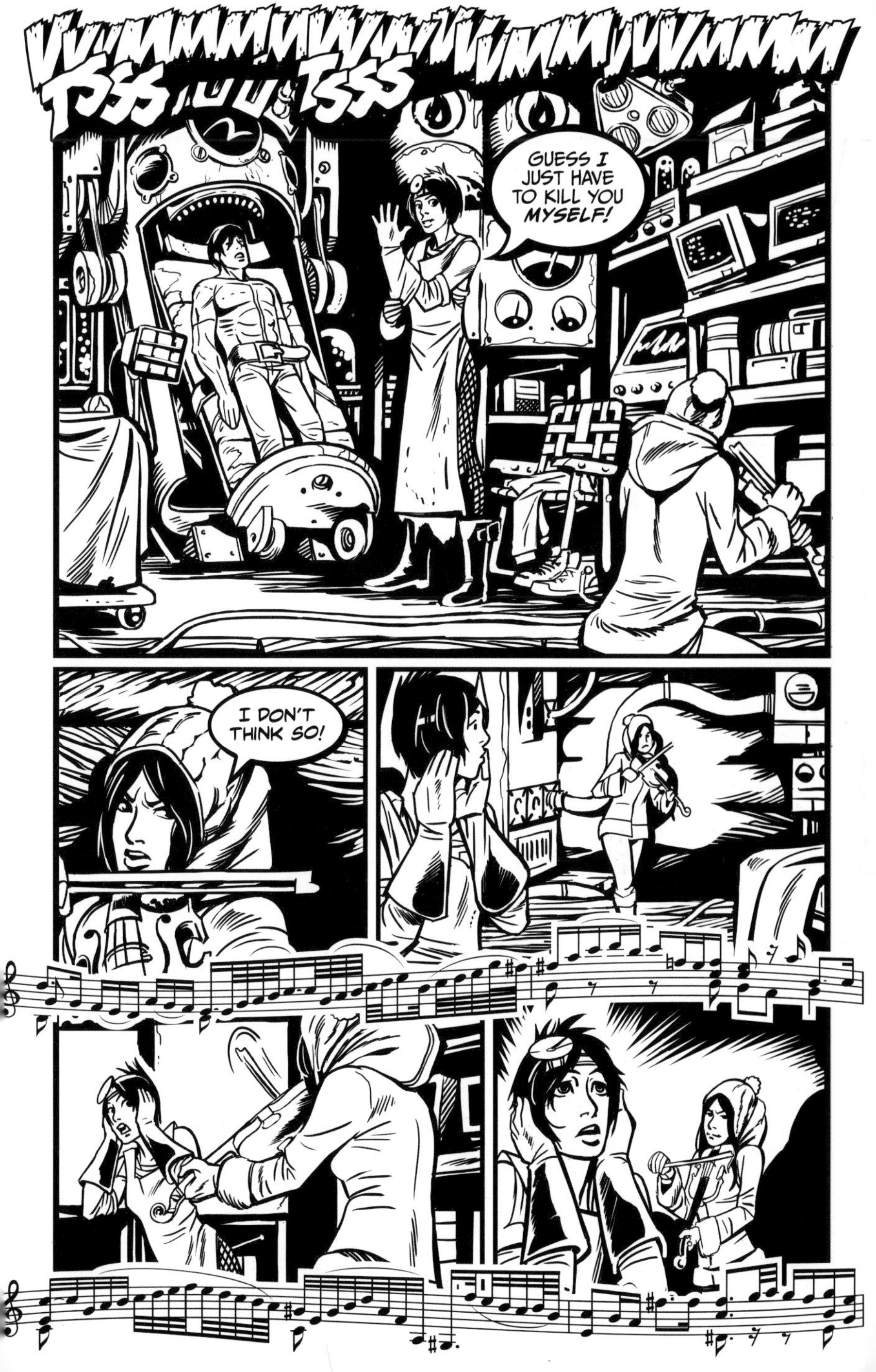
GUESS I JUST HAVE TO KILL YOU *MYSELF!*
I DON'T THINK SO!

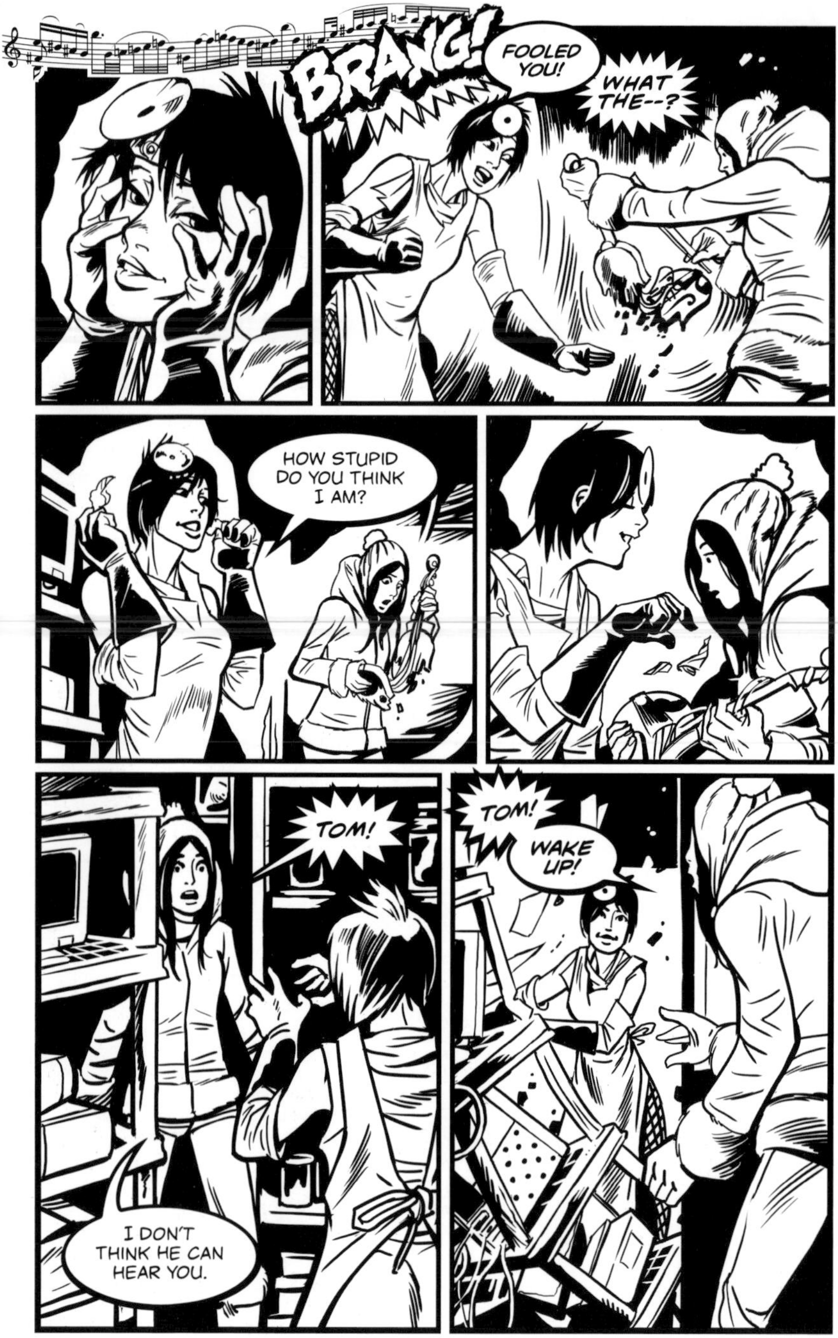
BRANG!
FOOLED YOU!
WHAT THE--?
HOW STUPID DO YOU THINK I AM?
TOM!
TOM!
WAKE UP!
I DON'T THINK HE CAN HEAR YOU.

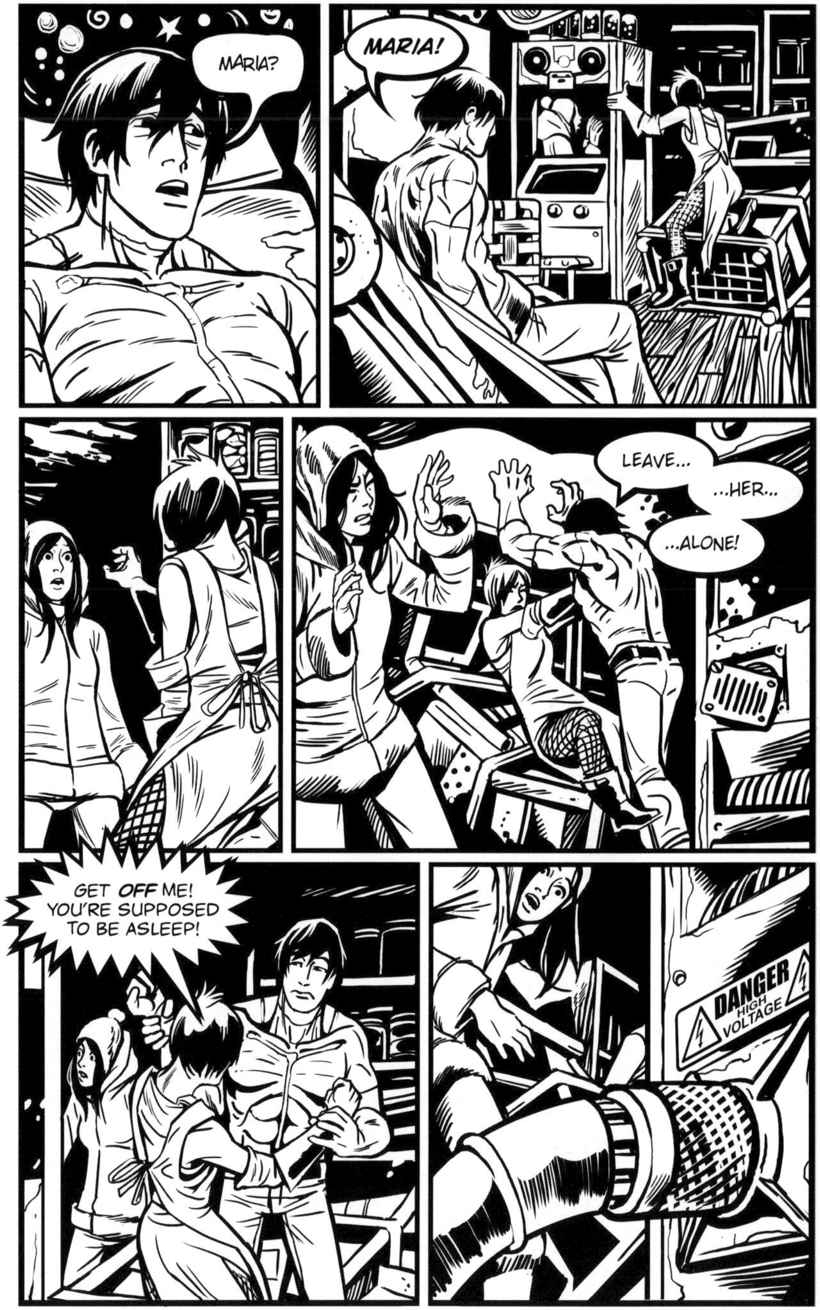

MARIA?
MARIA!
LEAVE...
...HER...
...ALONE!
GET OFF ME! YOU'RE SUPPOSED TO BE ASLEEP!
DANGER HIGH VOLTAGE

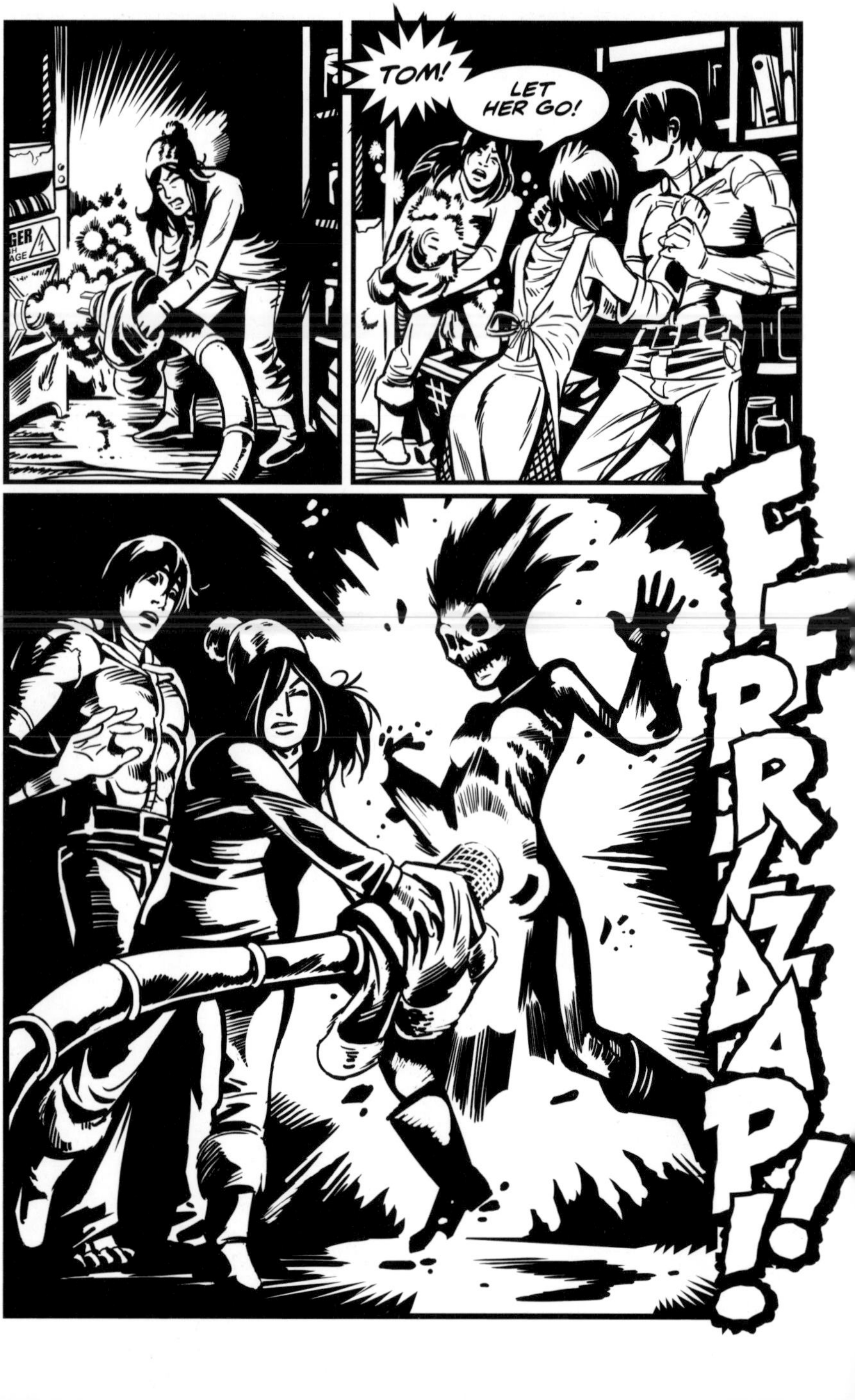
TOM!
LET HER GO!
FRRZZDAP!!

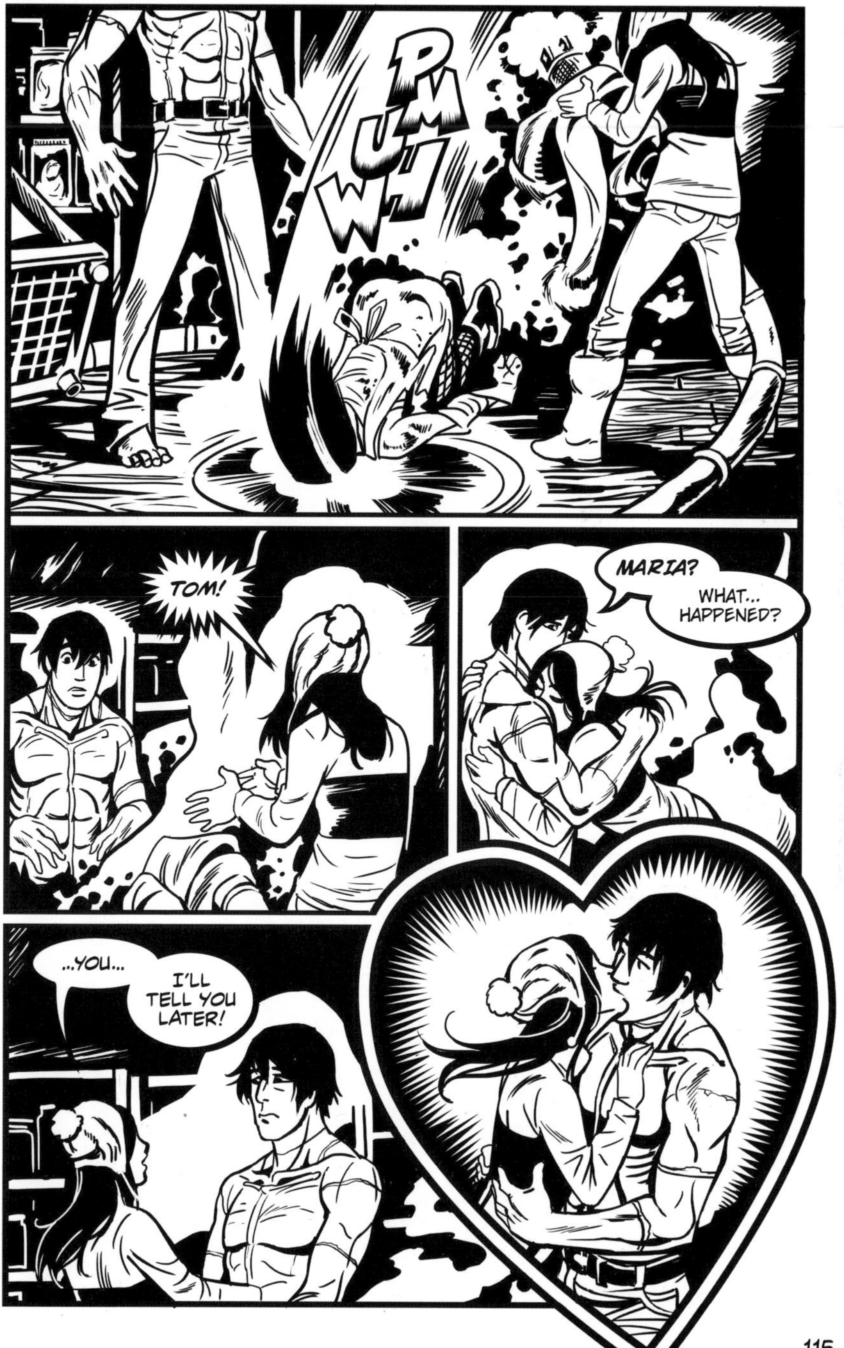
WHUMP
TOM!
MARIA?
WHAT... HAPPENED?
...YOU...
I'LL TELL YOU LATER!

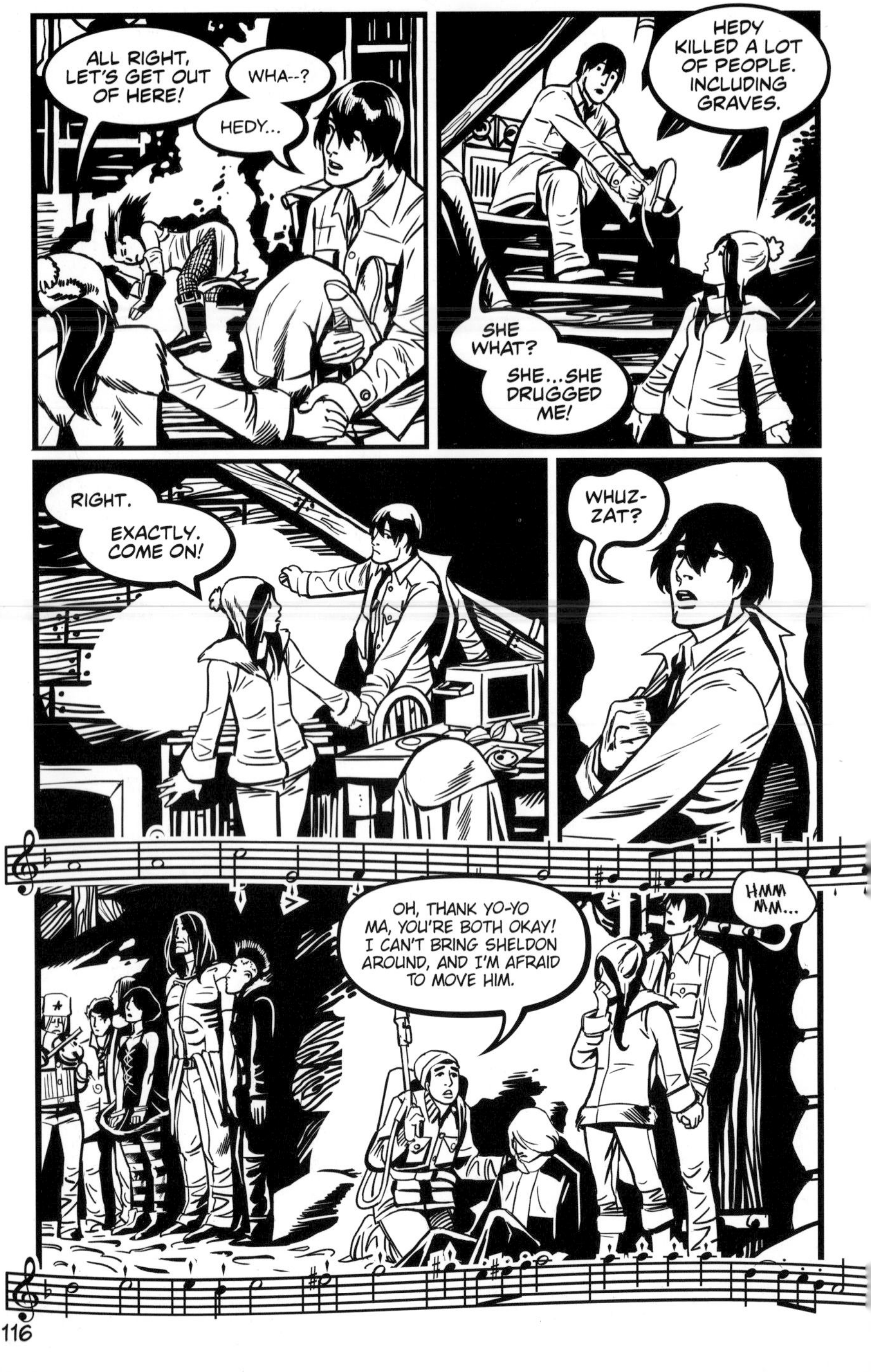
ALL RIGHT, LET'S GET OUT OF HERE!
WHA--?
HEDY...
HEDY KILLED A LOT OF PEOPLE. INCLUDING GRAVES.
SHE WHAT?
SHE...SHE DRUGGED ME!
RIGHT.
EXACTLY. COME ON!
WHUZ-ZAT?
OH, THANK YO-YO MA, YOU'RE BOTH OKAY! I CAN'T BRING SHELDON AROUND, AND I'M AFRAID TO MOVE HIM.
HMMM MM...

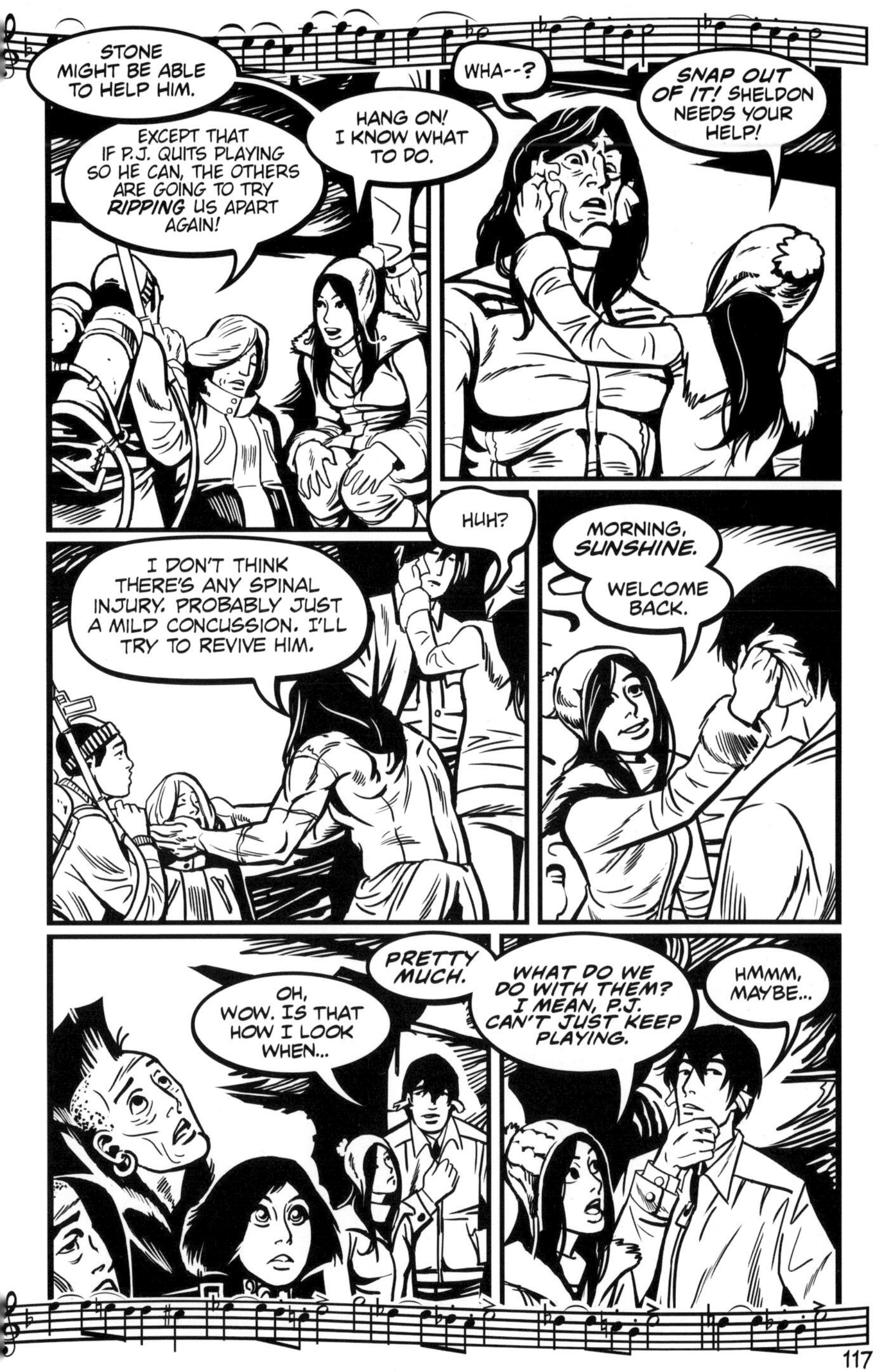
STONE MIGHT BE ABLE TO HELP HIM.
EXCEPT THAT IF P.J. QUITS PLAYING SO HE CAN, THE OTHERS ARE GOING TO TRY *RIPPING* US APART AGAIN!
HANG ON! I KNOW WHAT TO DO.
WHA--?
SNAP OUT OF IT! SHELDON NEEDS YOUR HELP!
I DON'T THINK THERE'S ANY SPINAL INJURY. PROBABLY JUST A MILD CONCUSSION. I'LL TRY TO REVIVE HIM.
HUH?
MORNING, *SUNSHINE.*
WELCOME BACK.
OH, WOW. IS THAT HOW I LOOK WHEN...
PRETTY MUCH.
WHAT DO WE DO WITH THEM? I MEAN, P.J. CAN'T JUST KEEP PLAYING.
HMMM, MAYBE...

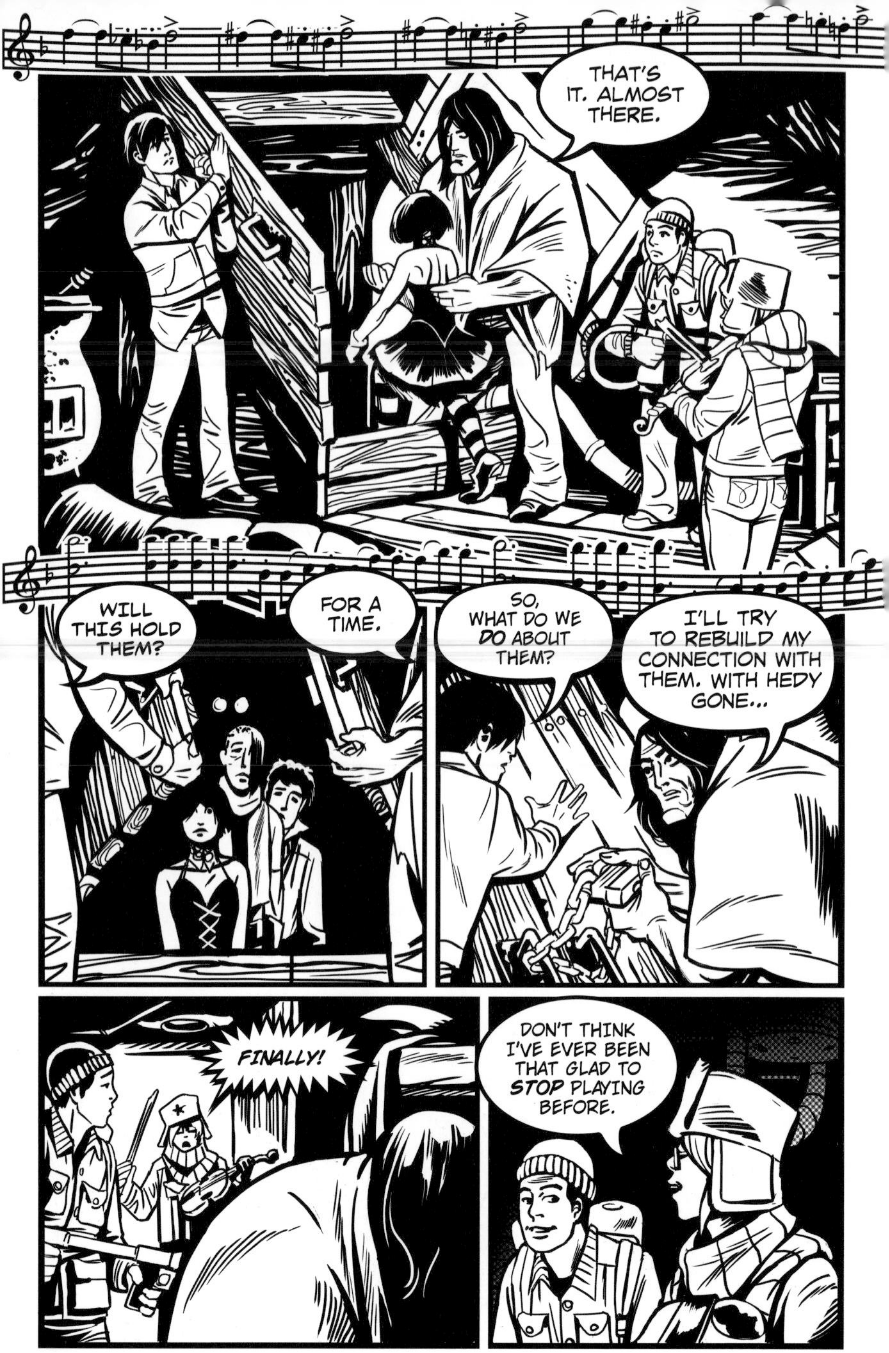
THAT'S IT. ALMOST THERE.
WILL THIS HOLD THEM?
FOR A TIME.
SO, WHAT DO WE DO ABOUT THEM?
I'LL TRY TO REBUILD MY CONNECTION WITH THEM. WITH HEDY GONE...
FINALLY!
DON'T THINK I'VE EVER BEEN THAT GLAD TO STOP PLAYING BEFORE.

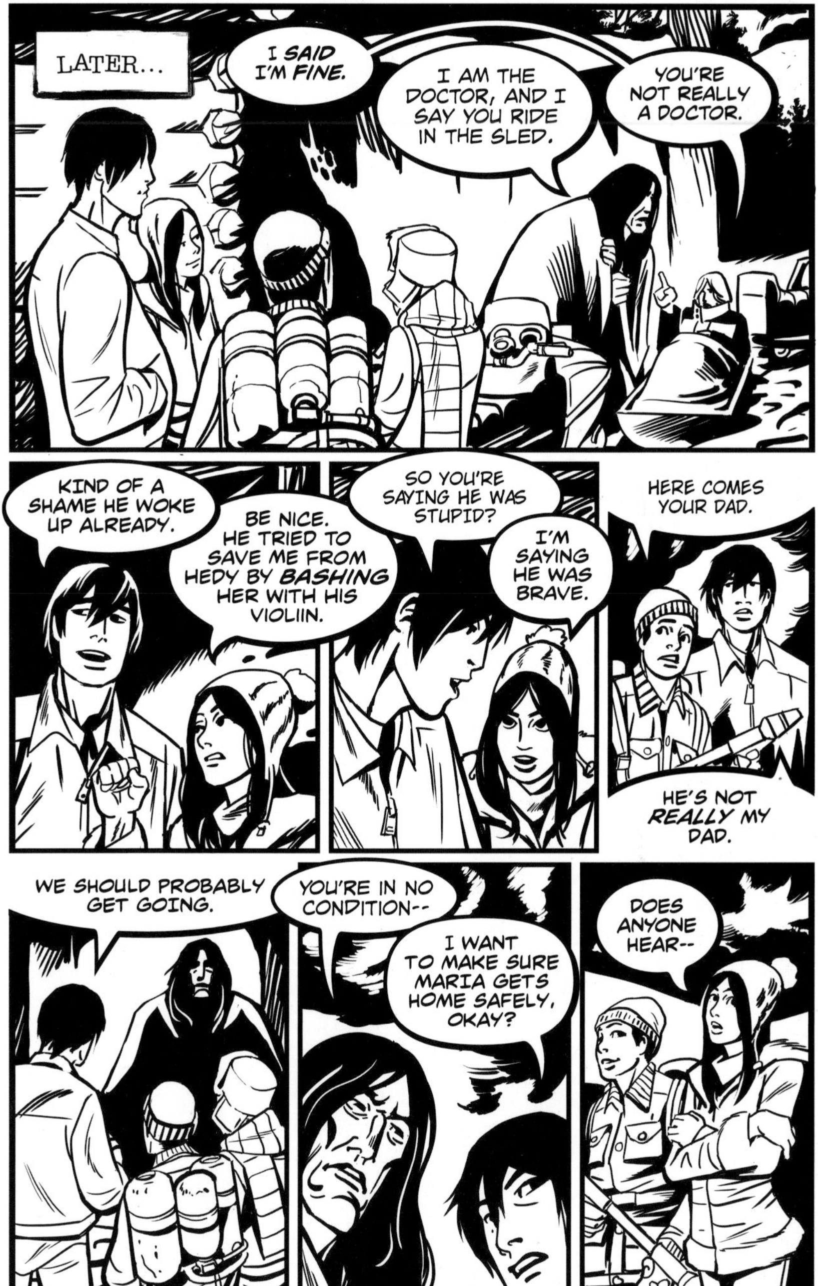
LATER...
I SAID I'M FINE.
I AM THE DOCTOR, AND I SAY YOU RIDE IN THE SLED.
YOU'RE NOT REALLY A DOCTOR.
KIND OF A SHAME HE WOKE UP ALREADY.
BE NICE. HE TRIED TO SAVE ME FROM HEDY BY BASHING HER WITH HIS VIOLIIN.
SO YOU'RE SAYING HE WAS STUPID?
I'M SAYING HE WAS BRAVE.
HERE COMES YOUR DAD.
HE'S NOT REALLY MY DAD.
WE SHOULD PROBABLY GET GOING.
YOU'RE IN NO CONDITION--
I WANT TO MAKE SURE MARIA GETS HOME SAFELY, OKAY?
DOES ANYONE HEAR--

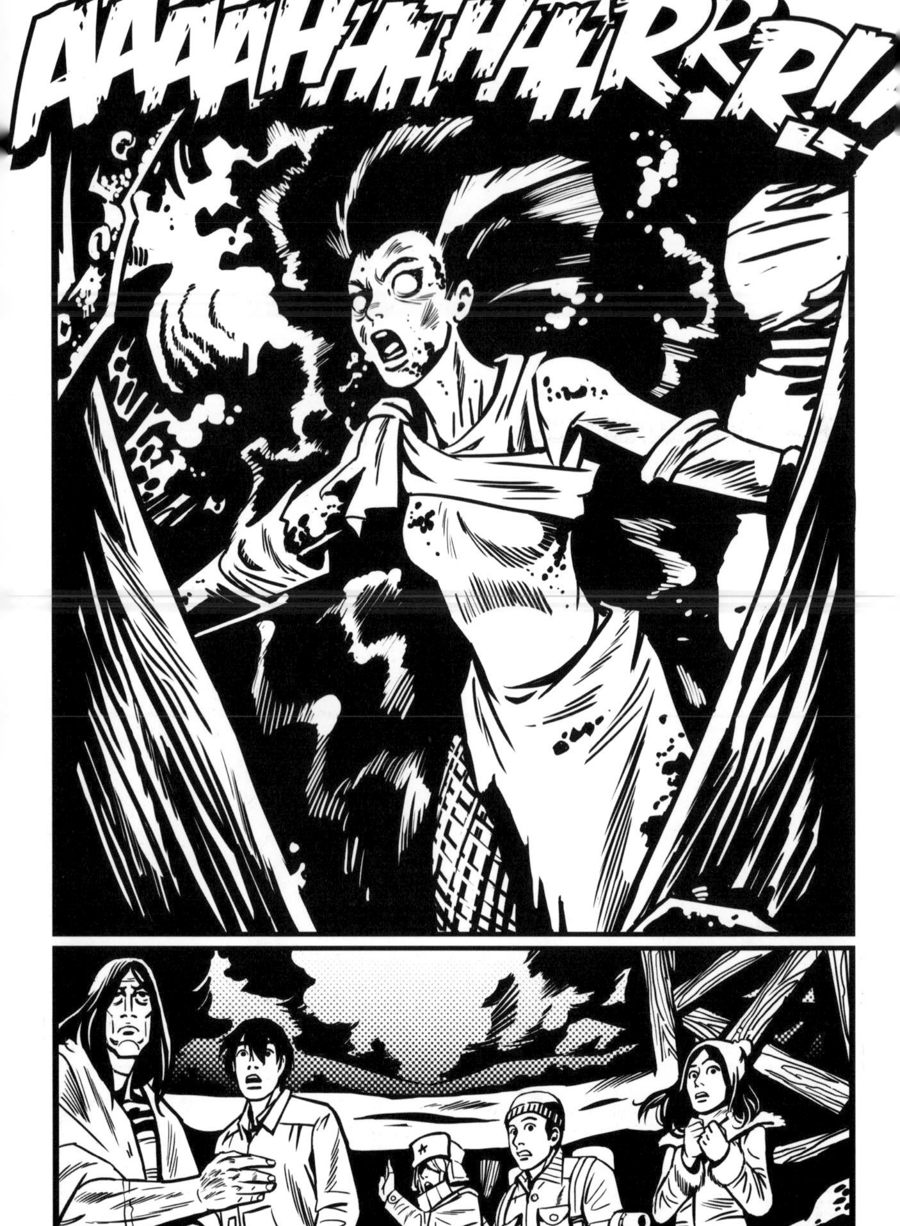
AAAAHHHHHHRRR!!

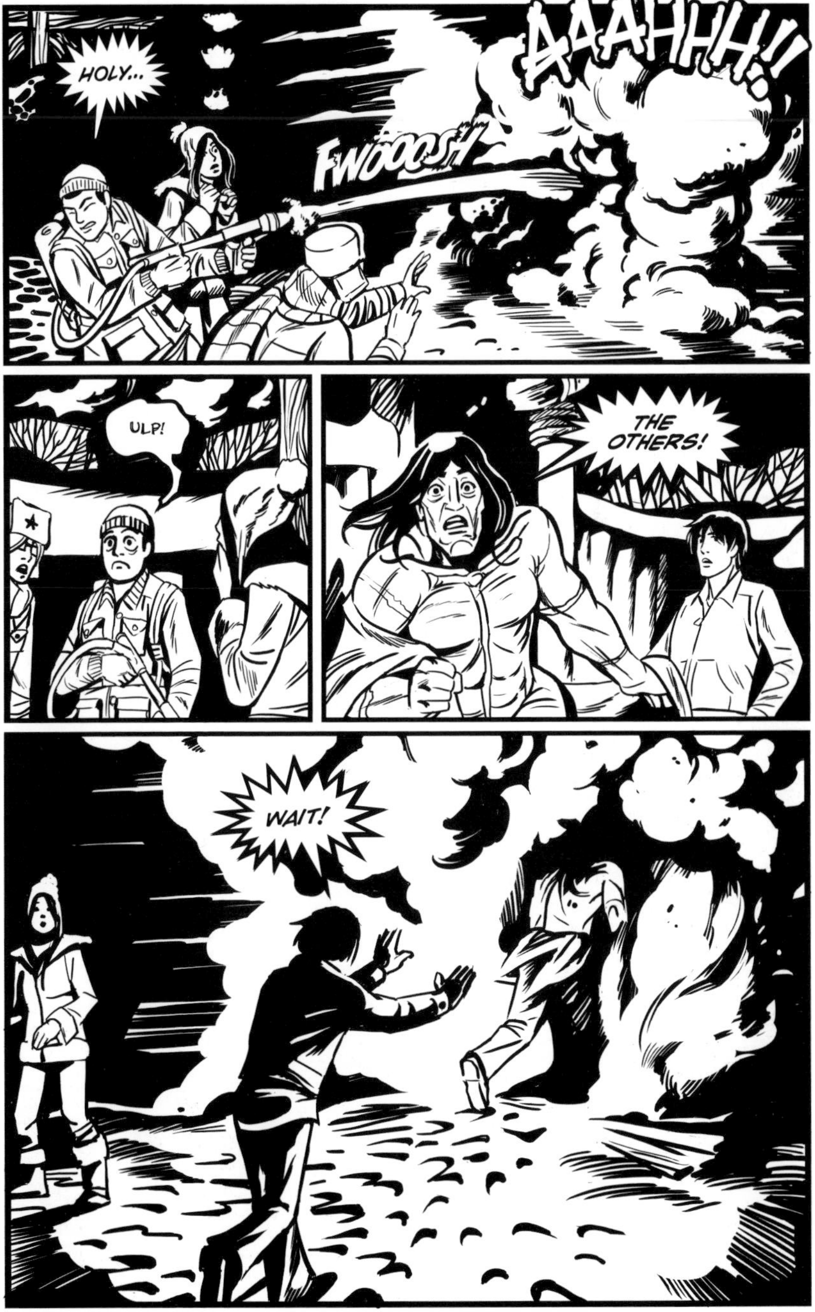
HOLY...
AAAHHH!!
FWOOOSH
ULP!
THE OTHERS!
WAIT!

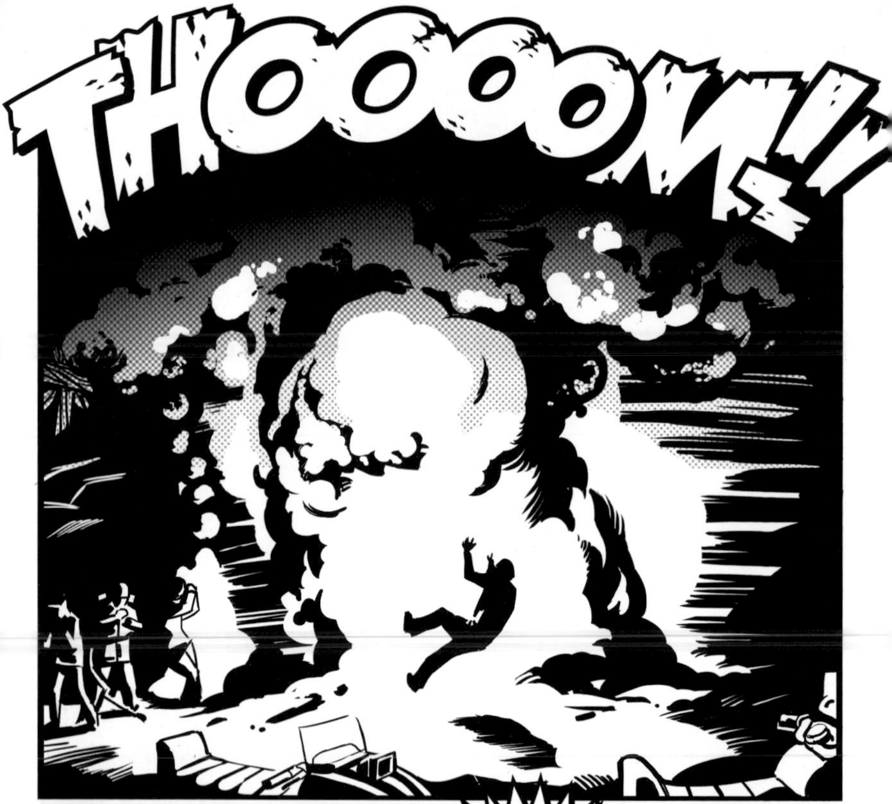
THOOOOM!!

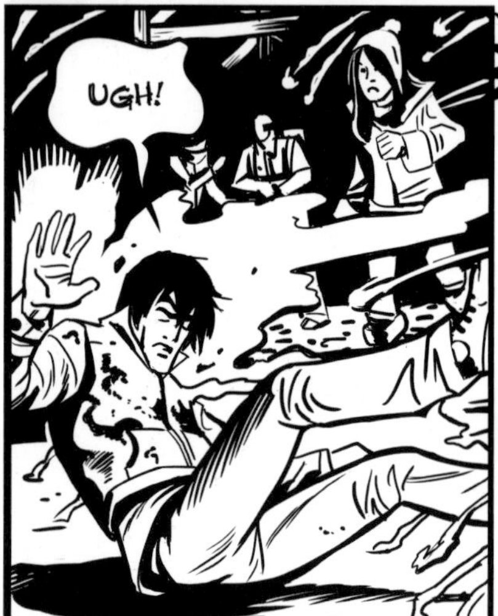
UGH!

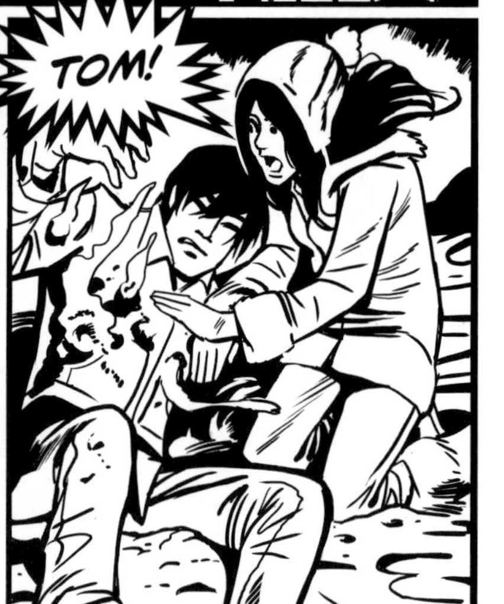
TOM!

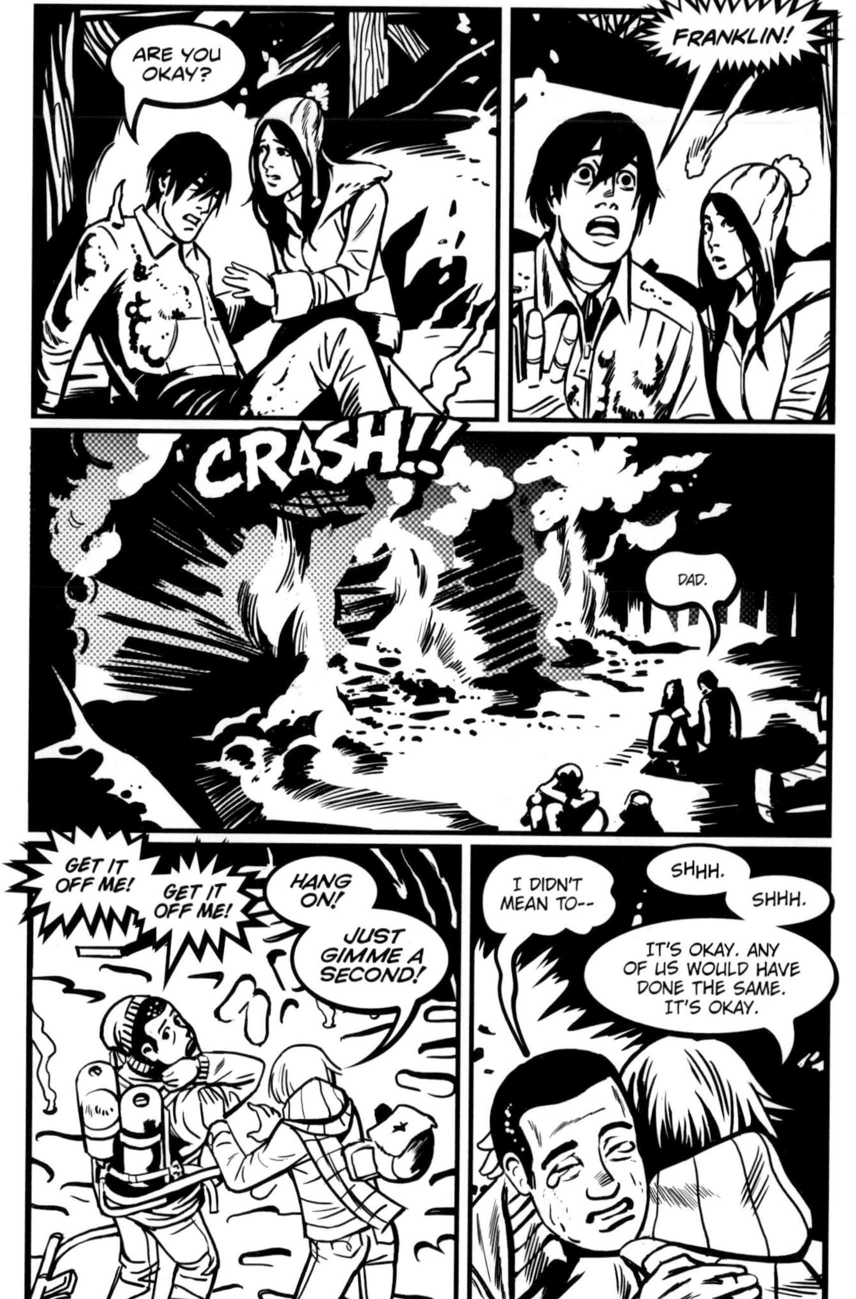
ARE YOU OKAY?
FRANKLIN!
CRASH!!
DAD.
GET IT OFF ME!
GET IT OFF ME!
HANG ON!
JUST GIMME A SECOND!
I DIDN'T MEAN TO--
SHHH.
SHHH.
IT'S OKAY. ANY OF US WOULD HAVE DONE THE SAME. IT'S OKAY.

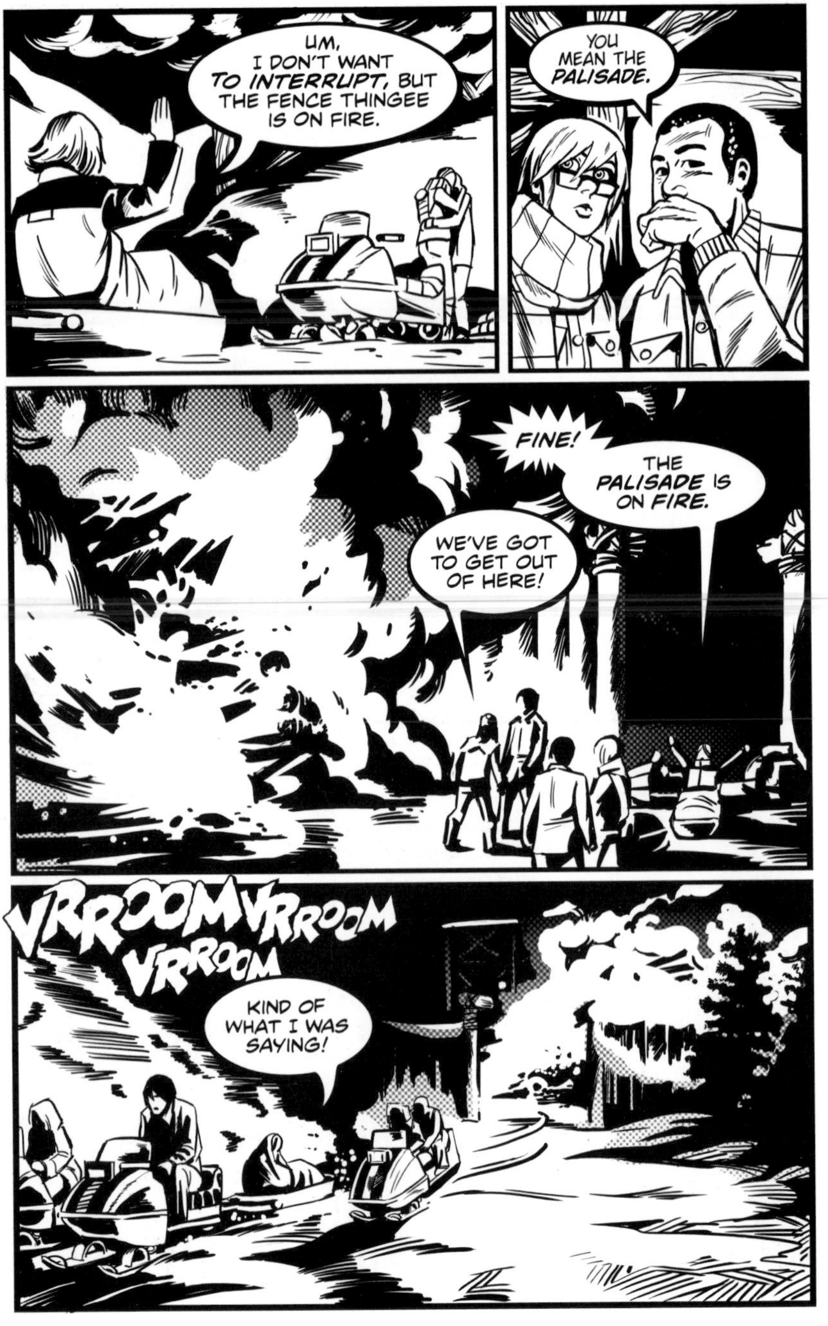
UM, I DON'T WANT TO INTERRUPT, BUT THE FENCE THINGEE IS ON FIRE.
YOU MEAN THE PALISADE.
FINE!
THE PALISADE IS ON FIRE.
WE'VE GOT TO GET OUT OF HERE!
VRROOM VRROOM VRROOM
KIND OF WHAT I WAS SAYING!

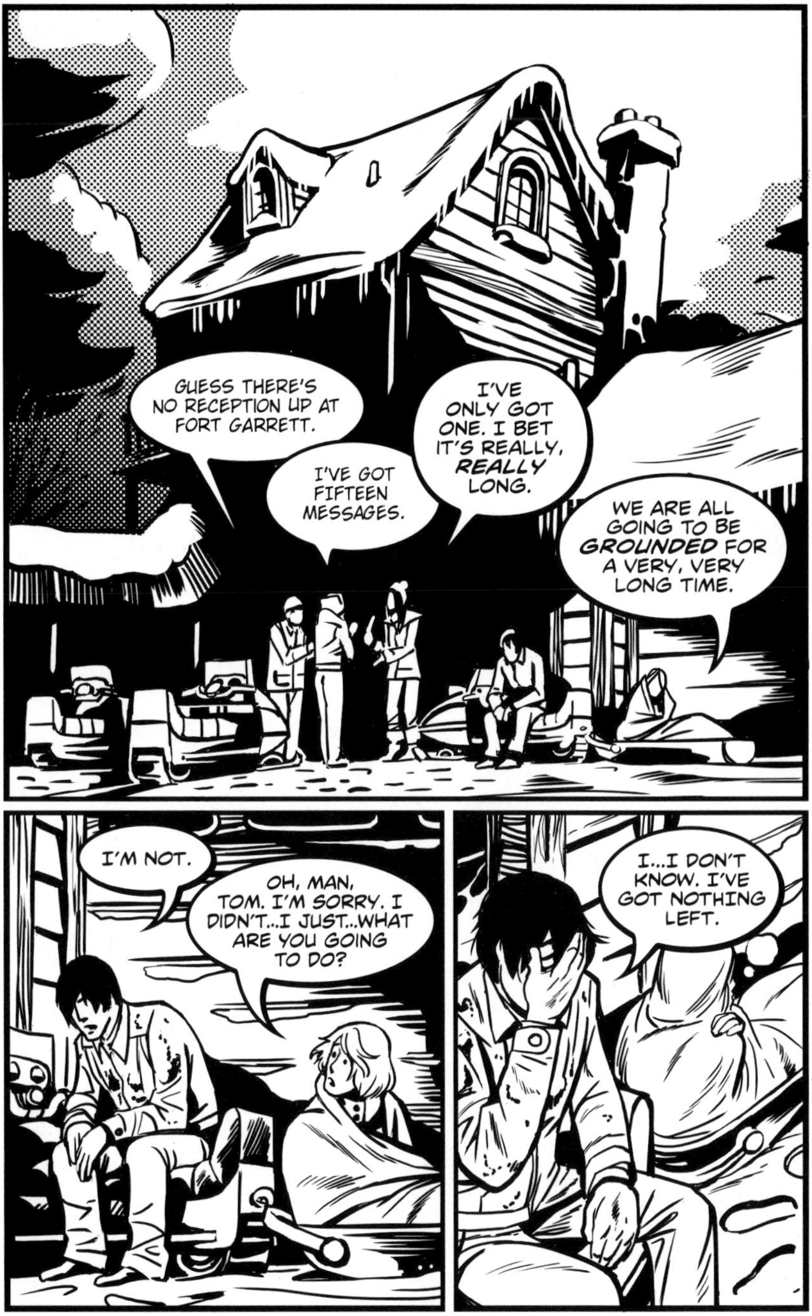
GUESS THERE'S NO RECEPTION UP AT FORT GARRETT.
I'VE GOT FIFTEEN MESSAGES.
I'VE ONLY GOT ONE. I BET IT'S REALLY, *REALLY* LONG.
WE ARE ALL GOING TO BE **GROUNDED** FOR A VERY, VERY LONG TIME.
I'M NOT.
OH, MAN, TOM. I'M SORRY. I DIDN'T...I JUST...WHAT ARE YOU GOING TO DO?
I...I DON'T KNOW. I'VE GOT NOTHING LEFT.

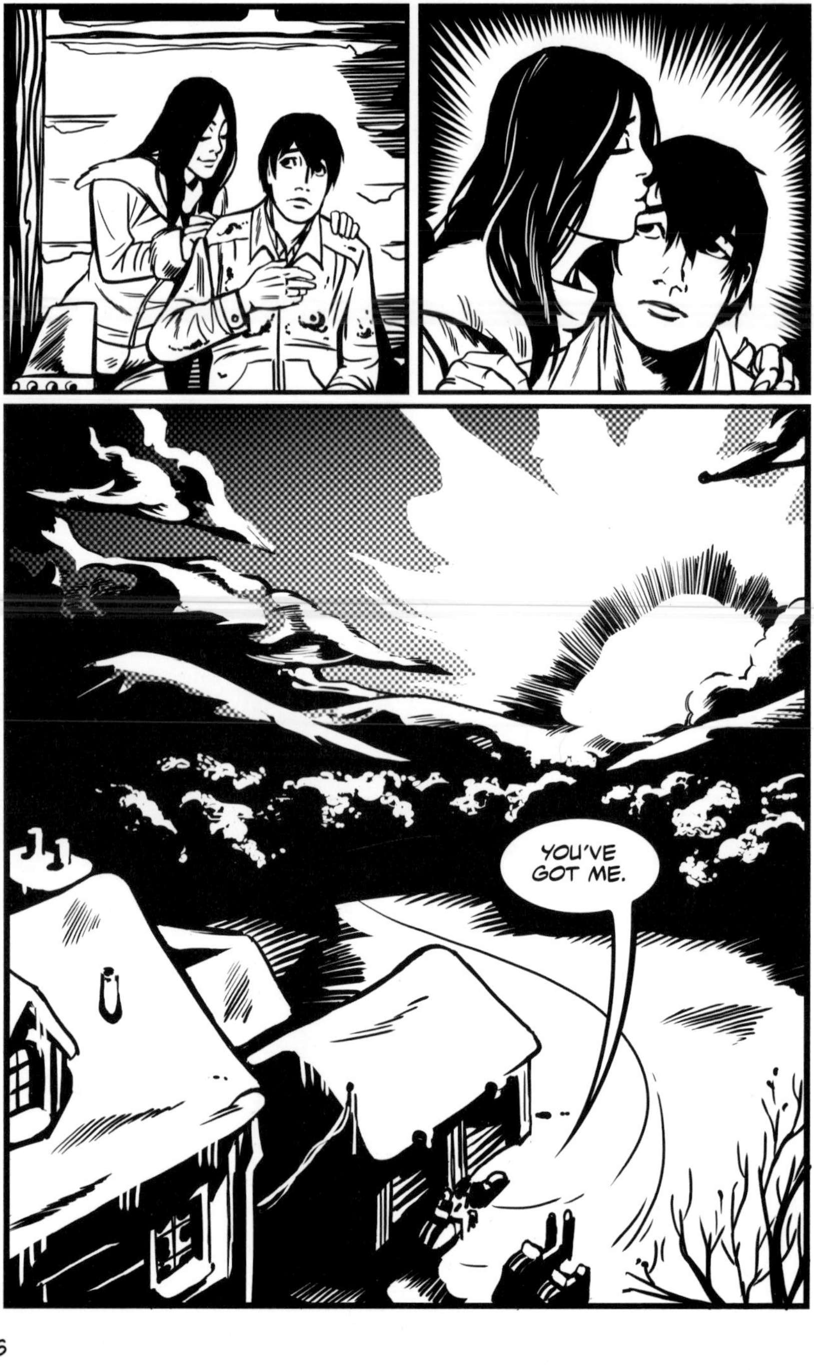
YOU'VE GOT ME.

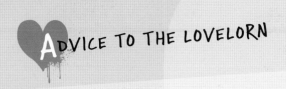

ADVICE TO THE LOVELORN

ELSA C. WRITES:

When you date a Frankenstein, do you have to be careful not to accidentally pop some stitches?

MARIA REPLIES:

Not anymore, Elsa. But good question. In the old days, surgical techniques and medical supplies weren't as good as they are now. Back then, if you held hands with a Frankenstein, you had to worry about ending up holding just a hand. Today, you can be confident that parts are going to stay put!

JENNIFER B. WRITES:

Why would you want to date a Frankenstein? Aren't they all ugly?

MARIA REPLIES:

You'd be surprised! Anyway, who says that it's all about looks? A great-looking guy might be a really ugly person on the inside. And sometimes the more you get to know someone really special, the more attractive they are to you. Sounds hard to believe, but it's true!

MARY S. WRITES:

Frankenstein is the name of the scientist, not the monster. Why do people always get that wrong? It makes me crazy!

MARIA REPLIES:

Not really a question about dating, Mary, but it's true—that's a common error. In the original novel, *Frankenstein, or The Modern Prometheus*, the monster doesn't have any name at all. But soon after, people started calling him Frankenstein. I guess it's because Frankenstein is a lot easier to say than Frankenstein's monster. Maybe the author should have given the monster a catchy name.

ABOUT THE AUTHOR
AND THE ARTIST

PAUL STORRIE was born and raised in Detroit, Michigan. He has returned to live there again and again after living in other cities and states. He began writing professionally in 1998 and has written comics for Caliber Comics, Moonstone Books, Marvel Comics, and DC Comics. His titles for Graphic Universe™ include *Hercules, Robin Hood, Yu the Great,* and *Amaterasu.* Other titles he has worked on include *Robyn of Sherwood* (featuring stories about Robin Hood's daughter), *Batman Beyond, Gotham Girls, Captain America: Red, White and Blue, Mutant X,* and *Revisionary.*

Creator of the webcomic *Astray3* at www.astray3.com, ELDON COWGUR is a seeker of action and adventure. Whether he finds it through the point of a pencil or far afield, where there is derring-do to be done he is there. Most times, he can be found at his humble northwest Arkansas dwelling, drawing wild tales of curious locations with his roguish pet conure Quetzal. When at leisure, he may be found enjoying the outdoors or studying the art of comics. Eldon is also very fond of robots.